CUPS OF FORTUNE

Lenore Tolegian Hughes

all good Fortune
Lenore Tolegian Hughes

DEDICATION

To
Mom Jahn,
My good fortune

CONTENTS

1 THE EVIL EYE CUP

to know your past is to know yourself

The day I was born, I was cursed by the evil eye and nothing could be done about it.

Masha took everyone by surprise.

Masha looked much the same as she had in the Old Country. She had the same intense green eyes that so worried everyone. Her hair was still dark and long, her face powdered white, and her lips and finger nails colored bright red. The only difference was that her shapely body was completely covered by a long, black coat, as she sidled into St. Luke's Hospital in Los Angeles, California, as stealthily as a snake. Without delay, she made her way to the third floor maternity ward. She shuffled along the walls of the corridors, so as to avoid the attentions of my grandmother, who had just arrived herself.

Unaware of the approaching disaster, my beloved grandparents Mama Jahn and Bobeeg Jahn moved with light and happy hearts. Mama Jahn carried her specialty—shakar locum. The shortbread cookies carefully packed in an empty one-pound See's candy box, were intended for the nurses who were taking care of my mother. When Mama Jahn laid eyes on Masha, this mean-spirited woman she knew well from the Old Country, she caught her breath. Dread drove away her happiness. Shoving the cookie box at Bobeeg Jahn, she sprang to try to stop her enemy.

It was too late. Masha was at the nursery window, staring down at me, as wicked as a Turk at the door. Out came the words, hissed to my grandmother: Atchkeed louis.

I was only an hour old and behind glass. What did I know of the superstitious, topsy-turvy Armenian culture I had been born into? It would

1

take many years and endless explanations to understand what was perfectly clear to everyone but me—spoken words had an effect opposite their meaning if spoken with malice. Armenian evil eye givers say one thing but mean another.

Atchkeed louis sounds innocent enough. It means "light of your eyes," an expression Armenians declare in congratulations. However, Masha didn't love or even care about us, except as an object of envy. Her only intent was to cast the evil eye, which she did particularly well because she had those green eyes. And because an evil-eye giver spoke the words, the lovely traditional Armenian blessing had the opposite meaning.

What Masha, with her dark and jealous heart, really meant by "congratulating" my grandmother was: "May you lose your sight so you'll never see this beautiful baby, this light of your eyes, grow up into a lovely woman."

Then before Mama Jahn could act, Masha made it even worse by declaring, "Azadouhi will marry a rich Armenian who will bring great honor to your family." Mama Jahn's eyes grew wide with panic. She knew that again nasty Masha meant the exact opposite—that her first grandchild's fate was to marry an ahnlee odar (a saltless outsider), that dishonor to the entire family would follow, and her anoush balah jahn, her sweet baby dear, would be lost to the family forever.

This second curse was almost worse than the first! Turning away from the malicious visitor, Mama Jahn threw her hands up over her ears and scurried down the hospital hallway as fast as she could to avert the first curse. Surreptitiously, because my mother didn't believe in curses and counter-curses, Mama Jahn entered my mother's room. Seeing that she was napping, Mama Jahn plucked flower petals from a bouquet of pink baby roses on her night stand and rubbed them across her eyebrows so she would never lose sight of her lovely new grandchild, me, Azad.

When I was about seven years old, my Hayrig, father, told me: "Listen, my little hokis (my soul's delight), that second curse meant that circumstances will keep you from remembering what the Turks did in the great genocide. But Azad anoush, sweet one, never, never shall we forget that the Ottoman government ordered the extinction of the Armenians and their 3,000-year-old culture. Never, never shall we forget!" he repeated. He explained that all Armenians believe that forgetting the genocide is the same as forgetting a million and a half of our blessed people who were dragged from their houses and savagely murdered just because they were Christians." If I forgot to remember, Hayrig insisted, no one would tell my children the history of their Armenian ancestors, and the loss of all those lives would have been for nothing. "What is not remembered is sure to be repeated," my father and my other relatives said, over and over again.

It seemed so unlikely. Was I really doomed to forget Auntie Makoush who was sliced through her pregnant belly, because her murderers were looking for family jewelry she might have swallowed to keep from being stolen by the Turks? How could I ever forget that they hung her baby next to her, by his umbilical cord from the apricot tree in her own garden? Hard to imagine that any force, even an evil eye, could purge such a ghastly vision.

Shuddering in sorrow that morning, Mama Jahn had murmured to her devoted husband in Armenian, "Yervant, there might still be time to keep the curse from entering her soul, if I pinch her three times, cross myself and say the Hayr Mer (the Lord's Prayer)." Pinching is powerful medicine in Armenian superstition, a cure-all for the insults of jealous hearts, as I was about to experience in my lifetime.

So my grandmother hastened to the nursery room and, standing over my crib, repeated the Hayr Mer, then pinched me hard three times. As the Catholic nuns came running to see why one of their charges was wailing at the top of her lungs, Mama Jahn loudly chanted the Hanganag Havado (the Prayer of Saint John Chrysostom), just for good measure. Then the Soorp Soorp (Holy, Holy), as she bowed at the waist and crossed herself after each prayer, like an overly zealous Der Hayr (priest), reciting the Divine Liturgy. The nuns and nurses tried, in their solicitous way, to quell this little tempest of a grandmother, but Mama Jahn would not be stopped.

Her impassioned performance had an audience of all the relatives of new babies and maternity nurses, who looked through the window into the nursery in amazement. I might have been embarrassed, even as an infant, with this clearly un-American welcome, yet I know that some part of me also felt that the prayers and even the pinching were full of love.

Masha's second curse also meant that one day I would leave our Mother Church and become a protestant. Devout Armenians were very bothered by the evangelical American protestants who dared to proselytize in Armenia, the land of the first church to accept Christianity in 342 A.D. Who were these foreign protestants to collect converts the way tourists collect souvenirs as they distributed food to the starving Armenians? "Amot kez (shame on you)," the Armenian clergy chanted from the windows in their incense laden vestibules, while shaking their fists at these odars, outsiders, who went from village to village telling our Armenian Apostolic Orthodox people that they needed to be "saved" and "born again." "What utter nonsense! These Americans mean well but they do not understand or appreciate the ancient Christian religions of the world," our Surpazan, Bishop, would say. Like Masha, any Armenian knew that the curse of becoming a protestant was a very ill fate indeed for a newborn.

That's how it is with Armenians. No matter where we are, we are always in the minority. Originating in the Middle East surrounded by many faiths other than Christianity, we're immersed in superstitions like evil eyes. And

Armenians have to work extra hard to get around these terrible ill wishes, like the kesh (bad), ol' Masha put on me before Mama Jahn could protect me with the blue bead, the small, round, button like blue and white amulet that keeps away the evil eye. Armenians have to pray harder and longer than any other Christians who had Turks as neighbors. An evil eye is rotten luck and a lifelong problem. I don't know if I'll ever get on the other side of it.

Reflecting on all this on my birthday, Mama Jahn's fears mounted. As other calamities would surely happen because of the curse of Masha's evil eye, I'd most certainly grow up to be the type of woman who would use margarine for her baking instead of butter, or, worse yet, I'd use cake mixes from the grocery store instead of making Armenian pastries from authentic ancient recipes. Mama Jahn had already planned to teach me how to make all of her recipes as soon as I could hold a spoon, like pilaf and cheorag, beorag, anoushabour and khadayeef and cata and shakar locum. Under this spell, the secret recipes hidden between the cracks of Mama Jahn's wooden bowl would certainly be lost forever.

Mama Jahn was utterly alone with her anxiety, because Masha's curse didn't bother my mother at all. In fact Mother laughed it off, something she learned to do in America where such Armenian ways were ridiculed as backward beliefs of ignorant immigrants. "Oh, Mama Jahn, there's no such thing as the evil eye," she admonished from her hospital bed. "Please, stop it right now . . . I don't want you passing on Old Country peasant ideas like this to my child."

Like the good Armenian grandmother she was, Mama Jahn nodded in agreement saying, "You right, Siroon." She covered her worries and counter-protections in feigned compliance as she scrambled to get home to prepare the house for my arrival. As she was discovering, it was menz, big, work being a new mama jahn. Her first move would be to brew a demitasse of strong Armenian coffee where the specific solution to this curse would certainly be revealed.

Of all the ways my Mama Jahn tried to track evil and stay out of its way, the demitasse was the most crucial. Every day at three in the afternoon Mama Jahn drank her coffee slowly while she waited for the day's stories to align themselves for her interpretation, as her mother had done and her mother before her, for as far back as anyone could remember. The only thing my grandmother did differently from her ancestors and other Armenian ladies was to read her own cup.

Even our Der Hayr acknowledged Mama Jahn's gift. I know because years later he told me, "Your Mama Jahn's readings make very good sense out of life and sometimes she can see future. You listen to her." With the Armenian priest believing in her powers I paid attention and listened to them both.

Reading cups was as necessary to Mama Jahn as breathing.

The day of my birth, the curse day, was distinct in one important respect. Mama Jahn was in a big hurry and hadn't read her fortune before coming to the hospital. She might have been able to stop the curse if she had read her cup before her first visit to me.

So, now that Masha had beaten her to the nursery window, she had to get busy as soon as she got home. Instead of sipping the pulverized brew, she gulped it without really tasting it to get to the grounds quickly. Swallowing the last dot of liquid from the cup, she flipped it cupside down onto its saucer to wait for the sediment to drain down the sides of the cup. Out of sight, the residue settled into revelations while Mama Jahn waited impatiently.

At last, when the bottom of the cup had cooled, Mama Jahn turned the cup right-side up. The dark brown ooze from the dense coffee grounds had made sensual curves, celestial swirls, dark blobs and dots on the sides of the cup as it always did. These patterns contained a secret language known only to those like Mama Jahn who had the gift—the gift of seeing. Peering into the cup, Mama Jahn was quick to see the number three very clearly etched in the coffee grounds on the right side of the cup, next to the handle. She knew that three was a very desirous number for any kind of good luck because of the Holy Trinity. Nothing was more fortunate than having God the Father, God the Son and God the Holy Spirit on your side, and especially on your side of the cup.

Then, as she turned her cup a bit to the right, and as clear as the big dipper constellation in the night sky, she saw the ancient shape of the Armenian cross, and, next to it, square stones that she recognized to be the turquoise jewels that everyone knew warded off the evil eye. "Tanks God, tanks God, tanks God, for showing me what to do to save my anoush Azad from the evil eye," she cried in gratitude for the insight of this fortune.

With that, my Mama Jahn headed straight for her bedroom, pulled open her top dresser drawer and, between her index finger and thumb, shook one of her linen hankies, in which she then wrapped a wad of money secured with a thick rubber band from the Sunday newspaper.

She had been secretly saving this stash of money for her Armenian Orthodox funeral. It would cost dearly to get the impressive twenty-five member Armenian male choir to sing all the appropriate sharagans (religious chants), and hymns. She knew that the honorable Surpazan would require a good size honorarium to officiate when her time came, especially if she wanted him to say highly complimentary things about her at the funeral dinner. Masha's evil eye, however, constituted an emergency.

With specific instructions, she sent her unflagging minion, Bobeeg Jahn, with the funeral money to Ara the jeweler to buy three solid gold Armenian crosses and three of the truest, largest, most unblemished turquoise stones he had. This was no time to cut corners. Nothing but the best to protect her anoush bala jahn, from Masha's curse, even if it was after the fact.

When Bobeeg Jahn returned from his mission, together they carefully unfolded the white tissue paper, within which each piece of jewelry was tightly wrapped. They laid them out on the creamy-white, satin-covered baby yorgahn she had made for my little cradle, then picked up the ornaments to eye them individually. The crosses weighed heavily in her hand, which meant they were loaded with gold. Just to make sure, she tested by biting down with her teeth. Immigrants are very wary of being gypped, because they often are, even by each other. Yes, Ara had sold Bobeeg Jahn the real thing. She put the turquoise stones close to her discerning blue eyes and looked through them into the sun shining in the dining room window. Bobeeg stood by with apprehension, but she deemed them to be perfection. With a quick clap of her hands, Mama Jahn smiled in approval, Bobeeg was relieved.

Next she began placing the precious jewelry in specific places in the house, according to the code revealed in the coffee grounds as dots and dashes. She loosened the threads in a corner of the yorgahn and nestled one gold cross and turquoise bead in the wool batting before sewing it up again.

The next cross she placed under my mattress. The third cross and second turquoise blue bead she hooked together on a diaper safety pin attached to my undershirt, out of sight from the prince of darkness and his evil-doers. Fire was known to be cleansing and protective, so she put the final turquoise jewel in an empty demitasse and stashed it behind a book on the fireplace mantle.

With all this, I would be protected from the evil eye for sure! Mama Jahn could finally relax and anticipate my arrival home with celebrations featuring pastries she made only for Epiphany and stacks of baby clothes she had for months been gathering and then washing in 99% pure Ivory soap before ironing them.

When we arrived home from the hospital, my mother was first to see that Mama Jahn had attached the gold cross and blue bead to my swaddling clothes. She wanted to remove the strange combination of hidden jewelry pinned to my undershirt—the Christian and the pagan, side by side.

"What's the harm," Hayrig said as he rocked me in his massive arms, insisting that it was best to be protected completely in circumstances where matters of the unknown were concerned. "After all, what do we really know about the power of evil?" adding, "Coochie , coochie coo," which means the same in any language.

Mother did not disagree. But she could not care less about such things. She was more concerned about losing the weight she'd gained in her pregnancy so she could wear that stunning royal blue silk V-neck dress she had bought for Leila's wedding, which was only two months away.

That night, when Mother removed Mama Jahn's safety-pin, gold cross and blue bead charm broach to change my clothes, she bit down hard on the cross and took a close look at the turquoise stone. "I wonder where Mama

Jahn got these? They must have cost a fortune," she thought. Then without skipping a beat, she immediately looked at the event through the ever-present lens of her own priorities: "No one bought me any jewelry for having a baby." This was my mother's first whiff that my birth meant sharing Mama Jahn's attentions.

When Mother was changing the sheet on my mattress, above which an oil painting already hung, depicting me as a grown woman surrounded by her gaggle of children and a proud Armenian husband, she found the other crosses and jewels there and in the yorghan. In no time Mother was on her way to Ara the jeweler, clutching two gold Armenian crosses and two turquoise blue stones. When she plunked them down on the glass counter, Ara of course recognized them but craftily said nothing. Wily merchant that he was, he purchased them from her for much less than what Mama Jahn had paid for them. Like Masha, Ara too had a jealous heart that kept him from doing the right thing.

A 3.5 carat ruby necklace caught Mother's eye while she was waiting for him to get the money from his safe. Oh, what a beautiful piece of jewelry, she thought before quickly rationalizing: I deserve it and, after all, ruby is the birthstone for July, and that's when I became a mother.

When Mama Jahn discovered the jewelry was gone from all of the hiding places, except for the safety pin broach that was always on my undershirt, she had a suspicion. And when she saw Mother wearing the ruby necklace to Leila's wedding, she knew for sure. But even my birth wasn't going to disabuse my mama jahn of her long habit of indulging her daughter, even though she immediately loved me best and closest.

The curse on me gave Mama Jahn something else to add to her list of things to worry about for the rest of her life, something else about which to pray endlessly to the Virgin Mary, who understands the pain of a woman's heart, something else to try to change, something else to blame herself for and something else to look for in the grounds of her coffee cup.

When I was old enough that all this was discussed, I asked my hayrig why Mama Jahn slipped up on my birth day . . . why she didn't see Masha's evil eye coming?

And, just as always, Hayrig knew the answer: "As you know, hokis, your Mama Jahn has a heart so pure and gentle and kind that she has great difficulty seeing evil. This causes her to miss the wickedness in the hearts and minds of mischief-makers, mischief-makers like Masha."

Nonetheless, Mama Jahn remained vigilant. She never stopped blaming herself for not putting a gold cross on me before anyone with an evil heart could lay eyes on me. I was never allowed to take off my bead and cross. She constantly pinched me on my vodeeg when we were in the presence of jealous women. And she rubbed flower petals on her eyebrows every day after my curse-day.

My father too and my other relatives who lived with us continued to work hard to make sure the second curse—which might make me forget what it was to be an Armenian—couldn't take hold. From the curse day forward, I would listen to atrocities in all their gruesome detail over and over again. No one ever read me fairy tales. Instead I heard horror tales of massacres, genocides and evil eyes. And every night they'd kiss me many times before I went to sleep, saying asdvadz kesi byieh, anoush Azad, may God keep you, dear Azad.

2 THE DEATH CUP

better to die of embarrassment than to live with shame

Mama Jahn sat on the front porch in her straight-backed wicker chair, sipping her afternoon cup of Armenian coffee. She drank her coffee down to the grounds as she did every day, then flipped it upside down on the saucer, turned it three times, and waited for her fortune to form inside the cup. Simultaneously, a sudden burst of cold wind stirred the leaves from the lawn and she pulled her shawl up around her shoulders. The old man across the street started up his lawn mower and Mama Jahn muttered a curse to him in Armenian for ruining her silence. She used the same curse as when someone dropped an egg in her kitchen: "Azdouzo garagit janit topee," which means "may the fire of God come down upon your soul." Only an odar would mow his lawn on Sunday, she thought.

Then she turned her attention back to her coffee cup. Mama Jahn knew that she was not supposed to read her own cup, that doing so was frowned upon by Middle Easterners, but she chose to ignore this tradition, dismissing it as a superstition.

She lifted her cup from its saucer and began to read her fortune inside the cup. Instantly, she was struck with fear. Her hands faltered; the saucer of her demitasse dropped to the floor. She clutched her head in her hands and dragged her fingers through her hair over and over again, until her tidy bun was pulled completely apart, all the while desperately wailing in Armenian, "Ahmahn, ahmahn, ahmahn, (oh my), I see death, blackness." The sounds of the lawn mower muffled her screams, so no one phoned the police, but from my bedroom where I was examining my zits in the mirror, I

9

heard her call for me at the top of her lungs: "Azaaad, shood, shood (fast, fast), come now, Azad!"

I ran to her, shaking with apprehension, not knowing what to expect. When I found her, she was slumped on the porch, sobbing, holding her head in her hands. "Mama Jahn!" I cried with terror, falling to my knees to look at her more closely, "What's the matter? What's the matter!"

"Azad," she wailed, "I dying, I dying. Take me to my room. Shood, shood."

"Dying? What do you mean you're dying? Sit here, don't move. I'll call an ambulance."

"Votch, no hospital, I die in my own bed."

I looked at her with fear in my ten-year-old heart. "What's going on? Why are you dying, Mama Jahn? I don't see blood. Is it your heart? Where does it hurt?"

"My cup, my cup, I see in my cup I going to die today," and she gestured to the far side of the porch, without raising her head.

I turned to look where she was pointing and saw Mama Jahn's favorite blue demitasse cup that she got in China Town. Mount Fuji was painted on it, which she thought was Mount Ararat.

She must have seen something horrible in her cup. I could feel myself grow pale and cold as I realized what this meant. "The cup," I whispered to her. "Is it in the cup?"

"Haa, haa, yes, yes, in my cup, I going to die."

My heart sank, as I understood: There was no need to call an ambulance, because if it was written in her cup that she was going to die, there was nothing doctors could do.

Mama Jahn collapsed her round, short body onto me and I helped her as she limped slowly to her bedroom. I sat her down on the stool at her dressing table. Then she proceeded to order me around like Mr. Mamoulian, the famous Armenian Hollywood movie director who was her best friend's second cousin twice removed. "Azad, change sheets . . . don't forget pillow cases . . . votch, no flower sheets, use all white sheets, only white . . . fluff yorgahn, comforter, close drapes… turn on lamp. Votch, votch, only put on bottom light."

And then she raised her right arm while I undid her corset of one hundred and eight hooks-and-eyes and helped her put on a white satin nightgown that she had been saving for just this occasion. She brushed her hair back into her usual neat bun, just like the shape of a cata, sweet bread, fastening it at the nape of her neck with black hairpins. She did not yet have enough white hair to use the silver hairpins, but they were waiting in the top of her dresser drawer for when she was old. She was definitely too young to die.

I helped her get into bed where she could be braced on all sides by her collection of bed pillows. Holding her maroon, leatherette-bound phone book, she began calling everyone she loved in alphabetical order, to come and pay their final respects because she was going to die. Over and over again I heard her describe the death cup she had just seen to each of her friends, and with each conversation she sank a little lower in the bed. She was completely lying down by the time she reached the Zadigians.

One by one, the rest of our family arrived home. My mother was first, coming through the door with her arms full of grocery bags. Tearfully, I told her what Mama Jahn had seen in her cup, and she snapped at me, "Darn Mama Jahn and her cups. She'll be the death of me. I'd better start frying the gatlets (Armenian hamburgers), she's got ready for dinner since she's gone to bed. Your hayrig, will be home soon and he'll be starving."

Uncle Mono, who took a shot of rakhi when he heard the terrible news, yelled at my mother who appeared so callous, went into his room, and shut the door.

Aunt Zov, tears streaming down her face, rushed to Mama Jahn's side, taking her a glass of hot tea with quince preserves. "Asdvadz mer, eench khidarag (God of ours, this is horrible)!" Mama Jahn nodded in agreement while eyeing her favorite quince preserves and wondering out loud if a dying person should have cravings for jam.

Hayrig, when he returned home, was not surprised that Mama Jahn believed she would die that night because of what she saw in her cup. He was worried that it would happen because she believed it would. He ate his gatlets and pilaf somberly.

And poor Bobeeg Jahn, my dear grandfather who lived to make Mama Jahn happy, sat in his upholstered paisley-print rocker positioned in front of the television showing only the test pattern, staring and worrying in silence, refusing to come to the table even for his favorite dinner.

As I filled Mama Jahn's hot water bottle, the doorbell rang. Our Der Hayr had arrived wearing his black cassock and carrying a pyx containing a consecrated holy wafer, a nushkhar, and a small cruet of holy muron. No one knew that Mama Jahn had called him. She did not tell anyone that she called her friends, either, and I didn't think it was my place to say anything. Out of embarrassment, my family pretended they were expecting him, and Hayrig gravely showed Der Hayr to Mama Jahn's bedroom.

Der Hayr stood over her, praying for her soul about to depart this earth in the tradition of the last sacraments of the Armenian Orthodox Church. When Hayrig saw how upset I became, he tried to calm me by explaining everything in a whisper, "Hokis, listen to me. Der Hayr is anointing her feet, hands, forehead and mouth with the muron, the holy oil made every seven years in Etchmiadzin, the Holy Sea of all Armenians. The making of the muron is an ancient practice," he continued. "A long, solid-golden arm relic, containing some of the bones of St. Gregory the Illuminator, who is the Patron Saint of Armenia, is used to stir the mixture of oil of balsam and the old muron in an enormous cauldron encrusted with precious jewels."

Hearing this, I reflected on Mama Jahn's arms. They should be contained in a golden relic, too. She did all kinds of wonders with her hands and arms, like rolling out dough, hanging clothes on the clothes line, ironing clothes with no creases anywhere, rocking babies and hugging me . . . not lying there, with her arms crossed over her chest waiting to die.

Mama Jahn should live, live to see that golden arm and the cauldron with all the jewels. She always said that gold and jewels made a woman feel like a takoohee (a queen). Hayrig went on to say, "According to our Christian tradition, the old muron contained traces of the oil that the apostles themselves used to cure people."

I solemnly prayed that the muron would cure Mama Jahn of whatever it was she was dying from rather than anointing her before she died.

Before Hayrig had a chance to speak with Der Hayr, the doorbell rang again. I heard my mother's shocked exclamation as she rushed down the hall to change her clothes and put on fresh lipstick. From the peephole in the door, she had spotted the first of the mourners.

Soon, a solemn procession of Armenians clothed in black with downcast eyes filed into our living room, each lady carrying a hankie and the men holding their tesbih's, obsidian worry beads the shade of unfiltered honey. When all the visitors had squeezed into the sofas and armchairs, the men carried in the dining room chairs and placed them along the edges of the room for the overflow.

Mama Jahn always had a delectable array of her homemade pastries ready in the kitchen cupboard for unexpected company. And this was as unexpected a time for company as I had ever known. My mother, Aunt Zov and I decoratively arranged the cookies, catas and other sweet breads on doilies and passed them on silver-plated trays to the mourners. Cousin Osheen kept the samovar full and steaming with hot chi, which Hayrig and Uncle Mono passed in tea glasses encased in metal holders, alongside shots of rakhi for those who needed more astringent bracing.

"Zvart just starting to enjoy her life after all her hard work. Is just terrible," one of her friends softly cried, under the lace-trimmed hankie Mama Jahn had crocheted for her sixtieth birthday.

Another friend recounted the hours Mama Jahn had helped her make layers upon layers of paklava dough for the lightest, most flaky, delicate tasting and highest paklava anyone had ever eaten. People would say, "When you bite into a piece of Zvart's paklava, it is so crisp and delicate that its crunch could even be heard by a deaf sheepherder in Beiruit."

Uncle Mono vowed that, if God would spare her life, he would never again make Mama Jahn nervous by making curry, which she hated because it splattered and stained the walls in her kitchen yellow and sent the smell of curry throughout the entire house, obliterating the subtle perfume of her clarified butter and permeating the furniture, rugs and draperies for days.

My mother—regardless that she didn't believe in fortunes from cups—put a framed photo of Mama Jahn, taken of her when she was all dressed up for a bridal shower, on our shiny ebony piano and lit a red votive candle next to it, being careful to put the candle on a saucer first, knowing that was what Mama Jahn would be concerned about if she knew.

Bobeeg Jahn continued his silent vigil from his rocker, quietly fidgeting with his tesbih and still staring at the TV test pattern as though it were a window to heaven.

After taking all this in, I went back to position myself at the foot of Mama Jahn's bed, looking up at the new icon of the Virgin Mary that hung above her. The icon, which I'd hung for her the week before, was a gift from a visiting Greek priest whom the Der Hayr had brought to our home for dinner. She had baked khourabia for dessert. The Greek Der Hayr said it was like none other he had ever eaten, except for those his long deceased mother in Cypress made when he was a boy. That was the first time I had seen a priest cry over a cookie.

I had never told anyone, but the reflection of the Virgin Mary and her immaculate heart often appeared to me in our O'Keefe and Merritt glass oven door. That convinced me that Mary, the Mother of God, was always in the kitchen with Mama Jahn. Therefore, I took this opportunity to hope and pray the Mother of God would understand and ask God to change His mind about taking Mama Jahn at this time. I prayed to the Virgin Mary like I had never prayed before. I begged her to tell me why Mama Jahn had to die, this lady who lived only to make the lives of her family happy by nurturing us with her glorious food and holding us in her wondrous heart. She doesn't deserve to die, I earnestly prayed. This brave, hard working, precious soul still had yet to finish the yorgahn for Cousin's baby shower. She still had walnuts in the ground waiting for the day when they'd be cured and ready to dig up to make into the most delectable walnut preserves anyone has ever eaten. And, she had to live to see me grow up! I blinked back my tears.

Mama Jahn opened her eyes, looked at the clock next to her bed and saw that it was eleven. Only an hour to go. With one eye open looking in my direction and with a tilt of her head she motioned for me to come close. I bent over, placing my ear close to her mouth to hear her. I wondered if I should get paper to write them down. They might be her last words. Slowly, she whispered to me that she had to cheesh, and asked me to help her to the bathroom, which I did as a final gesture of gratitude and pleasure for my dearest, sweetheart of a grandmother whom I loved more dearly than anyone else in the entire world. She could have cheeshed in my hands, I didn't care.

I was so sad and tortured that she was dying and soon I'd never see her again. I held back my tears so as not to upset her anymore than she already was.

After I put her back to bed and tucked her in, smoothing the hairs that had come loose around her ears, she lay there for a while looking at the ceiling. Her gray-blue eyes looked clear and she appeared to be thinking very hard. I was amazed at how alert she looked for someone about to die.

As it got closer to midnight, I saw no change in Mama Jahn. I got desperate and I promised God the Father, God the Son and God the Holy Spirit that I would be the good Armenian girl that Mama Jahn always wanted me to be and learn everything I could from her to grow up exactly the way my family had planned. I'd iron Hayrig's shirts so the collars didn't have any wrinkles, I'd marry a rich Armenian and never even look at a blond blue-eyed American boy again, I'd never talk back, I'd go to college and beome a teacher like Hayrig planned for me, and I'd become the best Armenian baker in Los Angeles.

As the minutes ticked by, Mama Jahn closed her eyes, grabbed at the center of her chest, took a deep breath, let it out, and then just lay there. The palms of my hands got sweaty, my breathing got faster and my mouth dried up. I sank into the rug, covered my eyes and cried so hard that tears came out of my eyes and my nose. Because Mama Jahn wasn't paying attention, I was able to wipe my nose on the hem of my dress. I looked up to Mama Jahn then to the Virgin Mary and back again to Mama Jahn, as her eyelids fluttered and she said to me, "Remember, Azad Jahn, yes kezi shad ga serem."

"I love you very much, too, Mama Jahn, very much," I answered like I did every night before going to bed.

By this time, Bobeeg Jahn, Hayrig, Mother, Uncle Mono and Aunt Zov were in the room to help me wait for Mama Jahn's last breath. We waited and waited. Nothing happened.

I smelled the luscious fragrances of the cata, paklava and shakar locum cookies that the mourners were eating wafting down the hallway into her bedroom. So could everyone. I heard Mama Jahn's stomach growl.

In a weak, thin voice, she asked everyone except me to go back and visit with the company in the living room. "It's ahmot (shameful) to leave company alone." They did as she asked and filed out of her room, glancing backwards at her with tear-filled eyes. When they were all gone, she sat up, told me to get the "death cup" she had left on the front porch. I ran to get it and gently put it in her hands.

She wiggled herself up into a sitting position, bolstered by her many pillows, and exclaimed in her best, broken English, "Look, Azad Jahn, before I die, you look. I show you where fortune shows I die and you learn, you learn to read cups."

She slipped her eyeglasses around her ears and we struggled to fit both our heads into the tiny cup, to see the prediction that she would die by the end of the day. It was easy to see the long, thick, jagged line of dark coffee grounds running vertically from the bottom of the cup all the way to the lip. That was the line that signified immediate death. It was now twelve-thirty in the morning and the people in the parlor were nodding off and now the stale smell of cigarette butts had taken the place of pastry. I heard her stomach growl again.

"This kind of line always means death," she murmured, handing me the cup with a mournful sigh and sinking back down into her pillows.

I held the cup not knowing what was expected of me. I was nervously running my fingers up and down the sides, when my thumb slipped and swiped away part of the coffee-ground death line. I looked at the black sediment on my thumb and thought of Ash Wednesday when Der Hayr puts the sign of the cross on our foreheads with black ashes from burned palm crosses. With a heavy heart I turned my eyes to peer again at the fortune. It was then that I saw that my thumb had uncovered a crack in the cup. "Mama Jahn, did you know there was a crack here?"

"Wat you mean crack? Broken? The cup broken?" she snapped as she pushed herself up to take a look. "Show me," she insisted. She grabbed the cup from me and looked inside. Within a split second, I saw her face change from worry to anger. She took her hankie and swiftly wiped out the remains of the coffee residue from the crack, revealing the source of her fortune. A dark shadow came over her face.

"Vie ahmahn, ahmotos medmim (from this embarrassment I die)! Dis cup is broke!" she cried implacably. "Dis line what supposed to mean I die, it is a broke in the cup. Why you show me this? Vie Ahmahn, I not going to die tonight!"

I realized with a shock that instead of being thrilled and relieved that this was not her death prediction as she had understood it to be, my grandmother was spitting mad. Mama Jahn ranted, but I paid no attention. I knew that my prayers had reached the ears and heart of the Holy Mother of God and that's why she didn't die. That's why we found a crack, now made visible. I crossed myself in my head at least twenty times in grateful thanksgiving. "God," I said, "I will never forget what you have done."

Mama Jahn reached for the glass of rakhi that Der Hayr had forgotten next to her bed and drank it down in one swift gulp. "Oh, what I going to do?" she wailed.

"What do you mean, Mama Jahn? You're going to celebrate! You are going to get up and have cheese and cheorag and hot chi with quince preserves and olives and simit and shakar locum with all of your friends."

She shook her head, "Votch, votch. I supposed to die. Ahmot, ahmot, shame, shame, everybody waiting for me to die."

"Come on, let's get up and tell everyone the good news."

"Che ha, che, ha (no yes, no yes)," she repeated over and over again.

She turned her back on me by rolling over onto her side.

"Why you show me, Azad? Why you do? To die is better than to be amot. Go way."

Now I too had been banished from her room. I left, her words stinging even through my joy and relief to find Hayrig. He would know what to do because he could always solve horrible problems. I found him reading one of Mama Jahn's favorite Armenian poems to the group of mourners. When they all saw me, there was an immediate hush as they turned to hear the news. "Hayrig," I said, "Mama Jahn needs you. Now." He solemnly closed his book and followed me down the hall towards Mama Jahn's room. As we walked away, I could hear the room of mourners erupt into fresh sobs and the clicking of their tesbihs move into high gear.

"Hayrig," I said in a low voice, "We have a big problem." I quickly told him what had happened. Hayrig nodded to me and looked pensive for a moment. Then he patted my head and went to Mama Jahn's side, kneeling next to her. He cupped her hands into his and told her how relieved he was that God had spared her and not to worry, that he'd handle everything, that this was nothing to be ashamed of, that she'd be able to hold her head high when this was over.

She stopped crying, kissed his hand and let out a long sigh. "Kourken Jahn, khelket sirem, I love your brain. You save my life."

Hayrig straightened up and walked purposefully into the parlor to face the mourners. As they raised their heads in his direction, fully expecting to hear that Mama Jahn had passed into paradise, the click, click, clicking of their tesbihs, came to a halt. When he held everyone in rapt attention, Hayrig announced in a slow and booming voice: "There has been a miracle!"

The room full of Mama Jahn's dearest friends cried out with joy. With his commanding presence Hayrig continued, "Our one and only Holy One, our merciful and benevolent Asdvadz has interceded and spared Mama Jahn because of the earnest prayers, holy muron and heartfelt tears of her dearest friends and family. Where there is such deep and abiding love, there is God."

The room erupted into shouts and prayers of thanksgiving and Der Hayr cried like the Greek priest.

People were quick to go home because of the late hour and very soon the house was left to us, Mama Jahn's immediate family.

It was not until everyone had gone that Mama Jahn finally emerged from her bedroom, back in her everyday flannel nightgown and flowered robe, and we all sat around the dining room table and ate what was left of the pastries. She was soon her old self, chastising my mother for not serving string cheese with the cheorag and asking her how could she have forgotten to serve the Blenheim apricot jam she had just finished bottling to her friends?

"She's going to send me to an early grave, that woman," muttered Mother, as she left the table.

The rest of the family went to bed too, but Mama Jahn and I remained at the table. She had rested all day and was wide awake. My eyes were wide open too, in awe of the miracle that had just occurred.

And then there was another miracle. Mama Jahn, who kept family secrets as sacred stories between God and herself, said to me, "Azad Jahn, I going to tell you everything about our family. I'm going to give you everything in my heart and you must promise you will never forget. If I died tonight all the stories would have died with me. Maybe that not the best ting."

I crossed my heart and made the sign of the cross. "Yes, Mama Jahn, tell me . . . but do you mean you're going to tell me everything? Even the ahmot things?"

"Eye-o, yes, I tell you all the ahmot things too . . . everything honest," she promised, looking up to God. "For many years I save coffee cups with special fortunes…fortunes too important to wash out because each one has important story to remember."

Now all the mismatched demitasse cup and saucer sets we had made sense. "Where are all these cups, Mama Jahn?"

"In hall closet, in pocket of my old coat I never wear anymore, is green and black cup. A red cup with a gold heart decoration is wrapped in piece of white silk in your mama's hope chest. In drawer of my dressing table, folded in nice piece of red velvet, is dark blue cup with sev black Easter lamb on front. And on shelf in garage, where Uncle Mono hides his ahmot magazines, is candy box with a yellow cup."

As she remembered each hiding place she became more distant. I could see it in her eyes. She was living in those cups as if they were the stage upon which her life was centered.

"Tomorrow we start. That's enough now. I tired," she announced then wandered off down the hallway to bed. When she had her hand on the doorknob to her bedroom, she paused and turned to look back at me,

"Remember, Azad Jahn, yes kezi shad ga serem."

I love you very much, too, Mama Jahn, very much," I answered as I did every night.

3 THE MISSING CUP

always believe the worst
and trust nothing to be as it seems

When I returned home from school the next day, Mama Jahn kept her word about revealing the truth about our family.

"Number one and most important story have no cup," she began, as she admonished me to pay close attention to what was about to unfold as though it was a matter of life or death.

"Azad Jahn, I never forget fortune I see in missing cup many, many years ago," said Mama Jahn, as she sat at our kitchen table with her eye lids closed and her hands around a bowl of freshly pulverized coffee beans, which permeated the warm afternoon air hanging heavily around us. "It was very bad time, very bad."

I held on with both hands to the seat of the blue plastic kitchen chair I was sitting on, my right leg doing a new thing under the table—shaking up and down like my Uncle Mono's leg did—as she began revealing her memories by saying, "now I telling you what I remember."

Throughout my childhood, I'd overheard pieces of stories in an Armenian dialect that I didn't really understand, which the grownups used when I was near. I was always left out, with the really great details right there but out of reach. I had to live with the emptiness, to live with the dullness and stillness of it along side the person I was becoming, but as Mama Jahn began to talk, that emptiness quivered and quaked, like a butterfly flexing its wings for the first time from inside its cocoon.

So settled in with both fear and fascination, I listened as Mama Jahn took me back, way back, to the time when she was an 18-year-old woman in the Old Country and married to her first husband, Sarkis, with whom she was madly in love. Another grandfather! I never knew I had any other grandfather besides my Bobeeg Jahn. This was the kind of thing I was hoping to hear—real stories about my family, which meant I would know more about me. My leg stopped jumping around and I began to pay close attention to her every word.

"In these times," Mama Jahn began, "bad peoples in government in our town in Russia steal from good people, peaceful people. They steal and beat up every body's. They murder for no good reasons."

She explained that Grandfather Sarkis was a Tashnag. I knew where the Russian town was on the map (near the Caspian Sea in today's Azerbaijan) and I knew we hated Turks, but I knew nothing about the Tashnags. Mama Jahn explained that they were a political group who believed that the only way for social change was through violence. Sarkis used his earnings to finance his revolutionary party, and for the same purpose, Mama Jahn secretly made clarified butter that her maid sold for her in the bazaars and door-to-door in the neighboring villages. Still the discrimination persisted. Even the priests had abandoned their hopes for peace when their meetings, pleadings and earnest prayers had failed to keep the Russian government from confiscating all their church properties. The clergy begged the Tashnags for protection. Sarkis and other Tashnags fought to defend the Church of the Holy Transfiguration, but only Sarkis was caught and arrested.

"Azad Jahn, Sarkis was in prison and I always afraid he die there because they beat him every day." Her eyes misted as she remembered. I put my hand over hers. "But I not let this happen! No. I make up my mind I going to save him." With that her face took on a determined look, and she continued, "And I decide I do everything I can—everything—to get Sarkis free."

Then she turned to me with a new sadness in her eyes. "I have to pay high price. Not just rubles."

Throughout the months of the long Russian winter Sarkis's devoted wife, Mama Jahn, sneaked around the jail house where Sarkis was being held captive, looking for the guards whom her friends had told her were open to bribes for his release.

"Azad, I start buying everything—every guard want someting different. I do everyting I have to do to get Sarkis home again."

She found that the guard at the main gate wanted French perfume for his sweetheart and cigars for himself. Clearly, he didn't know how much more she was willing to pay. The guard at the inner door wanted rubles. Lots and lots of rubles. He did know. But the guard who held the key to the jail gate wanted the most costly favor. He lusted after sexual favors with a certain woman in the village, Masha, who was Mama Jahn's age.

Sex! I got to hear about sex? My leg started up again and wiggled even faster than Uncle Mono's. Sex was a subject in my family like many others that was never discussed. I knew about it from listening to the kids at school. But from Mama Jahn? I was amazed!

Mama Jahn continued, explaining that she knew very little of Masha—just that she was an unfortunate woman whose parents, when they were alive, were unable to make a suitable marriage match for her because they had nothing to pay for her dowry. When her parents both died from influenza one winter, she was left all alone as a 14-year-old girl. With no relatives to take her in and care for her, and no one to give her a place in the social system, Masha had to take care of herself in a fashion that was to become her way of life. So she had to take care of her own needs for money, for companionship, for the need to be needed, by secretly being available to men outside her village for performing intimate sexual acts that wives wouldn't allow.

Mama Jahn wrestled with her conscience. She was a churchgoing Christian woman who knew right from wrong. She knew that what Masha was forced to do to make ends meet was not how any woman would want to live if they had a choice. Masha would rather be married to someone like her Sarkis, who had a good business, social status and was able to take care of his wife and family. But, how Masha lived was her business, and she could use the money. Who was Mama Jahn to argue the morality of how Masha lived her life? The main thing was that she could use the money and Mama Jahn could use her services to help get Sarkis released from jail.

So Mama Jahn was determined to meet with Masha and arrange for her to visit the jailer and give him whatever he wanted, over and over again, for as long as it took for him to turn the key to let Sarkis free.

"What I know? I tink doing business with Masha like buying leg of lamb at butcher—I say what I want, I pay money, and I go. What I know?"

Mama Jahn started out by foot to the next village where Masha lived, then got a lift in the back of a hay cart the rest of the way from a passing farmer. By the time she found her house she was exhausted. She wanted to get this over as fast as she could, so she could get back to her comfortable home and family.

When Masha answered her knock at the door, Mama Jahn entered and was startled to see that Masha lived in a nice home that was decorated with lovely turmeric, saffron and cinnamon-colored silk pillows of all sizes, drapery made from thick brocades and oriental rugs stacked at least six deep. Masha was doing well. She could smell the unmistakable aroma of freshly baked simit cookies. Sesame seeds were expensive. This was not a woman to be pitied as she had been thinking.

"After I see how Masha living, I not sad for her and I no worry about doing business with a boze ," Mama Jahn said.

Masha was not beautiful in the way Armenian women were considered beauties. The signs of a woman who worked hard were obvious from the roughness of her manner and the hardness carved into the lines in her face. But she had rings on her fingers and many coins decorating her head-band. Her hair was black, shiny from oiling and luxurious and curly as it flowed in a long length down her strong looking back. Her tallness made it easy to look down on Mama Jahn, which made my grandmother feel uncomfortable until they both sat down. Then they were just two women staring into each other's eyes.

"Masha ask me, 'Why you here? It can't be for coffee or locum. We know each other for long time and you never come to visit before.'

I take a breath then explain that I need pay her to service Sarkis's jailer.

"'Oh, I see. You need me,' Masha say.

"'Yes, I do.'

"'You need me do something you will not do. Is that right?

"'Yes, when you put it that way, yes, you're right.'"

Mama Jahn felt attacked, like Masha was trying to pick a fight. But she also knew she had to hire her because the jailer specifically requested Masha. She took a chance and challenged her.

"Do you want the job or not? I can go elsewhere, and with what I have for trade, I'll not have trouble hiring someone else." And with that she stood and stared Masha down.

"'Sit, sit, Digeen. Let's negotiate. I'm not a hard woman, just a business woman. Sit.'"

Besides rubles she bargained with Masha for a complete wardrobe made from the finest silks and brocades from Sarkis's sewing studio. He had been putting the finishing touches on the collection to sell to the mayor's wife during the time when he was arrested. Masha couldn't resist and agreed as long as Mama Jahn never told anyone how she acquired the clothing.

As Mama Jahn talked, I kept thinking that both these women had such a hard life, nothing like life of women in America.

Mama Jahn heard from Masha a few days later that Sarkis was to be set free. Throughout the months of the long Russian winter she and Sarkis's loving mother Nooritza had planned what they would do when, not if, Sarkis returned. They included Mama Jahn and Sarkis's daughters, eleven-year-old Zepure, and little six-year-old Siroon (who would become my mother) in the discussion. As soon as Mama Jahn received the news, the women of the household began preparing all his favorite foods and decorating the walls of their home with yards of silks and brocades gathered from Sarkis's sewing studio. They scattered plush, oversized pillows covered with lush fabrics for their guests to lounge upon. From the ceiling hung oil lanterns, covered with cutouts of stars and moons.

Everything had to be made perfect for his homecoming, but in the midst of the happy preparations, Mama Jahn's memory of what she had done to get him out of jail buzzed at the back of her mind like a swarm of blood-sucking flies all over her flesh. And as happy as she was, Mama Jahn couldn't forget what Masha had to do even though it was something she did willingly. Mama Jahn didn't let her bad feelings interfere with carrying out preparations for his homecoming as long as no one, especially Sarkis, found out that she was no better than a pimp and that she had given all his expensive clothes away to a known boze.

When the lanterns were lit, their light danced around the room with flickering shadows of images mimicking the night sky. A fire from the kitchen warmed the entire home and its chimney sent forth the perfumed scent of cardamom and cinnamon from the steaming anooshabour (sweet rice pudding), into the village, signaling a celebration in the making. All who were in range of the evocative spices knew that they were invited. And then before long, just as Masha had said, there was Mama Jahn's dear Sarkis at the door.

Sarkis's mother Nooritza heated the water, and Mama Jahn poured it into a large tub, which sat in the middle of the kitchen floor. Zepure and little Siroon dissolved essence of roses into the warm water and floated dried flower petals they had gathered in the summer.

Sarkis closed his eyes and soaked in his luxurious bath, breathing in the perfumed air that swirled around him as the steam that arose encircled his bruised and tortured body. Mama Jahn and Nooritza wordlessly observed the lacerations that scarred his body and tried not to think about the pain he had obviously suffered at the hands of his captors. Blinking back their tears, the women began the work of gently sloughing away the damage of months of abuse to his skin. When he began to flinch under their ministrations they quickly dropped their cloths, perched on stools and showered him with fresh, warm water that cascaded over his head, as though re-baptizing him into his life of comfort and safety while laughing and singing a simple Armenian bath-time chant: "wonderful nice, wonderful nice, wonderful nice."

As he stepped out of the tub, Zepure ran to fetch the thick Egyptian towels they had purchased on the black market. Only Turkish towels were sold in their bazaars but they would never have anything Turkish in their home, not even a towel.

The women circled him with raised arms holding the towel up to block any bit of a draft that might cause him a chill and patted him dry. Siroon handed her mother his soft flannel caftan into which Mama Jahn had sewn a small Armenian cross with the thinnest of gold threads months ago in anticipation of his homecoming. But before dressing him in his robe, Mama Jahn carefully and lightly applied her precious oil of hyssop onto his abused skin, from the top of his head to the bottom of his feet. It was as though she was anointing him. That's how much she loved him.

Sarkis stood, warm and clean, gazing at the smiles of his wife, his mother, and his daughters, whom he had thought he might never see again, and felt in that moment that his heart could not possibly hold more happiness. He opened his arms and pulled them all into a tight embrace.

Then Sarkis rested on his back with his arms outstretched on a pile of handmade, wooly yorghans so deep he was unaware of the ground below and fell asleep.

Mama Jahn paused in the storytelling to pour me a cup of honey tea, and as much as I wanted the tea I wanted her to keep talking. "Mama Jahn, sit down and keep talking. Let me get the cheese and olives to go with our tea." So she continued.

Throughout the village, everyone was talking about how Sarkis had been released from jail after months of imprisonment without a trial or hearing. This was a fate he had been prepared to suffer for his allegiance to the radical Tashnag political party. "Finally," he thought, "finally someone in a position of power realized who they were dealing with and set me free." This made him feel very proud. Mama Jahn was the only one, besides Masha and the guards, who knew why he was really freed. And she wasn't ever talking.

But, tonight was reason for celebrating: Sarkis was home and he was alive. This was the time for Sarkis's family to wear their festive Armenian clothes that they had folded away in a wooden chest the day their papa was taken away. They wore their deep eggplant-colored velvet skirts with matching boleros and decorated their arms and necks with what remained of the family jewelry: gold chains, gold bracelets and gold ankle bells for the girls. Zepure danced and giggled and Siroon jumped up and down, delighting in the tinkling of the tiny bells.

Tashnag by Tashnag, the neighbors all gathered to rejoice at the good news of Sarkis's return. One by one, with many tears and hugs, the men and women of the village approached Sarkis and shared their thanksgiving for his safe return. Then, the musicians arrived, playing the soulful oud (lute), pulsating duduk (drum), and the clear, reedy clarinet. And then the party began. The women snapped their fingers and let out cheerful, high-pitched sounds of delight, *dasheeg, dasheeg,* and the men performed intricate folk dances, suddenly feeling younger and fuller of life than they had the day before. Drink and food were the star attractions of the evening. Usually, at such village parties all the women helped in the kitchen, but not at Sarkis's home. He had hired help and tonight all the servants were on hand to prepare for the feast. Rakhi poured freely into their glasses and the singing became louder.

When Mama Jahn told me about the food, it was like magic. Throughout the evening the servants carried in trays of foods high above

23

their heads and set them with a flourish onto pillows on the floors strewn with oriental carpets. And they kept the food coming as if the platters were being delivered from a secret passageway connected to a prestigious restaurant from the center of the city. Mama Jahn had planned for the meal to be remarkable: thirty varieties of mazas, cooked skewers of ten different lamb and chicken kebabs and stews, fifteen assorted pilafs, stacks of warm unleavened breads, and finally the trays of disarmingly imaginative and delectable pastries that no one in the village was capable of executing except for Mama Jahn.

Only sheer exhaustion on the part of the revelers could end such festivities. As the villagers returned to their homes, the servants made quick work of cleaning everything and restoring the home to normal. Zepure and Siroon had long since fallen asleep on cushions in the corner of the room. The servants made up the bed for Sarkis and Mama Jahn in their usual place on the oriental carpets and departed into the dark evening leaving them alone together.

Mama Jahn made Sarkis a demitasse of strong Armenian coffee, and as she presented it to him, he took a sip through the thick foam and uttered a satisfying "ahhh." He then offered her a sip from his cup. Together they sat and finished the coffee to the dregs, finally turning over the cup in preparation for a reading. When it was time, Mama Jahn righted the cup and read what she saw aloud, pointing to the shapes of the coffee grounds in the cup. Her eyes sparkled as she described their upcoming trip to Greece.

All signs showed that it was going to be unlike any holiday they had ever had. Here was the big ship that they would take for their journey. Here the interesting new land they would explore together with a fingernail sliver of a moon above it. It was just what they both wanted to know. Sarkis held her face in his hands and kissed her, feeling the warmth from her lips permeate his body. Sarkis laid his head in her lap and my Mama Jahn gently stroked his hair, both feeling the bliss that came from their being together once again. And as he drifted to sleep under his yorgahn, with his family surrounding him, he thought he had died and gone to heaven.

It was the most romantic story I had ever heard.

4 THE CUP OF SACRIFICIAL LAMBS

fear the man who does not fear God

"Next day after Sarkis's party, Azad Jahn, I very happy sleeping. I tink I dreaming when I hear heavy boots marching. Closer and closer the sound come and I wake up. This not dream, I say to myself and I sit up very scared."

Hearing this, I sat up in my chair very scared too. Without any warning, Mama Jahn told me, continuing her story, Russian soldiers stampeded into their house right through the front door, ramming it with the butts of their rifles. Before anyone could figure out what was happening, these terrifying men in uniforms yanked Sarkis out from under his yorgahn, and dragging his legs, threw my grandfather into the street like a twisted sack of potatoes.

Hearing Sarkis's front door being smashed had made the hair of everyone in the neighborhood stand on end. Was it just a few hours since they were guests in Sarkis's home celebrating his return from jail? Before the dust had settled from Sarkis hitting the dirt, the village men had gathered, standing close enough to observe, but at a safe distance from any involvement. Their families nervously looked from behind curtained windows and partly cracked open front doors.

Zepure and Siroon peeked out from behind Mama Jahn's dress. Transfixed with terror, the three of them watched from the front porch as one of the soldiers yelled at their papa and another soldier held him down. They forced him to kneel before another man in a fancier, more decorated uniform, who demanded, *"Renounce the Tashnags and go back to your family, or be murdered as a traitor to the government, in front of all your family and friends."*

"My Sarkis was very brave man, Azad. Very brave," Mama Jahn said sadly. I held her hand, afraid to hear what would come next.

25

"I will never renounce my allegiance to the Tashnag Party," Sarkis said. Then looking skyward he screamed, *"Death to all who suppress freedom, and to those who take away our voice as independent Armenians, death to all of you!"* These were the last words she and his children heard their papa say. Then Sarkis tekelled (spit), on the face of the head soldier as he stared at him straight in the eyes.

The decorated officer in charge pulled his sword from his side, and with pursed lips, sent his sword slicing through the air like a streak of lightening, and in that flash Sarkis's life was over.

"Papa!" Siroon and Zepure screamed, *"Papa Jahn, Papa Jahn . . . our lovely Papa!"* They turned their heads away from the unimaginable sight and buried themselves in Mama Jahn's dress.

"Both Siroon and Zepure go crazy like me," Mama Jahn told me. "I see Siroon hitting the floor with her fists crying over and over, *"What have you done to our family, Hyrig? What about us? Aren't we are more important than the Tashnags?"*

It was too late for questions.

The neighbor men averted their eyes to the ground, as they quickly joined their families in their homes. Mama Jahn and her daughters stood alone while window shades came down all around. She overheard the baker say to his wife as they scurried away, *"A dead jackass is not afraid of the lion."* His wife hit him across his head with her large open hand, which just made him run faster to his shop, into which he pulled his wife, locking the door behind them.

Mama Jahn screamed and cried at the same time, pulled at her hair, threw handfuls of dirt and pebbles after the soldiers, ripped the bottom of her dress to shreds and stumbled into her house, now without a door to close out the world, unable to look at, much less tend to, her Sarkis's dismembered body. Back in the house, from the gaping opening where the door used to be, the girls stood, transfixed watching their papa's blood drain from his severed head onto the hopscotch lines in the street where they had played the day before. Later that night, a few Tashnag friends came out of nowhere and quickly took Sarkis, all of him, away and buried him in the church graveyard. All that was left of their papa, Mama Jahn's husband and Nooritza's son, was his reddish brown blood flowing down the street and puddling at the curb.

This was no story for a child my age. But my mother was even younger than I am now when she saw what happened to her father. Hearing about Sarkis's death for the first time, I was horrified, but I was also somehow calmed, because coming to understanding my family's brokenness was the beginning of my becoming whole. I stared at Mama Jahn quietly, waiting to hear what would happen next. She had tears on her cheeks.

Sarkis's blood ran down the street, ran through his children's bodies, and now they themselves ran—ran towards a new life. My mother as a little girl ran with Mama Jahn from the soldiers' swords; ran for cover so they, too, would not be killed; ran to dig up their secret money buried in the backyard to purchase black market passports and exit papers to leave immediately for America where Mama Jahn knew they would be safe; ran around the house for family treasures that contained the memory of who they were—the pair of Mama Jahn's solid gold engagement bracelets, Papa's gold pocket watch and Mama Jahn's mother's wedding ring—some were sold and the rest were sewn into the linings of their clothes.

Mama Jahn had used most of their rubles for bribes to get Sarkis out of prison. She had assumed that when he was out of jail he would soon make more money making clothes for the very wealthy in his design studio. But now all hope was lost and those who knew told Mama Jahn that there was an execution list filled with names of people associated with Sarkis. They had to leave the Old Country where there was nothing for them now, except worry, sorrow and more death.

They ran to find a temporary home with Grandma Nooritza. Mama Jahn couldn't afford the passage for three tickets unless she sold her engagement bracelets. She and Nooritza agreed that it would be a shame to sell such exquisite jewelry that held such significance for the women in the family. Mama Jahn rationalized that she would make a lot of money in America, where everyone became rich so that she could send for Zepure right away. Nooritza cried that she couldn't bear to lose her son and both granddaughters in the same week, and then assured Mama Jahn that she would take good care of Zepure, with whom she had forged a special loving attachment over the years. She insisted that Mama Jahn and Siroon not worry but leave right away and be safe. Nooritza was moving to the home of relatives in a distant mountain top village, where she and Zepure would be safe from the government.

Finally, out of time and out of breath, they all looked at each other and realizing what it meant to leave Zepure behind, they cried and cried.

After several train trips they arrived at a port at the Mediterranean Sea, where they boarded a Greek ship bound for America. Mama Jahn and Siroon huddled at the back of the steerage section on the ocean liner that would bring them to America. They clung so closely to each other that their breathing had the same timing, their breath the same smell, and their hearts skipped the same beats. They clung closely to each other because all they now possessed in the world was the shared memory of Sarkis being beheaded in the street right in front of their eyes. They looked backwards most of the time, knowing what was behind them but with no idea of what was yet to come. In seventeen days they would be in the land of the free, the land where Christians lived in peace, the land where Sarkis's blood could not follow them down the street.

Endless hours of being violently shifted back and forth by the movement of the heaving waves made them sick to their stomachs. Added to that was the lack of good food and fresh water. The hole for a toilet was in a wood plank set over a pan whose contents they had to dump into the ocean when it was full, making them sicker and sicker. At home even the odor of overcooked stew made Siroon nauseated.

The wooden floorboards of the ship stank with the smells of previous refugees who had sat like rotting apples on other voyages. The clothes the people wore in steerage had the stench of sickness and pain. Siroon longed for the pretty dresses her papa made for her.

Each day Mama Jahn got weaker and felt sure they were never going to see America. The round, prosperous figure, which she had proudly carried beneath lovely clothes Sarkis had fashioned for her, was withering and beginning to take on the dreaded skeletal look of a DP, or worse, a victim of starvation from the genocide. (Between 1895 and 1897 the Turks massacred as many as 300,000 Armenians, and in the first genocide of the twentieth century, 1.5 million Armenians died and many, many more were displaced.)

Every day Siroon thought about Zepure, wondering what was she doing, what Grandma Nooritza had made for her dinner, and was she happy to have all the dresses for herself? And every day Mama Jahn thought about Zepure, too. Did she cry for her Mama Jahn? Was she eating enough? Was she well? Had the soldiers come looking for them?

The men aboard the ship had devised a way to make a small fire. Over this they kept a constant flame under their Armenian coffee, which they consumed all day and night while they smoked cigarettes and sat cross-legged together, mostly in silence. The aroma from the coffee found Mama Jahn and circled round her head, giving her no peace from her disastrous misreading of their coffee cup the night before his murder.

"Over over I blame myself, Azad Jahn," she told me. "I hate myself and cry to myself because I make such terrible mistake." Mama Jahn vowed that she would never again presume a cup reading based on what she thought she knew. She would always be on guard for the unwanted fortunes lurking in the cup. She now knew the meaning of the Armenian saying, believe the worst and trust nothing to be as it seems.

On the fourteenth day of the journey, Siroon woke up in Mama Jahn's arms to find her head pounding and a wet latchag (cloth), wrapped tightly around her head. She had fainted because she hadn't eaten in two days. They had run out of rubles, but their destination was still a few days away. Siroon could see the pain in her Mama Jahn's eyes. Frantic with worry, Mama Jahn suddenly caught the glare of coins being unwrapped from a hankie concealed between another passenger's ponderous tzeezeegs. They were Masha's large breasts! She didn't know Masha was making this trip until now.

Even though they were not friends, Mama Jahn reasoned that she and Masha had forged a special connection. And Masha had money. A lot of money! And even though Masha was a boze, it didn't matter to Mama Jahn where her money came from right now. She had money that could buy food. And no doubt that some of it was her money.

Mama Jahn turned to Siroon, nervously massaging her hands together as she muttered to herself, *"I see Masha has money. What should I do? I cannot ask her for money to buy food. It would be ahmot. Sarkis would be horrified. I would bring dishonor to his name by asking for money, especially from her. But Sarkis is no longer alive. And we are starving. I must put aside my pride now for the sake of my child. We must survive."*

With a determined resolve, she carefully approached Masha in a way she never thought she would ever have to do. In her most articulate and polite, flattering Armenian, she said, *"Masha Jahn, you are known as someone with a kind and generous heart. Please can I borrow a little money to buy eggs for my little daughter, Siroon, and me? We are sick from hunger. We beg of you to have mercy on us."* And then she went one step further and kissed the top of Masha's hands, like how we kiss the Der Der's hand after the Holy Badarak (Divine Liturgy).

Masha looked down from her perch on an overturned crate where she watched everything going on and enjoyed the sight of Mama Jahn begging and groveling at her feet. It made her feel equal, if not superior, to this fine lady who never had the time or interest even to have a cup of coffee with her before and who had hired her to prostitute herself for her husband's release from prison. Reluctantly, Masha gave her the money while admonishing her to remember that this was just a loan. Not that it was much money, just a quarter in American money, but she wanted to have something to rub Mama Jahn's nose in.

"Yes, of course, yes, of course it's a loan. I wouldn't have it any other way. I will never forget your kindness," Mama Jahn insisted as she backed away.

Mama Jahn immediately bought two hardboiled eggs from the steward who walked through the deck several times a day rattling hardboiled havgeets in his pockets, looking down on the peasant passengers he knew would eventually do anything for one of his precious pocket full of eggs.

Slowly and deliberately Siroon and she each ate their eggs, saving the crunchy shells for dessert.

Two days later they arrived at Ellis Island where the blessed ground settled their equilibrium, their stomachs and their broken spirits. Like all the passengers, they were first held in a holding area to be sure they weren't sick or carrying any infectious diseases, and then when that period of waiting was over, they were on their way out.

Speaking through an interpreter, an immigration official as big and round as a wine barrel, with eyes as blue as a blue bead and hair as red as Grandma Nooritza's face when she had too much rakhi to drink, looked down at Siroon and asked, "What's this name, See-roon?"

The interpreter answered, "Siroon in Armenian means 'pretty one.'" She went on while holding Siroon's cheeks in her hand, "And you can see that this child is truly a pretty one."

"What a ridiculous name for a little girl," he huffed. "Well, kid, you're in America now and I'm going to give you a real American name. Let me see…yes, that's it: Jane. Your name will be Jane. Jane is a good American name."

Siroon's name, which had been passed on from her mother's mother to her mother, and her mother before that for as long as anyone could remember, was officially changed to plain Jane—a word as foreign to her as hot dog, hamburger, baseball and chewing gum. The official stamped their papers with a bang and then bellowed, "Next!"

With that Mama Jahn and my mother were ushered into the streets of New York City. Cousin Hagop was waiting for them has he had promised to do when he heard of their immigration to America.

"You will come with us to California. It is warm there. Armenians prosper there. There are other Russian Armenians and cousins who will show you what to do. We will find you a job and teach you how to fit in to this new country. We will introduce you to a good, hard working Armenian man to marry to care for you and Siroon. Then you can bring Zepure, and you will all be together."

Her future was clear to Cousin Hagop, but not to Mama Jahn. Too sick to think, and too scared to want to think, Mama Jahn was confused. There was so much to consider. Then Hagop said the magic words: "Sarkis would approve." And that's all she needed to hear to set her mind to go with him to California, which in any case, is where many Armenian immigrants, including Masha, wanted to live because it was always warm weather there.

Everything happened as Hagop had said. They went to Los Angeles, where his wife made a place for Mama Jahn and Siroon to stay in their home, which was a simple bungalow with red bricks, tile roof, stucco walls and a patch of green grass in the backyard where Siroon could play.

There wasn't a lot of food in the house, but there were peaches. A delicacy in any country, they thought. Cousin Hagop's wife worked in the peach canning plant and could bring home all the ripe peaches she could carry for free. Right away Mama Jahn was given a job in the same peach plant. Her job was to pit the peaches. Siroon never left her side, as one by one, peach by peach, day after day except Sundays, she pitted peaches. Siroon learned to play many games with the pits, including jacks. She liked the way her pockets bulged with them. The sound they made when they clicked together in her pockets made her feel prosperous.

And the first thing Mama Jahn did with her first pay check was to find Masha to repay the loan. Even though it was a small amount of money, Mama Jahn didn't want to be in debt to anyone, especially someone like

Masha who might harbor resentment toward her. She soon saw Masha at the grocery store and took advantage of the opportunity to return the quarter.

"Digeen Zvart, there is no reason to bring up that sad time. It's such a small amount of money. Please you insult me."

Mama Jahn insisted she take it but Masha was firm. It would be an insult.

"I tink that Masha have good heart," Mama Jahn told me. "I go away tinking I do her favor by not making her take money. Oh, that Masha so clever."

On Sundays, Cousin Hagop, Mama Jahn and the rest of them went to the Armenian Church services, in the Masonic Lodge hall, a few blocks from where they lived. At church, everyone was Russian Armenian as they were, and being there made Mama Jahn feel close to home for the first since time since leaving the Old Country so fast. On the second Sunday they attended church, Mama Jahn was introduced to Yervant Stempadian, who loved her right away. Three weeks later they were married, and they moved into his Spanish style bungalow on Esperanza Street.

"And this is how our life start in this new country—fast, fast just like when we leave Old Country—everything fast, fast."

Yervant was captivated by Mama Jahn. She was smart and beautiful. He knew he was very fortunate to have such a splendid wife. And she brought with her a lovely daughter, and another lovely daughter, Zepure, was waiting to join them. He would work very hard doing extra jobs to earn as much money as possible to make her life easy, healthy and full of joy, and to bring Zepure to America. To that end Yervant dedicated his life.

Yervant wasn't educated and talented like Sarkis, but he was very hard working; he loved his family and was committed to their happiness. If he were given the choice of death on the spot in exchange for renouncing his political party and going home to his wife and children, he would choose life. Mama Jahn knew that. All he required of her was respect and admiration for his hard work and dedication to their family. And sweet iced tea in the summertime.

Even though Mama Jahn had lost the husband she dearly loved, her high-class life style and beautiful things—wedding plates, etched chi glasses, gold-rimmed demitasse cups from Greece, stacks and bolts of handmade laces and silk materials for dresses and window curtains—she kept her dignity. The most important thing for her was to retain her untarnished reputation. She would rebuild her former style of living. The checkout lady at the supermarket would no longer look down her little odar nose at her as another one of those D.P.'s. And to this end she dedicated her life.

She was a proud woman whose sense of self worth was outwardly expressed by the way she carried herself, like a queen because of her wonderful posture. Her back was as straight as a chair because of the corset she wore every day. She knew that somehow she would someday have a place of honor in the Armenian community again. One day those who now felt sorry for her would look up to her again.

So Mama Jahn had accomplished her first goal—to reestablish her status as a married woman in the Armenian community with her marriage to Yervant. But she never relaxed in her pursuit of regaining her social position. She knew that tragedy was always around the corner waiting to happen, and she knew she wouldn't be blindsided again. She remembered that the grounds of the coffee cup always hide the warning signs of imminent disaster.

"Sometimes I sit alone at kitchen table, Azad Jahn, and I tink about all the tings I leave in old country, especially my acheeg (daughter) Zepure. Even though I make my mind to bring her here as fast as I can, save enough money, I very sad.

I wish I had that cup from the Old Country, to look into it one more time, to see what I miss, and figure out what I see wrong."

5 THE BRIDE'S CUP

the wolf eats the sheep separated from the flock

Even though my family got far away from the terrible Turks and Russians, they could always count on Cousin Zaba Dikranian and his son Osheen for trouble. And even though Cousin Zaba had been blessed to be the czar's favorite waiter, it wasn't enough. Cousin Zaba was mean and unpredictable, and Osheen was just as bad, maybe worse, even when he was young. That is why Mama Jahn worried when Osheen got old enough to marry. Whenever she read his cups she only saw problems.

Cousin Osheen met Araxie for the first time when she served him a demitasse of Armenian coffee in the parlor of her parents' home. It is traditional for a young Armenian woman to be judged by how she makes a cup of Armenian coffee. Is it strong enough? Is there enough of a thin layer of foam at the top of the coffee? Is it bitter? Is it hot enough? After all, what kind of a wife would she make if she couldn't prepare the perfect cup of coffee to serve to her husband and his friends and acquaintances?

She was also judged on how she served the coffee. Was she demure without being self-deprecating? Was she modest without being painfully shy, which would make others uncomfortable? Was she graceful enough? Was she pleasant to watch as she served everyone? Would she be willing to be seen but not heard?

So on this day, at this very moment, all Araxie's years of making and serving coffee to her parents and their friends were put to the test.

With downcast eyes, so as not to appear brazen or forward, she presented Osheen with a cloth napkin that she had taken great lengths to iron properly, the way her myrig (mother), had shown her already when she was nine years old—all the corners touching, and all the wrinkles removed by steaming a damp towel placed over the napkin as she ironed. Indifferently, Osheen unfolded the napkin, stroking it smooth over his knee, not noticing how perfectly it was ironed, as a future mother-in-law would have discerned while taking heed of any possible fault.

He was busy studying her curvaceous body as she moved towards the tray of coffee cups resting on the low table that Cousin Hagop had intentionally positioned across from where Osheen would be sitting. He put it there so it would take no effort on their guests' part to eat from the homemade selections of pastries on the sweet tray while he sipped his dark brew. Osheen noticed that the slim navy dress she was wearing outlined her shapely and sturdy hips in a manner that was revealing without being crude or obvious.

As she bent over to pick up his cup and saucer to pass to him, the cup with the most foam on top, a shiny thick lock of her thick, raven black hair fell from the white mother-of-pearl comb that held it in place at the back of her neck, and gently, very gently, bounced.

"Ahmahn, Araxie murmured under her breath while shoving the lock back into the comb with her free hand.

Araxie had been so involved in cleaning the house prior to his arrival— ironing the napkins and table cloth, polishing the furniture, brushing the carpets, making the pastries with her myrig, then grinding and finally making the coffee—that she hadn't spent enough time making sure her hair was securely fastened. This could be the end, she thought in a quiet panic. What will Hayrig and Myrig say when Osheen rejects me because I rushed to fix my hair?

But when Osheen saw the renegade curl fall and deliciously jiggle, he imagined Araxie to be his. Without a single outward sign on his face indicating his pleasure, he made up his mind to have her.

He thought that she might inspire creative thoughts in him, her physical beauty and charm would stimulate his sexual appetite so she would produce many sons to carry on the Dikranian name. And perhaps she might be talented in music or recitation to soothe his spirits when he was feeling low. So his silent imaginings continued.

The women watched Osheen with anticipation as he sipped his coffee, while the men talked about things the women didn't really care about. The important things were to be found in Osheen's cup when he had gone. For this the women counted the minutes until his departure. The men didn't know it, but my Mama Jahn, well known as the coffee-cup fortune teller and referred to by her given name as Digeen Zvart, waited in the kitchen for the arrival of Osheen's cup.

The main thing of interest to the women was the secrets uncovered from reading his cup when they got it into the kitchen to scrutinize every last ground of coffee.

The only thing of interest to Cousin Hagop was if Osheen would be attracted to his wonderful daughter. The money Osheen would pay for her would help out so much because Cousin Hagop hadn't been able to work since injuring his back falling from a ladder.

The only thing Osheen was interested in was getting this done as fast as possible. He was ready to move on. Ready to start his family and make his fortune in this new world.

With a final slurp to get the last bit of coffee, he masterfully avoided the heavy sediment in the bottom of the cup, which is never consumed but sometimes hard to avoid. He turned his cup over onto the saucer and briskly wiped his mouth with his napkin—removing traces of powdered sugar from the locum that had settled on his moustache. He stood up and motioned to Cousin Hagop with a quick upward jerk of the head, like a secret baseball gesture between catcher and pitcher, and they both understood that Araxie was acceptable—and the deal was struck.

While the men said their goodbyes and Osheen paid the agreed-upon amount, the women calmly walked to the kitchen carrying the trays of dirty cups and plates. Once they got inside the kitchen door the three began chattering at the same time as if their mouths had just been untaped.

"Oh, Myrig, look at this—I see a very long trip with no way back," exclaimed Araxie. *"What do you see, Digeen Zvart? Please tell me I'm wrong."*

"Of course you're wrong, Tzakus (dear one). Yes, there is long trip, but there will be many trips back and forth—see...over here?" She pointed to a long line running along the side of the cup in an unbroken circle. *"This is the way back. Don't worry. This is very good cup. He will make you a wonderful husband and, look, look over here...see these pebbles? You will have four children. Park Asdzoo, thanks be to God. I see only good things."*

Before this meeting Araxie worried if Osheen would find her to his liking. Now that she was chosen to be his bride, she worried if she would be good enough to please him.

And now, a month later as Araxie prepared to approach the altar where Osheen soberly stood in front of the sanctuary with the Der Hayr, the colors from the stained glass window of the Church of St. Gregory the Illuminator cast a long, colorful shadow on her trailing wedding dress.

The Armenian Church was always beautiful, she thought, but especially so when days were bright and intense sunlight beamed through the windows. She stood ready, at the back of the church, waiting to walk down the aisle with her dear hayrig.

Up until now Araxie's only experience with men was her relationship with her sweet and gentle father. After escaping the genocide in Armenia, she and her parents had lived a quiet life in the city of Los Angeles. They were not interested in finding those streets lined with gold that they had heard about on the ocean liner filled with other D.P.'s. Money brought trouble. The Turks murdered and stole for money. Some people they casually knew, and even some who were good friends, had killed for money. But Araxie's family was looking for peace and quiet in America. They would die for each other, but they would not die for money.

Turning to look at her daughter from the front row, her myrig thought that Araxie herself looked like a piece of stained glass. She seemed fragile and transparent, even as she brimmed with all the colors of the rainbow. As a cloud passed over the window, however, the shadow of dark lead that outlined the stained glass was all that remained on her white satin gown. Her myrig tried not to read a meaning into this but instead reminded herself of the good fortune Digeen Zvart had found in Osheen's cup, including the four pebbles. There was nothing to worry about, all will be well, she thought.

And so Osheen and Araxie were married that morning, just as the fortune in Osheen's coffee cup had predicted.

Osheen decided they would live in Fresno, California, far away from her family. He wanted to be her only one.

Back at her family's home, while Osheen was loading her two small suitcases into the trunk of his Ford coupe, Araxie's myrig pulled her aside. She held her daughter close as she gently pressed a tidy, thick bundle of money wrapped in one of her linen hankies into her hand, telling her in a low whisper, disguised as a kiss on the ear, *"Tzakus, quick, hide this money, and when you get to your new home put it in a secret place to use just for yourself. And don't tell your husband."*

As she slipped the hankie it into her pocket, Araxie—knowing how poor they were— wondered how her myrig managed to save so much money. She was surprised and moved by the gesture, but didn't understand the need to keep it a secret from her husband.

The first thing she did when she got in the car was to show Osheen the money. And the first thing he did was to take it. All of it. She never did that again.

Cousin Hagop leaned into the window of the passenger side of the car, cupping Araxie's head with his wrinkled hands. He kissed her face with anguish and muttered Armenian prayers of protection and thanksgiving for her life. He couldn't bear the thought of his beloved child moving so far away.

This parting burned a hole deep inside, colliding with the existing agony that lay buried from his childhood–the heart-wrenching pain of his mother being pulled from his embrace and then speared through her neck by a young Turk in the village of Yosgat where he was born.

Breaking down from the pain, he cried onto his coat sleeve while Araxie kissed his forehead to console him. As if taking a cue from her hayrig's tears, the light drizzle turned into a downpour, quickly drenching him.

Increasingly irritated at this intense display of emotion between father and daughter, Osheen pressed his foot down hard on the accelerator, propelling the car forward. Cousin Hagop, flung aside, landed in the muddy driveway, the unrelenting rain pounding him in his wedding-day suit.

Araxie craned her head out the window and gestured back towards him. "Hayrig, Hayrig," she cried. But the louder she howled, the faster Osheen drove.

Her tear-flooded eyes snapped a picture she was fated to carry with her for the rest of her life—of her hayrig helpless, lying face down in the mud.

Araxie gave birth to a little girl, Sossi, a couple of years before I was born. Osheen's sons were still-born. Everyone thought it was best there were never any more men born in their family, considering how mean they were. Eventually, Osheen, Araxie and Sossi moved back to Los Angeles, so our family had a front row seat to all the misery he caused.

Mama Jahn was reading her cup on a quiet spring day where she saw the outline of a cat eating its young and it came to her in a cold shudder down her back. "Yervant," she called out to Bobeeg Jahn in Armenian, *"Come fast! I see that Cousin Osheen is very 'ner-vez' again and he going to beating up his wife and Sossi."*

Knowing what she knew, she put down her cup, picked up the phone and asked her nervous cousin to come for dinner. Bobeeg agreed that this was the right thing to do.

Mama Jahn telephoned him, speaking tempting words of mouthwatering promises he couldn't refuse in their shared Russian Armenian dialect, "Osheen, remember when the czar requested my mother's dolma for his fortieth birthday lunch and asked your father Zaba, his favorite waiter, to serve him? Well, today I have an overwhelming urge make it if you can come to dinner."

How could Osheen refuse?

Mama Jahn got right to work in the kitchen, energized by her ambition to soothe Cousin Osheen so he'd be in a good mood and not beat the hell out of his family. She ground a sirloin steak twice, using the grinding mill she vigorously turned by hand and then added it to a well seasoned rice mixture. This was the filling for the dolmas. After the young and tender cabbage leaves were blanched in lemon water to retain their light green color, she set them aside to drain and then, bringing out the tomatoes she had bottled last summer, she went about making a sweet and sour tomato sauce in which the dolmas would eventually simmer. Next she sprinkled in a generous amount of fresh sweet basil leaves gathered from her garden. While the tomato sauce bubbled away over a low gas flame on her stove top, she gently folded in the unusual ingredients of dried apricots and prunes that, when cooked alongside the cabbage rolls, released their sweetness and depth of flavor. They transformed what could be thought of as ordinary cabbage rolls into a delectable masterpiece fit for a czar and for her nervous wreck Cousin Osheen, the wife and child beater.

Mama Jahn knew that anything reminding Cousin Osheen of his carefree younger days, when life was filled with delicious surprises and the expectation that his future would be as marvelous as his father's, and of his father before him, would put him in a good mood. She knew that he and his brothers and sisters were weaned on fanciful stories of dinner parties at the czar's palace in Russia, as they sat eating the banquet leftovers brought home by his father. They mused over bits and pieces of trash his father had secreted away from the palace, which to his family were snatches of magical moments in time. The paper ring from a cigar wrapper from Alexi Alenandroff, the Prime Minister of Public Affairs, the opalescent blue sequins that popped off the bulging bodice of Natasha Marinikoff's ball gown and the silver button that sailed across the room as Mr. Petrovich swung his velvet cloak over his shoulders when he departed the party early because of an attack of gout—such memorabilia were almost as tasty as the royal leftovers. All those kinds of remembrances made Osheen feel good about himself and life again—that, and all the empty compliments Mama Jahn lavished on him.

"Osheen, you alone are like the czar—may he rest in peace—who understands the beauty of the delicate balance of fine flavors like the cabbage and the apricots and prunes. You alone bring to my table the pride of all Russian Armenians who are no longer with us. And because we all love and cherish you for your handsome face and strong tall body and fine mind, you will always be admired." They both crossed themselves.

Her plan was working because Osheen's belly and head swelled with satisfaction like a puffed up piece of fried khanamee khapur pastry. After Mama Jahn's feast of words and dolmas, he left for home a happy man.

Because of the success of her dolma dinner, Mama Jahn could hardly wait until the next day. She was dressed and ready early in the morning waiting for Bobeeg Jahn at the curb, and before he could get out of the car from his night janitorial jobs, she told him to hurry and drive her to Osheen's house where she would show up unannounced to see for herself the effectiveness of her intercessions. They were both eager to see that no one was injured. For Mama Jahn it was important to prove to herself over and over again that she truly did have the gift of seeing into the future . . . and, that if the future was bleak, she could do something about it, as she had been unable to do for Sarkis.

She entered Osheen's house and saw that everyone was happy and unbruised. "Oough, Park Asdzoo (oh my, merciful God)" she uttered as she crossed herself three times in thanksgiving.

"Every body's safe. Tanks to God!"

Under his breath Bobeeg said, "Real tanks to Mama Jahn."

Mama Jahn decided not to hurry home. The cata dough rising on the kitchen counter could wait, and so could the hungry family at home hoping for a special blini breakfast. This was much too important an occasion not to savor. So she stayed for morning tea with Araxie, proud Bobeeg Jahn at her side.

Mama Jahn never reminded anyone that if it weren't for her seeing "all good things" in Osheen's cup when he came to ask for her to be his harse, Araxie might not have married him. Araxie might have had a different life, a life without an abusive husband. Later, Mama Jahn realized that years ago she should have been looking into Araxie's cup for her fortune. Osheen's cup showed "all good things," because this marriage was good for Osheen. It wasn't good for Araxie. From my perspective, though, if Araxie hadn't married Osheen, Sossi wouldn't have been born, and I couldn't imagine the world without my sweet Sossi.

6 THE SERPENT'S CUP

to be hungry is better than to be in debt

One morning, not long after Mama Jahn and Bobeeg were married, after church and before the usual Sunday church picnic, Mama Jahn told me that she had peered into Bobeeg's empty demitasse to find the image of a serpent in the coffee residue, winding its way from the bottom of the cup up into a tree and into someone's heart. Mama Jahn turned the cup this way and that and couldn't figure out what was going to happen—and to whom. She had no idea what would happen, but she knew she had to do something.

Her first thought was to stay home and not go to the picnic but Bobeeg wouldn't hear of it. "What's the matter wit you? Are you khent (crazy)? No snakes in American parks. Who's going to make khorovadz (barbeque shish kabob), if I don't go? We going." Bobeeg had his job to do and he wasn't going to be kept away by snakes in coffee cups.

So she prepared herself. *To be forewarned was to be forearmed.* She had no idea that this well-known Armenian saying existed in the American culture, too.

She stayed up late to finish sewing the V-neck, cream-colored sheath dress so she could wear it to the picnic. This way no one would be able to say she wore old-fashioned clothes. Using tricks she had learned long ago from Sarkis, she copied the style from a dress in the window at I. Magnin department store in downtown Los Angeles, the one priced at one hundred and twenty-five dollars. The gossipy ladies would not be able to make a derogatory remark about her dress that day, as they looked forward to doing at picnics. *"Ah,"* she thought out loud in Armenian, *"that's most likely what I saw in the cup—the ladies making fun of that old dress that everyone has seen me wear many times before."* Siroon was so used to Mama Jahn sacrificing everything for her that she must've thought, If myrig has time enough to make one new dress, I wish it had been for me. I long for clothes as beautiful as I am, the clothes I had to leave behind in the old country.

The family looked forward to Sundays for two reasons—Sundays were picnic time in good weather and everyone looked forward to going to church.

I had my own impressions of church by the time Mama Jahn told me the story, so I knew first hand that the incense burned intensely enough that by the time the Nicene Creed was sung the entire church looked like it was engulfed in a Fresno tule fog. I had also fully assessed the Armenian ladies, who dressed as beautifully as they could, often in two-piece tailored suits with matching gloves, hats, purses and sometimes with real fox furs draped around their shoulders. The fox heads were still attached to their little long fur bodies, so no matter what pew I sat in, the foxes' beady little eyes followed and unblinkingly stared at me during the entire service. There was nowhere to hide from them.

Proud, handsome men were dressed in dark suits like they were going to an important meeting or to a funeral, with starched long-sleeved white shirts closed at the wrist with cuff links. Those who had been to Armenia on a pilgrimage were hadgis (pilgrims), and they had a tattoo of the Jerusalem cross on the inside of their right wrist that I could glimpse when they crossed themselves many, many times during the service. Forever marked with the cross of Jesus as an Armenian Christian, identified always as members of the martyred, starving Armenians, they were set apart.

After a full week of hard physical labor, picnics after church services became a ritual as it had been in the Old Country. The Russian Armenians discovered Elysian Park and that became picnic headquarters. This was the one time that my Mama Jahn could sit and relax with our people for the day and feel the sun on her face. There was no need to pick up the house and have it perfectly cleaned on Sundays, because there was no chance anyone would come to the door for a visit and catch her off guard, with no pastries to serve and wearing an apron over a housedress purchased from Sears and Roebuck basement sale rack. *"No one to catch you off guard. This is freedom,"* she'd tell my mother in Armenian.

Because seeing a serpent in a cup is not a good cup reading she readied herself so the serpent, whatever it was, wouldn't be a sign of her oversight. She mentally prepared herself to pinch hard every time she got a compliment and she made sure to pin a blue bead in Bobeeg's pocket and hung blue beads to the gold chains that held their crosses, and, further ordered Siroon to stay at her side the entire day.

Marinated, skewered and grilled lamb shish kabob was the centerpiece of the Sunday picnic meal. In the Old Country, a lamb was slaughtered and carved on the spot at the picnic site—which was usually on the edge of mountains where there was a clearing. But here, in downtown Los Angeles, outdoor slaughtering wasn't an option. The night before the picnics, the men cut up legs of lamb, purchased from the local Chinese butcher, into one-and-a-half inch cubes, then submerged them in lemon juice, onions, pepper, oregano and oil to marinate overnight. Sometimes Bobeeg Jahn would sneak in a little red wine into the marinade when Mama Jahn wasn't looking. She said wine made the meat taste like stew and he countered with "Wine? What you talking about? I never use wine."

The meat was always grilled under Bobeeg Jahn's watchful eye. He knew nothing about cooking but knew everything about how to grill kebabs to perfection. He always prepared the fire the same way, from little sticks and small logs he gathered from the various fruit trees on our property, because they burned down to a perfect bed of hot white coals that imparted their own flavor to the lamb.

He turned the skewers a quarter turn at a time until all the sides were evenly seared so the juices wouldn't escape. By the time it took him to sing his favorite childhood school song from beginning to end, the meat was cooked to just the right doneness—lightly pink in the center. Mama Jahn told me that my mother was always first in line for what he called "samples," the first meat off the skewers. It was the best way to eat the meat - directly from the hot pokers and into the soft lavash.

Just as the Der Hayr had put wine soaked bits of holy wafer into their open mouths earlier in the morning at church, the kabob was the second communion feast of the day. The children took the bread and body of *this* sacrificial lamb and ran to a place under a table, far away from everyone else, so they could eat in complete privacy. If the old ladies spotted the children eating Bobeeg's samples they'd wag their fingers towards him saying, "Dun't do! Children must to eat pilaf first." He always dismissed them with a quick sideways toss of his hand like he was waving off irritating flies.

The smell of the lamb turning from its raw to cooked state on the grill drew everyone to the table. It caused the musicians to miss a beat, the dancers to lose interest and drop each other's pinkie fingers, and brought an end to the tavloo (backgammon), games from the men who had had enough of their bad luck, while the men enjoying a winning streak reluctantly yelled for them to come back to finish the game.

Everyone watched as Bobeeg took the meat from the fire, grasped it with soft lavash and pulled down from the long metal skewers into a big pot where the juices from the meat collected at the bottom and soaked into more lavash. Next, Bobeeg liberally sprinkled salt onto the cubes of lamb and tossed them up in the air to coat the meat with chopped parsley and green onions. Then he tossed them into a large, wide rimmed restaurant-sized stainless steel bowl.

When the lamb was on the table, all the women came forward unwrapping their covered pots, pans and platters, and proudly displayed their cooking and baked goods on crisply starched white tablecloths while they secretly scrutinized the cleanliness and presentation of each other's offerings. They were always hopeful that someone would have a spotted tablecloth or a messy platter they could gossip about the next day over a demitasse.

Pilaf from rice with browned vermicelli noodles was a staple. It was always made with chicken broth, browned vermicelli noodles, salt and just the right amount of clarified butter. If there was too much butter it would collect at the bottom of the pot in a puddle. Not good. If there wasn't enough butter, the rice would be sticky and bland. It had to be just the right amount to give the pilaf the slight toasty, nutty taste that clarified butter added to a dish, along with a very light yellow color, like the delicately yellow of an American egg custard. Mama Jahn discovered a brand of long-grain rice she liked to use for picnic pilaf called Uncle Ben's and she referred to it as "the sev mart's brinz" (the black man's rice), when she made out her shopping list for Bobeeg. The grains of Uncle Ben's rice had the enviable property of not sticking and withstanding reheating without changing the texture of the pilaf.

You couldn't have a picnic without lavash, the flat cracker bread the women made together every Saturday. They rolled out and baked dozens of rounds of thin crisp lavash, which they stacked high in piles and then wrapped in muslin for each of them to take home for the week. When they were ready to use the breads, they sprinkled them with water and wrapped them in big, white clean kitchen towels until they were soft enough to use as wrappers for string cheese, parsley, roasted eggplants, and red chili peppers to roll up and eat with their fingers, along with all the many varieties of wrinkled black olives. And at the Sunday picnics the lavash held the juicy kabobs and Armenian salad in a compact roll that made it easy to eat with your hands.

By the time Mama Jahn displayed her offerings on the communal food table, she had forgotten about the serpent in the cup. She was excited about her platter of Russian Armenian beet-red, pickled eggs that *Der Hayr* had specifically requested she prepare, and was putting them on the table at the same time five other women were doing the same thing with their contributions to the already groaning food table. Digeen Masha was one of the five.

The women remarked about Mama Jahn's dress and how beautiful it looked on her, how brave she was to wear a cream-colored dress and carry pickled beets, and how expensive the dress must have been. Mama Jahn pinched Siroon, Bobeeg and herself on the vodeeg many times throughout the day to ward off the evil eye. She thought to herself, "A-ha. I was right. It is my dress. The serpent is the evil eye waiting to attack because of jealousy over my dress."

Digeen Masha listened as the women continued to lavish compliments on Mama Jahn and seethed inside. Her face turned red, her eyes bulged, her fingers nervously clutched at her handbag, her nose twitched and her tongue licked her lips. Even her head seemed to shake. Mama Jahn felt the tug of Siroon holding onto her dress from behind, tighter and tighter. "I sensed it," Siroon said afterward. "I could feel something was about to happen!"

Then Digeen Masha burst. She stepped in front of Mama Jahn's face with her tall, imposing body, and yelled out in a voice loud enough for all the women to hear, *"Zvart, it's well past time you paid me back for the egg money you borrowed from me on the ship to America. You have enough money to buy fancy dresses. Why don't you pay me back?"*

Mama Jahn stood mesmerized by the intensity of the venom in Masha's eyes and in her words. She remembered well that she had offered to pay her back but Masha said it was an amount so small that it was an insult to her to even offer.

Masha ranted on. *"You begged me for money to buy food for you and Siroon on the ship and you said that you'd never forget that I saved your lives. Well, you forgot."*

Mama Jahn's face turned completely white, as white as an odar. Finding it impossible to speak, Mama Jahn took a few steps backward, stumbling into Siroon and dumping the purple eggs from the platter onto herself. She caught many of the eggs in the hammock of her upturned dress as they tumbled down. As the eggs cracked against themselves, the purple beet dye bled into the fabric of her dress and stained it in a pattern that looked like blotches of blood. The rest of the eggs rolled down the grass to a resting place under weeds.

Over and over again Mama Jahn wailed in anguish, *"Ahmahn, ahmahn, ahmahn, ahmahn… vie, vie, vie… eench neghoutooin,* what a disgrace…*ahmahn, ahmahn, ahmahn."* There was no witness to her offer to repay Masha. She had been tricked.

The women averted their eyes and lowered their heads in shame for Mama Jahn and walked away from the table while muttering *"ahmot, ahmot, ahmot"* under their collective breaths. It was clear for whom the *ahmot* was intended because there was no shame in the eggs falling, only shame on Mama Jahn for supposedly neglecting to pay back the debt to Digeen Masha.

Ahmot, shame, is the dark and dreaded word Armenians whisper under a cupped hand over the mouth, with a strong emphasis on the last syllable, which creates a slight spit when pronounced. It is a word with as much foreboding to an Armenian as hunger and starvation. Mama Jahn was shamed by Masha in front of everyone and there was nothing to do. Pinching, crossing herself and saying prayers wouldn't work to remove the ahmot.

Later Siroon would say, "I thought we would never have to run away again." Nevertheless, Mama Jahn followed her instincts and grabbed Siroon by the hand and ran away. "We ran and ran until we reached a big oak tree. Armenians at the picnic looked small like black zatoon (olive) pits, when we looked back."

Once out of sight Mama Jahn looked up to the sky, shaking her clasped hands back and forth in front of her mouth as if she were praying, and made an audible determined vow to Almighty God and the devil, not knowing who was actually in charge of these things, that she would never borrow or be in debt to any person as long as she lived. No one would ever have the opportunity to cause her ahmot ever again, even if it meant starvation. She would rather die of starvation than of shame.

From then on, Mama Jahn insisted that Siroon stay home and do housework with her. Keeping the home spotlessly clean, baking the finest baked goods, washing all things that were white in bleach to keep them white and starching and ironing everything until every wrinkle was gone, just to keep from feeling *ahmot* again. My mother hated housework and eventually hated being home. She would rather have been at school and in the school library where she could read stories about fascinating people and places in books and the latest magazines like *Vogue* and *Atlantic Monthly*, instead of at home worrying about peasants passing judgment on the family.

This incident made Mama Jahn even more fanatical about keeping her home clean and picked up all the time so an unexpected guest wouldn't find anything to gossip about. She always had a full box of home made pastries at the ready to serve at a moment's notice, whether or not anyone was expected to call. And she never borrowed anything from anyone ever again.

Whenever the family was invited to someone's home for dinner, she fed Siroon before they went. No one could ever say that her child was hungry, or worse yet, starving, or ate with a huge appetite like a farmer, or that her manners were reprehensible, or that she didn't get enough to eat at home. It would be ahmot.

And as the years went on she added other things to the list of shameful offenses like chewing gum in public, having girlfriends who smoked cigarettes, getting "B's" instead of "A's" in school, being too religious, not being religious enough, wearing clothes that showed thighs when legs were crossed, wearing make-up, and, of course, marrying an odar. She became obsessed with honor, pride and reputation.

7 THE MARRIAGE CUP

lies, lies, lies, lies, everything is a lie

Mama Jahn cared most about what other people thought, but her daughter Siroon did not. She wanted what felt good to her and what was beautiful. In America it was everyone for themselves and my mother liked it like that. It was unspoken, but everyone knew that my mother was the precious one. She wore an invisible jeweled crown on her head that all could see.

With a broad, proud smile across her face, my Mama Jahn told me that when my mother was a young woman her favorite amusement was to sit in the wing-backed, pale green brocade chair in the corner of the living room and read. Even when Mama Jahn was clanking her cleaning supplies around the room and vacuuming around her, Siroon sat comfortably for hours in the one chair in the living room that wasn't covered with plastic, oblivious to the commotion, while her legs dangled over one arm of the chair, and then shifted to the other arm. She read from the stack of her high school books and everything from the library that she could get her hands on, including fashion magazines. Her reading material reached all the way up to the top of the chair in two, teetering parallel piles. Even when she wasn't in 'her chair,' it was an unspoken rule that no one else was allowed to sit in it.

When Siroon swooned over a new dress she saw in *Vogue* magazine, Mama Jahn told Bobeeg, "We get one more customer for yegh (clarified butter), and I can buy dress for Siroon." And if Siroon woke up in the morning saying, "I feel like eating manti for dinner," Mama Jahn sent Bobeeg to the market to buy the ingredients to make manti, even though it was time-consuming to make. To Mama Jahn's way of thinking, giving Siroon everything she wanted was how she recaptured her former life with Sarkis so she could live in the present and in the past at the same time.

Whatever Siroon wanted was what Mama Jahn wanted. All the things Siroon wanted cost money, so she looked forward to getting a rich husband who could pamper her even more than Mama Jahn did. She had read in a book that it was just as easy to fall in love with a rich man as it was with a poor one. And Mama Jahn agreed. It made sense in Armenian and in English.

American high school was a place to become smart and learn how to play sports like tennis, to figure out how the American government worked, how to do arithmetic, read and write, and how to engage people in conversation. The one thing it wasn't good for, in Mama Jahn's opinion, was encouraging the socialization of the two sexes. The American way featured dating, then falling in love and marrying a man, just because your heart fluttered when you saw him. This was nonsense to Mama Jahn. "Crazy Americans," was her favorite way of expressing her disappointment in this and other American practices with which she disagreed.

Marriage was a contract in which a woman needed to make the best arrangement to secure her future. So, even though many American boys asked my attractive mother to dances and parties, they were never considered an option for marriage. Siroon had to wait for the right situation, an arranged marriage with the right Armenian. And until then she should be satisfied with her books, her home-life and the many pretty things Mama Jahn bought for her. Never mind that all the things Siroon wanted and got, took away from the money they were saving to send for her sister, Zepure.

As Mama Jahn told me all this, I wondered if Mother had any idea what she had missed by not having dated American boys.

When Siroon was eighteen and finishing her senior year of high school, an Armenian family came visiting. Mama Jahn had been expecting them to call. She saw their visit in Siroon's cup. She knew they would bring gifts as a way of asking for her hand in marriage. It was the Armenian way for the boy's family to claim a harse (bride), for their son. This was very clear in the way the swirls encircled the heads of the two figures standing in front of the Der Hayr in her cup. There was no mistaking what she saw.

The son in the family, Dicran Buchacklian, was twenty-nine years old, handsome the way Turkish Armenians were handsome; dark, a thin, trim mustache under a slender nose and a slender figure to match. He also had style; he looked like the men standing next to the female models in *Vogue*. Siroon liked that about him right away. He was quiet in manner with eyes that looked down most of the time unless he was spoken to.

"Good sign. He bashful, timid boy," Mama Jahn thought.

Not good sign he looking down instead of straight ahead, Bobeeg considered to himself. I no trust "carpet-weavers," people who look down all the time.

Dicran's mother was stocky, had short curly hair with a diamond clip in it, and was unprepossessing, the way some Turkish Armenian women looked at her age, with exaggerated facial features, which made her look manly. Siroon thought that the only attractive thing about her was the expensive jewelry she wore. She had a big smile she sustained even while she talked, which was disarming and friendly. She made you want to smile, too.

I wonder what she hide behind smile? mused Mama Jahn.

I want gold tooth like hers, Bobeeg Jahn reflected.

The father isn't at all a typical Armenian man whose bad haircut, bad suit of clothes and bad breath are out of place in America, thought my mother. This man knows how to dress and look American. But that mother-in-law, that awful flowered dress of hers...I wouldn't be caught dead standing next to her.

Baron Buchacklian was tall, had slicked down hair, was wearing an expensive looking dark blue suit, and had stylish shoes in patent leather, like the rest of his family. Mama Jahn was aware that expensive shoes meant that the family had money. They were not Russian Armenians; they were Armenians from Istanbul who were considered to be of a higher class than the Russahyes because they were more educated and had more money.

Mama Jahn knew only one thing about Baron Buchacklian, but it was everything she needed to know to feel sure they were a family honored by everyone who would then bring honor to their family with such a marriage arrangement.

The month before, the Head of the Armenian Church, the Catholicos from the Mother See of Etchmiadzin, presented Baron Buchacklian with the Medal of Honor in a special ceremony, after the Divine Liturgy held in the Episcopal Cathedral in downtown Los Angeles. The Episcopal cathedral was chosen because it was the only place that could accommodate the packed-to-overflowing members of all the Armenian congregations from California. The list of important guests included local civic officials and ecumenical dignitaries from various denominations. Everyone came to see the head of all Armenians present this once-in-a-lifetime honor to a man who had given most generously of his money and time working for the Mother Church in the Diaspora—Baron Buchacklian. There was no greater honor.

How could she have known that on that day of days, Baron Buchacklian was quick to notice the bulging cash collection bags from the service, left unattended in the narthex of the Cathedral by the ushers? While the faithful lined up for the last blessing and the rare opportunity to kiss the hand of the Holy Leader of all Armenians and receive a gold-looking Armenian cross from him, Baron Buchacklian sized up the situation and in a split second snatched up the money bags.

He stealthily slipped out the side doors holding the bags behind his back and tiptoed down the stairs as nimbly as an Armenian Fred Astaire. And there he tossed them into the trunk of his black caddy. The money was never seen again, leaving the ushers to accuse each other of theft ever after.

When the Der Hayr in charge of the service learned what had happened, he bellowed, "Worse than ahmot. Dis teef he vill go to hell and burn."

Baron Buchacklian himself phoned Mama Jahn a week after receiving the Medal of Honor to ask if he and his wife and son could come to visit. Mama Jahn said to come for tea. She wished she could ask him to wear the medal so she could see it up close. She couldn't wait to tell all her friends who was coming for tea.

To come for "tea" meant you would be served coffee and tea with an array of homemade pastries. Everyone knew that if the man in the family called to make the appointment to come for a visit that it was for more important things than local gossip.

Siroon was well known in the community as a beauty. She had stunning blue eyes which were unusual for any Armenian. Armenians had eyes that were either brown or black, unless their parents had married an odar. This was definitely not the case, since both her parents were as Armenian as Mount Ararat, with Lake Van water in their veins and pilaf on their brains.

Siroon was very glamorous without trying to be. Whenever she was out in public everyone turned to take a second look at her because of her breathtaking beauty and her striking resemblance to Elizabeth Taylor. She had the same lovely hair, the same shape face and the same mouth and eyebrows. She had bad eyesight and, because she thought wearing glasses took away from her beauty, she never wore them in public.. She'd ignore acquaintances who smiled and waved at her from a distance because she couldn't see them. This gave her the illusion of being aloof. All the eligible Armenian bachelors were crazy for her but Mama Jahn wouldn't let her be seen with any of them. They weren't good enough.

Mama Jahn was waiting for the right family to come calling for her hand in marriage. A Russahye family would not be good enough for her takouhii, (queen). The family for her Siroon would have to be a family of significant financial means with a wonderful reputation in the Armenian and American communities, and their son would have to be as handsome as Siroon was gorgeous.

Someone in the Buchacklian family had done their homework. When they arrived for tea they walked in carrying all the appropriate presents for such a visit to a Russahye family, more than Mama Jahn had ever heard of before: a pyramid of large gift boxes from all the right stores—Haggarty's,

Bullock's, I. Magnin, a round hat box from Shaffer and Sons, topped with three blue Tiffany boxes. The contents of the boxes were as spectacular as their presentation, enough to make Siroon and Mama Jahn swoon.

Out came an enormous round sterling silver tray stacked high with delicate deep fried pastry covered with powdered sugar, made by Dicran's mother's own hands. The name of this khanamie khapogh pastry, translates into "fool the in-laws pastry" because when the dough is fried it puffs up into a light and delicate bow shape that is, in substance, less than it appears stacked high on a platter. This is the traditional pastry for a visit in which asking for your daughter's hand in marriage is the intention, with a tall box of Armenian rakhi for the man in the house included for good measure. Dicran's mother's khanamie khapogh was delicate and delicious—the powdered sugar flying in all directions with every bite, and the rakhi was mellow and spirited.

After the right amount of time was spent in pleasantries, Dicran's mother pulled a diamond necklace out of her handbag, and struggled to get up out of the down-filled sofa, Mama Jahn's most cherished piece of furniture. When Dicran made a quick glance to his father who indicated with a forward snap of his chin for him to help her, Dicran eventually pulled her up. His myrig secured the necklace around Siroon's neck as she kissed her on each cheek and then stood back with her hands clasped in front of her, admiring her beautiful future harse. Now it was time to leave. Baron Buchacklian wasn't going to chance losing his wife again to that soft sofa.

Siroon had always intended to marry well. She never envisioned herself in want of anything. As I've already mentioned, Mama Jahn and Bobeeg worked hard at menial jobs to provide her with everything she desired, but she wanted more. She wanted a house that would be the envy of all the Russahyes and Americans, a swimming pool, a red convertible car of her own, "real" jewelry, a bed with a canopy and all the newest fashions as they were advertised in the women's magazines. Clearly, Buchacklian was the family to provide for her, thought Mama Jahn.

Siroon's counselor at school had another idea. "American young women go to college instead of getting married right out of high school. And your daughter is smart enough to become a nurse and maybe even a doctor. Her grades are all A's and she's made the highest test scores in the school in science and mathematics. She needs to go on to college and then medical school before she gets married." The counselor looked at Mama Jahn for a response adding as an additional incentive, "And we can get scholarships for her so you won't have to pay a thing."

"Siroon should get married, be nice houzlady and have wonderful nice children. College no important for Siroon." Mama Jahn was being kind to the counselor by not saying what she meant directly. She didn't want Siroon to work every day like this lady giving advice to her. It would be ahmot for a beauty like Siroon. It would be like saying to all the Armenians that Siroon had something wrong with her, that no wealthy family wanted their handsome son to marry her and continue to care for her like a queen. It would be ahmot.

Then the counselor looked at Bobeeg for support saying, "Dad, what do you think is best for Siroon?"

"Whatever Mama Jahn says," offered Bobeeg Jahn. He still didn't like the carpet weaver eyes of the pessa, but he knew it wasn't his decision. This was Mama Jahn's daughter and therefore her responsibility to make the decisions for her future. And he didn't want any trouble at home from voicing opinions that differed from hers.

When Siroon was asked what she thought, she put the onus on her mother, saying, "Mama knows best for me."

The day before the lavish wedding Mama Jahn saw a bad omen in Siroon's cup.

"*Vie, vie, vie*, wat I going to do?"

"What do you mean, what are you going to do? Do about what?"

"Should I tell you bad tings I see in your cup or not tell you?"

"You know I don't believe in that nonsense; just keep it to yourself, I'm going to marry into this wealthy family and have everything I ever wanted on a silver platter."

"Ahman, I vorry for you!"

"Keep your worries for yourself, Mama. I'm not worried. Your fortunes never come true anyway."

The wedding day was glorious in every way—the elegant Armenian Church wedding service with the Armenian Bishop and three Der Hayrs presiding, the expensive filet mignon, five-course dinner reception for two hundred people in the splendidly appointed Roosevelt Hotel in downtown Los Angeles, replete with crystal champagne glasses, plush red carpets, comfortable upholstered chairs, elegant table linens and orchids flown in from Hawaii for the flower arrangements. Even the wines complimented each course of the meal and the bottles had corks instead of twist caps.

Everyone in attendance was spellbound. "Ahman, ahman, in my whole life never I see this kind of wedding," was heard throughout the dining room, all night long.

The culmination of the evening's surprises were rum-lit baked Alaskas on parade, carried high above the heads of the white gloved waiters though the darkened ballroom while the full-sized society orchestra, Harold and the Troubadours, played "Here Comes the Bride." Nothing Armenian at the reception meant that it was a high-class affair and everyone was suitably impressed—and every detail of the evening was tended to by Baron Buchacklian. This was his opportunity to show the Armenians how successful he was as an American businessman, "a bigga shot" as everyone thought of him, and to show off his *harse*, known to be the most beautiful of all Armenian young women, a guarantee that his grandchildren would be magnificent.

No one had any idea that *their* money that *they* had put into the collection plate, when the Catholicos visited from Etchmiadzin, paid for all this splendor. One guest after another thanked him with heartfelt admiration and profuse gratitude for being included, almost bowing down when they talked.

The surprises kept coming for Siroon. The honeymoon was upstairs in the penthouse at the bridal suite of the Roosevelt Hotel. Siroon wore the white peignoir Auntie Gladys gave her at her wedding shower while she waited for her husband to join her in bed. Dicran said he needed to buy some cigarettes. He wants to give me time to be alone to get ready for him, Siroon thought. How very thoughtful and sweet.

Hours later she fell asleep, exhausted from the wedding day and from sobbing while waiting for Dicran to return. He didn't come back until morning, carrying racing forms under his arm and smelling like cigarettes and rakhi. How could she have known before marrying him that the only thing that excited him was the thrill of playing black jack and horse races?

The next day she was packed and ready for what she thought was to be a secret destination honeymoon. Maybe Paris, France. Or Niagara Falls. But instead they drove directly to the Buchacklian family home in Beverly Hills.

Siroon was surprised and disappointed but she knew that Armenian women were expected to follow their husbands. Maybe a trip would come later.

She was filled with anticipation to see the inside of the magnificent house that was to be her home. After their engagement she and her family had driven by the house many times trying to imagine what it was like inside; which of the many rooms would be hers and how they'd be decorated. She'd read enough French history to identify the architecture and to know what elegance was, and this house was definitely elegant and splendid. It made her giddy just thinking that she would soon be living there.

When she walked through the double, carved mahogany doors she was instantly struck with the grandeur of the large white marble-floored entry, the enormous Waterford crystal chandelier handing in the middle, and the living room beyond. The vision quite literally took her breath away as she gasped and clutched at her throat trying to breathe.

She stood at the entrance to the living room admiring the enormous pastel-patterned oriental carpet reaching from one corner of the room to the other, as her husband said he was going to get gas for the car. She didn't care how long he was gone because she wanted time to look at everything herself.

She never knew oriental rugs were made with pastel colors or that they were woven in such large sizes. Maybe Baron Buchacklian had it custom made. He certainly had enough money to buy whatever he wanted, and he was in the rug business.

Hesitantly, she entered the living room and walked ever so carefully so as not to leave a footprint trail of her trespass in the plush carpet. She ran her hands over the backs of the white-upholstered furniture without plastic coverings, realizing that they were covered with silk, and that all the tables were gold leafed. Her eyes went to a place in the bay window, overlooking the manicured sunken backyard gardens. The window was draped with yards and yards of pale peach colored silk fabric, gathered, swagged and gently flowing on the carpet. She pictured herself reading in that corner.

Beyond the Bacarrat crystal vases, antique silver platters and Lalique statues on the shelves that lined either side of the marble fireplace, she looked for books. They must be in another room, a library or den, with deep red leather sofas and chairs and walls all covered with carved mahogany, she thought.

Maybe a chaise lounge in the corner instead of a chair for reading. Who knows? The sky's the limit now that I'm married into a wealthy family. Who cares if he never comes to bed as long as I can read, shop and go to parties.

All of a sudden it dawned on her that the in-laws weren't here. Where are the khanamies? She found it strange that they weren't here to greet her with flowers and more jewelry. They must be tied up somewhere . . . I'd better look around fast before they come and insist on giving me a tour.

So she walked down the hallway from the living room that led to the red velvet dining room filled with ornate gold leafed vases and cabinets full of gold and cobalt-blue rimmed china dinnerware and crystal glasses of every size imaginable. The dining room table was wide enough to hold platters of food all down the middle and long enough to feed two big Armenian families at once!

While on her hunt for the library she discovered that these three rooms were the only ones in the entire house that were decorated. All the other rooms, including the bedrooms, were furnished with furniture like the kind she had grown up with. It was all junk. Except in Baron Buchacklian's bedroom, all the floors were pinewood with cheap scatter rugs here and there. She thought, Baron Buchacklian is a tremendously successful rug dealer. This is very odd. Where are all the oriental carpets and the beautiful pieces of furniture and draperies like the ones downstairs? Maybe they're re-decorating everything now that I'm the harse. That must be it…they're redecorating and they're waiting for my ideas.

She found her suitcases in a bedroom turned out to be hers alone. It was painted white, had a double bed against the wall under a painting of Mount Ararat opposite to a painting of an Armenian monastery. The bedspread was a heavy white one that had the potential for breaking her legs if she lay under it. Her mother-in-law had crocheted it. Her husband had the room next to hers with an adjoining door to her room. She was also to discover that it would never be opened from her amousteen's (husband's), side.

Even though she knew this was a Middle Eastern marriage arrangement, she couldn't help thinking that her marriage was nothing like she had imagined or read about in romance novels. Where was the money, the passion, the pay-off for her?

This was the great awakening. Siroon's marriage into the Buchaklian family had made her mother-in-law the hanum, Turkish for Queen of the Home, and herself the harse. Just like in the Old Country the harse was taken into the pessa's home to be the handmaiden of the mother-in-law, who was the 'boss' of the household.

Siroon's husband was out every night gambling. Her father-in-law made all the household decisions like who got how much money, what appliances to buy, and everything they would do socially. His wife, the hanum, made the decisions about the meals, assigned Siroon's daily chores and decided what clothes she and her harse would wear. The hanum's taste was J. C. Penney in contrast to Siroon's taste, which was I. Magnin. And it soon became clear that there was no redecorating plan for all the junk rooms that were out of sight of anyone who came calling.

Siroon might have been the daughter of peasant immigrants but she was smart and well read, so, after two weeks of marriage, Siroon began looking for a way out of this mess her mother had gotten her into. During the days when she was supposed to dust Baron Buchacklian's office she poked around everywhere—in his desk drawers, under furniture cushions, in the lining of the drapery—looking for information on their financial assets or anything incriminating, but she never found a thing.

Then one day she was so uncomfortable in the chair she had confiscated for her reading that she jumped up, picked up the cushion and stomped on it in a fit of anger. When she had calmed down she unzipped the cover and began to fluff up the stuffing from inside. That was when she discovered the church collection bag from the stolen cathedral money.

What an enormous esh Baron Buchlakian is, she laughed out loud to herself. Maybe his wife, the hanum, had put it in the cushion, to save for one day when she might need to use it to get her husband to do something against his wishes. Maybe God put it there. However the bag got there, my mother was thrilled to have found it. She kissed the bag and said to herself that this was her ticket out.

She waited until everyone was out of the house and then she phoned for Bobeeg to pick her up and take her home. Mama Jahn said an emphatic votch, so Siroon explained.

"Mama Jahn everything about this family is soud, one big lie... and my so-called husband never comes home at night. He sleeps all day, and he never speaks to me."

"Vie, vie, vie, ench ga ses? What are you saying?"

". . . and I'm expected to scrub the toilet bowls—*the toilet bowls*—and wash and massage the hanum's feet every night, and iron that eshag Baron Buchacklian's shirts and even his vardeegs . . ."

"Ahmahn, ahmahn, ahmahn . . ."

"...and she wants me to make the most difficult pastries like *sou beorag* and to even make rojig. No one makes rojig. You buy rojig in Fresno. I've never been treated like this in my entire life and I'm not going to stand for it now. Next I'm supposed to learn to make lahmajoon."

"Ench bede allah, ahmahn, park Asdzoo, ench bede alah?" "What will happen, oh my, God, what will happen?"

And, saving the worst for last, Siroon screamed, "and they have no money . . . they are as broke as peasants . . . they lied to all of us."

"Medeem, I'm dying . . . How you know he's poor? Maybe he just cheap."

"No, no, I saw for myself that he is a thief and a liar. I have proof. I need to get out of here right now."

Mama Jahn was mortified, to say the very least, particularly when she heard the "proof." "Vie, vie, vie, aht inch ahmot, medeem. I will die of embarrassment," she moaned, continuing her ranting along the following lines in Armenian: *"How could I have been taken in by these people? Every Armenian is sure to laugh at me and happily tell the story of this marital fiasco well after my death for being tricked by this family of eshes. And my takouhii, Siroon, now no decent Armenian will ever marry her. She is doomed to be a working woman for the rest of her life, living in shame."*

For herself, my smart mother figured a way out that would save the honor of her family and her reputation. In an extended Armenian family, there is always a professional who knows what to do. Cousin Osheen's uncle, who was an immigration attorney, told her that the marriage could be annulled instead of having to go through the disgrace of a divorce for one irrefutable reason—because her marriage had never been consummated.

Siroon gave Cousin Osheen's uncle the money-bag for safekeeping, then made her announcement to the eshag family, "I want an annulment. Immediately. Or I'll tell everyone you were the thieves who stole the church money."

Cousin Osheen's uncle had advised her to ask for a financial settlement as well, but Siroon didn't want anything to do with stolen church money.

So that's what happened. And amidst barbaric shouting, hysterical gestures and threats of violence against Siroon and her family from the eshags, Bobeeg Jahn picked up Siroon at the curb and they sped away from the disgraceful marriage arrangement, with a new sense of freedom ringing in Siroon's heart and images of an empowered Scarlet O'Hara declaring tomorrow to be another day. Siroon discovered the beginnings of a sense of independence and pride in herself.

After Siroon was home and had poured out all the stories about the eshag family, she realized how the news of her failed marriage would damage their standing in the Armenian community. Mama Jahn cried so hard she was just about to faint dead away until Bobeeg Jahn undid the hooks on her corset and made her drink a stiff glass of rakhi.

Everyone in the family avoided going to church and didn't answer the phone when it rang because they needed time to sort things out. Mama Jahn badgered herself with questions like how could she not have seen that this family was not what they appeared to be? How could she have given her precious Sirooneg to this horrible family to be treated as a servant instead of a queen? And most of all, why hadn't she insisted Siroon pay attention to the bad omen in the cup on the day before the marriage?

She decided that she would have to find the right man for Siroon immediately, before making more yegh to sell, before sewing a new yorgahn for Aznif's grandson, and certainly before Christmas, or they would have to move far away where no one knew them. This next pessa would have to be someone to bring honor to the family, or all was lost. But first, Mama Jahn saw in her cup that she must tell a known gossip a secret that would save their reputation without breaking the contract Siroon negotiated for her annulment. She was sure this secret would be told to everyone with one phone call to the Der Hayr.

"Der Hayr, I have some bad news to tell you about Siroon. It's a menz secret."

"Wat's happen? She's sick? You know I never tell wat you tell me."

"No, she's not sick… but you must never tell to anybody's…."

"Sure ya, you can trust me…"

"Her marriage is over because husband is manchaghchig!"

"Vie, vie, vie, poor Siroon. I never see before dis myself but I hear about dis kind of man in another family. Dis other family move far away to separate their son from his boyfriend, but he just find a different one, lots of different ones. Better Siroon know now so she can get away. I always tink something wrong with Buchlakian family because too much show off peoples and show off peoples always have something to hide."

And so the rumor spread about the eshag family, like fire under skewers of kabobs, and Siroon's reputation was not only saved but she was held in high regard for her suffering.

Nevertheless, Siroon became very depressed. She wore her robe all day, sat in the green chair all the time, not reaching for the library books on the pile and not eating much. Every night she had the same dream, of eating her way through the large round silver tray filled with the khanamie khapogh while staring at the idiotic smile on the hanum's face. The only thing that made her happy in the dream was that the hanum's constant smile was replaced with the gnashing of her golden teeth as she scrubbed the toilets.

Siroon was soon to meet someone else who had also made the wrong marriage. It was their jagad (destiny).

8 THE CUP OF DESTINY

the curtain reveals as much as it hides

Kourken Avedisian was a dignified Armenian, born in the unofficial capital of Armenian America—Fresno, California—and living in Los Angeles. He was gaining popularity as a master of ceremonies at Armenian American cultural events in town. People spoke of him as an eloquent man whom they were proud to have represent them in American society. He wasn't snobby or embarrassed by being Armenian. He didn't change his name like the Samuelians who had become Samuel and the Georgorians who had become George. He was proud of his heritage and would never think of dropping the 'ian' at the end of his name.

Armenians called Kourken Avedisian their *Pro-fes-sor* as a sign of admiration, but he was actually an immigration attorney. He wrote Armenian and English poetry that reflected the inner feelings of his people in the Diaspora, he was the founder and editor of *The Victory*, an English/Armenian newspaper whose platform was the ongoing dispute with Turkey regarding the genocide of Armenians. He cared about people and their problems, he gave one hundred percent of himself at work as a lawyer, and he volunteered his time at the International Institute where immigrants from all cultures were transitioned into becoming Americans. As a man and as an Armenian, Kourken Avedisian had much to recommend him. However, with Mama Jahn deliberating over which man Siroon should now marry, the best news about Kourken was that he was an orphan with just an uncle and a sister to call family. No khunamies to deal with.

The ladies who drank coffee together reported that his mother died from a stroke after she found her husband in a sexual embrace with her visiting seventeen-year-old cousin. And next, this same husband, Kourken's father, died after falling off the roof of a house he was building. Firsthand witnesses sweared they saw him smiling with his arms outstretched like he was enjoying gliding down to earth. Why? He had been told from his cup reading that he would fall from such a roof, so he had no fear. He told others who heard about the fortune that the fall would not kill him. No one could say, I told you so, because Kourken's father was instantly killed the moment he hit the concrete.

Kourken was devoted to his father's older brother, his Uncle Mono, who took care of him during his years in high school when he was orphaned. Kourken had earned enough to put himself though college, by writing letters and filling out immigration papers for the droves of DP's from all over the Diaspora, who had come to Fresno to get jobs picking grapes and working in fruit packing houses. He'd set up a little tavloo table in the park in downtown Fresno and wait for business to come to him. The men played tavloo with each other while he worked with one of them at a time. He had stationery made with his name and phone number that stated, "Teacher and counselor in citizenship and naturalization."

Mama Jahn knew family honor came from monetary wealth or from holding a respected position in the American culture. It was too much to hope for both anymore. It seemed that Kourken was destined to be the man to bring honor to Mama Jahn's family even though he wasn't rich.

Everyone knew that Kourken had one major flaw—when he drank, he lost his temper, but because his fulminations were usually directed at the Turks for the genocide, people loved him for his righteous anger. The church ladies who knew him and his family from Fresno said he inherited this trait from his father. But Kourken's one flaw didn't bother Mama Jahn because she knew all about the many ways women dealt with this kind of problem. She liked that it was out in the open. No more surprises.

Kourken had a past. About the same time as he had received his PhD from UCLA, he fell into the clutches of a very wealthy Turkish Armenian woman by the name of Sylvia. Sylvia was twelve years older than Kourken, she wore black horned-rimmed glasses, had a large Roman nose, pasty white skin, a trim medium-size figure and a tremendous amount of money. She wore Chanel suits when she went out and flimsy nighties when she was home. She believed in drinking at least eight glasses of water a day as long as they were well diluted with eighty-proof Scotch, and she had her mind made up to marry Kourken.

Sylvia's enormous wealth came from her first husband who invented the Hula Hoop. He had just launched the sales of his new invention when he died suddenly at the race track in Hollywood Park. Overnight Sylvia was instantly a very wealthy woman, getting wealthier as the Hula Hoop craze swept across the country.

Kourken was vulnerable to Sylvia's advances for two reasons. The first was an attraction to financial security. He had been without all his life and her money seemed a way to enjoy the good life that all Armenians dreamed of having. But he couldn't marry someone just because of money which meant that Sylvia had to resort to desperate measures.

She wanted this prize of an Armenian man for herself so she did everything she could to snare him. In addition to her wealth, which could make Kourken's life comfortable, Sylvia had an even more seductive attraction—she appreciated his mind. She made him feel like a Greek god by doing everything in her power to massage his ego. As he was telling stories she sat enthralled on the edge of her chair. When he described his travels or discussed the differences between the Rumgavars and the Tashnags she didn't take her eyes off of him. She clapped, sang out cheers of bravo and marveled at his ability to quote the poetry of Alfred Lord Tennyson, Swinburne and Shakespeare, especially when in reference to everyday situations.

Kourken used impressive, little-used English words in his conversations, like *medley* when referring to a mixture of vegetables and *obsequious* to describe a groveling waiter. Sylvia had never met anyone like him, Armenian or American.

She loved his brain and, he loved that she thought of him as disarming and marvelous, because he knew he wasn't really what was regarded as handsome. He was big and strong and his manners were powerfully impressive, which gave him the allure of a cultured English gentleman. His face wasn't smooth because of acne scars, but his curly hair was plentiful and his dark eyes were penetrating. She marveled at his gregarious personality and affable nature. He won friends as easily as someone giving away dollar bills on a street corner. Like her Cutty Sark scotch, he was irresistible and she couldn't get enough of him. And he loved being consumed by her awe of his many charms. So they married in a brief civil ceremony, attended and witnessed only by his Uncle Mono and Aunt Zov before leaving for a first class grand tour of Europe on an ocean liner, which she paid for.

But, once home and ensconced in daily life, over time her demanding and imperious nature wore him down. He used to complain to his odar friends that married life was just too damn daily. It wasn't long after their honeymoon that he felt like an indentured servant. She'd interrupt his studying and writing with her demands, veiled in the guise of favors. "Kourken, do me a favor and get me more ice. Kourken, do me a favor and find my glasses. Kourken, rub my back. Kourken, I'm all out of cigarettes. Please go to the market and get me more ciggies, and while you're there would you pick up a box of Kotex." That request was extremely distasteful to him.

Being a student of the romantic poets he constantly wondered why he was squandering his youth with this old woman who had no charm or grace for him to adore. But the final blow to his ego came when she blurted out in public—in front of their circle of friends—that she was the man in the house because she held the checkbook.

She was unable to conceive children and that made her very angry, so she drank more and more, and he accepted more and more master of ceremony engagements to get out of her sight. He thought of her as *the great destroyer* and she completely stopped thinking of him. She replaced him with a maid to do her daily fetching and a subscription to *The New Yorker* magazine for culture.

One night, while Kourken was out of the house giving a lecture to the Young Armenian Cultural Club, her maid, Inez, put Sylvia to bed after she passed out—a routine part of her job. But then Inez did something out of the usual. She made sure Sylvia was indeed completely passed out and in a deep sleep, then went to the back door and waved in her Puerto Rican boyfriend, who had been lurking behind the oleander bush. Just as they had been planning, she showed him where Sylvia's money was hidden and opened the jewelry drawers for him to empty. For some reason, Sylvia awakened and screamed. Without any struggle the Puerto Rican boyfriend suffocated Sylvia with her expensive, satin-covered, down-filled pillow. That night, Inez and her boy friend left the country and got away with her valuables and her murder.

Soon after Sylvia's murder, Kourken learned that she had a will he knew nothing about and all her money went to the Armenian Protestant Church. He felt sure Sylvia did this because she hated his violent reaction to Armenians singing protestant hymns. He loved the rich history of the Divine Liturgy and its poignant and mournful sharagans (chants). They often fought about the differences between the two churches.

He walked away with the things that were his—his many books, his suits, his custom-made shirts with French cuffs and cuff links. The only household belonging he took was the large, white ceramic bowl with a pedestal that he once filled with champagne for a party he gave as a bachelor. At that party an odar woman had invited him to lap up champagne from her large, pink tzeezeegs after dangling them in the bowl of bubbly.

After that erotic experience the vase took on new meaning. While he was married the vase was used to catch the daily mail but it also held a sense of male pride when Sylvia was at her worst. And after her death the vase held the promise a fresh start.

Months later a fateful event occurred. Kourken Avedisian appeared at the Wilshire Ebelle Theatre in Los Angeles, to introduce a new Armenian arrival to America, the awe inspiring mind reader, Emmanuel the Magnificent, who had entertained the crowned heads of Europe and the princes of the Middle East. His given name was Manuel Mushagian but he learned that Emmanuel meant "God is With Us" so he added the "Em," dropped the Musagian and became Emmanuel. A very American thing to do to change your name.

It was well past the advertised eight p.m. starting time of Emmanuel's performance and all eyes were fixed on the red velvet curtains, including Siroon, who was sitting in the middle of the front row with her girlfriends. By eight-thirty the time had come and gone for Kourken to give his introduction and no still one appeared. The crowd became more and more agitated and began stomping their feet until the formidable professor stepped out from stage right, motioning with his arms for the crowd to calm down. Kourken announced that Emmanuel was not coming out until he felt positive vibrations from the audience. He went on to say, "Fellow Armenians, Emmanuel the Magnificent confided in me that he can only perform for you tonight if he is surrounded by true believers. Until he feels your positive energy he will not perform. So please, everyone, yes ga khuntrem, I beg of you, control yourselves, relax, breathe deeply and open your minds so this remarkable fellow can come out."

Slowly the audience quieted down, and people looked at each other, wondering how to summon positive vibrations. Soon Kourken could see them physically relaxing into their seats as he had beseeched them.

In actuality Emmanuel had passed out from too much rakhi, and his agent and blond girlfriends were trying to revive him with Armenian coffee in the dressing room. Until then, it was up to Kourken to quiet down the crowd so they wouldn't riot and demand their money back.

In front of hundreds of people, all on the verge of walking out, and without even a few lines scratched on note paper in his hand, Kourken began reciting what he decided was something this group would viscerally respond to, the epic poem, *Baghdassar of Sassoun*, which he had recently translated from Armenian to English. As far as he knew no one had ever recited it in the USA before, and surely not in English. And so he began, using his booming voice and the eloquent words of Varoujan to bring his people into his world of great literature:

" . . . Greetings to the all –powerful giant of Sassoun!
Your voice has reached to the throne of God.
And soon He shall grant you a child.
But hear me well, O lord of the mountains,
On the day God grants you an heir,
On that very same day you and your wife will die...."

You could hear the ash drop from his cigarette as he told the legend of heroic *Baghdassar of Sassoun*, mesmerizing the audience into submission for forty-five minutes. Kourken then ducked behind stage to confirm

Emmanuel's revival and re-emerged. It was as he swept his arm in front of the curtains and they parted, that Siroon and he locked eyes across that crowded auditorium, and each knew that they had just met their destiny, their jagad.

Kourken, though smitten, somehow proceeded to introduce with great flare the "most prodigious extrasensory clairvoyant, whom we are proud to claim as a fellow Armenian, that great master of precognition and transcendentalism, Emmanuel the Magnificent."

When Kourken got closer to Siroon at intermission, her remarkable beauty captivated him, but he was drawn even more to her melancholy as evidenced by her downcast eyes, her sad demeanor and the dark halo that hovered over her lovely head of hair. He knew he could make her happy. It was his jagad. This Armenian word means, your future written across your forehead. Siroon was the future that Kourken saw written on his face that enchanted evening.

He soon heard that this rare Armenian beauty had been tricked into marrying a manchaghchig, so he knew she would be a virgin. That thrilled him to know he would be her first love. And when Siroon looked into his eyes she knew she could make him happy. He needed a woman who admired him but a woman who also gave him someone to admire. She was that woman. It was her jagad.

As Siroon got to know Kourken over the next few weeks, she recognized that he was who he said he was, and she could envision herself living her life with him and having a family. Cleverly, she also saw her mother and father living with them because she hated housework and cooking. Living with an extended family was fine with Kourken who brought along his Uncle Mono and his sister Aunt Zov to live with them, too. Kourken believed that living together was the Armenian way and "some of our ways had to be preserved or we would completely loose our identity as a people."

Siroon had accepted her jagad and realized that even though money made life enjoyable being married to a good man would give her happiness.

Kourken had accepted his jagad and realized that even though money made life easier, a wonderful wife gave him reason to live.

Mama Jahn confided in Bobeeg Jahn her deepest thought about the marriage, *"They are right for each other in many ways and they are both a little used."*

So in the house that Kourken bought at the top of a hill in Silver Lake, they all lived together, prayed together and ate together, while they waited for me, Azad, to appear on the scene. And after I arrived, Masha's evil eye curse galvanized not just Mama Jahn, but pretty much everyone, except perhaps my mother.

I knew all about my future long before I had a chance to live it, thanks to my family. Because "nice Armenian girls" never left home until they had a gold band wrapped securely around their ring finger, I accepted that my destiny was to live with my family in Los Angeles in my little turquoise bedroom until I was married. And wasn't my future all there on my bedroom wall, in the painting Uncle Mono had done to honor the Armenian mother I would become?

Mother became a librarian so she could read books all day long, and left my indoctrination into domesticity to Mama Jahn. Mama Jahn repeatedly told me, "You have to be good wife. You have to take care you husband's shirts . . . you have to wash, nice starch and iron per-fect . . . no wrinkle—especially collar—everybody notice collar. And you have to listen everything he say. Be nice houze lady and never make him nervous and you be happy woman." She'd always make her final point waving a serrated steak knife as an extension of her index finger saying, "You listen me. I know what I say. I see everything in the cup and I know what I see." I believed her.

Hayrig made all major decisions regarding my life, which he had already projected into a future as tidy as Mama Jahn's starched collars. At my sixth birthday party Hayrig lifted me up in his huge arms and onto our brick patio wall and announced in front of our family and my little neighborhood friends, "Azadouhee Jahn, your play days are *over*." Enthusiastic applause from the adults motivated him to continue.

"Now that you are entering your seventh year you must think about your life. You are an Avedisian and even though you were unlucky to be born a female you cannot be ordinary or unproductive."

With all the fire of an evangelical protestant preacher at a revival, Hayrig cast his eyes upwards and with his basso profundo voice boomed, "You are part of the plan to replace all the teachers and intellectuals who were massacred in the genocide. You will make us proud and bring honor to the family name by going to college and becoming a teacher. This is your jagad."

This was pretty heavy stuff for six-year-olds. His speech got foot stomping and cheers from everyone except the little odar kids, who just wanted to cry. My odar friends came to the party expecting to play Pin the Tail on the Donkey and Musical Chairs, but instead they got Uncle Mono calling out, "come on, let's poke the esh in the vodeeg," and Hayrig's zealous genocide reparation speeches.

This was where I had to thank God for my mother, who loved decorating with colorful American crepe papers, paper plates and napkins. To spare the odars mazas made with garlic, she served vanilla ice cream and white cake with pink roses from the local bakery for the odars and me.

Afterward, I looked in the mirror for my jagad. My olive skin had freckles. If I connected the dots, the freckles made the outline of a hot dog bun, but I didn't see anything written across my forehead.

9 THE SECRET INGREDIENT CUP

even a sharp onion has its place on the table

On Saturday mornings, while other kids on the block were running around playing dodge ball and riding bikes—I was inside helping with the baking or washing or the war against ahmot. Finding dust was one of my biggest assignments. Mama Jahn deployed me to scrutinize under beds and crawl into hard to reach corners behind dressers and cabinets. Soon I was old enough to learn how to devour the dust with her most prized possession, a top-of-the-line, Proctor Silex vacuum cleaner, the sort that looked like a dachshund—a long, round tube that rolled along low to the ground.

A great play thing for me under the guise of housework equipment. For many minutes on end, I pulled on the self-retracting cord then watched it travel at high speeds into the dog's vodeeg! My fertile imagination was incubated in this environment of cleaning up the daily dirt of our lives and creating opportunities for cleaning by emptying drawers or cupboards and re-sorting and organizing things while happily waiting for Mama Jahn's praise for a job well done. "Azad Jahn, you do vonderful vork. You make me very proud. You are good girl."

When the war was won for the day, I would sit with Mama Jahn on the flowered sofa in our living room, learning how to knit a ruffled shawl using a scallop design that she remembered from her mother in the Old Country.

In my mother, the genetic predisposition to home economics seemed to have skipped a generation, but in me domesticity was dominant. I enjoyed making things with my hands. Rolling grape leaves into sarmas and folding the delicate lace-like filo dough into triangles around sheep and goat cheeses didn't feel like strange ways to spend Saturday morning. Neither did knitting.

All colors of leftover yarns were in a basket by the radio in the living room. I especially liked the plush lipstick-red yarn leftover from a scarf Mama Jahn made for Auntie Zov when she went to Chicago to look for a husband. The lucky blue yarn was from a vest Uncle Mono wore when he went for his first driver's license test. It was the shade of turquoise blue that kept away the evil eye. The creamy yellow and white yarns were from the afghan Mama Jahn made for a church lady's baby shower and for my baby doll.

For my shawl project, I picked the lavender yarn that remained from the sweater that Mama Jahn made to send to her daughter Zepure, who was *still* in Armenia. (We found out later on, after Aunt Zepure received it, that she sold it on the black market for rent and food money. It was hard to imagine that Aunt Zepure lived for an entire month on the money from that sweater.)

I picked the lavender color for my shawl because it reminded me of the ribbon a pretty girl at school named Penny wore to tie back her silky smooth, blond ponytail. I loved watching Penny's hair bounce when she walked down the hall—not like my hair that just stuck straight out because it was so Armenian and ugly—fuzzy-curly, like the poodle next door.

As I knitted—over and under, over and under—I proudly showed Mama Jahn my stitches and she was happy to see that I had a natural ability for making shawls. "It not easy pattern to make, Azad. You have to make lots of concentration to knit all those fluff-fuls. Anoush acheeg (sweet girl), you make wonderful nice fluff-fuls. I very proud."

She never mentioned the mistakes I made, but late one night when I got up to go to the bathroom, I saw Mama Jahn pulling out the rows I had knitted in the daytime. I stayed long enough to see that she was re-working the yarn to the place where I had stopped, taking out all the mistakes along the way. I never mentioned what I had seen. Mama Jahn and I both pretended that my work was without a single flaw.

We spent a lot of time together knitting. Mama Jahn talked and I listened while I added rows and rows of yarn to my shawl. I watched as it grew to cover my knees then slowly drape to the floor in layers and layers of flouncing waves.

When my mother walked by she'd get very serious as she bent down to touch the ruffles and say, "How I wish I could think of a way to make money from these shawls. We have enough of them to keep all the Armenians in the Diaspora warm."

Mama Jahn talked about her childhood and about her young mother dying of a ruptured appendix and of the pair of her solid gold engagement bracelets that she intended on giving me one day when I became engaged to some *wonderful nice* Armenian boy, and how my eyes were the exact color of her father's eyes and why Armenians used an ohlaghvee—a length of wooden doweling—to roll out pastry dough, instead of an American rolling pin that I thought was the best invention ever, even though I didn't tell my beloved grandma that.

Mama Jahn recited poems she had memorized in grammar school. She thought about, then decided what to make for dinner, after which she stopped to look in her demitasse cup for messages of what was happening with the relatives in Armenia. When she did that, it was usually time for a break because she invariably saw something that made her cry. Then she had to clean her eyeglasses.

With so many people living together under one roof, our house was never empty. There was always someone at home. And as time went on, the strands of our individual lives were woven together under one roof by our deep love and genuine concern for each other and by the continuity of our individual longings and heart's desires. Just as Mama Jahn unraveled the mistakes of my shawl in the late hours of the night, so family members helped each other rework the familiar patterns from the Old Country into fresh new ways of being in our chosen City of the Angels, in the "New-nited States of 'mericas'."

Mother, Hayrig, Uncle Mono, Aunt Zov, Bobeeg Jahn and I came and went during the day, but my Mama Jahn was always there when I walked in the door, and as I called out, "Parev (hello), I'm home," she would reply with, "Parev, anoush acheeg!"

Then I would go into the kitchen for a delicious piece of something Mama Jahn had baked, like cheorag, a golden, sweet, buttery Armenian bread roll with the extraordinary scent of mahlab. "This cheorag fragrance is angels' perfume," she'd tell me as the scrumptious fragrance filled the air.

On most days she and I would sit across from each other at the kitchen table eating cheorag. She sipped hot coffee made fresh from her mysterious dark blend of pulverized coffee beans. She always drank out of her special demitasse cup and I sipped chi through a sugar cube in my special glass. And then we would talk about what I had done at school that day.

One horrible day I came home from school, slammed the front door shut and did not answer when Mama Jahn called out to me. I ran past the kitchen, straight into my room, and closed the bedroom door. Hard.

Right away Mama Jahn came to my room and knocked on my door. "Azad, Jahn," she called out, "What's the madder?

"Nothing, you wouldn't understand anyway."

"Come out and have something to eat with me. You'll feel better."

I did not answer her. I could picture Mama Jahn wringing her hands with worry as she padded away in her red velvet slippers muttering, "Vie, vie, vie."

"Telling me, please telling me what's wrong, Balah Jahn (baby dear)," she came back to say.

From behind my closed door I screamed out, "IT'S MY HAIR! They said I look like a porcupine because it sticks straight out."

"What you saying?"

Throwing the door open I continued my tirade while picking at my horrid hair. "I do look like a porcupine! I hate my hair," I screamed as I tugged at it and stomped my foot hard on the ground. "It's awful. It's ugly. Combs break and get stuck in it and it hurts! Even brushes won't go through it. In the rain it gets frizzy and gets bigger and bigger. It looks like it's growing right in front of your eyes!"

Mama Jahn nodded her head in agreement. "I know many Armenians who have same hair as you."

"I bet they hate their hair and that they were teased in school, too."

"Votch, no, in Armenia almost everyone has hair like yours. When a person is different is when everybody's make fun. Like now, with you."

"Why does my mother have beautiful, wavy hair and I don't?"

"Never mind you mama's hair. You have your hayrig's hair. Very curly. You make very short like Hayrig and no stick out. No good luck you get Kourken's hair."

As if I had to be reminded of my curse.

"Well, in my school I'm the only different one!" I cried, "And I want to have straight hair like the other girls at school. Like the models and movie stars in magazines and on TV!"

"Let's make your hair short, like Cousin Raffi."

"I don't want it cut," I insisted. "I'll never be able to put it in a ponytail the way the other girls do if it's short. I want it to bounce up and down when I walk, not stick straight out like a broom. And I don't want short hair. I'd look like a boy. I want to look like *Barbie*!!!"

Not knowing what else to say, Mama Jahn again said, "Come to kitchen and have something to eat—you'll feel better."

I followed her into the kitchen and watched as she made me my favorite meal, a sandwich made with crunchy bacon and little diced potatoes, fried to a crisp in bacon fat and clarified butter. Then Hayrig came into the room. "Azad janus, einch-beses? (How are you?)" Seeing me with red eyes he became worried and asked, "What's the matter, my sweet child?"

I was chewing between crying so Mama Jahn answered for me: "Children in school make Azad cry because of her hair."

"What do you mean?" he asked, the pitch of his voice rising higher and higher in his excitement. "How can she be teased about the most beautiful dark brown hair of any Armenian girl I have ever seen? I love every hair on your head. Who is saying things to hurt my anoush acheeg?"

Hearing Hayrig's raised voice, Uncle Mono and Raffi came running into the kitchen.

"What do *you* think of Azad's hair, Uncle Mono?" asked Hayrig.

Uncle Mono rubbed his bald head. "I give anyting to have hair like Azad," he said. "Anyting!"

"For that ugly hair?" said Raffi, pointing at Azad's head. "You don't want her hair. She looks like a frizz ball. And you should see her in the morning when she's slept on one side and all her hair sticks out one way and is flat on the other side. It's weird! She should wear a wig."

"That's enough, Raffi," said Hayrig.

At least my mother didn't wander through and pat her perfect hair in front of me.

Just then Mama Jahn said, "Azad, I have something I show you about your hair."

"What is it?" I asked between swallows and sobs.

"When you finish eating I show you," said Mama Jahn, and she left the kitchen.

I wondered what Mama Jahn had to say. Maybe she would tell me to wrap my hair in a latchag as she did every night. Maybe she would use pins and clips and combs to flatten my hair so it wouldn't stick out anymore. Maybe she had some secret potion or cream to pour on my hair to make it straight and smooth. Maybe she knew exactly what to do. Maybe I would be beautiful. Maybe.

When I was finished eating, I ran into Mama Jahn's room announcing, "I'm ready!"

Mama Jahn took me back into the kitchen. "I need you to help me make the cheorag for tomorrow."

"But what about my hair?"

"First," said Mama Jahn, "help me with dough." This was quite something because cheorag was one thing she never let me help with.

She brought out her big wooden bowl that was filled with risen dough. "Look, dough ready because when I put my finger in it, it makes hole and hole never go away."

Then we punched it down and kneaded it more with our fists.

"When dough feels soft like your ear lobe, it's ready to make shapes."

Mama Jahn had secrets like these about everything.

"Now watch me," she said. She took a piece of the dough and plopped it in a sprinkling of flour. Then she rolled the dough into a long tube. Next she made two more lengths of dough the same way. Lining them up beside each other, she began to twist the tubes together. "Under, over, under, over, under, over. "You do,' she told me, and so I did—over, under, over, under, over under until all the lengths were bound together.

When I completed working all the dough, Mama Jahn put the rolls aside to rise again, then into the oven to bake. "There," she said, "Shad lav (very good). Soon we have fresh cheorag. "

"Now will you show me what to do with my hair, Mama Jahn?" I had almost forgotten about my problem while I was helping her with the dough. But not completely. The pain was still there, like I had swallowed piece of chewing gum and it was stuck in the center of my chest.

"Now your hands know; your hands will show you." And she turned towards the stove to make another jezvah of coffee.

I walked to my bedroom. What had Mama Jahn shown me? All we did was make cheorag.

I began to brush my hair. It stuck out, but I kept on brushing. My fingers parted my hair into three sections in the back and I began looping and crossing the different parts, over and under, over and under, over and under, as I had done with the dough and with the knitting needles. It was easy and quick. As if my fingers had always known what to do. The knowing was like knitting without looking at the yarns, like tying shoes without thinking. Soon my hair was in a beautiful long braid. My ears stuck out but I tried not to notice. I couldn't handle more than one problem at a time. So I pinched the end tightly and went to find Mama Jahn.

"Baligus, baby darling!" exclaimed Mama Jahn, "Your hair. It look beautiful! So smooth and nice ... I see your big, brown, dancing eyes much better."

"I know Mama Jahn, I love my hair this way, but I need a rubber band to tie it so it won't all come apart."

Mama Jahn went to her special dresser drawer and took out a length of silk red ribbon that she had taken as a keepsake from Aunt Zepure's hair, before leaving her in Armenia. She had tied it around her rolled up citizenship papers. Now she tied it around the end of my braid.

I wrapped my arms around her thick middle and squeezed, squealing, "Thank you, Mama Jahn. I feel beautiful."

We went into the kitchen to see how the cheorag were baking and to make some fresh chi so we could sit and talk and talk and talk, all about red ribbons worn by little girls in the Old Country and in the new country, and about why dough rises and about the difference between hurts that need only love to heal and those that need bandages too.

Slowly, as the hot chi melted the sugar cube and intertwined with the sweet buttery flavors of the warm cheorag bathing my taste buds, Mama Jahn's words rolled into my heart and I was filled with comfort again, and all was well.

10 THE CUP OF FEAR

what the eye truly sees, the heart never forgets

At three in the morning Baron Hamalian put his finger on our doorbell and didn't let up until Hayrig came out. When Baron Hamalian saw Hayrig he fell on his knees and cried, "Professor, we need help...please you come with me to the police station...my boy, Arsene, vostigan (police), take him to jail."

"Arsene is a good boy . . . what's he doing in jail, for God's sake?"

"They say he have no green card and they going send him to Armenia on Monday."

"Eshag (asinine), police. Why don't they pick on some other race?"

"Professor, you know he born here . . . you see his baptism . . . he no need green card. I no understand."

"Come in, come in and calm down. Wait until I get dressed and we'll go right away to straighten out this mess."

Mama Jahn sat Baron Hamalian at the kitchen table. She was already at the stove with the jezvah making his coffee. I toasted yesterday's cheorag while he sat with his head in his hands, lamenting "vie, vie, vie" over and over again.

Hayrig and Baron Hamalian went down to the police station and we all went back to bed. In the morning we learned that he had raised his eyebrows instead of his voice to get Arsene released. That was easy. What wasn't easy, he said, was changing the minds of the law enforcers who looked at young Armenians as trouble makers because they were different.

That morning, it was hotter inside the house than it was outside. The scorching summer days in the Los Angeles basin silenced the Saturday sounds and activities that typically came from our household. It was at least a hundred degrees outside so everyone in the family went in different directions to find a cool, quiet refuge.

The men in the house, who usually sang loudly with Caruso records and played enthusiastic tavloo games in which they'd bang down the pools yelling out the numbers on the dice shesh-oo-besh (six and five), were silent.

The cluck, cluck, clucking of the ladies gossiping was normally loud above the rhythmical movements and sounds of the rolling oghlavee pressing out circles of dough for lavash, which the ladies made by the dozens to stack for use over the next two weeks, but not that day.

Even the annoying noises of Raffi running in and out of the house, banging the screen door each time, were silenced during the hottest time of the day, in the hottest time of the year. Instead he sat watching his trains go round and round on their tracks until they derailed. Then he'd lie on the floor, the caboose upside down in his hand, wheels spinning in the air, until the monotony of all that whirling lulled him to sleep. As his body relaxed, his thumb found its way into his mouth and he began gently sucking. His other hand held tightly to the caboose anchoring him to planet Earth.

"Dun't bother me anybodys, I tink-ing," Uncle Mono pronounced—which meant he was taking a nap on the sofa under the open window. I could see him straining his neck in his sleep to catch the tiniest breeze through the window that occasionally slipped through the Japanese Elm tree growing in our front yard. In his sleep Uncle Mono smiled and made little whimpering sounds while "tinking." He was probably dreaming of sailing on the ship he always talked about traveling on one day. "Some day my ship's coming," he'd say, thinking he was clever with words like a successful American businessman.

I peered into Auntie Zov's room, to see what was going on. I loved it there. My auntie was a total romantic. Hanging from satin covered hangers all around the room were peignoirs in every pastel color imaginable against the backdrop of her rose patterned wall-paper in pale cream and light peach colors. When I opened the door, the diaphanous fabrics billowed, as they usually did when the windows were open. But that day it they had none of that life of their own, fluttering and twirling on their hangers. There was no breeze whatsoever.

I loved to visit with Auntie Zov in her room, doing our nails and listening to the radio, but that heat made adorning myself in her hot pink feather boa or her pink feathered spring-a-later slippers impossible. I plopped down in her overstuffed floral covered arm-chair and began flipping through her movie star books from the large stack next to chair.

"Come on tzaks," which is Armenian slang for "hun," she'd say to me. "Come with me to the picture show. You'll cool off and maybe you'll see some cute boys," she'd continue, while primping in front of the half mirror in the hallway.

Auntie Zov went to the movies where the air-conditioning made her forget that it was hot. She fluffed up her ratty old fur coat, which I called "Bear," to take with her to the movie theatre in case she got cold there. Bear had the same color fur as her home-dyed hair—reddish sable brown. It was embarrassing watching her go out the door wearing Bermuda shorts, a starched sleeveless batiste blouse and leather Bandolino sandals with bobby-socks and Bear draped over her arm. She looked screwy and very "Old Country," even to other Armenians.

Maybe if we'd had a full-length mirror she could have seen for herself how stupid she looked in her getup. As bored as I was, I wouldn't go with her to the movies. I'd absolutely die if my American friends saw me there with her. It was hard enough being an Armenian in school without her making me look more foreign. Bobby-socks with sandals! Fur coat in the summertime!

She was a total embarrassment.

Mother was in her favorite place to relax after a busy week at the library, her bed. She went to ladies' luncheons and hair parlors and nail polishing and serving as president of the prestigious ladies council of the Armenian parish when she wasn't working but she loved her bed the best.

She liked to stretch out on her side, reading a romance paperback while lounging on top of one of the cool white cotton sheets Mama Jahn ironed for her. (Mother had read that the Queen of England slept on ironed sheets.) My mother liked reading romance stories she borrowed from her friends. I eagerly looked through them when she was gone. Once, written in the back of the book, was a list of page numbers in pencil of where to find all the good stuff. I learned all about how to kiss like a sex maniac from a book titled, Sex Maniac Doctor and His Sex Maniac Nurses.

Even in the intense heat and after being out all night with the Hamalian family, Hayrig was working at his desk. He loved working. He didn't understand anyone who wasn't working. Whenever he saw a man relaxing, having fun riding a bike, for instance, he'd say, "What a ridiculous activity for a grown man? Can't he find something better to do with his time?

"But Hayrig," I'd say, "Americans like to have fun and riding a bike is fun."

"Fun? Fun? Fun is for children. Azadouhi, we never know when our time in this world will come to an end so we can't waste a second of it." And then he'd yell, "What would our relatives have done differently if they had known they were going to be slaughtered by the Turks, or the Russians like your grandfather, when they woke up in the morning? Their freedoms, even the freedom to ride bikes if they had them, were taken away. Those damn Turks. They'll never kill the Armenian spirit as long as one of us is alive!" And then poking at his chest with his index finger he'd go on exclaiming, "Especially this Armenian. It's our job—the job of the survivors of the genocide—to live strong, healthy lives, become college educated and continue being good decent people who are a living testimony to our heritage as the first Christian nation."

In addition to his school-year job as a law professor, Hayrig volunteered at the International Institute on Boyle Avenue as a lawyer, helping Armenians and other immigrants settle in America. And every bit of free time he had, including his summer vacations, he spent building and fixing things around the house or translating Armenian poetry into English or tracking down the location of the lost British newsreels showing the slaughter of the Armenians by the Turks. He'd give lectures explaining, "The Turkish government had gotten their hands on all the newsreel films that were made of the genocide and destroyed them all. But one British reel escaped them and I vow to track it down if it's the last thing I do."

He heard the newsreel was being held for safekeeping by Roman Catholic Armenian monks in the Monastic Headquarters of the Mekhitarian Order of St. Lazarus on the island of San Larenzo, off the coast of Venice, Italy. He saw himself going there one day, finding the film and making it available for everyone in the world to see the massacres for themselves. It was his mission. When Americans, trying to get to know him better asked, "What is your hobby?" he'd say. "Collecting facts about the genocide is my hobby," and boy, were they sorry they asked.

In the summertime you could be sure to find my academician father in his den, typing with two fingers racing on his portable Remington, wearing only his white boxer shorts with the fly sewn shut. Mama Jahn had sewn all of Hayrig's boxer shorts closed after the day, as he was sitting in the kitchen eating lunch, his fly was wide open and the first and only cleaning lady we ever had quit. She dropped the pail of dirty water she was using to clean the floor at his feet, grabbed her purse and yelled, "You crazy, filthy Armenians . . . animals, animals!" as she drove her '57 Chevy out our driveway and away from our house forever.

"Oh, Kourken, what were you thinking? Dressing like that when an odar is in the house?" my mother chastised.

Hayrig just kept eating his madzoon (yogurt), with a large soup spoon, tapping his feet in the cool scrub-bucket water under his feet, while commenting, "Curious, how prone to hysteria women are."

All of us were accustomed to Hayrig's summertime practice of wearing just his boxer shorts, which sometimes—depending on how he was sitting or bending down—would expose his jooge.

"Oh, Kourken, what are you thinking, dressing like that?" my mother would again chastise.

"This is my home... I can do whatever I choose to do in my own home!"

"You can wear men's shorts."

"I will never fall victim to American, Madison Avenue advertising . . . trying to convince me that I need to purchase a special article of clothing to wear to be cool. Never!"

We made a point of looking only at his head or his feet and never at any of the middle part of his body, not until the weather cooled off and he wore long pants again.

That morning, Hayrig sat in front of an oscillating fan on his desk placed directly in front of his face. He smoked one Lucky Strike cigarette after another, ashes flying in all directions, sometimes singeing his chest hairs on their way into oblivion, as he worked on his translations of Armenian poetry:

Where does the stone
Lie, now,
That will be
The headstone over my grave?

Who can tell,
In my roaming life,
I've not sat, grieving,
On that stone?

He was in a world of his own, like everyone else in the family.

Of all the places to be in the house, my favorite was the kitchen. I was most comfortable there with my Mama Jahn.

Hoping she was making something wonderful for dessert, I entered our completely white-tiled kitchen with the big wood table in the center, looking for a chance to taste. Tasting was the way I looked forward to one delight after another, and a kind of game I liked to play, determining the ingredients in whatever she was making. That was important to me because she didn't write down recipes and her foods always tasted different, depending on what she intentionally or unintentionally left out or put in. Only in home cooking could the same meal taste different each time it was made. Not like canned food or take out foods, which followed a formula that never varied.

Frequently, someone at the dinner table would say something to Mama Jahn like "this is the best dolma you ever made." Then she would respond with an answer like "I use wonderful nice fresh basil today, not dried one; that's why."

Today there was nothing to taste or lick except my dry lips. Mama Jahn was standing at the back screen door fanning herself with a folded issue of the Armenian Church's monthly bulletin, The Mother Church, and drinking hot tea instead of coffee, while thinking out loud about grapes ripening in the intense summer heat, which always led to her say, "I very sad, very sad."

On most Saturdays Mama Jahn brought out a dessert to amaze us. In the summertime we congregated as a family on our backyard deck that looked out onto the vast expanse of our City of the Angels. I'd sit on my favorite yard chair that rocked back and forth that Mama Jahn had covered with my old baby flannel sheet to protect the cushion from dust and leaves. Everyone had his favorite spot to sit, and we all looked out into the night lights or up to the sky, lost in our own thoughts until Mama Jahn appeared with the main reason for the day as far as I was concerned—one of her delectable desserts.

Was it cata—sweet bread made with yegh, layered between delicate thin sheets of folded dough and filled in the center with a sugary mixture of clarified butter and granulated sugar; or would it be five-month-old aged walnut preserves ceremoniously disinterred from the earth in their sealed jar; or bourma, thinly rolled filo dough sprinkled with butter, wrapped around a round stick after being stuffed with crushed walnuts and then pushed together at both ends to resemble a length of ruffles and, after being baked to a delicate light brown, drizzled with a thick lemon-sugar syrup; or stacks upon stacks of handkerchief-thin blini slathered with her homemade apricot jam; or crumbly shakar locum, shortbread-type cookies cut in the shapes of diamonds and decorated with a whole almond on each piece?

When Mama Jahn came up the stairs with her sweet creation we'd all hover round while she told the story about what it was, when and where she was when she first ate it, and how she learned to make it. "When I make anoush (sweet) foods, I remember my mama jahn."

Feeling excited, comforted and then completely content after experiencing her buttery shakar locum, I sat back and let my mind wander, usually thinking about the family in one way or another. No matter what she prepared for dessert the grown-ups could always be assured of a demitasse of strong Armenian coffee. How would anyone know what was happening in their lives until their coffee grounds were read? Except my mother, that is, who didn't believe in them.

I thought my father was the strongest and smartest person in our family. And my Uncle Mono, without trying to be, was the funniest; my Aunt Auntie Zov was the best at embarrassing me; my mother was the prettiest; Bobeeg Jahn the sweetest; and Cousin Raffi, who lived with us, the meanest. But my Mama Jahn was the best of us all. I could see that she held the family together. And I was the one most grateful for her. I was the only one who always lit a candle for her in church, the most important candle, right in the middle, under the painting of Virgin Mary, the Mother of Jesus. Mama Jahn would have been Jesus' mother if she had been born in another time. I was sure of it.

When it was this hot, Mama Jahn usually drank Armenian coffee from a demitasse cup and played solitaire with a deck of airline cards, which Cousin Gladys had brought back from her trip to Las Vegas with the church ladies. It was a very serious sadness she was experiencing when she did both at the same time, like today. It meant that she needed to know something important and she'd either learn it from the cards or by reading the coffee cup or both.

She played solitaire on the blue-checkered, oil-cloth covering the kitchen table while sipping her hot coffee. I never understood how the hot tea she drank in the morning and the hot coffee she drank in the afternoon kept her cool, but she said that it did, so I believed her. Today she cried whenever a picture card came up from the deck, wailing, "Oogh, oogh,oogh, Sarkis Jahn," when she saw the jack of eights. "Agh, agh, agh!" over and over again as pictures of horrible things must have been swirling around in her mind.

We were all used to her being sad and crying for her daughter, Aunt Zepure, still in Armenia and her brother Berge because he lived far away in San Francisco and she couldn't see him every day, and she was crying for her dead mother and father. I knew it was best to leave her alone with her far away and dead family on these days.

The heavy heat of a day like this reminded her of the fires the Turks set that burned down hundreds of people in their villages. She told me all about it last year on a cool, windy day. I understood that a day like today took her right back into the fire and the horror of the experience. We all needed distractions to save us.

I told Mama Jahn I was going out and she yelled after me to be careful. "Stay close. Ouz-goush (careful), I see khatches (crosses), Asdvadz, Asdvadz, el ench, el ench? (God, God, what else, what else)?"

The heat bothered me too, but not as much as being alone in a house full of people taking up all the cool air with their lives. Outside I made the rounds of the neighborhood, looking for Caroline or Elizabeth or Bradley to play with. The only kid around was playing alone on his front porch. He was part of the new family that had moved in just down the street last week. I went up to him and we started playing jacks together until his mom came out. "Jimmy, you and your little friend come on inside now and help me make my chocolate ice box cake. Lord knows I can't do it all by myself in this heat . . . the cream will melt before I can get it put together."

In their green and white tiled kitchen, Jimmy's mother gave me a box of thin round chocolate cookies and told me to pass them one at a time to Jimmy, so he could spread them with cream she had sweetened and whipped up stiff. She pushed one on top of the other until the cookies were gone. With the remainder of the cream she completely covered it so that all you saw was what looked like a fluffy white log covered with snow.

"This will set up in the fridge, and in a while I'm going to need you to taste it for me. Will you come back to help me taste it, you darlin' little children?" She scooted us out to the front porch where we found a big box of clothes and fabrics to play with.

I twirled in place while Jimmy wrapped silky white curtains all around me. "Now you stay there while I go and get your flowers," ordered Jimmy. He picked some red geraniums from the front yard and positioned my hands like a bride holding her bouquet. He put on a big black jacket and was the groom. After we went on our honeymoon to China, Jimmy decided he wanted to be Tarzan and I was Jane. And then I was the cowboy and he was the Indian. We ran from one palm tree to another playing hide and seek and catch-me-if-you-can. When I played with my other friends I never got to be Jane or a cowboy or the bride. With Jimmy I was everything I wanted to be.

Both of us made an important discovery the first day we played together. He thought I would taste like vanilla ice cream and I thought he'd taste like chocolate. We were both wrong. As we licked each other's arms and cheeks and fingers we discovered we tasted the same even though our skins were different colors.

And his mom's chocolate log held a magical surprise, too, because when she cut the roll it uncovered layers of brown and white stripes that were nothing like Mama Jahn had ever made before. The dark brown was chocolate and the only things we ever had in our house that were chocolate were Hershey's cocoa and Sees candy. Right then and there I knew I had two new friends for life—chocolate and Jimmy—and each reminded me of the other.

The recipes Mama Jahn made in her Armenian kitchen were all pastries and sweets she grew up with in the Old Country made from dried fruits and nuts and honey and sweet butter and white sugars and flour. Many of the breads and pastries she made were glazed with an egg and water wash to give a golden brown finish to the top, but the insides of her creations were all shades of white-white to creamy white which I never noticed before now. Nothing she ever made was as dark as chocolate unless it had burned.

My experience with Jimmy and his mother convinced me that chocolate was the most fascinating American food.

When I excitedly announced at dinner that night what I had just discovered about chocolate, everyone in my family was interested and asked questions. But when I told them about the discovery Jimmy and I had made, about how we tasted after licking each other on our honeymoon, they all exploded at the same time.

"Never such a ting happen in this family. Ahmot. Shame on you," shouted Uncle Mono while dropping his fork and knife at the same time onto his plate with a loud crash. "His family maybe come to our house with big sticks and beat us all up, just like in Old Country."

My mother, who believed that everything wrong with the human body and mind could be fixed with cleanliness—inside and out, shouted, "She needs an enema."

"Azad's getting an enema! Azad's getting a spanking!" sang out horrible Raffi.

"Ahmahn, ahmahn, ahmahn. What are you? Animal?" my Mama Jahn muttered to me from the side of her mouth, which was littered with traces of mashed potatoes. "Never I hear in my life this story. Evil eye follows you everywheres."

"Is this Jimmy cute?" wondered Aunt Zov aloud.

And even sweet Bobeeg Jahn had something bad to say, "You better be careful, God pinch you."

I was waiting for my father's long arm to reach across the table to hit me. It was odd to me that it didn't.

As I sat there, my head swirling and my stomach in turmoil, I wondered what was wrong with what I had said. I thought they'd be happy about my discovery. I didn't eat Jimmy. I just licked him.

Just two days later, in the middle of the night, we were all awakened by the sound of screeching brakes and loud sirens. I got up quickly, pulled on my jeans and tugged on my tennis shoes, so I could go along with Hayrig and Uncle Mono to see what was happening down the street from us where all the fire trucks and police cars had stopped.

Flames were jumping way up in the night sky, big pieces of flaming embers flying across the lawn into the street, and we could feel the heat from way far away where we were standing. There was a huge wooden cross in a blaze of fire in front of Jimmy's house. The flaming cross was standing straight in the ground like it was growing out of the ground.

In a frightful flash of terror, as a piece of fire landed a few inches from my feet, I thought my licking Jimmy was the reason for the fire. Was God punishing us? Is this the work of the evil eye? I hid behind my father's massive legs so no one would see me.

The men in my family spoke quietly to each other in Armenian about the Turks and something they called a clan while shaking their heads back and forth.

I heard a neighbor yell from across the street, "No one's safe in this neighborhood anymore." And then I saw Jimmy and his mother and father in a big car being driven away. His face was pressed against the window in the back seat. He and I waved to each other.

The next morning my father told me about the famous Armenian General, Andranik Pasha, who was honored all over Armenia because of his brave efforts fighting for Armenia. "The entire Armenian community collected money from all over the Diaspora to thank him for his devotion to his people and they used it to build him a magnificent home in Fresno where hundreds of Armenians settled, including my father's family.

"Azad," he continued to tell me, like I was a grown up, "the Americans who lived in Fresno did the same thing to the general's home as was done to Jimmy's home last night. They burned a cross on the front lawn and wanted to drive him out of town because they didn't want foreigners—Armenians— to live in a style better than them."

"But Hayrig, I thought the United States was a safe place."

He gathered me up into his big strong arms and said, "As long as I'm alive I'll keep you safe. Don't you fret."

I waited and waited for Jimmy and his family to come back to their house but they never did. My hunger for chocolate kept reminding me of Jimmy —as dark as Armenian coffee and as disarming as Jimmy's smile when he was my groom, placing flowers in my hands.

My father and Uncle Mono installed floodlights in our front yard. They switched them on every night, lighting up our house like a comet against the night sky. And they slept with American baseball bats under their beds . . . just in case we were next like General Andranik in Fresno and Jimmy in our neighborhood.

My family wasn't mad at me for long for licking Jimmy. Hayrig got them to understand the need I had to discover differences between people for myself. The problem with being Armenian was that because our skin color and facial features weren't different enough from most Americans, no one felt sorry for us and no one defended us against those who thought we were less than dogs. If I had been black like Jimmy, I thought maybe I could look mean people in the face and say, "What are you staring at? I'm as good as you." But because I couldn't do it looking more white than black, I knew I couldn't do it if I were black. It's a curse, this inability to stick up for what I believe in because of fear. This is all a curse much bigger than being Armenian.

11 THE CUP OF GARLIC

life without hardship is like bastrauma without garlic

The longer I went to school, the more I noticed the differences. No one else was eating bastrauma (cured beef made with garlic), wrapped in lavash, worrying about the evil eye, and remembering how the Turks massacred thousands of Armenians. Other girls wanted to tap dance in shiny black shoes as Shirley Temple did at the time, but none of them were holding pinkies with a long line of hairy Armenian folk dancers instead.

Most of all, I wanted to eat plain, white-bread sandwiches and have a mother with straight, blond hair like the girls at school, and like the mother of the girl on the wrapper of Barbara Ann bread. I was convinced that she made plain red Jell-o and spent her days looking at ladies' magazines instead of fluffing yorghans.

My mother, who was entirely caught up in her job at the library and work on Armenian women's committees, didn't stop Mama Jahn from making my lunches with sarmas and kuftas and beorags and other foods no American can even pronounce, much less eat for lunch. I dreamed of white-bread with cardboard crusts cut off, on either side of ham and cheese, or roast beef and pickles, or peanut butter and grape jelly, or cheese and tomato, or chicken . . . anything—anything - but Armenian foods.

My Mama Jahn didn't know how important it was for me to be American, *especially* at school, and especially at lunchtime in the third grade— and I didn't know how to tell her. She had her own ideas of what lunches should be. She didn't understand that real American kids ate only white-bread sandwiches for lunch.

For Mama Jahn, food was the single most important ingredient in life. She held us all together with it. Preparing food was her gift to everyone. Being at her side every day after school, I knew how much thought went into her preparations, and what went through her head as she talked aloud to me while planning the family's meals. Her foods were like prescriptions she filled after personally diagnosing our every need.

"Kourken, he looking skinny. For breakfast I make him date omelet instead of plain scamble eggs."

I nodded and got the dates from the cupboard, knowing that the ingredients had to be mixed together and then sit overnight in the fridge.

"I see Bobeeg's eyes looking tired...he work too much. I make nice turkey zoop. He sleep very good with wonderful nice turkey zoop. And then I make khash for to make Siroon's bones more strong and to make Mono's sourpuss personality go away."

One day she pronounced: "Today, I make berashki for Zov because she has no mama. It will make her feel wonderful nice, like she had mama cooking for her again."

I watched Mama Jahn spend the whole afternoon making Auntie Zov berashki, by first making a huge stack of thin blinis, one-by-one. Then, she rolled them with a stuffing she made with minced beef with sautéed diced onions and seasoned with salt and black pepper. She added chopped hard-boiled eggs when the mixture was cool. After that, I helped her bread the logs by first dipping them into beaten eggs and then into the bread crumbs she had made from toasting and crushing day old French bread. Finally, we fried the berashki in clarified butter in her big black cast-iron skillet until they were a delicate, golden brown on the outside and soft and juicy inside.

But Auntie Zov came home carrying a big brown bag of take-out food from "The Mexicatessan." She walked past the berashki on the stove, oblivious to Mama Jahn's annoyed reaction to her Mexican take-out feast, and started unpacking enchiladas, tacos and burritos from the grease stained brown bag, with the unmistakable smell of jalapeño chili salsa masking the delicate scent of the clarified butter in the kitchen. She said to a stunned Mama Jahn and me, "It's nice to have something different for a change, huh, ladies? Mmmm, this smells so good don't you think?"

"Khent es, eench es," Are you crazy? Mama Jahn exclaimed in Armenian and in English. "I make you wonderful nice food and you bring home Mexic food!"

"But, Mama Jahn," Auntie Zov replied, "this is delicious stuff. You should learn how to make it. It's so much easier for you to make than Armenian foods—look, just look at this burrito. It's just like your berashki – but the filling is all rolled up in a tortilla instead of a blini!"

"Ahmahn, ahmahn!" Mama Jahn cried, and I watched in horror as she threw the entire pan of berashki into the trash and stomped out of the kitchen cursing the burritos.

After that, Auntie Zov ate her take-out foods hiding in her car.

The way things were, I knew that there was no way I could ever ask Mama Jahn to change my lunches from Armenian foods to American-style lunches. And I couldn't explain how painful it was for me to be so different. The kids at school noticed everything: the color of my socks, what kind of underwear I had on when I was on the swings, if I had plastic or metal barrettes in my hair, if my sweater was handmade or bought at the store, and they especially noticed my lunches, which made lunchtime in the third grade a gruesome experience.

"Azad has *garlic meat* again!" Amy would say, laughing and pointing, her beautiful blond curls bouncing on her shoulders.

"And it stinks more than last time!" someone added.

And then, "Peeee you!" all the kids would chant at me as they pinched their nostrils closed and looked sick to their stomachs.

In my most convincing tone of voice, like Der Hayr giving a sermon, I would say, "Bastrauma is a filet mignon steak!" as proudly as if I were announcing that Hayrig was the President of the United States. There was no way I would ever show the other kids how embarrassed I actually was.

I considered my options. I could tell them everything I knew about bastrauma: that it's good for cleaning your pores, because, besides being saturated with what my Uncle Mono calls "life-giving garlic," it's covered with twenty different kinds of hot spices all ground together into dark red cheman, that kills all kinds of germs, and then for months it's hung out to dry, like a bat in a dark room somewhere in Fresno. And I could add that my grandmother says that only rich Armenians can afford bastrauma. None of that would matter to odars.

Instead, I said: "My Uncle Mono says bastrauma is a miracle food. It kills all kinds of germs like the ones in pneumonia and stops you from vomiting and cures sore throats, and he's seventy-six years old and he's never been sick in his whole life *and* he still goes surfing!"

Immediately they settled down. I could see them trying to imagine my skinny old, bearded uncle, whom they had all seen at Open House, eating bastrauma on a surfboard. I took advantage of their silence and changed the subject to something I knew I was admired for, "So, who wants to be on my team for handball?"

"Me, I do, pick me, Azad," they pleaded, and soon another lunchtime was over. It seemed so unfair to me that I had to work so hard at lunchtime.

I squashed what was left of my lunch into my napkin and pitched it in the trashcan. I had lost my appetite, anyway. It was hard work defending my lunch.

I spent my time on the playground playing to win, while my stomach growled from hunger. I couldn't stop thinking about all the tasty foods I had thrown away because I was so angry. In my mind I saw myself rolling the bastrauma together with string cheese in softened lavash, and I tried to imagine feeling full while I smashed the ball into the backboard, scoring another point for my team.

One day, when we returned to our classroom after lunch, our teacher, Miss Jones, said we could play "Heads Up, Seven Up" while she finished correcting our spelling papers.

We all put our heads down on our desks with our eyes shut tight and Miss Jones picked six kids and me to tiptoe around and gently touch someone's thumb before standing at the front of the class in a line. The seven of us each had to guess which of us had touched them. I smugly smiled to myself. Amy would never guess that I picked her. I always fooled everyone because I had a lot of practice looking like I didn't know anything when I wanted to escape trouble at home, like all the other jarbig Armenian kids.

But this time when the teacher said, "Heads Up, Seven Up," Amy stood next to her desk, looked around at everyone and pointed her finger straight at me and announced loudly, "It was Azad! She's easy to find—the smelly Armenian."

The class roared with laughter; I wanted to sock her.

It wasn't enough that the bastrauma stank up my lunch box, but now I found out that it stank on me. I realized that it didn't matter how good I was at spelling or telling jokes or sports or anything because bastrauma would always keep me from being American even though I was born at St. Vincent's Hospital in Los Angeles, California, USA.

Once home from school I noticed Mama Jahn first and she noticed everything all at once with her dancing eyes: the cheorag, if it had risen enough and if it was time to bake, if Cousin Raffi had washed his hands after playing outside before touching anything in the house. And she wondered where Mother had gone in such a hurry that she didn't finish her chi and, when she saw that I had just gotten home, said what she said every day without the slightest interruption while washing out the two big stock pots she was cleaning at the kitchen sink, "Azad, herishdagas (sweet angel), park asdoodzo, tanks to God, you home safe. Now take out garbage, herishdagas, and come back fast to help make haladz yegh. I have lots of orders."

I did what I was told even though I thought, whoever heard of an angel taking out the garbage, and what if I don't want to make clarified butter right now? I prayed that some miracle would happen and I would instantly be changed into an American kid with maids to do all the housework.

I watched as Bobeeg Jahn heaved onto the kitchen table two huge bags of butter that he had brought home from work at the Challenge dairy the night before. The bags contained smashed up, distorted bricks of butter that were damaged in the processing plant where he worked as a janitor. He told us they were sold cheap to the men who worked there.

My job was to remove the twisted and tangled wrapping papers that had smashed into the rejected, shapeless blobs of butter and then to dump the pieces into Mama Jahn's huge stockpots.

"Today my cup show big Armenian feast," pronounced Mama Jahn after she read her afternoon coffee cup. "I see big table filled with wonderful nice foods made with my haladz yegh and everyone happy!"

But this news of her fortune didn't change the unhappy feeling inside of me, as one by one I unwrapped all the mangled Challenge butter sections and plopped them into the pots, until each was half full. Then, Bobeeg Jahn, who was always nearby when we were working in the kitchen in case Mama Jann needed his strength to lift or pull or bend or reach for something, hoisted the heavy pots up to the stove top.

Mama Jahn set the gas burners to the lowest flame. "Yervant Jahn, bring steps for Azad to stand," she directed and I climbed the step stool next to her and, being careful that my apron didn't catch fire, I hovered above the pot, mesmerized by the sinking yellow globs as the butter started to melt slowly and slide down into itself. This was my favorite part.

"Haladz yegh day! How glad I am to have come home early!" boomed Hayrig as he walked in through the kitchen door. "There is nothing like the fragrant aroma of haladz yegh. It takes me back to the beginning of my memories of every tasty morsel of food I ate growing up." Hayrig turned to me, "Azad, you must never forget, hokis, that clarified butter is the highly prized, extraordinarily valuable staple of every Armenian kitchen. It's Armenian gold."

"But Hayrig, why don't we just use margarine, like Americans do?" I asked. "It's so much easier than melting all this smashed butter."

"Margarine?" my father huffed. "What nonsense are you speaking, child?"

Mama Jahn had heard of margarine at the church ladies auxillary meetings. The church ladies were all trying it out in place of butter. "Never I change. Never I make cata, beorags and simit without haladz yegh.

"All best foods need yegh," added Mama Jahn. "Everything enlee (flavorless) without butter, just like some odars."

"But, our food doesn't always have to be Armenian all the time, Mama Jahn," I blurted out. "We can also have very good American foods, made without yegh."

"Azad, stop talking gibberish and pay attention to your job," ordered Hayrig. "Be careful now as the butter melts down to a billowy foam of bubbles, then cascades against the insides of the pot."

I didn't need him to tell me anything about clarified butter. I'd been doing this job since I was born.

Mama Jahn and I watched our pots of melting mixture without talking. Hayrig gave a running commentary, like a sportscaster, as he stood behind us.

"Look, look here it comes," he said excitedly. "The transformation is beginning. The waves of frothy foam are settling down and the opaque liquid is slowly turning transparent, as the grains of impure residue sink to form a thick, salty sediment on the bottom of the pot. Azad, can you see how this process is similar to the proper making of Armenian coffee?"

"I guess so," I offered, without enthusiasm.

He continued as the sediment started to turn from white to yellow: "Now the golden liquid mass continues to cook to a pale custard color as it begins its final transformation into a deeper golden honey hue, the intensity of yellow found in a buttercup flower or a free-range egg yolk. As the liquid spurts from its center, hear how it splatters, bubbles, and talks to us with spits and sputters like an active volcano, becoming transparent and making visible the sediment, which is turning a medium golden brown at the bottom of the pot." He paused for a moment and peered down his glasses at us. "Pardon me, ladies, as I take my leave. I need a nap. This unparalleled fragrance is driving me mad." And with that Hayrig left the kitchen.

Mama Jahn didn't understand Hayrig's fancy English, but she was content that he took her yegh seriously. "Azad," she said happily, "I'm going to make you number one, best bastrauma and eggs for lunch tomorrow with yegh from this fresh batch."

And with that, without any warning, I exploded, just like when Auntie Gladys' new pressure cooker blew its lid and sprayed the ceiling with stuffed bell peppers. I turned to Mama Jahn and yelled in a voice that shocked even me, "No! No more bastrauma for my lunches! Never again bastrauma for school!"

I felt as though I had threatened her with a shish kabob skewer pointed straight at her heart. I dared not look at her, not even sideways.

"Fine," she said in Armenian as she tilted the pot back to check the color of the sediment, "Why you yelling? I hear you. No bastrauma for lunch."

I was stunned. Fine? She said "fine"?

"Instead, I make you dolma or kufta or batleejon (eggplant)."

Exasperated, I sighed. "No," I insisted, "no Armenian lunches. Only *American* lunches. I want sandwiches." Mama Jahn looked at me, confused. I continued, "Sandwiches made with soft, fluffy white bread - not lavash! - and ham slices that come from a plastic package, with yellow mustard on one side, and squares of orange American cheese slices and lettuce. That's a real American sandwich."

"What you saying, Azadouhi? Who put these khent (crazy), ideas in your head?

And I want potato chips to eat with the sandwich, and I want Twinkies and Ding-Dongs . . ."

Mama Jahn was baffled, "What is Twink, Dong-Dong?"

I went on, blurting out every horrible thing I had ever thought about her lunches. "I don't want any more wrinkled Greek olives or tabouli salad or string cheese or feta cheese or paklava packed in a bowl dripping with syrup from the Old Country! No one at school eats paklava! No one brings bowls! And they're called "Twinkies," not "Twinks." You see how right I am? If you don't know about Twinkies and Ding-Dongs, then you don't know the first thing about being American! Twinkies and Ding-Dongs are little vanilla and chocolate cakes with a surprise white fluffy filling inside and they're already in their own cellophane bag. You just rip it open with your teeth and eat it in two big bites . . ."

"Now you want to eating like animal, tearing open bags with teeth? . . . ahmahn, Azad, you crazy!"

". . . and definitely, never ever again do I want that nasty, smelly bastrauma in my lunch! Never!"

And just at that moment, we both smelled something terrible. Looking down into my pot, my heart sank: the buttery daffodil-yellow color of the yegh that signaled it was time to turn off the gas had now turned to a dark butterscotch color. It was the end of the butter. I invisibly crossed myself. Mama Jahn cursed her usual curse and screamed for my mother, "Sirooooon, Sirooooon, come fast. Azad make big trouble."

"Vie ahmahn, vie vie vie!" Mama Jahn yelled when my mother came running into the kitchen, grimmacing as she smelled the awful burned odor. Mama Jahn pointed at me, "My yegh! All my yegh is ruined because of Azad. Because she not want to eat Armenian food and look what happened to my yegh!"

"See what happens because of that evil eye?" Mother said as a joke.

"It's *not* the evil eye!" I cried, "I've been cursed by bastrauma! Horrible, nasty bastrauma! It's ruining my life!" I looked at the shocked faces of my mother and grandmother. They had never heard me speak so vehemently before. I ran down the hall to my room.

"How can bastrauma be nasty? It's only meat!" I heard Mother ask.

I fell onto my bed, sobbing. From my window, I saw Bobeeg Jahn load up the pots of burned yegh into his station wagon. God knows where he was going to dump them out—somewhere far away from home, in some empty lot, I suspected.

At the dinner table I said nothing and only picked at my food but I listened as everyone else had something to say.

Hayrig told a story. "When I was a young lad attending elementary school in Fresno, all the Armenian children and the odar children sat mixed together in the classroom. But, after lunchtime, the Armenians were herded together—like black sheep—to sit in the back of the room, while the non-Armenians, the white sheep, all sat up front. This was because we smelled of bastrauma from our lunches."

"Yes, Kourken," Auntie Zov said, "and, in Azad's situation there's one big difference: she is the *only* black sheep in her class. You weren't alone. You had other Armenians sitting with you. But she is the only garlic-reeking Armenian in her classroom."

Uncle Mono exclaimed, "No Armenian is ever alone! I helping her. She bring all her friends to here and I show them beautiful bastrauma hanging in my shed."

I inhaled in horror. I never wanted my classmates to know we lived that close to so much bastrauma.

"But," Auntie Zov spoke again, "maybe if she ate enough parsley with her lunch, it would take away the garlic odor, or chewed Chiclets," she offered.

Then Bobeeg Jahn said in Armenian, "He who pities his lamb cannot eat shish kabob." I guessed the meaning to be that you can't eat bastrauma if it upsets you to smell like garlic.

There was a murmured agreement all around, and Mama Jahn said "amen," lowered her head and crossed herself.

And then my Mother offered her definitive answer to the problem: "I just know Azad would feel better if she had a new sweater...one of those cute angora ones at Haggarty's. I know it would make *me* feel a lot better."

I walked back to my room and closed the door. Food was my enemy tonight.

In the morning, a toasted slice of cheorag with butter already melting in all the yeast holes waited for me at the kitchen table. Mama Jahn handed me a cup filled with hot tea and sat down next to me.

"I tinking about yesterday's fortune in my cup," she said to me. "I see one day Armenian foods be in everyone's lunch. Odars will eat Armenian foods. Even the Mexicatessen peoples will eat Armenian foods. The best American restaurants will serve lavash and peda breads, and sarmas and bastrauma -yes, bastrauma - and filo cheese beorags, paklava and pilaf. Non-Armenians will make long line to find place to sit. Great American chefs will be begging for our ancient and delicious recipes. You wait and see. This is feast I see in my cup."

I didn't know what to think about that. I couldn't imagine blond Amy from school and her American family waiting in line at a fancy restaurant to eat cheese beorags and pilaf for their dinner. I just knew that right now I couldn't be Armenian at school anymore. "But, what about now, Mama Jahn?"

"No body's want you be nervous. Everybody's want you be happy, so today, Bobeeg Jahn taking you to market and pick out foods for American lunches. And then I make 'samwich' for you."

And just like that, I became an American girl at lunchtime, with sandwiches made with peanut butter and grape jelly one day and bologna with yellow mustard, or ham and cheese on another day. All of a sudden, I was like everyone else at lunchtime. Soon, I even traded Sam Stevens a Twinkie for a cinnamon crumb doughnut. The kids actually wanted to trade foods with me!

But, one day Mama Jahn started making my sandwiches with cut-up kuftas and slices of shish kabob with humus spread like mayonnaise another day. The first time I saw one of her "wonderful nice samwich specials" I could feel my heart beat faster and faster as I worried about the teasing starting up all over again. If it did, I decided I was never going back to school. But, to my great relief, no one noticed the fillings in my sandwiches because the Armenian foods were hidden between the slices of soft white bread. And, I was surprised to find out that I liked the way they tasted, so I decided not to say anything to Mama Jahn about it. My sandwiches were a lot like I was becoming - American on the outside and Armenian on the inside.

Deep down I know who I am with my family. They are my flock of sheep. We are the black ones huddled together in the room. When I'm with my family, I am myself, covered with lots of Mama Jahn's wet bacheegs (kisses). I know this best when I go to bed and she bends over to kiss me good night and her long braid of thick hair feels like lamb's wool on my cheek, and I can't tell if the bastrauma smell is coming from her or from me.

I never tell anyone how much I look forward to Saturdays because of our usual breakfast, bastrauma and eggs, which leaves all day Sunday to eat parsley and chew Chiclets.

12 THE FORTUNE-HUNTER'S CUP

one man's treasure is another man's loss

As I went to bed each night, Bobeeg Jahn left for his jobs all over the city, proudly driving his powder blue station wagon through traffic lights that were just turning red—a great American thing to do.

He got home around six in the morning, when I was waking up. Bobeeg Jahn always entered the house quietly from the kitchen door and went straight to the laundry tub to wash up under the spigot. Mama Jahn had a towel warming in the oven for him next to the yogurt setting, above the heat of the pilot light.

After washing off the grime of the evening, he stripped down to his oatmeal-colored long johns, brushed back his thick graying hair, and put on a hefty terry cloth robe with fancy interlocking letters "H H," the monogram of Hilton Hotels, on the pocket.

Sometimes he came home with a warm, oval-shaped loaf of bocon (Armenian flat bread), tucked under his broad arm and a thick package of pink butcher paper containing "meats ham," his special name for bologna, from Manoush's butcher shop—sliced very thin, the way Mama Jahn liked it.

"Yervant Jahn," Mama Jahn greeted him, "bocun hatz smell wonderful nice. Sit down, I make soft boiled havgeet and we eat."

This was our breakfast and his lunch—fried bologna, five-minute eggs, string cheese and parsley all rolled up in a generous torn-off wedge of bocon hatz—one of our favorite morning meals.

Bobeeg Jahn's smile was broad, knowing how happy his early morning grocery shopping made us. In fact his purpose and subsequent contentment with his life came from knowing what made us happy.

He never moaned about going to work. His secret for being content with himself was simple—he didn't confuse what he did with who he was.

90

Work was the means to earn money to pay for his family's wants and needs, and he saw working as a privilege that provided stability, joy and adventures for his family in this new land.

Bobeeg came to this country with his cousin. Hayrig told me, "Bobeeg and his family were forced to leave their village as part of the Turkish deportation of thousands of Armenians from their homes, leaving behind their properties, businesses, valuables, furniture and clothing, allowed to take only what they could carry."

Hayrig went on to say, "Bobeeg's father had already been tortured and murdered along with the other Armenian men in their village. All the women and children were sent from their homes on a march of death. His mother carried his little sister strapped to her back and Bobeeg Jahn, Yervant, walked by her side. After several days of walking in the scorching sun, with no water, no food, and being prodded and poked by the guns of the Turkish soldiers to keep moving, his mother went mad and ran into a field throwing herself and her little girl into a well so she wouldn't be taken and *used* by the Turks.

Yervant sat by the side of the road confused, practically nude, his shoulders bleeding from the afternoon sun beating down on the cuts that the soldier's guns made on his flesh, watching the human train of the people from his village walking into oblivion." (My hayrig always had two clean, ironed hankies in his pocket—one for his nose and one for his tears. He never stopped crying for his people.)

The Turks' genocide plan was that Armenians, the "black dog infidels" as they referred to us, would drop dead as we walked. All because the Turks hated us for being Christians. Yervant lay on the side of the road dying, until he heard someone call out, "Yervant, is that our Yervant?" He looked up to see a woman approaching him with her arms outstretched. "It is, it's Yervant," she exclaimed to herself. And my Bobeeg Jahn recognized her as his cousin.

"What are you doing here all alone, Yervant Jahn?"

"Two days ago Myrig ran to get water and hasn't returned."

She knew why his myrig hadn't returned and asked no more.

His cousin picked him up and took him with her, giving her a reason to survive. Eventually they came to America, where she raised him as her son until she died of tuberculosis two weeks after he graduated from elementary school. He went to work cleaning, wherever anyone would hire him, and he's worked ever since.

He found his jobs in Los Angeles by walking into one dive or another and then telling the owner, "Look like you needing good cleaning mans. You hire me—I gonna clean up everyting good for you." He was clever to realize that the bottom line for any businessman was money. "Whatever you paying for cleaning now, I charge twenty dollars less." He was right. He always got the job.

He roamed the bars and dives in L.A. like a nomad, like his ancestors before him who roamed the Anatolian plains at night. His Bedouin instincts were in tact but instead of riding on camels across the steamy desert in the company of a band of brothers, Bobeeg set out by himself, driving his trusty powder blue station wagon.

He single-handedly entered the bathrooms, waiting rooms and office buildings of cut-rate doctors and dentists who take out ads in the yellow pages using smiling pictures offering deals on dentures and abdominal operations.

He steam-cleaned concrete floors in warehouses and parking lots, waxed office linoleum floors, and polished the parquet flooring of fancy shops like the classy Boulevard Music Store.

And in the dark neon-lit bars on Main Street in downtown Los Angeles, Bobeeg Jahn the Bedouin, scrubbed and sanitized bathrooms, mopped up floors, emptied garbage from overflowing kitchen bins, tossed out cigarette and cigar butts that spilled from the sides of tiny ash trays and vacuumed carpets. He did all this while we were home, sound asleep.

Offices, stores, coffee shops and dives were his entrée into the American world of business. What reason would he ever have to go into the Boulevard Music Store if he wasn't cleaning it? In the wee hours of the morning, when all the clerks and doctors and dentists and bar keepers were home, Bobeeg Jahn was an American businessman. He was in the business of cleaning *and* looking for treasures to bring home to us. In bars he found rings, bracelets, necklaces, wallets, watches, sweaters, coats and even money on the floors or in the cushions of the red leather banquettes. He was on a treasure hunt every night he worked. And most mornings, when he came home, it was like Christmas.

"Look, Azad. Look Zvart. This sweater belong to some nice girl who drink too much whisky *and* she forgets her sweater in bar. She no more nice girl. Azad, you take this sweater."

Besides sweaters, Bobeeg Jahn sometimes gave me important insights he learned from his work. "Remember, Azad Jahn, when peoples drink, they loose things," he instructed. "Ladies never look nice when drinking. Better you never drink whisky when you grow up. You listen me, I know," he concluded, with an intense look in my direction.

"You're right, Bobeeg, I won't drink whisky, and every time I wear this beautiful sweater I'll think about that girl who went bad because she drank."

"Zvart, look what I find for you tonight...lots of nice money," and he unraveled a wad of bills. Her eyes lit up and she laughed out loud, putting her hand over her mouth and exclaiming, "Vie, vie, vie. Wonderful nice money, Yervant Jahn. Tanks God. You think this enough money to buy washing machine I see in magazine?"

On another occasion he came home announcing, "Tonight I find green matneek (ring). . . just right size for you finger, Anoush. Go ahead…put on you finger. You enjoy."

I wore the ring when I went to play with my cousins the following Sunday, and while I was pretending to be a princess going to the ball, Auntie Lucy saw it. She grabbed my hand, looked closely at the ring and blurted out, "Azad, what are you doing with this ring? You stole it, didn't you, you naughty little girl."

Before I could say a thing, she pulled it off of my finger and was biting down hard on the gold band with her front teeth. She brought the stone close to her half-open right eye and then as quickly as she could, she ran to my mother, with my cousins and me running behind her. She couldn't wait to tell Mother that I stole a real emerald ring. My mother quietly said it wasn't an emerald and assured her I hadn't stolen it.

I took off the ring to go to bed that night. When I awakened it had disappeared. For the longest time I thought I had lost it and was afraid to tell anyone. I never saw it again until it appeared on my mother's little finger. Mother loved jewels, loved them much more than I did, so I didn't say anything. Like everyone else, I liked it when she was happy.

Bobeeg Jahn's treasures weren't just about finding lost jewelry and money that kept the family going. Behind the bar he loved "finding" bags of beer nuts, packages of Black Jack chewing gum, boxes of crunchy brown Boston Bean candy, and little tins of aspirin. He'd stuff just enough candy and gum in a metal fishing box he kept on the floor of his station wagon's back seat to "sue-prize" the children in the neighborhood and in the family, to make us happy. He saw this bounty as his fortune, luck and his right, since his bosses had so much. In Bobeeg Jahn's mind, America was all about sharing. The rich *could* give to the poor and he helped them.

As Bobeeg Jahn cleaned the outsides of the liquor bottles behind the bars around the holidays, or when Mama Jahn was going to be entertaining at home, he transferred alcohol from the bars into jelly jars to pour into his own liquor bottles. He didn't take much from one place; just a little from each bar he cleaned. He filled the liquor bottles with tap water to bring the level up to where it was before he helped himself. At home he used the same bourbon, scotch and vodka bottles he'd had for years, over and over again in this way—his never-diminishing bottles of cheer. He liked to offer high balls to the men in the family when they played tavloo. Again, this was all a demonstration of largesse; he himself only drank the sweet iced tea with lemon that Mama Jahn made just for him.

And then, all of a sudden, without any explanation, he stopped bringing things home.

"Why you no bring home any presents, Yervant?" Mama Jahn would constantly ask, but Bobeeg Jahn just looked at her without answering. After days of nagging, he grabbed Mama Jahn by the hand and said, "Come, come Zvart, I show you . . . I have cigar box in glove compartment . . . you open only if you sure you want to know why I no bring presents anymore."

"Azad, come, too," she giggled. "Bobeeg have big surprise for me."

"It's no good surprise. It is a terrible thing to see," he warned, but she ignored him.

"What's the madder you?" she impatiently snapped as she elbowed her way to the box.

But even my Mama Jahn wasn't prepared for what Bobeeg Jahn had found in the bathroom trash at The Pussy Cat. Yes, it was a treasure but one he didn't know what to do with. It was a huge diamond ring, which was the most valuable and amazing find he'd ever had, but, there was a catch—it was still on the middle finger of its owner!

No wonder Bobeeg Jahn had been so quiet.

When I saw the awful finger, all shriveling and smelly, I jumped back, falling off the curb, but Mama Jahn moved closer in to see. She wasn't the least bit upset seeing a dismembered body part; I figured this was because she was used to cooking heads of sheep and cows and eating out their brains and eyeballs. Body parts didn't bother her, but what did upset her was that now she had a treasure that she didn't know what to do with. That was a very new thing for her to ponder.

"What's the madder you, Yervant? Pretty soon police-mans come over here looking for this. "Go hide it again. I going to tink about what we do."

By letting Mama Jahn in on his secret, Bobeeg Jahn had also relinquished responsibility. She was now in charge of the *ring-finger* and of thinking about what to do with it. We waited for her idea. And as we waited, life went on.

I never wanted to go to sleep on Saturdays so the day would last as long as possible. I was allowed to stay up very late, while we sipped chi and ate strings of Armenian cheese that Bobeeg Jahn got fresh from the Long Beach dairy. Around nine o'clock, when it was time for Bobeeg to go to work, sometimes Mama Jahn went with him, and I liked to go too. Hayrig didn't mind my going, but Mother thought it was degrading. She never wanted anyone to find out that her father was a janitor. For that reason, I usually didn't go with Bobeeg and Mama Jahn unless my parents were out to parties. When they came home it was too late to say I couldn't go because I was already gone.

One night at a dentist office, Mama Jahn and I dusted the furniture that was always covered with a film of white powder. Mama Jahn told me, "When you teeth get rot the dentist grind up with drill. And when American people are cremated after they die this is what happens to their bodies. Turn to dust."

That information turned dusting into a religious ritual for me. I prayed very hard for those people whose teeth I was wiping up and away. I was glad Armenians didn't believe in cremation so my remains wouldn't some day be wiped up in someone's dust cloth.

While Bobeeg Jahn did all the hard work, I read all the magazines in the waiting room and Bobeeg said I could have the ones in the trash to take home. And he gave me some from the tables if they looked overly used.

After a couple of hours of cleaning doctor's offices the three of us drove to Bobeeg Jahn's next job at The Spot. The Spot was one of the first hamburger stands in our neighborhood and it was the best place of all to clean. I loved rubbing my hands across all the stainless steel counter tops in the kitchen after Bobeeg shined them up. It made me feel as if I could make a wish and it would come true.

It was so peaceful in The Spot when it was closed and yet the energy from the cooking that took place when it was open to the public still felt palpable. I walked all over, looking at the tall orderly stacks of paper cups and checkered paper plates and millions of packages of burger buns and giant cans of ketchup and relish and mayonnaise.

After about an hour, three police cars pulled up to the stand and approached the take-out window. I was terrified. How did they find us? Would Bobeeg Jahn be carted off with the finger? Would Mama Jahn? Would they think I was an accomplice?

I was alarmed to watch Bobeeg Jahn pull the little window open.

"What's cooking, tonight, Pete?" one big policeman asked, poking his head through the window. (They nicknamed him "Pete.")

This was a flabbergasting turn of events. *What? They're friends?!*

"Is Mama Jahn with you tonight?" another cop piped in, trying to squeeze his head in the tiny window, too.

"Oh, yes, I here," she called out to them. "You wait, I gonna make you best samwich."

As if she was some kind of sorceress, Mama Jahn immediately stepped up to the grill she had just cleaned and turned the flame up to high, then began mixing beef patties she got from the walk-in refrigerator into Armenian hamburgers. She mixed ground beef with minced onions, parsley, Ketchup, diced chili peppers, salt, pepper, and dried sweet basil she found in a jar that was rolling around in the knife drawer. In no time she tossed the Armenian burgers onto the grill and they were sizzling and spitting out their juices in all directions.

She got down the giant poppy seed buns from the top shelf by knocking them with the end of a broom handle. She topped the big burger patties with chopped tomatoes, shredded iceberg lettuce, grilled red onions and yellow

American cheese slices. With one hand she topped the burgers with buttered toasted buns and with the other she wrapped them in waxed paper squares.

Those burgers were oozing and dripping in all directions. Her remarkable results were not borne from accidents. It took secret touches. For these burgers she purposely did not add the cheese while the meat was still on the grill. She wanted the cheese to be a little firm on the meat, so it would have a more definite taste that wouldn't melt away on top of the cooking meat, so, instead, she laid it on the hot meat, after coming off the grill to gently soften, retaining its cheesy taste and texture.

As the cops pulled up, dismounting from one car and motorcycle after another, to line up for their midnight snack, "Pete" served freshly brewed coffee. The policemen stood around outside, feet up on the benches, their leather jackets unzipped and big black guns fastened at their sides looking like friendly toys rather than deadly weapons. They talked and joked with each other while chomping their burgers and sipping coffee, at the same time half listening to the calls coming in over their car radios. I watched in amazement as steam and burger bits escaped their mouths when they laughed with one another.

Flipping on the radio, Bobeeg Jahn hunched himself over the speakers, turning the selector button ever so slowly, in his attempt to find the Armenian music station that didn't exist. Growing tired of concentrating so hard and not finding Armenian dumbags and oud, he settled for a station playing Mexican love songs.

He and Mama Jahn began dancing Armenian style, with their hands up over their heads swaying back-and-forth, their feet moving to a gentle two step mixed in with some fancy turns. Mama Jahn clicked her fingers to the beat of a school song she hummed to herself and Bobeeg pulled out his white handkerchief to twirl in the air as he jumped up and down like a Cossack letting out a few "ah-yaah" shouts.

I sat on a stool enjoying every second of the merriment, my chin resting in the palms of my hands, and all the cops wildly clapped to the beat of the music, enjoying the "love dance" going on in front of them without regard to the age of the couple dancing . . . or knowledge of the ring finger a few feet away from them in the glove compartment of Bobeeg's car.

My grandparents were the most wonderful, magical people on this earth. I was terribly impressed that they were feeding all these men, whom I had been taught in school were very important, these important men who knew my grandparents by name, and I was thrilled to watch Armenians dancing to Mexican music in a burger stand that wasn't even theirs. Out of nowhere they created a joyful party on a dreary, cold Saturday night on a street corner in Los Angeles. Good food, happily prepared, lively people well fed, and a hefty side order of larceny—the perfect combo meal for a hearty and lusty life.

When I asked Bobeeg Jahn why he fed the policemen, he laughed like I asked a really silly question and said, "Because they hungry."

And Mama Jahn added, "Remember, Balah Jahn, it very good ting to be friends with police mans."

Bobeeg Jahn took us home before going to his other jobs that night. By the time we got to bed, I was too excited to sleep. My heart was thumping, thinking about the dancing and the fleshy ring finger, with the cops who were unaware it was just a few feet away from where they were eating Armenian hamburgers.

In an attempt to relax so I could fall asleep I rolled over in bed and reached for the brown leather music box Bobeeg Jahn had given me last month from the Boulevard Music Shop. I opened the lid and wound it up. By the time it had finished playing "When You Wish upon a Star," I was asleep.

The music box was magical. Everything was magic in the late nighttime.

Mama Jahn deliberated about the problem of the ring finger by looking into her coffee grounds many days in a row. At last, she told Bobeeg to take the finger back to where he found it, put it in their garbage disposal and then to quit that job.

"But Zvart, what we do with diamond ring?"

"We keep ring, and we give tanks to God for our good fortune."

"But it not belong to us."

"Yes, that's right, but if person have no finger, why they need ring? That person have no more use."

"Better we give ring back to person or bad luck come to our family," said a fearful Bobeeg Jahn. He was conflicted—fearful of God's vengeance and afraid of Mama Jahn who wanted to keep it.

When Mama Jahn sensed his hesitation she said, "We do this. Every time we go someplace we look for some body with no middle finger. When we find, we give back ring. Okay?"

They agreed that this was a very good plan. And Bobeeg Jahn decided not to 'find' any more things until the ring was returned so misfortune wouldn't be visited upon our family. Again.

13 THE COUSIN'S CUP

you spit on the camel or the camel spits on you

Weekends could be very dramatic for a variety of reasons.

I had no problem in going to church nor any real problem with believing in a living God who saw everything going on in the world and punished naughty children who put their hands under the blankets and touched themselves at night. I just didn't understand anything going on in church. The three-hour long liturgy was all said, sung and chanted in the language of classical Armenian. And like conversations around the house, everyone looked and acted as if they knew exactly what was going on except me.

Since first grade, I had become a practiced faker and eager to fit in. So during the Divine Liturgy service I tried to mouth the words to the sharagans and pretend I knew what was being sung. During the Lord's Prayer, we had to hold our hands together with palms upward signifying a state of openness to whatever God had in store for us. *Including being raped and slaughtered by the Turks?* I presumed irreverently.

Churchgoers paid a dollar for candles that they lit and put in front of the painting of a beautiful yet unapproachable blond, blue-eyed Virgin Mary, who had been donated to the church by an Armenian artist from the old country. This flickering, together with the thick creamy while candles in long candle holders held by altar boys, cast dancing shadows on the walls and ceiling of the church. I eagerly anticipated the wax drippings falling on the hands and heads of the altar boys and loved watching for their surprise jumps and squeals when they were unexpectedly burned.

The sumptuous liturgical vestments the clergy and the other participants of the Divine Liturgy wore took my breath away. The vestments and altar curtains were made out of heavy velvets and thick brocades. The Bishop perspired profusely under the weight of the jewels and yards of fabric sewn with ancient designs of cranes, flowers, crosses and ancient religious symbols. Our clergy wore vestments made with resplendent fabrics of iridescent silks in rich hues of ripe eggplant purples, deep blues reminiscent of the Dead Sea, luscious pomegranate reds, and all covered with jewels from treasure chests bursting with alabaster pearls, burnished golds and glistening silvers. Only spun-gold embroidery threads were used to hand sew onto the edgings of the altar linens, the crosses on the backs of the shabigs (choir robes), and on the fair linens that were used in preparing the sacrament of the Last Supper. Even the tiny Jerusalem crosses were delicately stitched onto the little cloth used to wipe the bishop's brow when he perspired.

Ball gowns actresses wore in the movies weren't half as opulent as what our priests wore for church services. I loved this Sunday show, but sometimes my cousin Sossi would call me on the phone begging, "Azad, please come to my house for the weekend, *p l e a s e*!" So, if Mama Jahn didn't need me to help her roll out paklava dough or hang laundry, I got to visit my cousin, sometimes staying for overnights. I liked being with Sossi, mainly because both of us hated being Armenian and we both hated her father, Cousin Osheen.

Their house had a big front porch that her father built. It wrapped all around the house like a deck on a ship. We played wedding day with our storybook dolls, and hopscotch, jacks, and jump rope, and we colored in our coloring books all day long while snacking on simit cookies and Oreos.

Sossi's mother, Araxie, had mesmerizing hazel eyes.

Late one Saturday while I was playing with Sossi, Araxie came home from a day of shopping loaded down with bags of shoes, dresses, a billowy frosty-pink negligee that looked like cotton candy, and a little black box of midnight-blue eye shadow. Sossi and I watched her get dressed for the evening. Watching Araxie get dressed was like watching a movie star.

We committed her every move to memory. Using a Q-tip, she carefully smoothed the midnight blue eye shadow under her thick black eyebrows that she had made shiny by applying Vaseline with another Q-tip. She spread the color across her deep eyelids up to the bone then picked up the black mascara from the red Maybelline box. She got the right consistency by gently spitting on the black color brick in the box before rubbing the little applicator brush in the paste. Next, she layered the mascara onto her eyelashes in long strokes. She blinked, looked side-to-side at herself in the mirror and smiled. She glided Revlon's *Fire Engine* red lipstick onto her generous lips, after which she smacked her lips together, then blotted them onto a piece of tissue, tossing it into her gold wastebasket.

At this sight, I sucked in my breath with a big gasp. Even Araxie's blotted tissue looked beautiful, like a princess butterfly on a white cloud, floating into oblivion.

After snipping off the price tag, she slipped on the sleeveless, V-neck poufy, black taffeta dress, over yards and yards of a red taffeta petticoat.

When she sat down on the bed to put on a pair of black peau de soie high-heel shoes and all her skirts flew up to her face, we all laughed.

"If I'm lucky I'll be dancing all night and I won't be sitting in this dress," Araxie said, "because it's not really a 'sitting dress'!"

"Yes, Mama, it's a twirling dress and you can't twirl if you're sitting!" Sossi exclaimed excitedly.

Araxie dabbed some of her French perfume on our foreheads after putting it behind her ears. Even though she had dark hair, she looked divinely American, with all her movie star makeup, movie star clothes and movie star shoes. I knew that I would never be so close to a more beautiful person, not in church, not anywhere.

She said goodnight to us and we settled down under our yorgahns, giggling, listening to the click, click, click of her high-heel shoes and the rustle of her red petticoat floating down the hall as she sang out sweetly, " Ooh-Sheeen, I'm ready, yertank, let's go."

We were so excited at the thought of Cousin Osheen seeing how amazing Araxie looked all dressed up, nothing like she looked when she was doing housework. I thought he might even give her such a big kiss that we'd hear it down the hall where we were. We got quiet so we could hear his reaction.

What we heard was not what we expected to hear.

Sossi's father went nuts, screaming and yelling like a crazy man. And at the same time, we heard Araxie scream, "Osheen, what's wrong? What's wrong?"

We immediately jumped up out of bed, and after getting wire coat hangers from the closet to protect ourselves, ran down the hall. (Years with Cousin Osheen had taught us that we should always be armed.) We stayed out of sight, watching. There was the terrible Cousin Osheen, spittle spraying from his mouth and his nostrils fanning in and out like an enraged bull.

He screamed, "You tourse ungatz boze (fallen street whore)! You tramp! Get back to the bathroom and take off that tourse ungatz make-up before I hit you across the room." He thrust her neck back by pulling her long black hair from behind and, as we watched in horror, pushed her to the bathroom as if she were an upright vacuum.

Out we came, a fearless miniature brigade of two. We attacked him with our silly weapons, hitting him over and over again on his legs while covering our heads with the other hand in case we got hit, too. "Get away you pests, you can't hurt me. You're like little flies attacking iron," he yelled. Moving away from us, he shoved Araxie to the ground and walked away, adjusting his French cuffs and then smoothing his hair as he walked unsteadily down the hall away.

Sossi rushed to her myrig's side—bracing her up with her little body. Someone had to take care of her mama. I didn't know what to do except watch with compassion and rage. There, on the ground, in the middle of a heap of black and red taffeta, Araxie sobbed and cried and wailed, harder and harder, until all her eye makeup dripped onto her cheeks and onto Sossi's tear-soaked shoulder. I couldn't believe how quickly the sublime happiness that had filled my entire body while we were watching Araxie get dressed had changed to outrage and terror.

Sossi had a lot more experience, since this monster was her father. She learned how to live with her father's angry rages from listening to what her mother advised over and again: "We mustn't make him nervous."

The two of them learned what to do and what not to do to appease his temperament. Sometimes they were successful in taming him and other times they were not.

Even I learned, but we had to watch him like a hawk. When he patted his breast pocket with his right hand, we knew he was looking for his cigarettes. Right away we'd run to get them and grab an ashtray and matches too, so he wouldn't yell, "Can't you see I have no matches and no ash tray, you morons?"

When Cousin Osheen strode in each evening from work, his dinner was always ready the moment he walked in the door. An Armenian meal was always waiting—not too hot and not cold, but just the right temperature. This would soothe him like the giant in *Jack in the Beanstalk*.

I was there once when Digeen Araxie gave him coffee that was too hot, and he threw it across the room at her while she was standing at the kitchen sink washing the dishes. Seeing it coming, Sossi and I yelled, "DUCK!" as we had learned to do in dodge ball at school, and we all hit the ground as we did at school during bomb drills. Araxie covered us with her body and apron and luckily the boiling hot liquid cooled down enough as it flew through the air so the burn didn't scar her arm.

And it was best that the family didn't eat together because something would always make Cousin Osheen nervous. He would start picking on someone for no reason—pick, pick, pick, until they began crying and had to leave the table with half eaten food falling out of their mouths while running to a bedroom to get away from his rage: "Why is your bike outside? What kind of an ungrateful child are you, not caring what happens to something that cost so much money? I could have bought a lawnmower instead. I'm going to break that bike into a million pieces to teach you a lesson." Or another time when I was there he started picking on Araxie with, "Over and over again you leave one piece of meat on your plate at dinner time. Eat it up, now!"

"No, I can't eat one more mouthful," she had answered.

"What! Talking back? Sossi get the strap and I'll teach your mother to talk back." We'd run out the door instead. Did he really think we'd get the weapon to hurt our beautiful Araxie?

Cousin Osheen could be entertaining and interesting, but he almost always ended up picking on someone no matter what. I wondered what made him lose control and fall into such rages. Sossi and Araxie didn't analyze him like this. Their position was that there was no use trying to understand; the important thing was to keep his temper under control. This was the family's job—to figure it out and learn the formula, so they could keep it from happening again, explained Araxie. With practice, Sossi and Araxie got good at predicting his moods, and they always behaved in the most pleasing ways, so he would stay calm and peaceful around the house.

I had the misfortune to see Sossi fail at this task twice. Once, when she was thirteen she grabbed back her diary that Raffi found and gave to her awful father, who was reading it out loud to all the men in the family. And it was her birthday. They were all laughing at her most private feelings. When Sossi asked for the book back, saying that he had no right to read it, her father took her outside and beat her with the strap.

The other time was when she wouldn't relinquish her position that an eclipse of the sun was indeed happening, even though it was raining outside and it couldn't be seen. Both times awful Cousin Osheen beat her into submission. I wanted to stay with Sossi, but I couldn't because my mother said it was none of our business and we went home. I thought Cousin Osheen was just as bad as a Turk. And I hated myself, too, for not going to her room and rescuing her and sticking around to comfort her wounded heart afterward.

Sossi was my dear friend, so I thought about her plight a lot. I continued to wonder why Cousin Osheen was such a bully. I didn't tell my family about everything I saw at Sossi's house, or they would never let me go there to play with her. She needed me and I couldn't jeopardize our friendship by telling anyone how mean her father was most of the time. It was always strange to me that he didn't want to act differently. Like Cary Grant or Roy Rogers. It would have been easy to learn to be like them, because all he had to do was watch their movies and copy how they acted, which was American, very American—handsome, smart, but most especially *polite and kind* to women, children and dogs, and always happy unless there was injustice to fight. And even then, they were happy to fight for justice.

Araxie couldn't stand up to him because she was afraid of what he'd do, so she asked Mama Jahn's advice. Mama Jahn told her that the Armenian way was to look for opportunities to get even, and like so much of Mama Jahn's special power, the revenge involved food.

Since Armenians, as starving refugees, didn't have antique furniture to pass down from one generation to another, they had smaller treasures like madzoon, which is cultured yoghurt, always made from the original culture. And madzoon became just as important as antiques, even though it wasn't worth money and you couldn't sit on it like an antique chair.

When Araxie and Cousin Osheen were first married, his aunt gave them a container of madzoon as a starter. The madzoon had been passed down from all the women in his family. A small amount of it was carried on the boat from the Old Country and used as a starter in America and the entire family had been using the same madzoon for years and years.

Cousin Osheen loved his madzoon. He especially loved its history and told the story many times to anyone in the room while he was slurping it with cucumbers or swallowing it cold, chilled with ice cubes or plopping it onto dolmas, pilafs and manti.

So, knowing how much this madzoon meant to Osheen, and with directions from Mama Jahn, Araxie took a big breath while standing at the sink one day and ceremoniously dumped the family "heirloom" in the garbage. She never told him that he was now eating store-bought madzoon from the A & P. This betrayal felt so good. She smiled secretly to herself every time he slurped it down his satisfied face.

Araxie also created small irritations that made his life harder than it needed to be. She loosened little screws on appliances, twisted pipes under the sink, put honey to attract bees where he stored the lawnmower, and under the hood of the car she tinkered with this and that. The occasions demanding that her husband figure out and fix something multiplied. All these repairs and problems tired him and took his focus off the family. He got mad at the car, the bees that attacked him and the twisted pipes instead of them.

Araxie even learned how to calm his wild temper. My mother kept Sossi's poor mother in good supply of Valium, which her nurse friend had taken from patients who left their medicines behind when they were discharged. Araxie didn't use the Valium herself. On Saturday mornings she'd put a pill in her husband's hot cereal to assure that he'd take a nap and be pleasant for the rest of the day. Once she discovered she could slip him tranquilizers when she needed him calm, she could relax and be happy at home, too.

One day Mama Jahn saw in Sossi's cup that she was going to have a big argument with Cousin Osheen. Because the coffee grounds showed one big jooge (penis), and one smaller one, Mama Jahn knew that the argument would be about a boy.

And the argument came to pass, just the way she saw it. And while Sossi was in her room crying, because Cousin Osheen was screaming that she couldn't go on a date with an odar boy, he suddenly clutched at his chest and dropped to the floor, dead. Just like in the movies.

As always happens in such cases, there were many opinions about Cousin Osheen's early demise. Some wanted to pin the blame on poor Sossi, the ungrateful daughter who made her father "ner-vus" instead of being a good girl and doing what she was told, especially about not dating odars.

I knew it wasn't Sossi's fault. Mama Jahn knew, too. She'd seen this kind of man many times before in her lifetime. Mama Jahn said, "Cousin Osheen die because his heart black and his soul even more black."

"This wasn't his fault," said Hayrig. "His temper came from his pain which was created by the meanness of his father and his father before him and what the Turks did to them all."

"But Hayrig," I piped in, "you're not mean and the Turks did all those things to our family, too. What's the difference between you and Cousin Osheen?"

"Cousin Osheen allowed himself to sink as low as a Turk instead of fighting back with his good heart. What the Turks did to the Armenians was evil."

"And now Digeen Araxie can wear all the mascara she wants," I pointed out, not daring to add "Sossi too."

Auntie Zov said, "Yes, this is what it is like in America."

And Mama Jahn added, "Park Asdzoo (God, Grant us mercy)."

14 THE CUP OF STUFFING

one hint is enough for a clever person

Even though I was already in the third grade, I didn't understand why Mrs. White, my tall, well-dressed, well-intentioned teacher, whose glasses kept slipping off her nose, spent so much time and energy on people she called *PilgrimsandIndians*. She dedicated the entire month of November to them. She had us make Pilgrim collars from white construction paper on one day, and feathers from colored construction paper—that ended up flopping like rabbit ears—the next. We took even more time using clay to sculpt dinner plates, pumpkin pies and corn-on-the-cob, then glaze them and fire them in our big school kiln. If this had been about the *TurksandArmenians*, there would have been a lot of blood instead of fake corn and feathers.

All these *PilgrimsandIndians* activities culminated in a play our class staged. Half the class sat demurely in their construction-paper white-collars, pretending to be thankful, while the other half, covered in the drooping, fake paper feathers, got to be loud and fearsome. The Pilgrims were motionless. Only the Indians moved. They banged on drums while chanting *oo-ga, ugg; oo-ga, ugg* and offering gifts of popcorn to the hungry, dopey looking Pilgrims, then swiped their arms across their chests in gestures of peace.

It seemed inevitable that I would be assigned the part of a loud, fearsome Indian. Even though I had fun in that role, I knew Mrs. White

105

thought I was in no way good enough to be a Pilgrim. And I was convinced that she was right. The pilgrims looked pure and confident, sitting with their hands folded in front of them as if expecting a test to which they knew all the answers. Mainly, though, the Pilgrims were blond. All the dark-haired kids— all six of us—were Indians, and I was their chief because I had the darkest skin and the wildest eyes.

I didn't fully understand Thanksgiving and especially the foods central to the celebrations. There were so many questions I wanted to ask. I had already learned, however, that some questions would make the other students mock me, so I was pretty careful with my questions, not asking, for example, was the turkey named after the Turks? And why did the kids talk about dark and white turkey meat as if taking up sides against each other? To me it was like the blond kids were the white meat and the brunettes the dark. I seemed to gravitate to the two kids in my class who liked both kinds of meat. And those were the kids who liked me, too.

In our home, for *every* big holiday and special occasion we ate *shish kabob*. It was always the same wonderful menu of rice pilaf, shish kabob, grilled plum tomatoes, cheese beorags, and those marvelous, unpredictable grilled Anaheim chilies which could be as hot as Uncle Mono's temper or as sweet as Hayrig's lovely compliments. I looked forward to our long established holiday menu as much as presents at Christmastime. Our succulent lamb dinner was as important to us as taking communion.

At school Mrs. White, pushing back her horned-rimmed glasses, passed out *Lady's Home Journal* magazines and said, "Children, I want all of you to find pictures of foods to illustrate a present-day Thanksgiving meal, the kind we all have with our families." In my brain, two thoughts vied for attention: First, if Mrs. White had an Armenian nose instead of her straight thin nose, her glasses wouldn't slip all the time. And second, I wondered if she thought that my family was fake, because we were not pure American but *Armenian American*.

Nowhere in the magazine could I find fancy wedding rice pilaf, smothered on top with a thick layer of raisins and slivered almonds sautéed in clarified butter, or sarma—rice and spices all rolled up and cooked in grape leaves, or filo cheese beorags in their familiar triangular shapes, or wrinkled salty black olives, or any of the foods we ate on special occasions. By now— after many humiliating missteps, Armenian missteps—I was becoming skilled at supplying teachers not with information that seemed correct to me, but with information they expected. I was like Pavlov's Armenian dog.

I found one image on a November page that I knew was a big part of this holiday—a great big fat golden brown turkey, and I cut it out to show my group. Mrs. White said, "That's, right, Azad, that's what everyone eats on Thanksgiving, a turkey." Everyone but us, I thought, but I kept my mouth shut.

Other kids cut out pictures of foods that I didn't realize were especially for Thanksgiving, like shimmering red Jell-O with nuts and cottage cheese floating in it, mashed potatoes with a pot-hole filled with a strange-looking brown sauce which the can proclaimed to be:

"A+ Number One Turkey Gravy,
the best you can get out of a can
and better than most Moms can."

I wondered about that.

Then Mrs. White asked us to say something about mushy-looking stuff that came out of the turkey's insides. She called this "stuffing." The kids talked about putting it in, and then, after the turkey was done roasting, taking it out. I tried hard to imagine all this. The way everyone spoke about stuffing made it seem like the most important part of the meal. I was even more astonished that everyone had such strong opinions about their kind of stuffing.

Jerry said, "Ours is made out of raisins and apples and old white bread, just before the green mold starts to grow."

"Yuck," several kids said.

The fruit part sounded okay to me, but not the old bread part.

Julie said, "No, that's wrong. Stuffing is always made with corn bread and celery and onions."

Lots of kids nodded their heads in agreement.

Mrs. White said that the stuffing in her family consisted of oysters and chestnuts. None of us knew what an oyster was, but it sounded iky so all of us stuck out our tongues and said eeeuuu! It was always wonderful when all of us scrunched up our faces and stuck out our tongues at the same thing.

Still, as my classmates talked about what they put inside a turkey and what it tasted like, I tried to imagine each combination. Its texture. Its flavor.

All I could picture was swollen, soft bread with the taste of a wet sponge.

Armenians stuffed grape leaves and red peppers and great big Vidalia onions and filo dough, but I never saw a chicken or turkey stuffed with anything but the bag of icky neck gizzards and livers that Mama Jahn pulled out with her hands *before* roasting them. She was brave about removing the slimy things I couldn't even bear to look at. She took exceptional pride in that clean empty space in the turkey. When she was through cleaning and drying it, our turkey's insides sparkled. Afterward she actually patted it on its bottom as if it were a good child.

Now the kids at school asked me what my family put inside of our turkey. I could tell by the smirks on a couple of faces that they thought it was going to be something with a lot of garlic.

Because we didn't stuff our turkey at all, my mind went blank.

"Well, Azad?" Mrs. White asked when I hadn't spoken.

I still didn't know what to say so I said the first thing that came to my mind. "My grandma always puts a *surprise* inside of our turkey," I blurted.

"A surprise!" they all exclaimed, looking at each other quizzically. "What kind of surprise?"

Now I *really* didn't know what to say, and I knew I was in deep trouble—because they were all staring at me expecting a terrific story. Even Mrs. White leaned to the edge of her chair.

"The surprise in our turkey is popcorn. My grandmother puts popcorn kernels inside our turkey."

Everyone's eyes got big and round, and they all squealed. "Gee! Wow! Popcorn in turkey! Imagine that!"

They believed me! When they went on squealing, even *I* believed me!

I had never realized that I had what might turn out to be a real flair for spur-of-the-moment invention. This felt like a sort of turning point.

Then Joey, the class wise guy who got A's in everything, had to ask, "But *why* does your grandma put popcorn in the turkey?"

This is when I let it all out, all the Armenian jarbig in me—the sheer cleverness of who I was becoming.

"Everyone knows that when the popcorn is popped we know the turkey is ready to eat," I said as matter-of-factly as I could, looking at him as if this was something he should already have known.

"Oh, of course," he said, and looked away.

I had done it! I had no idea where this was coming from inside me. Some wonderful American gift I had because I was born in the City of Angels? Or perhaps, it struck me, only because of the evil eye had I become such a big liar—and could be so happy about it. But I put that out of my mind.

"Sure, that's what we do at our home, too, Joey," added Shirley as she put her arm around me. "Didn't you know that?" With that gesture of camaraderie, I got my first American best friend.

Mrs. White dropped back into her chair again, pushed her glasses to the top of her nose, and continued on with the lesson.

Back home that afternoon, I made my announcement: "Mama Jahn, I made a big discovery for Thanksgiving. Instead of shish kabob this year we need a huge turkey, just like the size of the one on Uncle Eddie's calendar."

I pointed at the calendar hanging next to the framed photograph of the Catholicos of all Armenians. Across the top of the calendar a banner read, "Compliments of Eddie Gosgarian's Service Station." Even though Uncle Eddie was Armenian, the people in the paintings weren't Armenians doing Armenian things in Armenian places, like climbing Mount Ararat, eating pilaf and praying in Holy Etchmiadzin. The picture on the November page was the Norman Rockwell painting of a family feast, depicting a grandma, proudly standing next to a grandpa seated at the head of the table, both of them staring at a big brown turkey. I got the calendar down off the wall, and with the Catholicos looking down from his photo, Mama Jahn and I pored over every bit of that painting together. The grandma was using all her muscle power to hold onto a heavy platter. The tablecloth was clean and white, with perfectly ironed creases, just like Mama Jahn's, and the grandma's apron was the same style as Mama Jahn's. Both women wore their hair pulled back in a bun.

But the food was very different.

"See, Mama Jahn, see? The turkey is on its way to the center of the table where everyone is waiting. The grandma and grandpa are smiling at it."

"Proud, they are proud," commented Mama Jahn. I could tell she was feeling the same pride as if it were she in the painting standing there with the huge platter, with Bobeeg Jahn at the head of the table and everyone else in the picture looking happy to be with each other.

Mama Jahn lowered her head and got up really close to the picture for the very first time, and took notice of what I was telling her with the same curiosity as when Mother showed her for the first time how to wrap a Christmas present with store-bought paper. "Eye-o, eye-o, yes, yes, I see. Wonderful nice big turkey and nice, white, starch table cloth. That woman good houze lady."

"See, Mama Jahn? There are creamy white mashed potatoes on the silver dish, with thick brown gravy. But most of all, there's stuffing inside the turkey. See how it's falling out of the opening, right there under the leg? That's what we have to have, Mama Jahn. We have to have stuffing, too."

"Eye-o, eye-o, yes, I see, Azad Jahn, I see."

"And there are some things you can't see in the painting . . . because they're still in the kitchen, ready to come out and be served with the turkey. Sparkling red gelatin—you know, gelatin, it comes in a box and you just add water to make Jell-O—with apples, celery and cottage cheese floating in it, and sweet preserves made with little round cranberries they call cranberry sauce and white fluffy bread called Parker House Rolls with lots of folds for butter to melt into."

Mama Jahn blinked at me with incomprehension. "Barker Houze?"

"Parker House. But that's not what's important. The stuffing is." I scrambled to show Mama Jahn the pictures of stuffing I'd collected from school, all the while telling her, "To be a real American you're supposed to have all these foods, but *most* important is stuffing the turkey in the space you've cleaned out in the center. That's what really makes it an *American* Thanksgiving. So, can you do that, Mama Jahn? *Will* you do it? P l e a s e!"

I hoped, deep down, that I wouldn't have to press too hard because I knew Mama Jahn and I shared the same passion for being American. Sometimes we would sit and look at the picture of the American flag on the

July page of Uncle Eddie's calendar and marvel at the handiwork, wondering how Betsy Ross made all those stars. "Big, big job. Lots of corners for every star," Mama Jahn had exclaimed between tsks, as she'd traced each star in the picture with her index finger.

The day she and Bobeeg took their citizenship test, she had Bobeeg Jahn stop at the butcher shop on the way home. "For dinner we make Ahmerican hawt-dawg because now we United States citizens."

That's why I wasn't surprised when now she answered me, "Yes, Azad, tzakus, sure, I try make stuffink for turkey. So, you tell me. What goes in stuffink?"

I stood there, tongue-tied. Then I repeated the various combinations of ingredients that had been mentioned in class, including Mrs. White's oysters and chestnuts. (I decided not to mention my popcorn stuffing.).

With every new assortment her head tilted back a bit and her eyes widened. "Mama Jahn, I don't think there's just one way to do the stuffing. The important thing is to have something "wonderful nice" inside the turkey, so when it's done and on the table, you can spoon it out and serve it along with the turkey meat and mashed potatoes and other foods."

Her eyes shifted their focus off me, and I glanced over my shoulder to see if someone else had come into the kitchen. But I realized Mama Jahn was staring into space—or rather, into her imagination.

After a pause she spoke. "You give me time. I tink about recipe. Then I do."

"It'll be American, right? Inside the turkey?"

"Azad. Too much you talking. Making me nervus. "Don't vorry, Azad. I make stuffink. I do everytink right for real Ahmerican Tanks-givink. You 'go vay' now."

How could I go away? I needed to know. This was no longer just about stuffing our Thanksgiving turkey. Stuffing had now taken on a life of its own as a defining element in my ability to fit in with the popular Pilgrims instead of being the leader of the minority Indian group. I was sick and tired of feeling like a second-class American—never good enough.

I opened the kitchen door a crack and squinted to get a look at what she was doing. I saw her tying back some loose strands of her hair but her wide vodeeg blocked my view of what she was chopping and mixing.

What was that Armenian smell I was getting a whiff of? I sniffed again. Dried sweet basil, that's what it was! No one in school said there was dried sweet basil in their stuffing and I distinctly smelled it. Lots of it. And mint. No one said anything about sweet basil and mint in their stuffing at school! I couldn't stand it anymore so I busted into the kitchen saying, "Oh, Mama Jahn, I can smell that you're doing it all wrong."

"Azad, you go 'vay or I going to stuff cabbage dolmas in the turkey!"

That stopped me cold. I had pushed Mama Jahn too far.

I ran off, and finding Hayrig, put my question to him, "Is turkey named after a Turk?"

"Yes, Azad Jahn, if you can believe it. This elegant fowl *was* named after the Turks. Turkey got its name from the turquoise blue stones found there."

"But the turkey doesn't have a blue stone. I don't get it."

"In the Turkish countryside there is a kind of bird, called a chulluk. It looks like a turkey but it is much smaller. Its feather coloring is a turquoise blue and its meat is very delicious. Long before the discovery of America, English merchants had already discovered the delicious chulluk, and began exporting it back to England, where it became very popular, and was known as a 'Turkey bird' or simply a 'turkey.' Then, when the English came to America, they mistook the birds here for chulluks, so they called them 'turkey' also."

"That's a very good revenge for the genocide, isn't it?" Hayrig agreed with me. I crossed myself thinking about a turkey standing in for a Turk in our O'Keefe & Merritt oven. But I crossed myself in my head because I knew any kind of killing was evil.

Next, I went into the dining room to help Mother set the dinner table. Mother was removing the vase of plastic, multicolored roses that Mama Jahn had won as a door prize at a baby shower two weeks ago. Mama Jahn had proudly plunked it down in the middle of the table for "dekoration." Mother was always trying to elevate Mama Jahn's taste level with regards to home furnishings.

"Azad, take these hideous artificial flowers and stuff them behind my coat in the hall closet. If Mama Jahn doesn't miss them, then we will put them in the trash." Instead, down the center of the table, mother laid a long garland she made using plants from our garden: dark green and variegated ivies, different varieties of ferns, small bouquets of fresh herbs, miniature marigolds and thin dark green grosgrain ribbon running throughout the garland. She had a knack for making anything she touched look elegant.

"Our Bulgarian china with the rims trimmed with colorful paintings of fruits and vegetables is perfect for fall," mother mused as she ran her fingers over the designs. She and I placed the dishes exactly two inches from the edge of the table, as directed by Emily Post in her etiquette book that mother kept on her bedside table. We flanked the dinner plates with silverware that mother had polished to a high shine, and we used the crystal water and wine glasses she got as wedding presents to complete the table dressing.

While we were putting the finishing touches on the dining room table, the smells and sounds from the kitchen were getting more pronounced. I heard Aunt Zov grunt as she struggled to release the Jell-O mold, Bobeeg Jahn running the carving knife in a succession of quick strokes against the sharpening rod, Mama Jahn ordering Aunt Gladys to sauté the raisins a little longer in the clarified butter for the topping of the white rice and, of most concern to me, the loud noise of crackling turkey fat and juices. They were mingling with Mama Jahn's stuffing creation, but what was going on inside the dark confines of the O'Keefe and Merritt oven as the turkey released its juices through the breast, down into the secret cave containing our family surprise would be a big surprise to me.

When it was finally time for dinner, Mother opened the doors to the dining room. Cousin Queenie clutched at her chest when she saw the table. It was as though she had seen a holy vision. She wasn't alone in her excitement. As each person entered they gasped at the sight of the table heavy laden with all of the Tanks-givink food heaped on platters. The platter of fancy rice wedding pilaf co-existed with mashed potatoes, and cheese beorags shared the same silver tray with white Parker house rolls dripping in Mama Jahn's clarified butter. There was a bowl of carrots and another bowl of Armenian green beans in tomato sauce, and the red gelatin mold that gently shook every time Uncle Mono raised his voice. The gelatin was dazzling with its vivid stained-glass red color. It looked even better than the magazine picture from school, much better. I could see right through the Jell-O mold. I tried hard not to laugh out loud when I saw Uncle Mono's large Armenian nose was redder and bigger than ever, as seen through the shimmering transparent gelatin.

Everyone clapped for joy at the sight of Mama Jahn carrying in our golden brown turkey, using all her muscle power to hold onto a heavy platter, just like the grandma in Norman Rockwell's painting. Mama Jahn put it in front of Hayrig to carve. I covered my eyes and peeked through my fingers as he cut through the string holding the drumsticks, releasing the stuffing. It tumbled out onto the platter and some of it spilled over onto the tablecloth. Uncle Mono grabbed it up with his fingers and gobbled it down and a shocked expression came over his face.

Oh no. What did that mean?

I was at the far end of the table so I couldn't tell what she had used to make the stuffing. As Hayrig spooned it into a bowl I worried that it looked like cracked wheat. Could it be bulgur? Did she make bulgur stuffing? My head dropped into my hands and I thought: *What a disaster.*

Then I heard words of praise coming from all around the table. "Oh, magnificent! What an aroma, what color!" When Mama Jahn tasted it, she exclaimed, "Ahmahn, ahmahn, wonderful nice this stuffink. Czar would go crazy."

When the fragrance reached me I was amazed. Mama Jahn glanced over at me and smiled. I forced a smile back. I still wasn't sure what I thought until I tasted it. When I did, I knew that Mama Jahn had outdone herself. While everyone was busy filling their plates with all the other foods, I was able to use my fingers to scoop up a taste of the stuffing from my plate.

Mama Jahn always said to understand and truly appreciate food you must not put anything foreign between your tongue and the food like a fork—only use your fingers to really taste.

Using as her surprise main ingredient—the crunchy texture and flavor of savory cracked wheat, she had combined bulgur and walnuts with soft, transparent Bermuda onions, which mingled with celery and the robust flavor of diced red bell peppers. I got a good taste of the flavor of her wholesome turkey stock too, which served to moisten the bulgur, releasing the heady, nutty essence that it's known for. The mélange was further enhanced by the unmistakable flavor and scent of her clarified butter, bay leaves, crushed dried mint and sweet basil, salt and coarsely ground black pepper and, of course, the natural turkey juices.

Until today I had always seen my Mama Jahn as a sweet, strong, smart, loving, coffee obsessed, wonderful nice peasant woman. Today I saw her as a chef. And I was entranced.

Mama Jahn, though not given to showmanship, tapped a spoon against her glass. The room went still. Then she said, "Azad ask I make American stuffink for turkey. I make everyting half 'na half—today, half American and half Armenian. I hope everybody enjoy."

Hayrig stood up, raised his wine glass, and said, "I hereby declare that Mama Jahn's new creation, using perfectly balanced proportions of heretofore unmarried ingredients, has initiated a new food on the Armenian-American culinary scene."

"Abrees! (Live!)" said Uncle Eddie.

"You said it, Prof," added Aunty Gladys.

Hayrig continued, "Heartiest of congratulations to Mama Jahn for creating this incredible new taste sensation, Bulgur Stuffing—a masterpiece of culinary inventiveness brought forth from the depths of her limitless capacity to create food that nurtures us from the bottomless, love-filled cavity of her soul."

Hayrig sure knew how to say things that made you feel proud, even if you didn't understand everything he said.

"We all toast you, Mama Jahn for your inventiveness and culinary mastery. Tzeerekt dahlar (may your hands always be blessed)."

"Ooof, Kourken Hokis, you make me embarrass," Mama Jahn said, wiping her forehead with the edge of her napkin.

Feeling happily stuffed with all the good Thanksgiving foods, I sat back in my chair and looked out over my family gathered around this memorable feast and, as I studied the faces of each and everyone, I fell in love with them. Their passion for delectable foods prepared with tender thought, care and love; their enjoyment of each other's company evidenced by their non-stop animated conversations the entire time they were eating; and their grateful hearts for being together here in this "wonderful nice" country led me to think of that clay food presented to the Pilgrims in school by the noisy, happy Indians. We Armenian-Americans were now both, the grateful Pilgrims in this new land and the Indians, the happy, noisy, passionate Indians. We were the New PilgrimsandIndians.

15 THE WISHBONE CUP

what the eye truly sees, the heart never forgets

After our Thanksgiving dinner, all the ladies helped clear the table and took the dishes to the kitchen. It was then that Auntie Gladys carved out the wishbone and asked mother to break it with her.

Just then Auntie Zov called out, "Make a wish. Make a wish. Whoever gets the larger piece after you two pull on it gets their wish. Come on everyone and watch," she added, herding the rest of the relatives into the living room. "Let's see who gets their wish."

"Wish? Wish! What you saying? You khent guneeg, crazy woman. We going to play meetkeseh," said Cousin Garo as he grabbed the wishbone away from Auntie Gladys and walked over to Uncle Mono.

"Don't let them do that to you, Gladys," called out mother.

"Oh, let them have it," Gladys said. "It will be fun watching two old men trying hard to remember and trick each other."

As the men agreed to a hundred dollar bet, they immediately grabbed an end of the wishbone and tugged at it until, *crack*. Uncle Mono held up the longer piece and handed it over to Cousin Garo who yelled, "Meetkeseh, I remember!"

I asked, "What are they doing?"

"It's an old Armenian memory game called Meetkeseh, which means "I remember" in English, and at their ages it's probably going to be over before we eat our paklava!" laughed Gladys. "And, come to think of it, I don't believe either one of them even has a hundred dollars to pay off a bet. Do you, Prof?"

"I can't answer that, Gladys, but I do know with the stakes that high they will both be playing to win and you know what that means? It's going to be a long time before someone does win," mused Hayrig.

"Well, stand back when someone looses," said Gladys. "These two have been trying to prove who's the most jarbig ever since they met."

And so the meetkeseh game began.

"You shoon shan vorti (son of a bitch), you tink you can beat me? I been winning this game all my life and I be ten times, a million ten times, more jarbig than you," blasted Uncle Mono.

"Vee vill see who is the jarbig one, you sarsakh, tootoum galogh (stupid picklehead).

"You go to hell, calling me a tootoum galough."

"Here," Cousin Garo said under his breath as he motioned with the smaller broken bit of wishbone for Uncle Mono to take.

Uncle Mono immediately said "meetkeseh," then grabbed the bit of wishbone from Cousin Garo's fingers. Using it to pick the dirt from under his fingernails, Uncle Mono walked away from his frustrated opponent.

That was how the game worked and how it began for Garo and Mono. After they pulled and broke the wishbone, whoever handed the other one something, anything—a pencil or cup of coffee—and they took it without first saying meetkeseh, lost the bet. And then the winner could yell, Yadash!, meaning, I got you, I win!

I had a lot to learn from these two men. Wasn't I myself becoming jarbig clever? I wanted to know more about what being jarbig meant, because living by our wits was how Armenians survived the genocide and got to America to make new lives and become successful in this new land of opportunity for those jarbig ones, clever enough to catch onto the American way of life. Without being obvious, I watched what my uncles did and I learned.

Uncle Mono put the turkey carcass in a bag and handed it to Cousin Garo saying, "Here, Garo, this will make a nice khash for your family." Cousin Garo started to reach for it and remembered just in time, declaring, "Meetkeseh, you esh."

Next, when Uncle Mono came in from taking out the trash, Cousin Garo handed him another bag of garbage saying, "Mama Jahn said to take this, too." Just in time, Uncle Mono remembered to say meetkeseh.

They had to be on their toes.

A couple of hours later when Mama Jahn was finishing reading the ladies' cups in the kitchen, Uncle Mono walked Cousin Garo to his car and passed him a big box of leftovers, saying Happy Tanks-givink, Cousin."

To which Cousin Garo replied, "Meetkeseh, you big aboosh."

"Big aboosh? I'll show you who is stupit, you menz eshag."

It was then that Uncle Mono and I realized that this wasn't going to be an easy win.

I looked up at the calendar in the kitchen and tried to imagine a painting showing our Armenian American thanksgiving. I saw Uncle Mono and Cousin Garo passing that wishbone back and forth to each other, and I saw the Catholicos covering his ears as the men cursed in Armenian thinking the children didn't understand what those curse words meant. Of course we knew. We weren't eshes.

The meetkeseh that started with the wishbone went on and on for two years. Everyone said, "Ahmahn," and agreed that it had to end sometime. But when and how?

One day we were all visiting at Uncle Eddie Goshgarian's house, and the men were outside in the patio where it was their custom to play tavloo. Cousin Garo noticed that Uncle Mono was deep in thought over his next move in a heated backgammon game with Hayrig. He desperately wanted to get even with Uncle Mono for not respecting him, for taunting him and making him feel like a fool in front of the entire family for so many years.

As I said, the bad feelings between them were enduring, much greater than this wishbone game. The inherent rivalry had escalated into discord due to a feud over a real estate opportunity that could have made Uncle Mono rich. Years before this game, Cousin Garo, who was a realtor, sold a piece of property to Uncle Eddie for his gas station, even though he had promised it to Uncle Mono, because he didn't want Uncle Mono to get rich. It was a dirty trick. Everyone said so. A few years after Uncle Eddie put up his gas station, that property was worth a million dollars to Los Angeles developers, which made Uncle Eddie a very rich man instead of Uncle Mono. And most of all, the loss of that property made Uncle Mono, who prided himself on being jarbig, shamed and ordinary. Even I knew that was a terrible combination.

So Cousin Garo, who was presently on the losing end, watched for the perfect time to get even. When Uncle Mono's dice flipped over the board and onto the floor, Cousin Garo saw his chance. He swooped up the dice and *handed* them to Uncle Mono who *took* them from him and tossed them onto the board yelling, "shesh ou besh (six and five)." In a fit of uncontrollable laughter, Cousin Garo yelled out, "*Yahdash! Yahdash*...you sarsakh (idiot)," and it was all over. Two years of meetkeseh was over and Uncle Mono had lost the bet.

The instant he realized he had lost, Uncle Mono jumped into the air and spun around holding his head with both hands in anguish. As he jumped up his knees propelled the tavloo board up into the air and everything came crashing down on the concrete patio floor; the pools scattered in all directions and little chips of mother of pearl from the inlay work on the tavloo board popped out and flew into the grass, sparkling in the sunlight.

Speechless and with long faces, we all stood around the broken board and our broken Uncle Mono. This was the reaction Cousin Garo had expected from Uncle Mono but it wasn't how Cousin Garo had anticipated the rest of us would react. He thought he'd be the hero because he was the winner, the jarbig one, the "bigga shot," the smart one. But he beat our beloved Uncle Mono and we were all in mourning for him.

There was only one thing Uncle Mono could do. It was inevitable. His honor as the jarbig one in the family had to be regained.

The two-year long meetkeseh game was over, but Uncle Mono's plan for revenge had just begun. When we got home that night he asked Mama Jahn make him a cup of coffee and to read his cup, which was unusual for him. He always said he didn't care about such things. And manly Armenian men really didn't believe in fortunes in cups.

After studying his cup, she said it was clear that in time he would prevail. She saw the symbol for his superior intelligence, a flying cape, hovering above an esh. We all knew who the esh was.

Uncle Mono knew that in order to exact the perfect revenge he'd have to wait for an opportunity. To Uncle Mono's way of thinking, an opportunity meant that he had to uncover something about which Cousin Garo felt strongly.

So, to think up an idea, Uncle Mono retreated into his private world, the room that I was forbidden to enter. His bedroom. Once when he was away for the day I went in. I knew it was wrong to go in when he was away but that didn't stop me.

Dominating the far corner of the room was his surfboard. His bed was a two-foot stack of oriental rugs he had acquired over the years. Who else slept on a pile of carpets? Still, I was old enough to understand because these magnificent works represented survival. The graves of our ancestors and our houses and land were not movable but the rugs were. For Uncle Mono, they were probably symbols of our exile.

I was astonished to see an easel erected behind a panel of room dividers with an array of watercolor paint tubes spread out on a card table like surgical instruments. Hanging on the walls, stacked three deep, were paintings of the ocean, surfers and Armenian monasteries. After discovering his paints I realized they were all *his* paintings. So that's what he did in there—he painted and planned his revenge on Cousin Garo.

Before Uncle Mono ever took me to Uncle Eddie Gosgarian's filling station, I knew about it from the wall calendar in our kitchen, the one with the Norman Rockwell paintings. His station was like an Old Country coffee house. Men only. The station sat on the one piece of land Uncle Eddie had kept from the sale of his property. He needed a place to go everyday with his friends, away from busy-body women who never went there, even for gas. Their husbands filled their gas tanks for them.

The men gathered to visit, learn news of their enemies, play tavloo and drink lots of Armenian coffee without their "silly" wives trying to tell fortunes from the grounds. "Men aren't interested in reading fortunes," Uncle Eddie would say. "They *make* fortunes."

On Saturdays children usually came along so mothers could have some of what they always yelled that they needed—*peace and quiet*. Cousin Raffi and I would get into the back of the Buick and go with Uncle Mono and Bobeeg to Uncle Eddie's garage. That's when I'd get a good look. Inside, the "repair boys" made only simple oil changes and tire repairs because they had no real education. Many times Raffi and I heard that we'd end up as repair boys . . . or maybe garbage collectors . . . if we didn't get a college education.

The "regulars" gathered at the front of the metal-siding building. From this vantage place, Uncle Eddie could see the customers, watch the men's tavloo games and keep a sharp eye on the cash box.

The men sat around a beat-up wooden table that was just the right height for the tavloo board. On the pock-marked stucco wall hung an out-of-date calendar, which Uncle Eddie kept because it featured a photo of a Middle Eastern girl.

The dominant aromas—and I could smell this on Uncle Mono's clothes when I put them in the wash—were of oil, cigarette and stale cigar smoke.

One day, while watching the men play an ongoing game of tavloo at the garage, I overheard Cousin Garo mention an idea he had for a business. I could see Uncle Mono's ears perk up like a fox in the woods who has just heard delicious footsteps on the approach. He hadn't forgotten.

Oh, he was a sly man, my Uncle Mono. As he subtly lifted one eyebrow, the other automatically shifted down. He started to breathe heavily and salivate, catching himself just as spittle started to drip from his lips, realizing he was in danger of looking overly interested. That could arouse suspicion, even in an esh. He knew he had to be cautious. He couldn't let his enthusiasm show, so instead of participating in the conversation about the business idea, he continued fingering his demitasse even though he had already reached the dregs.

Cousin Garo's brainchild unfurled: "Every night I have same dream," he said. "I dream I have very good business. I making tamales and selling them to Mexican restaurants all over Los Angeles and making big moneys." His plan met with laughter from the men who questioned his instincts for producing and then selling Mexican food to Mexicans, a culture about which Armenians knew nothing.

Uncle Mono was all nonchalance, feigning disinterest and never letting on that he had been hanging on every word his nemesis was saying, in order to identify the opportunity for his long awaited revenge.

Cousin Garo turned to Uncle Mono and asked him directly, "What you tink, Mono?"

Crafty Uncle Mono replied in a round about way by telling one of his favorite *Hodja* stories, "You know what Hodja would say, Garo? He would tell you about the dream he had that people gave him twenty gold coins. But he wanted thirty coins so he refused them and sent the men away. When he woke up and he saw that his hands were empty, right away he close his eyes and say, "Come back. I take the twenty coins.""

"What does it mean, Mono?"

"It means if you have a dream then you must believe in it and do it. It's like Mama Jahn seeing a fortune in your sourj. You can't turn your back on your fortune . . . if you believe in fortunes."

"Ahhh, I understand." Cousin Garo puffed up his chest, stuck a cigarette in the side of his mouth, lit it and as he exhaled he announced, "I going to do it."

"It's up to you," Uncle Mono responded with fake gravity.

The next week Cousin Garo appeared again at the garage, and sat down to play tavloo. Uncle Mono waited for the subject of his tamale business to come up but he offered nothing, so Uncle Mono nudged Baron Levon and whispered to him to ask about the tamale business.

"Garo, what happen your business?"

"I looking for office. I need office to take orders. When I get orders then I start making tamales."

"Look, Garo, across the street," said Uncle Eddie. "See that sign, *For Rent*. That be a good place for your business."

"You tink so?"

"Yes, it's a good spot. You can still come to play tavloo with us and run your business at the same time. Call number on sign and find out how much rent cost."

And that's just what happened. Cousin Garo rented the space, and the men helped him move in a desk, which Uncle Mono positioned right in front of the window looking out onto the gas station.

"Why you put desk there?" asked Garo. "I like in middle of room."

"You need lots of light from the window to do your business, so you don't have to waste electricity."

"Yes, yes, put it in front of window, I not want to pay extra for electricity," he agreed.

"Whatever you say, Garo. You the boss."

Cousin Garo had a phone installed and put out a stack of receipt pads and pencils on the desk ready to take orders. He advertised tamales for sale in the local newspaper and distributed mimeographed flyers he made at the church office. Garo's business plan was to take orders before deciding to hire ladies to make the tamales; that way he would only stand to lose one month's rent if he didn't get enough orders.

Day after day the men watched him at his desk waiting for the phone to ring. They watched as he read newspapers, squirmed, swiveled and slept in his executive office chair, waiting and waiting.

Every day he went to his office and waited by the phone, which never rang.

This ritual of Garo's provided much amusement for the other men, which in turn amused Uncle Mono. Finally someone said, "Someone call and give him order so we can see what he do next."

"Of course!" thought Mono. And he wandered over to the pay phone hanging in Uncle Eddie's office, dumped in some coins and dialed Cousin Garo's office.

The men watched as Cousin Garo woke from his nap, fumbled for the phone, and knocked it off the cradle before putting it to his ear. Uncle Mono heard him say, "Ei-o, er, yes, Tamale Factory, please you give me your order."

Uncle Mono pretended to be a Mexican restaurant owner on the phone and ordered twenty dozen tamales to be delivered in time for Easter in four weeks. Speaking with accents came easily to Armenians.

The men could see Cousin Garo's excitement from the window. After taking the order he stood tall, jumped up and down and waved the order form back and forth, like a flag marking a newly conquered piece of land, so the men could see his first order. They all lifted up their arms in unison and let out a happy cheer. "Abreez! Bravo!"

After that the phone didn't ring again until the next day, when Mono called again, ordering six dozen tamales for a gringo burger joint, then another six dozen for a Mexican dinner dance, five dozen for someone's daughter's quinceañera, and then the payload—a gross, one hundred forty dozen, for the country club in East L.A. for their annual golf tournament. Each time he called, Uncle Mono changed his voice and accent to match the order.

Cousin Garo was ecstatic. He had his orders so now he could go into production. He asked Uncle Mono to drive him to the wholesale food supply store where he bought big containers of cornmeal for the masa, enormous cans of lard, bushels of corn husks to wrap the tamales in, all the raw ingredients to make the chili so his tamales would have a very special flavor unlike any others, and pork, lots and lots of pork.

And then he added one nice touch. He used the embroidery sewing machine he invented to embroider white aprons with his business name sewn across them in red threads, *Garo's Tamales*. They looked great, professional and prosperous.

One by one, he interviewed and hired Mexican ladies to make the tamales. They worked between midnight and six in the morning in the small kitchen of a Persian friend's coffee house. As the orders were filled, the tamales were put into big rented freezers in his office space, waiting for pick up and payment.

Inevitably, the pick up dates came and went and no one showed up. Cousin Garo called the phone numbers Uncle Mono had given him and they were either the wrong number or the restaurant didn't know what he was talking about.

His head in his hands, he sat by the phone, day and night, waiting. Waiting for calls from all the people who had ordered tamales. Of course no one called.

At first Uncle Mono and the men watched from their vantage point at the gas station laughing hysterically as Garo struggled. His ravings with his hands and body movements while talking on the phone to the bogus customers were great entertainment. But when they saw the desk taken away and then the tamales tossed into the garbage dumpster, they felt bad for him.

But not Uncle Mono, he didn't feel bad. In his mind he had won back his title as the jarbig one. He had exacted his revenge. He barely remembered why he had to avenge his honor but then it all came back to him, how Garo tricked him into losing the meetkeseh memory game, and swindled him out of the filling station property.

Weeks after the failure of Garo's Tamales, Cousin Garo showed up at the filling station in a new suit, a dress shirt with French cuffs and cuff links with his initial outlined in diamonds, and a big fat cigar instead of the usual Lucky Strike cigarette dangling from the side of his mouth. He looked successful.

What was going on wondered Uncle Mono? He knew that he had crushed Garo's tamale business and had sent him away with his tail between his legs, so what was he doing pretending to be wealthy, acting like an esh again?

Uncle Mono would not give him the satisfaction of asking him what was up but Uncle Eddie did.

"Garo, what is this? You are looking very prosperous after your business failed."

Uncle Eddie continued, "This is an act he's putting on . . . he's just trying to convince us it doesn't matter."

Everyone nodded and laughed in agreement.

"I a very rich man and I didn't sell one tamale."

"What you mean, 'rich'? You mean you are rich with empty order pads!"

"No, not order pads. I have dollars, lots and lots of American dollars."

"What do you mean you have lots of American dollars, you esh."

"I tell you what happened. When I give my keys back to owner of building he see the embroidery stitches I put on my tamale aprons, still hanging on a nail, and he ask me who sewed words on them. I telling him about my machine I use to sew them and he get very excited. He very surprised that a sewing machine could work like a lady's hands, and even faster. Next day he talk with businessmans he know very good, and right away they come to my garage and buy my idea and my machine for big money."

These normally very talkative Armenian men were suddenly struck dumb with Cousin Garo's news.

He continued, "I owe my fortune to man who trick me to go into tamale business and phoned in orders," as he stared directly at Uncle Mono. "Yes, I owe Mono tanks for my fortune."

Uncle Mono knew that Cousin Garo had heard that it was he who caused his misery. In fact he counted on him finding out. So what did he want from him now? He had his money and his fame in the community as a clever businessman with this sale. As far as Uncle Mono was concerned Garo was still an esh, a lucky esh, but he was not jarbig.

Cousin Garo pointedly asked Uncle Mono for advice because he respected Mono as the smartest of them all. "Mono, tell me. I have no wife, no children, no one to share my good fortune with. Am I too old to getting married and starting a family?"

Mono was ready to walk away from him and then a thought came to him: Marriage and children is one way I can get that esh into a mess he'll never recover from, no matter how much money he has.

So Mono replied. The lonely man asked the Hodja: "Can a hundred-year-old man get married and have a child?" And the Hodja said, "Yes, of course he can, if he has lady neighbors who are twenty years old."

Uncle Mono had regained the title of the jarbig one in our family, which to him was like carrying around bags of gold.

Cousin Garo was rich beyond his dreams from the sale of his embroidery attachment to the Singer sewing machine people.

And I learned that an important part of being jarbig is to be ever vigilant, to be one step ahead of the other person. Some people call this "the American way." But I know it's not. It's the Armenian way.

16 THE CUP OF GOLD

marriage is growing old on one pillow

I believe in Mama Jahn and Bobeeg Jahn and my parents and my aunties and uncles and cousins, and in afghans and shawls, in evil eyes and the American flag, and in pilaf and string cheese and shish kabob, and in fortunes found in demitasse coffee cups.

And I believe in God and the Virgin Mary.

I also believe in wishes.

Once I wished that I could be a grown-up right away so I could eat just the center of the watermelon—the sweetest part with no seeds. And I wished for the day I'd never have to wait for someone to say "yes" before I could do something I wanted to do, like go to the movies instead of school and have a new blue bike and straight blond hair and blue eyes. I wished that the Turks had never lived and that Masha would drop dead because she hurt Mama Jahn so much and gave me the evil eye, and I wished that there was no crayola the color of brown; only red, yellow, pink, blue and purple.

There was never a time that I didn't wish to be like all the other American kids. I wanted to look American, act American and live like an American, but even though I was born in America, everyone I loved was from the Old Country. There was no escaping it—clarified butter and Armenian coffee were in my blood and so was the evil eye. It was the curse of the evil eye that kept me looking like an Armenian but wanting to look American. The curse had me locked in this horrible contradiction.

When it was my eleventh birthday in 1954, Mama Jahn brought out a tray of Armenian paklava that she made especially for me. It was saturated with rose-water syrup and dotted with lit candles. This was my birthday cake, my Armenian birthday cake.

Everyone in the family shouted, "Make a wish, Anoush, make a wish." I made an earnest close-my-eyes-as-tight-as-I-can-and-blow-out-all-eleven-candles-at-once wish. I wished that I could go to the beach for a real American vacation. My lungs and heart were fully committed to that wish, but my head was full of skepticism. Fat chance that would ever happen, because my mother hated sand and my father always worked in the summer—he didn't believe in vacations. Anyway, I doubted that candles and wishes worked with paklava. Surely, I'd have to have a real American birthday cake for wishes to come true! White cake with pink icing and a blond, blue-eyed plastic ballerina in the middle—that's a "real" birthday cake. Even though we lived in Los Angeles, the Pacific Ocean might as well have been on the moon.

And then, a few days after my birthday, our Armenian neighbor told Mama Jahn about a vacation place by the seaside that she could rent, because her brother, Garbage Man Baghdassar, had just bought it for an investment. Garbage Man Baghdassar heard that the city was going to tear down all the seaside buildings for a shopping center one day. When that happened he'd be rich and wouldn't have to collect trash anymore, but until then it was a vacation beach house like the royalty from czar's palace used to have.

My heart pounded with excitement at the news. I ran into my closet and secretly made the sign of the cross three times, because if once was good then three times was even better. This was my wish coming true even with paklava instead of a cake and even with the curse of the evil eye on me. *Oh thank you, God, thank you!* I realized that my wish was coming true, but because the wish was secret, and had to stay a secret, my family's role in this miracle was still up for grabs.

Going to the beach for a vacation was a "rich person's thing to do," according to my Mama Jahn, who also noted that Americans did rich things all the time, even those who weren't rich. I knew how much Mama Jahn admired things wealthy people did, not as much as my mother, but still quite a lot. She said that rich people lived longer because they didn't worry about money and they could go to all the places that kept them healthy, like desert hot springs for mud packs, massages and sulfur treatments, and they could go to the best doctors, who graduated from UCLA instead of the University of Yerevan, and they could live in houses by the seaside in the summertime, where everyone knew that the air was the best for your lungs.

That night Mama Jahn saw a flowered bathing suit outlined in her coffee grounds so I knew it was really going to happen. Right in front of my eyes I saw my wish come true in that demitasse. But I still hadn't told anyone about my birthday wish. I promised God I would not ask for straight blond hair ever again or complain about anything, if only I could go to the beach for a vacation. And He was making my wish come true. He knows how much I need to be a real American. It was obvious to me that my wish came true because I had wished hard and long enough and had kept my wish a secret. That's important. That's how wishes work. And I was going to keep my promise to God. This was the covenant of the paklava.

And sure enough, a couple of weeks later, Mama Jahn, Bobeeg Jahn, Auntie Zov and I excitedly climbed into Bobeeg Jahn's powder-blue Pontiac station wagon to make our way to the "bitch," as my Bobeeg Jahn called it in his broken English, Long Bitch, California.

All the traffic signals were working against us. Every time we approached a yellow light, Bobeeg Jahn brought the car to a screeching stop, lunging us forward then backward as he slammed on the brakes. I tried hard not to throw up so Mama Jahn wouldn't put me to bed when we arrived, or worse yet, turn around and go home! If only Bobeeg Jahn would miss all the yellow lights and drive faster.

All the starting and stopping got worse. We waited and waited at red lights until they turned green. Start, lunge, stop; start, lunge, stop, until Mama Jahn couldn't stand it anymore and gave him one of her "how to be an American" speeches.

"Yervant, ench gen ess mez? (Yervant, what are you doing to us?)"

"I very good driving."

"Kesh-heh! (Drive on!) GO, go, go, go. When you see yellow light never stop. You have to go. This is Americas. Every ting have to be fast in Americas."

So, having had permission from the family rule-maker and rule-breaker to disregard the very laws that Bobeeg had so studiously memorized with me to pass his driving test, he pressed his foot to the floorboard and straightened out his elbows. His hands firmly on the steering wheel, he stuck out his chin like one of his favorite wrestlers, The Cruncher, and flew down the boulevard. This was more like it, though it still took two hours to get from our little neighborhood near downtown Los Angeles to the bitch.

With the big windows all rolled down and the triangular, pointy, wing-vents blasting cool fresh air directly into our faces, we whizzed through all the yellow lights so fast that I couldn't even read the billboards except for the first letters of words. Now Mama Jahn was happy. And when she was happy we were all happy and I didn't feel sick anymore. We were a car full of happy Armenians going to the bitch. And it was all because of me. *My* wish made all this happiness possible.

As soon as we arrived, I stood in amazement on the asphalt parking lot looking out over the expanse of ocean in front of me. I was mesmerized at the sight of so much water all in one place. What made it blue? What land did it touch on the other side of it? Was it hot or cold? Could it spill out and drown the world? How deep was it? And the smell, this was the smell of the ocean. The mixture of salt and mist and rock and sand and fish and sky was like nothing I'd ever smelled before.

"Ahmahn! Tanks be to God for this wonderful nice place," praised Mama Jahn looking up into the heavens. A seagull buzzed her head and we all smiled.

"Let's go, Mama Jahn, let's get in the water!"

"Later we go wadder."

"Please, can we go now?" I begged.

Then I remembered my pact with God so I stopped arguing and quickly promised I wouldn't do it again, while crossing myself three times in my mind. I couldn't do anything to jeopardize this vacation.

"We go look at every ting first. Tomorrow we go in wader."

The Garbage Man's beach cottage was in the middle of a long row of identical ones facing the ocean. What made it different from all the others was the painting of a large blue circle with a yellow center he painted on the front door to keep anyone entering safe from the evil eye. Luckily, it looked less like a foreign talisman, a blue bead, than like a sun with a blue sky around it.

After hauling all the suitcases and grocery bags into the cottage, we went to the boardwalk to investigate our surroundings, as all wary and wise immigrants do when they're in a new place.

Our family motto was "know where everything is *before* you need it"— public bathrooms, markets, telephone booths, policemen, the places where the criminal types and "hobos" hung out so they could be avoided, and the quickest escape route in case of trouble. Very important for Armenians.

We held hands and walked two by two, Yerevan style, noticing with happy curiosity the unusual and strange things on the pier that none of us had ever seen before. Through a huge glass storefront window, we saw two people tugging at saltwater taffy. We went inside the shop and Mama Jahn bought lots of all the flavors to eat with coffee. Rich people spent money on things they really didn't need just because they wanted them, and on this vacation buying lots of candy made her feel wealthy too.

On the boardwalk people and foods and smells and music and men hollering for us to come close all caught our attention, but when we came upon a tall box with a glass window behind which sat a figure of a woman, her eyes closed and downcast above a glass globe the size of a tether ball in front of her, we were entranced. Her formidable presence bid us come close to investigate—but not too close.

Her name was printed in blue lights in a halo above her head: *Madame Rosa*. She looked like the women I'd seen in pictures from the Old Country. Gold coins dangled on her forehead strung from a thin band of ribbon that held down a colorful flowered scarf tied at the back of her neck, and for a moment I thought she was a real dead person, sitting upright in a glass coffin like an old Middle Eastern Snow White, still waiting for her prince to come. Her eyes reminded me a little of the Armenian lady who sat in the back row of church, watching everything as if she was memorizing life so she would hold onto it for as long as she could.

A young couple, who were holding hands and kissing on the lips every time they looked at each other, stopped near us, right in front of Madame Rosa. They put a coin in the slot.

The sign on the box, printed in fake Arabic lettering, said:
YOUR FORTUNE FOR A NICKEL

As soon as their nickel rolled into the slot, all the lights above Madame Rosa's head flashed on and began to blink, her eyes opened and her head lifted up. Right in front of our eyes, she came to life and her hands cradled the crystal ball glowing in hues of blue in front of her.

A red card slipped out of a heart-shaped opening next to the money slot, like a tiny flying carpet, and Madame Rosa looked straight into the eyes of the couple while they read their fortune. After reading the card they kissed again for a long time, and then the girl blew a kiss to Madame Rosa through the glass before they went away together, smiling and giggling. The lights turned off and Madame Rosa lowered her head and was again, frozen in time.

"I wonder what their fortune was," queried Auntie Zov whispering to me in English. "The way the girl acted she probably told them they were getting married," she added.

Mama Jahn overheard her and didn't miss a chance to say how she felt. "Never last, that marriage," pronounced Mama Jahn. "Boy no good!

"Mama Jahn, how can you say that? You don't even know him?" defended Auntie.

"He not wearing shoes."

"But," Auntie Zov challenged, "we're at the beach. This is the boardwalk. It's okay to go barefoot."

"Ne-ver you mind. Only no-good peoples, no-good families, no-good education peoples wear no shoes. Anyway, what kind fortune you get from some lady in box? Every bodies know you only get fortunes from coffee cup. Crazy Americans. Come on, we go-ink."

I protested to Auntie Zov behind Mama Jahn's back. "I want Madame Rosa to tell my fortune . . . look a nickel is exactly what I have in my pocket. I believe in her. She has a crystal ball that glows and lights that flash all around her head."

"First let's see everything else before we decide what to spend our money on, Azad. Let's go. There's so much else to see."

"Please, please, I want to spend my money now . . . right here."

"Later, we'll come later, on our way back."

I longingly looked back at Madame Rosa as Auntie tugged at my arm, dragging me along with her, while we ran to catch up with Mama Jahn, who was now talking to the Fat Lady about her enormous dress.

I was arguing again, and I told God I was sorry again, and I crossed myself three times again, but I felt that Madame Rosa could tell me something important. I just knew it. She knew a big secret about me and my secret was in that glass ball she had. Maybe she knew whom I would marry or how I could have smooth blond hair or how to get rid of the evil eye. She knew all sorts of important things. I was sure of it.

But on we went, bombarded with all sorts of things to stare at and scrutinize. Every person, booth, box, arcade and amusement in our sight was of intense fascination and wonderment. Madame Rosa soon faded to the background of my thoughts.

Pitch a penny into a plate and win a goldfish, a sign said.

"Cousin Lucy had some of those fish. One day they die and she sprinkle dead fish over parsley seeds in the garden," said Mama Jahn. "That parsley was best parsley I ever taste."

We all lost interest in the fish and walked away.

Step right up, shoot the ducks and get a big teddy bear, said another sign. Mama Jahn said the stuffed bear was full of dust and would give asthma to whoever won it. Her pronouncement ended any desire to shoot ducks.

Ride the roller coaster for the thrill of a lifetime.

"Come on Auntie Zov, let's get the thrill of a lifetime," I pleaded. It sounded like fun to me.

"What's matter? You khent? Crazy American idea. What's important in life is to be safe. Armenians have enough excitement from Turks," Mama Jahn proclaimed. "Show me ride about having fun being safe, then you can go."

Auntie Zov and I rolled our eyes behind her back.

After a couple of hours of walking and investigating more things than we could ever have imagined, like the Ferris wheel, Dr. Death, the House of Horrors, the Tattooed Strong Man, the Russian Black Bears and Elephants from India—all dangerous to Mama Jahn—I decided the best deal for my money was the carousel ride. I'd never been on a horse before and the painted horses were amazingly beautiful.

Mama Jahn quickly said, "Votch! Too much danger," but Bobeeg Jahn assured her that it was safe and she acquiesced. She was worn out from all the temptations and needed an excuse to sit down for a while anyway.

I never thought I'd ever be riding a horse, because the year before, Auntie Gladys had told Mama Jahn about an elegant Armenian lady she knew, whose entire life was ruined because she was thrown off a horse when a fly bit the horse on the leg. She was injured so badly that she was never able marry and have children, and she had to go to the bathroom in a bag that she wore taped to her stomach for the rest of her life. I didn't want to wear a bag under my clothes for the rest of my life or be childless, so I listened to her cautions about horses.

In this case, it was clear that a fly couldn't bother wooden horses. Still, my heart raced when I saw how high I would be sitting off the ground as I mounted mine. I couldn't show my fear or Mama Jahn would pull me off in front of everyone, so I acted brave. My horse was white with peach-colored roses around her neck and a flowing white tail with a mane braided with a garland of dark green leaves. She was magnificent.

As the carousel started up I realized that Bobeeg Jahn had gotten on the ride and was standing far behind me to calm Mama Jahn's fears. I pretended not to see him.

After I saw how easy it was to go up and then way down and not fall off, I was relieved and I could enjoy the ride. I felt so American sitting on my beautiful white horse. I felt happy and confident and proud to be me. Our speed picked up and I got into the rhythm of the carousel, humming the tunes and picking out a good name for my horse—I called her Susan—very American. Giddy-up, Susan! I whispered in her fake ear.

I saw Auntie calling something out to me as I went past her. I strained to pick out her words as she yelled, "The *r i n g*, Azad, pull the *r i n g*...the gold ring...get the gold ring."

What did she mean, *the ring?* I looked towards where she was pointing and then I saw it—a big gold ring, way up high above me to my right, which the girl in front of me reached for and missed. The next time around, I made a grab for it, but it was out of my grasp, above my head. That was the end of humming and talking to my pony. Instead, I focused all my energy on getting that gold ring. I couldn't miss out on a chance to be jarbig, to make my family proud.

As we went around again I mustered all my strength to slide way over to the edge of the saddle, stand up on the stirrup and grab for the prize. That time around I missed it by an inch. I wished hard to get it but I quickly saw that it wasn't about strength and wishing, it was about coordination, distance and timing.

In the name of the Father and the Son and the Holy Spirit, Amen, it's mine this time . . . I thought, as I tried to figure out a way to elongate my body and make my fingers just a little bit faster and longer. And then, like someone suddenly yanked the plug in the bathtub, my magnificent horse went down and stayed down. We lost speed and the music groaned to a stop as if the organ grinder had just croaked. My nickel's worth of time had run out. And I saw that the prize was in someone else's hand. A pretty girl, whose blond ponytail sprang up and down every time she moved, had the ring in the crook of her index finger. Being jarbig wasn't important if you were a blonde. People were staring at her and smiling, even *my* Mama Jahn.

Why had I wasted my money on that ugly old horse? The paint was chipping underneath her ears and "Susan" wasn't as fast as all the other horses. It was all Auntie Zov's fault for pulling me away from Madame Rosa. That nickel I had wanted to spend on Madame Rosa was gone forever.

By the time we walked back to our cottage we were starving. Mama Jahn wouldn't let us buy hot dogs from the fancy green and purple cart by the Ferris wheel. I love hot dogs.

"We go make kabob now," was her bidding.

Again I had to respect my promise not to argue. I promised myself not to ever make promises to God again. They're impossible to break, and this trip to the bitch was fraught with temptations to break promises.

We barbecued our shish kabob over a wood fire Bobeeg Jahn made in the sand, right in front of the ocean. I was accustomed to shish kabob that had been prepared on the ground behind the garage, on the cement driveway beside our house or in long barbeque pits at Armenian picnics, but never in the sand at the seaside.

Mama Jahn unfolded her freshly baked pita breads, holding them arm's length over the mellow charcoal, lightly warming them. The heat awakened the fragrance of fresh yeast mingled with butter and salt that bound the dough, and I started to drool as I imagined the juices of the lamb and vegetables saturating the bread.

She delicately drizzled olive oil and a sprinkling of salt and pepper over the skewers of marinated cubes of lamb, tomatoes and onions, which she slowly turned to perfection. Then using the pita, she pulled them off the skewers into her favorite heavy cast iron roasting pan that Bobeeg Jahn had brought home from one of his job sites that he cleaned at night, the Pink Pansy Bar and Grill. He tossed the lamb with chopped green onions and Armenian parsley.

"This is the only way to eat shish kabob . . . just like our sheepherder ancestors in the rocky cliffs of the Anatolian ridges of the Bosphorus," said Auntie Zov. "Outside, over an open fire, sitting on the ground with the stars covering our heads. Ah, this is the life. I wonder what the poor people are doing?" (I knew she wasn't talking about people without money.)

As I sat there eating my Mediterranean feast, I knew Mama Jahn was right. She was always right. A hot dog didn't compare to this. It would have tasted good at the moment, wrapped in its soft white American bun and nestled between yellow mustard and relish. Comparing the two was like comparing the ancient liturgies of the Armenian Church—filled with sweet-smelling incense, holy oils and ancient chanting—with the Evangelical Protestant Church my cousin went to with her family—with loud singing in English, preachers who yelled at everyone for being sinners and the smell of ladies' perfumes and men's colognes mingled with cleaning solutions in the pews. They were both Christian churches but with different ways of feeding the soul. Hayrig used to say that we Armenians felt nourished after our church services and Protestants felt disinfected.

After we finished off the last morsel of meat and the remaining puddle of juice soaked into the last piece of pita, Mama Jahn made Armenian coffee. The long handle of the jezvah was made for cooking coffee over the heat from the flames of an open fire. She thought of everything to bring along on this beach holiday. Even sugar cubes.

With the kind of contentment that only comes from having a full stomach from eating earthy foods like ours, I drank in the faces of my dear grandparents and sweet auntie sitting around the comforting fire. As I faced the ocean, watching Mama Jahn make the ritual Armenian coffee, as a priest at the altar prepares the divine feast for communion, with reverence and grace, I felt that we were made for this kind of life—outdoors, uncomplicated and peaceful—the authentic rich life.

After serving coffee to everyone else, Mama Jahn passed me a cup of coffee filled to the brim. This was a special treat! At home I helped her make the coffee but I rarely got to drink it. And she rarely told me my fortune. She would say she was too tired or her head itched or she had to yank out her chin hairs—there was always some reason why she couldn't do it. She had done this so often that I had concluded that she never told my fortune because of the curse.

So I was shocked that Mama Jahn passed me a full cup of undiluted coffee. She must have been feeling really happy because we were at the "bitch." I pressed my good luck by inverting my empty cup and turning it three times in hope of a good fortune and a good reading.

"Mama Jahn, read my cup, too."

This time she offered no excuses. Instead, she reached for my inverted coffee cup, and noted that, because the rim stuck to the saucer, whatever I had wished for would come true. Thank you God, thank you, I murmured. I get to visit Madame Rosa!

Mama Jahn turned it over and looked into it to read the grounds that formed a pattern on the bottom and edges of the inside of the cup. Looking first into the cup and then into my eyes, which were lit only by the burning embers from our fire, she said that my fortune was clear. She proceeded to "read" the settled coffee grounds in her Russian Armenian dialect, which was so beautiful, compared to her broken English, *"Azad Jahn, you are never alone. See the lady next to you…down here?"*

I *did* see her, enveloped in layers of draping fabric, and I think she was holding a baby, or at least her arms were together like she was.

"She will never leave your side."

Of course, that's my Mama Jahn, I thought to myself, and she will never leave me. And I smiled back at her, reaching for her hand to squeeze.

"And look over here, Azad Jahn . . . see the circle in this veil? That's your ring. It's your wedding ring…the most important ring you will ever wear."

"Why is it so important?"

"That's no big mystery, Azad," Auntie Zov jumped in. "It's the biggie, the main attraction for women, the splendid treasure from the King Solomon mines, the Midas touch and the Cadillac convertible, all rolled up into one perfect circle of untarnished golden perfection. It announces to everyone that you're worthy of being chosen to be a man's possession . . . to be his slave for the rest of your life. Not that I wouldn't want that fortune. You lucky thing you!"

"Amot, Zov, shame on you, talking like that to Azad," scolded Bobeeg Jahn.

"Ah, I'm only kidding. I just don't want the kid to get the wrong idea…the Old Country idea that the only thing a woman is good for is getting married. There're plenty of other things to do in this world besides getting married."

"Marriage is a necessary safe place for a woman," said my usually quiet grandpa in Armenian. *"The Bedouins in the desert thought more of marriage and their wives than you do, Zov Jahn. The men have a special cloak they put over their bride at the wedding ceremony while pronouncing to everyone present, 'From now on, nobody but myself shall cover thee.' He takes his* harse *under his protection, vowing to keep her safe and to care for her no matter what,"* added my quiet and gentle grandfather, slipping his big wool sweater around my grandmother's small, round shoulders.

With a softened attitude, Auntie Zov added, "The wedding ring is like a straight line that's bent and comes together, never to be broken—it has no beginning and no ending, and it's strong and soft at the same time. It represents how a husband is supposed to love his wife. Totally and completely, never ending. Let's face it, without women, men would never understand their purpose in life."

"Why is everyone talking about my wedding ring?" I interrupted. "I'm not old enough to get married. Anyway, I want a big sapphire ring, with diamonds all around it, sparkling, like the movie stars wear. The girls at school would all want to be my friend with a ring like that. I still have to go to college, then teach school, and then explore the whole world before I get married."

Mama Jahn looked at everyone and asked if they had anything else to add before she answered the question.

Bobeeg and Zov stared at her like naughty children being scolded by their teacher because they realized that they had spoken for her, and well, *no one* speaks for Mama Jahn. They tried to steal her stage and they did not impress her. She continued explaining while speaking very slowly in her very best Armenian as Auntie Zov continued to translate.

"Your wedding ring is the most important ring you'll ever have because it will connect you to all the married women who have gone before you. You will belong to the circle of married women from whom you will learn how to be a woman. You can make your marriage a chore or a blessing. It's up to you."

Taking off her own ring and holding it carefully in the palm of her hand, she stared long and hard at it and then continued: *"My mother used to say that being happily married was a matter of how you looked at life. Marriage can be small and restrictive, like the walls of a ring, closing you in and sealing you off from the world or . . ."* Lifting her ring up to one eye, she peered through it to the sky, continuing, *". . . it can be a safe place from which to explore the entire universe. See how big the moon looks when you see it through my ring pressed up against your eye?"*

She put her ring to my eye and I couldn't believe how huge the moon looked through her small gold wedding ring. How did she do that? How did she make the moon fit into the same space her tiny finger filled? I wished I were as smart as Mama Jahn.

"One day you will be married to a successful, good Armenian man and have a family of your own, and you will always be very happy. This is not only your fortune from your cup but my prayer for your life."

I took my cup into my hands to see if I could find anything more because I didn't want to be married to an Armenian man. I wanted an American one. One with blue eyes and golden hair, a straight nose and a big smile that showed white teeth with no gold. Of course I told no one what I secretly wished for because my wish was the same as part of my curse, to marry an odar. Let the curse do the work.

As I concentrated my gaze into the patterns of coffee grounds I saw them swirl and twirl in front of my eyes. The fire was playing tricks on me as I consciously blinked and shook my head to regain my equilibrium. I got a shiver across my shoulders and lay on my side on the sand, which was still warm from the intense summer sun during the day, and I stared into the night sky. The sky and ocean seemed to blend into one seamless stretch of atmosphere each reflecting off the other, so it was hard for me to tell where one stopped and the other began.

Auntie Zov took my hand and pulled me toward the water, saying, "It's time Azad; we've waited long enough. Let's go in the water!"

Tossing my cup into the sand, I sprang up and darted out with my auntie into the great, beckoning sea, without a single apprehension. No sooner had I run into the water than I fell into a trench that was several feet deep and made me lose my balance. As I grappled for my footing, I was struck down by a big wave that sent me spinning, disoriented by what seemed like clusters of constellations all around me. As I spun, unable to get to the surface for air, I saw sparkling stars outlining the lady we saw in my cup, illuminating the water with her presence. Is it Mama Jahn or is it the Virgin Mary? GOD, get me out of here!

I saw blue lights blinking around the lady's head, and she looked right at me as I tumbled and rolled and fell from star to star not knowing what would happen next. She looked like the fortune lady in the glass box, too. As she reached out to catch me, I felt like I could conquer anything—even the evil eye. I could hardly breathe, and I realized that I was holding my breath longer than I ever imagined I was capable of doing. Then, just as quickly as I had been tossed under the wave, I was washed up on the shore, gasping for air and absolutely exhausted from the struggle.

"You see! I tell you ocean is big danger," shouted Mama Jahn as she put our big picnic blanket around me and dragged me back to the cottage. Now, back to talking in her broken English, she scolded me saying, "Tomorrow you just sit and *look* at wadder."

But the next day Aunt Zov gave me a nickel to buy some candy, and instead I found Madame Rosa and, after kissing my nickel, I slipped the coin into her machine. I just knew I'd find my true fortune in her reply: "Your fondest wish will come true."

17 THE CUP OF BROTHERLY LOVE

everyone is a prisoner of his own past

During the summer when I was twelve years old, Mama Jahn and I took the train from Union Station in Los Angeles to San Francisco to visit her yeghpayr (brother), Berge, for the purpose of helping him make Christmas corsages to sell at his drug store later that year. But the real reason we went to visit him was because Mama Jahn loved any excuse to see her beloved brother.

We boarded the train lugging as many grocery bags as we could carry. For the duration of the trip, Mama Jahn and I vigilantly guarded the bags against would-be thieves. The bags were filled with homemade lavash, simit, cata, string cheese and jars of Uncle Berge's favorite quince preserves that Mama Jahn had made especially for him—just the kinds of things train robbers would want. I was getting to the age when I thought all this—the food, the lugging, the guarding—was a bit over the top, but I loved Mama Jahn so much that I went along with it uncomplainingly.

When we arrived, Uncle Berge brought out treasures from the store for all the ladies in the family. He didn't live in a big fancy house and didn't act rich, but judging from the beautiful things he brought home, I figured he owned a big store.

He brought Mama Jahn an authentic bottle of Chanel N° 5 perfume, imported from Paris, which she called "Channel Five." For each of the other women in the family he produced rose-scented body powder in turquoise glass boxes that seemed perfect for storing secret personal treasures when the powder was gone. And inside a brown bag were Revlon lipsticks—*Pink*

Flamingo, Red Hibiscus, and their favorite, *Orange Flip*; thin, silk neck scarves in all the colors of the flags at the International Institute's yearly Chinese New Year festival; and sparkling pieces of chunky rhinestone jewelry in the shapes of chrysanthemums, cymbidiums and camellias. Uncle Berge knew what made women drool.

Uncle Berge brought me candies to eat right away. They came in a double layered yellow box with a hinged lid printed with pictures identifying each chocolate by name and flavor, which took the guessing out of choosing so you didn't have to poke a hole in the bottom to find out before eating a nut one when you really wanted a cherry one. And best of all, he brought me my first-ever jeweled Orlon sweater in the softest color pink, completely covered in swirling leaf patterns with little white pearls and silver and white sequins. Of course I knew I couldn't wear it because it might get dirty—an important lesson Mama Jahn taught me early in life. It made me happy just to look at it folded away in its box, or opened up and stretched across my chest the way it *would* have looked if I could have worn it. I felt Uncle Berge was really generous, particularly when I learned that he only worked at the drug store and did not own it.

Uncle Berge showed us around his four-room, hilltop home. In the corner of his small dining room (which could become a living room when the table was made into a small end table by the removal of its two leaves), my uncle showed me an enormous brass chest carved with a hunting scene in an English countryside. He kept the box filled to the brim with red pistachio nuts. I liked running my hands through the red nuts and watching them cascade through my fingertips. I thought of them as rubies gathered in one gigantic golden box—just for me.

Uncle Berge had cleared out his chest of drawers for us, putting his own belongings in grocery bags that he lined up in the closet—one for socks, one for undershirts and vardeegs, and one for everything else, like nightshirts, hankies, bits of paper with notes written on them, and lots and lots of keys. Mama Jahn and I unloaded *our* grocery bags.

We didn't wait until after dinner to begin work on the corsages. Right after we unpacked, Uncle Berge pulled out cardboard boxes containing dozens of rolls of thin white satin ribbon, bundles of little pinecones and clusters of fake red berries, whose stems were attached to wires, as well as leftover bits and pieces of decorations from last year. The three of us sat around the one table and fashioned Christmas corsages for the next twelve days and nights until everything was used up. It was tedious work, but I loved it, because Mama Jahn cracked open pistachios for us to munch on and because of the stories I heard as brother and sister talked and because we didn't do any housework.

To be considered well-dressed during the holiday season in those days, every woman in the city wore a corsage on her coat or jacket. These were either fancy ones made from fresh flowers, mass-produced artificial ones from department stores, or simple made-in-Japan kinds from the local drug store. Ours were in a category of their own. If they'd had a tag it would have said: Made-in-San Francisco-by-Three-Armenians.

My job in the assembly line was to unwind the berries from their tight clusters and separate them into single stems. Uncle Berge did the same with the pine cones and Mama Jahn artfully arranged them together with the ribbons, finalizing the corsage with a quick twist of her wrist, tugging tightly at the ribbon in the center to make a secure knot. While I unwound what someone else had painstakingly twisted in Japan, where all the corsage materials came from, I tried to imagine who these people were, what they looked like, and what they were thinking about as they twisted. I wondered if they ever thought about someone untwisting all their work, and if they ever questioned why they didn't use something easier to work with that held the stems together instead of little pieces of wire, something such as rubber bands.

Our assembly process kept going, evening after evening, night after night, until we filled twenty-five cardboard liquor cartons to the brim with the most dazzling corsages imaginable. As we worked, brother and sister, Berge and Zvart, talked to each other in Armenian while I sat in silence listening and reflecting on what they were saying. Uncle Berge had no idea how to talk with me. He never knew what to say to me and I had nothing to say to him, so it was a relief to sit, do my job and listen to brother and sister do all the talking.

Fiercely loyal, Mama Jahn loved everyone in her family with her large heart, and we all knew we could do her no wrong, even when we hurt her by careless actions or painful words. She always excused us and saw our misbehavior as being out of our control. "That bad girl, she make you do this. I tole you never be with her." There was always something or someone else upon whom to blame my shortcomings and bad conduct. "Poor Azad, evil eye won't leave her alone. Not her fault."

When she sent her hard-earned money, gained from making yegh, with Uncle Berge to the Old Country to bring Zepure to the United States, the daughter she had to leave behind, he brought his own son instead—*and she excused him*! If it had been anyone else who double-crossed her like that, she would have lost her mind and spent the rest of her life trying to get even.

The day she told me this, I said to her, "Mama Jahn, why didn't you get mad, scream, throw things at him and never see him again? He did a terrible thing."

"Azad Jahn," she explained, "I love him more than anyone else in the world for one reason—because he is only person in my family who is not dead. And the last ting my myrig said to me before she die from pneumonia was to take care of Berge."

So, in her eyes, Uncle Berge could do no wrong. I was aware that Bobeeg Jahn, Berge's brother-in-law, did not share her blind affection, but I did not yet know why.

When Uncle Berge came for his annual summertime visit to the family in Los Angeles, Mama Jahn worked for days before his arrival, preparing for him the most mouthwatering foods she envisioned from the finest ingredients she could find. For weeks before his visit the rest of us had to eat one leg of lamb stretched into at least sixteen different meals so she could afford what she needed for Uncle Berge.

She lavished her most disarming personality and charm on their every moment together, showing him nothing of the nervous or volatile disposition that we, who lived with her, witnessed when things didn't go exactly as she wanted. And Mama Jahn could definitely get volatile, as we all knew from the year she was preparing cabbage dolma for Uncle Berge's visit, when her careful preparations were thwarted.

She had sent Bobeeg Jahn out to get perfect heads of cabbage from Mr. Tanaka, the greengrocer. Previously, she herself had gone to the market and picked out the plumpest, unsulfurized apricots and prunes brought in from Fresno—where she said they grew best—to use in a rich sauce she'd made from home-grown tomatoes—which she de-seeded, de-skinned and puréed— then seasoned with a delicate hint of dried rahan (sweet basil). She had everything ready—the rice mixture for the stuffing, the fruits, the tomato sauce bubbling away. But Bobeeg Jahn still hadn't come home with the cabbage. She nervously waited for the fresh spring-green heads, even going so far as to put the enormous pot of water with salt and lemon on the stovetop to come to a boil, so she could be ready to plunge the leaves of cabbage in as soon as Bobeeg Jahn walked through the door—yet he still hadn't appeared.

She paced the kitchen floor fretting aloud in Armenian that it was taking too long to buy cabbage. She needed it that second. He should be here by now. And as the pot of water came to a rolling boil, so did Mama Jahn.

When poor, unsuspecting Bobeeg Jahn finally did arrive, she was fuming from standing over the evaporating water, bone-weary because of the housework she had already done, and panicky about all the baking that still needed doing. The late cabbage, though a small matter, had burgeoned into a larger matter, made that much more offensive by Mama Jahn's knowledge that Bobeeg Jahn did not believe Uncle Berge deserved his place on Mama Jahn's pedestal. It was clear, though, as I studied Mama Jahn from a careful distance, that this was not a good time for late cabbage.

I met Bobeeg Jahn as he sauntered up the long row of steps leading to the front door, and though I gave him a meaningful look of warning, he stopped anyway to inspect the new growth on the juniper bush he had pruned a few weeks ago. There ahead of him stood Mama Jahn on the porch, arms folded across her chest and legs astride, telling him how long she'd been waiting, and in a louder voice adding that next time she would send the sickly, old odar neighbor man in his wheelchair to the market instead of him.

Whereupon, she reached into the grocery bag; and pulling out one puny, brown-leafed head of cabbage after another, she began hurling insults in Armenian—first at the cabbages, then at Bobeeg—for choosing such "*horrid, pale, withered, smelly clumps of garbage unfit for even a Turk much less my beloved brother.*"

With the agility of a professional juggler, or maybe a basketball player, my short, round, bow-legged grandmother gathered all the pitiful balls of cabbage into her apron and strode to the kitchen door. From there she turned, and threw them with a vengeance, one at a time, onto the grass with a special curse attached to each one.

I watched with my mouth open alongside Bobeeg Jahn as the cabbages went sailing across the patch of lawn, some coming our way. We evaded them like a game of dodge ball. On and on they came, skipping down the long row of steps like out of control bowling balls, finally landing at the curb in front of Bobeeg Jahn's station-wagon, with nowhere else to go except roll over one last time and spill into the storm drain, dropping out of sight with one final plop.

Without a word to either of us, Bobeeg Jahn put on his cap and left. We were told later that he had returned to the market and told the produce man that the cabbages weren't good enough for his wife and her brother. Without further explanation, Mr. Tanaka understood the problem and got fresh ones from the back. "I, too, have wife who has brother," he had said.

The American saying "Blood is thicker than water" didn't begin to explain Mama Jahn's profound connection to her brother. Maybe she would have been embarrassed if she could have observed her indulgences towards Uncle Berge with detachment. I don't know. But I do know that he was the only one who carried the picture of her as a young girl and remembered what made her laugh as they played together as children. He alone knew their myrig's face and how her arms felt as she hugged each of them good night before scooting them off to bed. He was the best man at her wedding to Sarkis. He remembered all the days of her life before coming to America because he lived them with her. Uncle Berge was not as in love with her or anyone else so much as he was in love with himself, but that didn't matter to Mama Jahn. She needed this relationship because it connected her to her past. And that was the only way she could face all her tomorrows. Her eyes twinkled like blinking Christmas lights in his presence, and all her worries seemed to fade away.

As a result, Mama Jahn gave Uncle Berge her marriage bed to sleep in whenever he visited. She slept in my bed, I slept on the sofa and poor Bobeeg slept on yorgahns on the floor in the living room. She wouldn't let Uncle Berge spend a penny of his money on anything when they were together. She bought his Black Jack chewing gum and Tums for his constant heartburn, and she paid his dry cleaning bill. It was as if brother and sister were members of a secret club—of two. Uncle Berge was the president and chairman of the board and she was his personal assistant, existing only to facilitate his desires. She did a lot of crazy things for him that Bobeeg couldn't abide.

I never saw Uncle Berge wear anything but well-pressed, three-piece suits with starched white shirts and subdued neutral tones of coordinated patterned neckties, held down with a diamond-studded, golden tie tack from the Shriner's Club. (He was never a Shriner himself. He found the tie clip on the bathroom floor at work and wore it every day after that.) And he wore a hat—always a charcoal-gray felt fedora to match his dark gray suits. His hair was wavy black and slicked down with pomade that glistened in the sunlight when he tipped his hat to passing women. He smelled of sweet sage, Black Jack chewing gum, and ever so faintly of nice smelling pipe tobacco. His teeth were perfectly straight and actually glistened. Mama Jahn taught him how to make a paste using baking soda that kept them pearly white. But my uncle's most disarming feature was his smile. He smiled not only with his mouth but his eyes. I saw women blush and stammer when he smiled at them. Even men were charmed—all except Bobeeg.

When Uncle Berge arrived at Armenian parties, he'd scrutinize the women guests who looked his way. He'd zero in on the quiet-looking married ones, a class of women he thought especially vulnerable, saying to Mama Jahn behind his hand covering his mouth, "I want to get to know *that* one." While pointing in her direction with one raised eyebrow he'd say, "She looks very sad."

He would proceed to introduce himself to her. Once seated in some quiet, dark corner of the room, he always said the same thing as a conversation starter. "You appear to be very unhappily married."

Bobeeg would angrily tell Mama Jahn in an intense low whisper, "There he goes again, Zvart—your brother Berge doesn't fool *me*." Bobeeg Jahn knew as well as Uncle Berge knew: If you ask any woman if she is unhappily married, she'll reflect on all the things her husband has done to upset her. And so Uncle Berge caught women in his web: he had them feeling sorry for themselves.

If one said, "Oh no, I'm happily married to a wonderful man," Berge would start to go away—but what woman doesn't want the attention of a striking single man? This prompts her to say, "Wait! You're right. I am

141

unhappy. How did you know?" And then he had her! Either way, Uncle Berge was irresistible.

Bobeeg was definitely on to him and his tricks, and it gradually dawned on me that Mama Jahn actually abetted Uncle Berge's dalliances with married women. That's why my grandfather Bobeeg disliked his brother-in-law. He didn't judge him for what he did as much as for involving Mama Jahn in his assignations.

One day I overheard them describe a time, when my mother was around ten years old, that Mama Jahn sent her along with Uncle Berge to meet a married lady in a dark restaurant so that the lady's husband wouldn't suspect anything was going on. My mother, facing the other way, sat in the back booth sipping a milkshake, unaware that her uncle and his lover were nuzzling each other's ears and whispering and giggling a few booths away.

All these years later Mama Jahn was still enabling her brother's trysts. The summer before our trip to San Francisco while he was visiting Los Angeles, Mama Jahn took her yarn and needles out to the front porch and sat there knitting and purling as innocent as can be. Meanwhile, Uncle Berge was with a married lady in Uncle Mono's shed behind our house. A man named Mr. Jorjorian showed up, hissing and spitting and screaming at the top of his lungs, because he claimed his wife was with Uncle Berge. Mama Jahn told him such a convincing lie that he questioned his suspicions and went home, apologizing to Mama Jahn for his jealous outburst.

As soon as the husband left, Bobeeg, who had observed the entire scene from our kitchen, got furious with Mama Jahn, telling her that her lying was just as bad as what Berge was doing with that tourse ungadz boze (fallen street whore), Digeen Jorjorian, and he would have no part of it. Bobeeg, usually meek and mild, flung open the shed door and directed the garden hose, with the nozzle on its most powerful setting, onto the two of them lying naked together.

Mama Jahn yelled out, "Yervant, Yervant, eench gunes!? Ghent es? (What are you doing? Are you crazy?)"

Of course, I came quickly because everyone was screeching and talking fast in Armenian. And what a show! With the harsh stream of water coming after them, Uncle Berge and Digeen Jorjorian ran around the yard looking for cover under crazy things, like the branches torn from the apple tree, the dome-shaped lid from the barbecue pit, and a pair of big leather gardening gloves. Uncle Berge covered his dangling jooge with one hand and tried to cover his eyes with the other (maybe so he wouldn't have to see what was happening) while Digeen Jorjorian used both hands to cover her flopping tzeezeegs, which jiggled and swung back and forth like pendulums while she ran and jumped as if dodging bullets. Then, just when she bent over to pick up her eyeglasses, without which she could not see clearly, Bobeeg pointed the hose directly in her vodeeg, the shock of which caused her to jump high off the ground and run as fast as a deer out the gate and down the street, completely naked.

The next day we heard that Digeen Jorjorian had somehow convinced her husband that she had been attacked by Turks. Incredibly, because all Armenians hate the Turks more than anything or anyone in the whole world, he believed her outrageous lie.

My revelations didn't end there. Mama Jahn did more than care for her brother, indulge him, and help him in his questionable assignations. During that summer trip to San Francisco, I discovered that the special connection between them held an even more shattering shared secret.

We sat together, night after night, making corsages while Mama Jahn and Uncle Berge talked and laughed and cried, sometimes even singing childhood school songs while twisting and untwisting family stories without any shyness or attention to my presence. I felt physically invisible, though I was always present. The only time they really noticed me was when it was time for me to go to sleep on the sheet-covered furniture cushions set onto the floor next to the bed Mama Jahn slept on, or to fetch something they needed.

Mama Jahn and uncle felt free to talk about anything at all. Because they thought I didn't understand a thing they were saying, it was as though I wasn't listening. Little did they know!

Though no one had ever sat down with me to formally teach me Armenian, I had already spent twelve years in our Armenian home. Mama Jahn spoke to me only in Armenian and broken English, and I always answered her in English since my parents wanted me to speak only English. She took for granted that I understood her only through her halting English. In addition, Uncle Mono, Auntie Zov and even Hayrig and my mother often talked amongst themselves in Armenian, which automatically infused me with a certain comprehension. So now, listening to Mama Jahn and Uncle Berge's stories—and understanding nearly everything—I realized how much Armenian I really knew, but I didn't let on because I didn't want them to clam up.

Their discussions were totally entertaining. There was their gossip about crazy Krikor, who was an embarrassment to his family in the Old Country because he sat in his chair in the living room, talking to himself and looking out the window, yelling at each woman who passed by. Once he ran out and started kissing every lady he saw.

"Imagine our cousin, married her beautiful only daughter off into their family. I wonder which of her children will be ghent (crazy), like Krikor," Mama Jahn had said, though in Armenian of course, half smiling as she imagined the worst.

"I would die from the embarrassment if that ever happened to anyone in our family," Uncle Berge answered also in Armenian, shaking his head in earnest.

One night, near completion of the corsages, Uncle Berge and Mama Jahn had sipped several glasses of Armenian rakhi. They talked very quietly— almost whispering— about Uncle Berge's wife in the Old Country. I was all ears, and it was hard not to stop my untwisting job and stare in disbelief: I never knew he was married! If I had stopped, they would have known that I understood what they were saying and changed the subject, so I kept on with my job without hesitation and stared downward though my heart pounded with excitement as I listened. Listening to them was like a serial movie.

"I'll never forget that night on the train when I was so sick I thought I was dying," said my uncle.

"But you were dying, Berge!"

"Yes, it was terrible—the high fever, the pain in my stomach—the cramps. I was shaking so badly I cut the inside of my mouth with my teeth. Luckily, my friends knew what was wrong and made me vomit."

Folding her hands as if in prayer, Mama Jahn exclaimed, "I thank God every day you were spared."

"Aghh, aghh, aghh, Zvart, how can I ever forget that she poisoned me? My own wife, the mother of my only son, poisoned me. How can a woman bake a special Easter cake, soak it in expensive honey—that should have been a clue in itself—and sprinkle it with cinnamon and nutmeg just to hide the taste of poison earmarked for her husband? What kind of tribute to the risen Christ is that?"

"She's rotting in hell for what she did, especially because it was on the most holy day of the Lord's resurrection," Mama Jahn added while crossing herself.

"And for what?" asked Uncle, lifting his eyes to the ceiling. "For what did she lose her immortal soul? For that morally disgusting, poor excuse of a man, with a dying wife and seven starving children. For that man I should be murdered?"

"For that she should be murdered!" retorted Mama Jahn. "You should not forget. You should remember. You should always remember how brave you were to go back on the train…how smart you were not to let anyone know what you were doing . . . going late in the night and coming back that same night so no one would ever suspect you."

It took every bit of restraint for me not to sit up straight and stare.

"I can still see them standing so close to each other on the bridge that you couldn't pass a communion wafer between them. I see that peece hodadz, (low-life rotten), man's face full of terror when he saw me coming from behind her. He never saw my knife but he knew I was going to kill him. That's why the coward pushed her into me so he could get away."

"Oh!" I cried out.

"Vat? Vat's wrong," Mama Jahn asked, suddenly suspicious.

"Nothing," I said. "I just poked myself with the wire that's all." I looked down, and resumed work as if nothing had happened.

After a few moments Berge went on, "So Knar turns to me, and on her face is pure fear. But my will is resolute. Before she can scream I plunge my knife through her lungs and puncture her heart. Meanwhile the man is running across the bridge. You should *have seen him, Zvart. He couldn't have run any faster if a Turk had been chasing him with a sword pointed at his jooge."*

By now I was fighting back tears, overwhelmed by this new image of my gentle Uncle Berge.

Did you ever find out what happened to him? Did he ever come back?"

"My spies tell me he never returned. That his sickly wife died. That he's afraid if he shows his face I will come back from America and kill him."

"God have mercy."

"Still, I worry someone will find out," Uncle Berge said with a shudder.

Mama Jahn put her arm around him. *"Rest assured, Berge, no one will ever know from my lips what happened. Your secret will always be safe with me."*

In my head I was screaming, "Hey, what about me? Are you at all interested in knowing what I think of all this?"

"Of course, Zvart, he said, while she stroked his gorgeous hair. *"I never question your loyalty."*

He sat up, and they resumed making the corsages.

"You deserved a good wife, Berge, not one who was having an affair behind your back and making a fool of you in front of your friends. And trying to kill you, Berge. Don't ever forget that! She deserved to die. It served her right," she said snapping the heads off the red berries with an extra hard twist of her pistachio-red stained fingers.

"She got what was coming to her, Berge. Asdvadz wanted it that way, or you would have killed him instead."

Under the strain of remembering, Uncle Berge broke down. Through heavy sobbing he went on, *"You're such a wonderful sister. What did I ever do to deserve you? You're my sister, my only true friend and now my mother . . ."*

Holding his head in her strong, corsage- and bread-making hands, she kissed dry his tears, pressed her cheek to his and took off his glasses to wipe them clean with the underside of her new slip from Macy's.

"It's time for bed, Berge. Enough talk of those days. We need sleep so we'll look good for the party tomorrow."

"I can never repay you for your devotion all these years. You're a saint . . . because you still love your nothing, horrible brother."

She pulled up his inverted demitasse cup whose fortune hadn't yet been told. *"Look, here in your cup...look at your fortune for tomorrow . . . you see . . . there that Digeen Kellekian . . . wearing her expensive gold and black silk shawl from Italy . . . she'll be at the party. And look, you see this open part down here in bottom of the cup— she's alone...her husband is still in Persia. That will be something good to think about while you go to sleep."*

They traded tender kisses on each other's foreheads, and he went to bed on the threadbare, gold-velvet sofa in the corsage-making room, while she and I went to his bedroom where she lay on the twin bed with me alongside on the red-and-orange-silk-covered yorgahn on the floor.

After all that excitement it was hard for me to fall asleep. I was afraid to show any emotion. What would happen if they found out I knew?

From my mat on the floor I could see the Golden Gate Bridge framed by the purple morning glories in the window. Uncle Berge had told me during the day that, because of the view of the bridge, this was his favorite room in the house. Now, at night, the scene held a darker aspect for me, with the white lights outlining the bridge against the black sky prompting me to wonder what other untold secrets there might be in my family.

From that summer onward, every time Christmas approaches and I anticipate the excitement of the holiday with its big delectable meals, the snow-flocked Christmas trees stuffed underneath with presents, and all the ladies wearing corsages, I also think about my Uncle Berge's attentions to married women and remember that he murdered his wife.

18 THE CUP OF GOOD MEASURE

the camel does not see its own hump

During the summer, not long before I started junior high school, my mother was putting away towels in the bathroom as I was drying myself and said, "Your breasts are filling in. That means you'll be menstruating soon."

"I'll be what?"

"Menstruating," she said again. "You're going to bleed and if that happens at school, you ask your teacher for a pad to wear so the blood doesn't leak everywhere."

And that was it, her total coming of age conversation. Educators must've heard about my mother and that's why Sex Ed was invented and was extended to week-long, in-classroom presentations, complete with slideshow and Q&A. From the moment mother made her offhand observation, I lived in terror of bleeding in front of all the kids at school, *from my breasts!* There wasn't a day that went by that I didn't worry about it. I even had nightmares of circles of blood staining my blouses and sweaters in big, drippy polka dots. I prayed that this menstruation, whatever it was, erupted in the summer so I wouldn't have to wear a jacket to school every day, in case I needed to cover myself up.

Imagine my shock when Mama Jahn and I were on our way to San Francisco by train, on our usual summer visit to see Uncle Berge, and I saw blood in the stainless steel toilet bowl on the train. Not just breasts would bleed? Now I'm bleeding elsewhere, too? To my hysterical cry for help, "Mama Jahn, blood, blood!" she simply said, "Don't vorry, it be normal, it be normal." She tore up her cotton J.C. Penney slip—rippppp, rippppppp, ripppppppp—and nimbly folded them into enough little pads for me to use for the next five days. All very "normal," just like other girls whose grandmothers routinely shred their underwear, I'm sure.

When we got back from San Francisco, mother lifted a thimbleful of maternal responsibility and showed me how to use an elastic belt with flat hooks that attached to what she called "feminine pads." They came in a box, *Modess*, with photographs of beautiful women wearing ball gowns with yards and yards of flowing fabrics, some in white, without a bloodstain in sight.

Even with three grown women in our house, no one ever bothered to explain *why* I was bleeding and how long it would last. So all summer long I fretted about this, along with other life changing things, especially acne eruptions, volcanoes that pushed out horrid pockets of pus, on my face. I learned fast that if I attacked by using my fingers, I could relieve myself from the sight of them for at least a day. It was a constant battle. I couldn't wait for September so I could mine the other girls for answers, as we walked to and from school.

On the morning of the first day of junior high, my mother, Hayrig and I sat at the kitchen table having breakfast while Mama Jahn made lunches.

"Too bad Americans don't understand all that yogurt can do for you."

"I couldn't agree more, Kourken. How about those long-lived Russians who eat madzoon every day? Our bodies need those microbes. And, Azad, if you'd just apply madzoon to your pimples at night, as I suggested, they would dry up and go away."

How embarrassing, I thought. This was my parents' idea of a breakfast topic? Even though their conversations were sometimes disgusting, you could see how much they loved each other when they were passionately talking about words and foods. It was their shared hobby.

While they were into their madzoon, I was thinking about the same thing I always thought about when I was going to be with kids my age—how Armenian and therefore different from them I was—dark hair, dark eyes and dark skin, now embellished with pimples, and for extra appeal, blood flowing from a secret dark place.

My family never agreed with me regarding any of my obvious flaws. Mama Jahn said to "tank God" for my straight nose. Hayrig applauded my outgoing personality. Aunt Zov said I should not show how smart I was. Bald Uncle Mono loved my masses of horribly curly hair. And Mother said I had a good figure. To me, it sounded as if they were discussing a poodle.

Gazing down at the fruit-print oil cloth that covered our kitchen table, I mindlessly outlined the shape of one of the pineapples and its decorative outer crosshatchings with my right index finger, and when I looked up at the clock, I caught Hayrig's eye. Without breaking his stare he reached into his shirt pocket and pulled out a shiny box. With his index finger placed squarely in the center of it, he pushed it slowly across the breakfast table towards me, saying, "Armenians girls with olive skin tend to be sallow in complexion. You'll need this for junior high school."

148

Immediately my covetous mother jumped in; "Amoussin (husband), what is this? Ahmahn . . . you never told me . . . what color is it, Kourken?"

I threw my arms around Hayrig and then ran to the closest mirror, still in total disbelief, twirling past Mama Jahn and exclaiming, "It's Revlon's *Coral Island* lipstick . . . . I can't believe it . . . lipstick for me! It's so sharp, thank you, Hayrig, thank you."

Mama Jahn couldn't wait to give her opinion: "Lup-a-stick; no-good girls wear lup-a stick."

I knew what Mama Jahn thought, that girls who wear lipstick are no-good, and that's exactly why it never crossed my mind to ask if I could wear lipstick. I thought everyone in the family would call me a boze if I asked for it.

But I was so happy with my tube of lipstick that I couldn't take Mama Jahn seriously. Instead I teased her. "Do you know this song? "Boze, boze, boze, I'm a junior high school boze girl . . . hey!"

"Oooff, Azad, go vay."

Ever since I was little, I had envied women who used lipstick. No tube of lipstick in a room ever escaped my eyes. I had inner radar that noticed women pulling out lipstick tubes from private hiding places.

Especially fun to watch were ladies who had been necking all through a movie at the picture show, then just before bright lights flooded the theatre, fumbled around looking for their tube of lipstick so they could quickly swipe it on. Otherwise the lights would have exposed their smeared lips. Desirous of being like them, I routinely went to the theatre's candy counter and bought big, thick, red, waxed lips and candy cigarettes, which I pretended to smoke.

My history teacher had a tube of lipstick in her top desk drawer that she used when class was just about over. She'd turn her back on us and then feign great interest in the map of the world while she refreshed her lipstick. But I saw what she was doing in the reflection of the glass on the picture frame.

Mrs. Hill, my P.E. teacher, never used a mirror or even so much as a reflection in glass. She pulled out her tube of lipstick from her tennis sock and applied it whenever and wherever she was in the mood—on the field, in the gym, at the equipment storage area—probably when her lips got dry because she was outside most of the time. She always wore the same color lipstick because it looked beautiful with her hair. I felt sure that it took lots and lots of practice to put on lipstick without a mirror.

In restaurants some ladies re-applied their lipstick after eating, right there at the table, and some, when no one at their table was watching, even re-applied their lipstick between courses.

Many women puckered their lips while they applied lipstick and then smacked their lips together to distribute the lipstick evenly.

Aunt Gladys used a lipstick brush to apply her lipstick that had silver letters on the side spelling *Stardust Casino,* more Las Vegas paraphernalia. The brush swiveled out of a red pencil-like tube that she used to paint her lips her favorite color, *Vegas Red.* The names of lipsticks like P*aradise Red, Ballroom Beauty, Plum Happy, Hibiscus Pink,* and *Orange Flip* transported me to dreamy places and romantic scenes of passion and abandon. Of *Coral Island,* all I could think was "aloha!"

Just as I never saw Mama Jahn *with* lipstick, I never saw my mother *without* it, except when she was sick or sleeping.

Hayrig and I had the same reasons for my wearing lipstick and I was thrilled beyond belief to be adult enough to have it. Hastening to make the most of "the big moment," I brushed my teeth, dried my lips and then took the new tube of lipstick, removed the cap, slowly swiveled out the luscious peachy-coral stick of color, and, with the never-before-used tip, carefully outlined the right and then the left side of my upper lip and then filled in the bottom lip. The process felt so natural, like coloring within the lines of a picture in a coloring book. And my lips felt like satin looked. Now I was a woman.

I smacked my lips together and smiled at myself in the mirror. I looked different, almost pretty. I'd been practicing putting on lipstick with my imagination for years, and now I was using the real thing. All of a sudden I felt so much more like the self I imagined myself to be. It was a start.

I excelled in P.E., becoming a star player in all sports and captain of the basketball and volleyball teams, because I knew how to play defensively. The Armenian in me. No coach had to tell me "don't give up, get in there and fight for the ball." Fighting for the ball came naturally to me. That instinct was in my blood—not like the girls I called "the cuties" whose group I both hated and mocked. I thought the way the cuties behaved was funny. *They were so stupid.* Their concern with their long fingernails—filing them, polishing them and growing them—made them scream and run away when the ball came towards them so they wouldn't break their nails. I loved watching them preen and then run scared. They cracked me up. But I also hated them. They didn't have to be smart or athletic or anything except cute. Even though the coaches were frustrated and angry with the girls too, I envied their ability not to care about winning a game or being a good player, much less the best player on the team. Being cute was all they needed. Cute and normal.

Strangely enough, I was popular with these cutie girls because I wore lipstick and their parents didn't want them wearing make-up. When these blond blue-eyed beauties whined to me, "Ah, look at Ahzie, (the "cute" nick name they gave me). She's wearing lipstick! I wish I could wear lipstick," or "Ahzie, you're so lucky."

I never went up to their faces gushing over their silky hair or lovely dresses. Why did they have to make such a big deal about the lipstick? They wanted everything even though they already *had* everything—blue eyes, satin straight shiny blond hair, light complexion, beautiful clothes and shoes. And now they wanted my lipstick.

Without thinking I blurted out in defense of my lucky lips, "But, you're not sallow!"

"Huh? Sallow? What's sallow?" they asked each other as they continued to walk down the hall to their next class.

I should have just kept my lucky lips shut and smiled. Instead I showed them that I was an imperfect third-class citizen even with my beautiful lipstick. I had something everyone wanted, and instead of encouraging adoration, I gave them reason to think I was unworthy of knowing, much less admiring, by talking about being sallow instead of lucky. I felt like a real idiot. These kinds of landmines are everywhere when you're an Armenian.

In elementary school people either got along with their teacher or they didn't. Teachers thought you were either an idiot or a genius. Going to different classes with different teachers for each subject and having four times the amount of students as elementary school made junior high a more interesting place. And I had lots of opportunities to mix with the other kids. I imagined myself walking down the hall and having kids call out to me, "Hey, Ahzie, looking sharp," and "Ahzie, see you in gym." And I'd call out to them similarly, "Judy, I like your new bucks," and "Hey, Jack, good for you—you beat your own best time yesterday." But I just couldn't get the words out fast enough and the kids just kept on walking. I was the out of place bowl of madzoon at an American banquet.

In junior high, everyone had many chances to get along and many opportunities to demonstrate idiocy or genius. As for me, I wasn't interested in math so I did the minimum amount of work and kept my head down. I was great in biology because learning about the human body was very entertaining—all those body parts and activities going on inside were fascinating, especially when we looked at germs under a microscope.

Even though I was not fascinated by English, I could put together a thoughtful and well organized essay and I was presumed to be a genius by the teacher because I could define, spell and use interesting words when I wrote my essays, words like *prerogative* and *obsequious* and even *sesquipedalian*. I knew more about vocabulary and literature than the other kids because Hayrig loved the English language and Mother loved reading. Also, I had read many books years before junior high, books like *Robinson Crusoe*, *Don Quixote* and my absolute favorite I could never put down—*Larousse's Encyclopedia of Mythology*. Zeus and his entourage on Mt. Olympus. I loved them all: the weak, the vengeful, the tortured, and especially the twisted. The English teachers loved me because I was the one person in their classes who understood their lame jokes that had literary illusions. Take, for example, Mr. Thomas's quip: "Whenever I'm reading really bad prose, I always remember it could be verse," to which I alone burst out laughing.

Even when I feigned ignorance to be more like everyone else, the teachers knew I knew. Being smart wasn't something American kids valued, so I downplayed my brain and tried to act dumb like Aunt Zov suggested. She knew.

Being cool was the one thing that *everyone* in the group knew about. Cool meant that you didn't show what you felt about anything. You were calm, cool and collected emotionally. All feelings were kept inside or you were un-cool.

Happily, I no longer had sack lunches to distinguish me from the other students. And even though the school cafeteria, the 'caf' was an unparalleled culinary adventure for me, I managed to keep a lid on my enthusiasm. No one else seemed as excited about it as I did, so I never mentioned my pleasure when spaghetti and meatballs were on the menu or my displeasure when they were gone by the time I got to the serving station. I never let on that I was mesmerized by the whole experience—the silver trays, the stainless steel counters that the trays slid across, the workers in their crisp white chef jackets and black-and-white check trousers, the immaculate counters in the kitchen, and, of course, the food. The food was basic, down to earth, everyday American food, and the more I ate, the more American I became. I kept thinking that the Bible said *we are what we eat.*

The one junior high-school class I had looked forward to was Home Economics. This was where I was going to learn how to make fabulous American foods and I was going to meet a teacher with whom I had a lot in common, a love of cooking. I would finally have my own American hero, or so I thought.

Since I had spent the greater part of my previous twelve years in the kitchen, making complicated foods with Mama Jahn, I knew I wouldn't even have to study for this class. This class is going to be so easy and so much fun, I thought, as I sat in the front row on the first day anticipating meeting my American kitchen Super Woman. As always, however, I tried to keep my cool.

I wondered what the teacher would look like, how she would dress, how old she was and what we'd be making first. Maybe we'd start with breakfast, since that was the first meal of the day and maybe, just maybe, it would be that amazing egg dish that transformed ordinary eggs into floating islands of gastronomical delight because of hollandaise sauce—Eggs Benedict. Maybe I'd find out who Benedict was, too. There was so much to learn and I was ready.

The final bell rang, and in walked the much awaited lady, trim figured but old with white hair. Right away she announced haltingly, as if waiting to overcome a seizure, "Um, I'm Mrs. Baxter, and um, please open your notebooks and write down the first, er, recipe we're, um, going to, er, make in small groups, er, tomorrow—Cinnamon Toast."

I laughed out loud, looked around me for others laughing, too, and blurted out, "Cinnamon Toast? This is a joke, right?" Mrs. Baxter didn't say anything to me, or look my way to acknowledge what I said. She had to be hard of hearing. What was going on? No smiles? No jokes? No darling organdy apron? Nothing wonderful at all. This had to be a mistake.

"She's going to teach us a recipe for cinnamon toast? Is that really what she said?" I then whispered to cute, long finger-nailed, Patty Jones sitting next to me.

"It must be. Look, she's writing it on the blackboard, Recipe for Cinnamon Toast," she whispered back.

I gave Baxter the benefit of the doubt and thought that she must be starting with the easy stuff and working up to the complicated foods. Yes, that must be what she's doing.

While she was writing on the blackboard, with her back to us, I looked her up and down. She had absolutely no style. She had shoes like Mama Jahn, old lady laced oxfords in oxblood brown. And she wore the kind of apron that was loose and fit like a dress over her dress, like Mama Jahn's aprons. An outfit like Mama Jahn's might suggest that she knew her way around a kitchen, but with no hips or vodeeg at all, she didn't even look as if she ate, much less cooked. When she turned around I saw that she wore no makeup and her gray hair was styled with pin curls that she hadn't brushed out. She made the old Armenian church ladies at a funeral look like the height of chic.

My expectations that Mrs. Baxter was to be my queen of the American kitchen, my Head Chef, my mentor, my guide to all American foods . . . toppled.

She pulled down a chart the size of a movie screen from the ceiling and said, as she walked out the door, "These er are the tools we're going to uh use in the kitchen. Use the rest of the period to copy them down in your notebooks."

The next day I spent my time counting how many times she said *um* and *er* in a sentence before we went into the room of kitchens.

I was hoping we'd be making the bread for the cinnamon toast. But instead she distributed one toaster and enough slices of store-bought white bread for each team to create one piece of cinnamon toast, which, by the way, was to be graded.

She had a check list with which to evaluate how well we followed directions, and we got points which collectively added up to a letter grade for things like color; if it was too light, too dark or just right; and if the butter was evenly distributed all over the toast including the edge so the cinnamon would stick on the toast, if the cinnamon sugar mixture was balanced—not too much of either sugar or cinnamon, and finally if it was sprinkled evenly on the toast, not in blobs. Of course, mine was done to perfection. But I stayed true to my general displeasure by not eating the finished product. I didn't want to give her the satisfaction of thinking I thought it was "wonderful nice." It was boring and stupid.

And the days to come were even worse. We had to make Milk Toast. When bread was toasted and buttered, warm and crispy outside and soft inside it was delicious as it was, but then she had us pour warm milk on top of it, which turned it into garbage. Milk Toast was for sick old people with no teeth. It's not in the caf' or in a movie theater or on any menu I ever heard of. Only people too sick to go on living would want it.

Then came making white sauce into which we added packaged corned chip beef and poured over toast again, resulting in what she called, Chipped Beef on Toast. They were equally disgusting.

It was toast, toast, toast, all the time toast. I didn't want to have anything to do with any of Baxter's toast dishes or anything else she had to offer. I moved to the last row, and challenged her to inspire me with my noncompliant attitude and body language, which communicated disapproval and disinterest. She never confronted me about my bad behavior. It didn't take me long to figure out that she wasn't deaf, though. She was ignoring me intentionally. We were ignoring each other.

It wasn't long before Patty passed me a note: "Come to my house after school and I'll show you my mother's new cookbook."

I looked her way and I nodded in the affirmative, my big eyes open wide with gratitude and surprise. This is the thing about the cuties: Even cuties can take you by surprise.

Just as I had never seen measuring spoons and measuring cups before, I had never seen a cookbook either. Prior to the illustrations on Baxter's kitchen tool chart, I only knew how to measure for baking and cooking by trying to match the amounts of yegh, sugar, flour and salt I'd seen in Mama Jahn's all knowing palms and to master the elusive pinches and sprinklings cascading from her dancing finger tips.

Patty told me that her mother was a stay-at-home mom who loved watching television and doing housework.

"Oh, hi, girls. You must be Ahzie. Patty told me that you really love to cook and that you'd like to see my new cookbook. It's fabulous." Meeting Mrs. Jones was kismet. Patty Jones, I thought, go paint your nails and leave me alone with your mother. I have to get to know her.

Mrs. Jones motioned to a place on her plastic-covered white sofa and asked me to "Come, sit down, so I can show you this new Betty Crocker cookbook. It's in its second printing. Isn't it beautiful? See here, look at all the pictures. The pictures show you exactly how to make the recipes in the book. It's so easy when you can follow Betty Crocker."

We sat in her neat, sterile living room, turning the pages of the cookbook filled with photographs and drawings, marveling at all the knowledge and excited about how doable everything looked, because of the step-by-step explanations and illustrations. Section-by-section, we turned the pages together starting with: *Special Helps, where Betty Crocker tells women how to make work easy:*

If you're tired from overwork,
Household chores you're bound to shirk.
Read these pointers tried and true
And discover what to do.

And if all her tips—like "harbor pleasant thoughts while working . . . it will make every task lighter and pleasanter" and "every morning before breakfast, comb hair, apply make-up, a dash of cologne, and perhaps some simple earrings . . . it does wonders for your morale"—don't work, then instructing, "If you are still tired and depressed, have a medical check-up and follow doctor's orders" will, and then you'll be a happy homemaker.

When we got to page one hundred eighty-three, Mrs. Jones said, "I just finished making this old-fashioned chocolate fudge recipe. Let's go in the kitchen and have some. Pat-eeee, fuuuudge," she called out. No one called out "fudge" in my home. Lots of other callings out like, bourma, paklava, shakar locum, halvah, simit, cheorag and, come, let's look in your cup and see what vee see," but no one ever said "fuuudge".

Mrs. Jones words floated when she spoke, like Betty Crocker's new recipe for lighter-than-ever orange chiffon cake.

I had finally found my American kitchen hero, Betty Crocker.

At home Hayrig didn't like that I was having conflicts with Baxter and said, "Acheeges (girl of mine), you should try to share something of your knowledge of cooking with the Home Economics class as a gesture of reconciliation."

"Oh, Hayrig, you don't understand. Baxter is a total idiot. She knows nothing about making good food. She makes disgusting food for sick people."

"Never you mind. No daughter of mine will grow up thinking she's better than anyone else. You use your brain and think of something you can do to reconcile. Forget about her. It's for the health of your soul that you find something you can give and something you can learn from her."

Hayrig made me promise, so I raised my hand the next day and told Mrs. Baxter and the class that my dad had bought the newest Servel refrigerator sold—with an automatic ice-maker. You'd think a Home Economics' teacher would be interested in such an announcement, but instead she ignored me and continued talking about the laxative properties of a balanced breakfast.

My mother said, "Forget trying to have her like you. It's clear she's jealous of our family because of our new refrigerator."

Hayrig said, "Never mind what your mother says, you try again. Share something about our way of cooking."

My parents—having grown up surrounded by other Armenians—weren't very useful when it came to problems I was having at school. They really didn't get it. Nonetheless, I thought and I thought and it came to me that I could teach Baxter about our Armenian secret, yegh, which is perfect for making sublime eggs. I would show her how, as the yegh melts in the frying pan, you can't help recognizing the aroma, which is like toasted nuts. She would then be swept away by the golden color as it turned liquid over a medium high heat under the frying pan and begins to spurt and crackle. At that point the yegh is telling you to pour in the eggs you've lightly beaten in a bowl with the long tines of the perfect fork you've been lucky enough to have from your grandmother, the fork she picked up at her favorite Chinese restaurant after eating asparagus beef with noodles. That fork blends the white and the yolk together perfectly. (I even decided to get Baxter one just like it the next time we went to General Lee's.) Then as soon as the edges of the eggs begin to solidify, you use a narrow spatula to pull the eggs in toward the center giving them a quick stir. The hot clarified butter puffs up the eggs from within, infusing and transforming them. A sprinkle of salt and pepper and it's perfection. And from there I can share Mama Jahn's date omelette. No one's ever had that before because Mama Jahn invented that recipe.

I was getting carried away. Yes, I'll share our Armenian secrets with her and Hayrig will be proud, I thought. So I asked Mama Jahn to put some haladz yegh into a glass canning jar. I couldn't wait to give it to Baxter. Maybe we could be friends after all.

Before class started, I went to her office and politely asked if I could see her for a minute. She invited me in and waited for me to talk. "Mrs. Baxter, you said we'd be starting to cook eggs this week and I'd like to give you something we Armenians use to make incredible egg dishes—clarified butter." I extended my hand with the precious jar of liquid gold, clarified butter, and put it on her desk. She looked at me without looking at the jar and said, "Thank you for the thought, Azad, but I'm going to have to ask you to take it home."

"Take it home? Why should I take it home?"

"We can't use it here. It's just too foreign for us."

That was it. I would never reach out to her again. Never.

When I told Hayrig how she reacted to the yegh, he said, "We must pray for her."

Yeah, pray for her to drop dead, I thought.

And Mama Jahn pronounced with a tsk and quick dismissive upwards jerk of her head that this teacher was typical of some odars she had met; she was ahnlee. Mama Jahn saw all this coming in my cup when school first started but didn't want to cause trouble by telling me.

Der Hayr talked about savorless, insipid food without salt when he gave sermons about uninspired and corrupted people, comparing them to useless, flavorless food which wasn't even good enough to use as manure without salt. He impressed upon us the fact that Jesus called his disciples the "salt of the earth," and instructed them that it was their job to prevent corruption and impart life like only good salt could do. Mama Jahn even put salt in her clarified sweet butter. It made it taste good. Everything is sacrificed for taste.

As the weeks went by Mrs. Baxter and I clashed on everything. She was definitely ahnlee, saltless, and I was most certainly not the example of the good disciple. I stubbornly refused to believe her or follow her teachings or respect her or admire her, because she knew nothing I wanted to know and she expected me to learn what she had to teach me, which was *nothing*. I didn't show what I felt. I played it cool. And I did what I was told within my assigned cooking team of American girls, which unfortunately did not include Patty.

Most days all three of them wore Lanz dresses with the signature zigzag on rick-rack edging and when they weren't wearing Lanz they had on matching monochromatic skirt and sweater sets. As the semester went on, these girls in my cooking group were a source of irritation. It wasn't long before their beautiful clothes with matching flats meant nothing to me because I saw their internal flaws. I couldn't believe that all of them, *without exception*, loved making and eating Mrs. Baxter's very own, secret prized recipe for Chipped Beef with White Sauce over toast! When they saw that I wasn't interested in eating my portion they actually fought over who was going to get my serving, and they didn't stop there. They lapped up the disgusting Milk Toast like it was a Pavlova. In my opinion, they proved themselves to be just as bland as milk toast. And when they oohed and aahed over the taste of scrambled eggs fried in melted Crisco, I knew I didn't want to be anything like them . . . even if it meant that I'd never have a Lanz dress and would be forever known as an Armenian with black frizzy hair instead of an American.

Mrs. Baxter was a fraud, so I decided to expose her. Since I had no sway with her, I deputized Patty into bringing in her mother's Betty Crocker cookbook to share with the class. I knew Baxter would ignore the book, and then everyone would see her for the pretender she really was, because Betty Crocker was the American food genius of the world. I had it all figured out. I was going to correspond with Betty Crocker and eventually meet her, and *she* was going to be my food mentor. I'd show Baxter who was the real cook.

With a confident sense of pride, Patty held up the Betty Crocker cookbook and announced to everyone in class, as she held it high and moved it to the left and right so everyone could see the colorful cover. "Today I'm happy to share my mother's new Betty Crocker cookbook, which is full of beautiful pictures and step-by-step directions for making all sorts of things."

There were nothing but blank stares from the other girls, who didn't have a clue as to what this extraordinary cookbook was all about. But Mrs. Baxter said, "I know all about that cookbook, and I want to go on record to say that Betty Crocker is a fake, a charlatan. Moreover, she doesn't exist. She's a woman contrived by the advertising department of General Mills.

How can that be? I knew for a fact that in 1945, *Fortune* magazine named Betty Crocker the second most popular American woman. Eleanor Roosevelt was named first.

"You may take it home, Patty, and never bring it back." Then, looking at every girl in the eye, except for Patty and me, she continued, saying without one stammer, "Girls, if you don't learn anything else from my class, then learn this: that the best recipes are those tried and true ones that are handed down to mother from mother and from her mother before her, like Milk Toast, Chipped Beef on Toast and good old fashioned American scrambled eggs with Crisco."

I wanted to scream, what about *my* family recipes, those passed down to my mother from her mother and from her mother before her? And what about all the people who voted Betty Crocker the second most popular woman in America? Are we all wrong? But I didn't. Lucky for Mrs. Baxter that it wasn't cool to let my emotions show.

I had failed to make a good impression on Mrs. Baxter, but I still had my lipstick, my one delicious luxury. Even though it added to the fact that I was different, as much as I wanted to blend in with everyone else I wasn't about to give up *Coral Island*. Lipstick gave me hope in the possibility of wonderful things yet to come when I was grown up, when I could live my own life my own way, without vapid girls and without milk and toast together in the same dish!

19 THE CUP OF CHRISTMAS

don't pollute the well; some day you might need the water

Armenians cried at happy occasions such as birthdays. Mama Jahn explained that it was hard to have a good time at parties because Armenians couldn't forget about family and friends who would never have a party again because of the massacres.

Except for my Auntie Gladys.

Whenever she came over to visit she made us all laugh. She knew how to tell a joke, play practical jokes, and do silly things when people got too serious. She made Mama Jahn giggle even when she said hello by giving her little bacheegs, all around her neck, and she called my dad Surpazan while bowing down low and kissing his hand as if he was the venerable Bishop. And we were all captivated when she started telling stories about people we knew who were in some kind of trouble:

"Did you hear about Sasha? He caught his wife with Dadour the butcher when he came home early from fishing last night."

When she saw us all horrified and the color drain from the women's faces, she continued while laughing, "Yadash! I got you!"

The ladies glared at her for joking around about what could have been a good bit of gossip.

Auntie Gladys, who was relatively young when she arrived in the United States, had learned how to be the life of the party by being around her American friends at high school. She learned that worrying about tomorrow made you forget you were living now, today.

Plus, Auntie Gladys did things that I had only known Armenian men to do, like smoke in public and go to Las Vegas to gamble. She had her own business and made her own money, so she had fun and enjoyed her life—this despite the massacre of two and a half million Armenians by the Turks in 1915, a cloud that hung over every Armenian-American I knew except Auntie Gladys.

When she was seventeen, she saw Leo Takesian leading the line dancing at an Armenian New Year's Eve party. The minute she saw him, she wanted to be with him forever. Everyone called him "The Armenian Fred Astaire," but of course without the tiny nose. He was the best dancer that anyone in her circle had ever seen — jumping like a Cossack high in the air and performing steps so complicated and energetic that everyone threw money at his feet. He didn't even break out in a sweat while he danced, while a cigarette dangling provocatively from his lips. Auntie Gladys just had to have him.

Two weeks later they were married by a judge in Las Vegas. This was a big, big deal in our community — being married by a judge rather than in the Armenian Apostolic Church with a Der Hayr presiding. This was a very American movie-star thing to do. "Ahmot, shame! Not what 'good' Armenian girls do," my Mama Jahn whispered to herself every time she saw Auntie Gladys.

"Gladys's myrig must have eaten raw oysters when she was pregnant," was Mama Jahn's explanation for Gladys's behavior for the course of her entire life. She saw the dreaded oysters, without pearls, whenever she read Gladys's coffee cups.

After this enormous break from tradition, and many, many smaller transgressions in between — such as swearing in English *and* Armenian, drinking while sitting on stools in bars, owning her own business, choosing not to have children and buying a car without a man to do the negotiating, Auntie Gladys knew she could do whatever she wanted, and she knew no one in the family would ever say a word to her face about her decisions. Oh, she knew they all talked about her behind her back, but she also knew that they would never outright confront her.

Immediately after their honeymoon at the Sands Hotel in Vegas, Auntie Gladys took a job working for Mr. Marvin at the local five & dime, called, fittingly, "Marvin's." Gladys recognized that the store, located in East Los Angeles where Russian Armenians like us had settled, needed to cater to the growing Mexican-American community that grew to encompass it. She convinced Mr. Marvin of this, and brought in whole new lines of merchandise, which in turn brought in a new stream of customers. So through hard work and brains, before long she became manager of the entire store. She and Mr. Marvin got along great—he called her 'Glady' and she called him 'Marvy.' When Mr. Marvin fell ill and had to retire, he offered her the opportunity to buy the store, paying for it over time, and she jumped at the chance.

Auntie Gladys still called the store "Marvin's," even though she owned it. When I asked her why, she said, "Hey, kiddo, look at the front. The name's already painted there. Why pay for another sign?" I think she also knew she could avoid salesmen and bill collectors if she kept Mr. Marvin's name on the sign because everyone would think he was still the owner. Over the years she had been used to telling salesmen that the boss was out of town but she'd pass on the message when he got back. So nothing really changed — except now all the profits, after the payments she made to Marv, were hers.

Meanwhile Uncle Leo, though an amazing dancer, was less than stellar as a provider. He worked as a commercial refrigeration salesman, but the piles of coils and refrigerator part samples that were in their backyard were a constant reminder that he wasn't on the road selling anything. Uncle Leo relinquished the task of daily work to Auntie Gladys, while he spent most of his time on the road supposedly selling, but really going to rodeos, shooting ranges, and stock car races with "low class bums," as Auntie Gladys called them. It didn't escape her that the places he spent his time didn't have telephones where he could be reached.

The more Auntie Gladys broke from the traditional Armenian way of being a woman, the less Uncle Leo behaved like an Armenian man. He didn't feel the need to take care of her because he didn't have control of the money. He wasn't even sure he liked being around her anymore. He called her "hard" in English and bagh (cold), in Armenian. Because she had financial security, she wouldn't tolerate him telling her what to do. She didn't like being bossed around, so expectations that she do his laundry and cooking like a "good" Armenian housewife fell on deaf ears. She sent the laundry out, she ate out and, when he complained, eventually she kicked him out.

After Uncle Leo had surgery to remove his gall bladder, almost dying from pneumonia during the recovery period, he decided to quit his "job" pretending to sell commercial refrigeration. His plan was to do little things that needed to be done for Gladys around their rented house and in the store. The one thing she didn't let him do was work the cash register. She wouldn't trust him with that.

When I turned thirteen, I thought I would have to spend the summer cleaning house, washing clothes, hanging them all out to dry, and ironing them, especially Hayrig's shirts with those awful French cuffs, *for-ev-er.* "No make wrinkle." Mama Jahn would say. I was thrilled when Auntie Gladys agreed to take me to work with her on Saturdays. I knew I'd be doing odd jobs in her big five-and-dime store for free, but I didn't care because she was rescuing me from having to help my mother and Mama Jahn. I'd been doing "howze-work" with Mama Jahn since I was really little, and I needed a change. Mama Jahn had seen this change coming in her cup, I'm sure, because all she said was, "You want me make you lunch to taking to store?"

Auntie Gladys would swing by the house in the brand new '57 red convertible T-Bird she'd won in the big spin at the Sands Hotel in Vegas. She'd be wearing lovely, fashionable sundresses made from Vogue patterns by her seamstress, from yardage she sold in her store. I felt as free as Auntie Gladys when we hit the road. I wished we could drive for hours together in that car instead of the mere ten minutes it took to get to Marvin's. The only drawback, I discovered from the first trip when I got into the store and saw myself in a mirror, was that the fresh air blew my kinky Armenian hair straight back so that it looked like it had been sucked up by a vacuum cleaner.

At first Auntie tried me out as a cashier because she trusted me, but she watched how nervous I got adding things up on a tablet and giving change. Gladys could add up prices in her head — "forty-five and sixty and seventy-five and, let's not forget to pay Uncle Sam . . . that'll be $1.85" — while I couldn't even get it right with pencil and paper. I prayed for people to have the correct amount, because the more flustered I got, the more wrong change I'd give out — and nothing got my auntie as angry as losing money.

Very soon she told me, "Kiddo, your place is out on the floor. Some people are made to handle cash, while others are born to make customers happy and get them to buy. I'll bet you're one of those."

She was right. I was much more relaxed out on the floor, folding, sorting, stocking, and talking with the customers.

That's when I discovered something else. One day the woman who usually did the store's window displays—which to my mind were boring and old fashioned—quit to have a baby. Auntie Gladys asked me if I'd like to try dressing a window.

"Sure, I would."

So I started in. It was the beginning of summer so I blew up dozens of beach balls and filled the space with them and had little stuffed animals lying on beach towels as though they were tanning themselves at the seashore. The colors, designs and various sizes of the balls were visually appealing and the addition of the critters took it out of the ordinary. That's what I was going for, out of the ordinary. I wanted to do what others couldn't do. The windows made everyone who saw them happy. My effort paid off. When Auntie Gladys saw my work she gave out a huge laugh, full of pleasure. "Azad, you're such an artist—these windows are alive! Having an eye for design and style is a whole lot better than having the evil eye, isn't it, Kiddo?"

When Auntie Glad went away for a week in Vegas, I wanted to surprise her with a magnificent design, my very best yet. I used bolts and bolts of the flashiest and most strikingly colored cloth, draping yards of velvet and polished cottons and silks every which-way, creating the look of a sumptuous stage curtain like the one I had seen at the Pantages Theater when my fifth grade class went to see *Hansel and Gretel.*

Then, I thought, why not hook up electric lights inside of Chinese lanterns, string them high and fill the space below with lines of wires covered with silver glitter that would sparkle under light from the lanterns. And from those glittery lines I would hang a rainbow of silk scarves we had just received from China. I could just see them fluttering like butterflies under the lanterns from the breeze I would create from a fan concealed on the floor. Imagine, I thought—Chinese butterflies in the middle of Los Angeles. All at Marvin's! I couldn't wait to do it and see Auntie's reaction.

When I'd finished—it took me four full days—my handiwork caught the eye of everyone passing by, even construction workers walking past or men in gardening trucks slowed down to look at the windows as they were driving by. People waiting for the bus peered into the window as if looking into a crystal ball—searching for something magical. As often as I could, I'd stand off to the corner inside the store and watch onlookers staring at the displays without their knowing I was there. Looking at them as they enjoyed what I had created inspired me to think of even more interesting possibilities.

Then, that Friday afternoon, Auntie Glad returned. I stood proudly by my creation and plugged in the lights and fan. To my horror, the velvet had drooped and got stuck in the fan blades, knocking down the line holding up the scarves. Electric sparks went flying in the air like swarming June bugs. Auntie Glad screamed.

I tried to correct the problem but she just went on hollering at me as she realized that I had used her most expensive materials—and that in addition these had faded from exposure to the sun. I spent the next few hours putting everything away. Auntie didn't speak to me for a week. From then on I was allowed to use only items that were inexpensive, wouldn't fade—and I was never again allowed to plug in anything.

It wasn't easy making tamale pots look as good as silk scarves. But I couldn't restrain myself. I started creating unpredictable scenes using strange combinations of materials, such as dozens of plastic rabbits in various poses, copper and silver scouring pads, and rolls of chicken wire. I positioned the rabbits in and out of the pots and pans with candy bar wrappers strewn all around, and chocolate smeared on their faces. All these rested on a bed of brightly-colored kitchen items, more than you could ever imagine in one place. I even made hats out of Brillo pads and ribbon remnants for the lady rabbits. The gentlemen rabbits carried walking sticks made from rulers. I was sure that at night they all had a great time.

By the fourth of July, I was back in Auntie's good graces, and she put me in charge of the displays and decorations inside the store as well as in the windows. My job continued into the school year on Saturdays. I couldn't have been happier.

By December, when I was on Christmas vacation, we went into high gear. I had so many plans for what to do, and so many things for Christmas to display, that Auntie Gladys brought in some of her poker-playing friends to help out, among them her closest friend, Roxie. Roxie was the first Armenian redhead with freckles that I'd ever seen, as well as the first woman I'd ever met who carried around a cigarette tucked behind her ear like a pencil.

To discourage shoppers from stealing, Auntie Glad also brought in a lady wrestler friend with the professional name of Goldie Locks. *Truly*. I had already met Goldie back when she arranged to have my picture taken on the shoulders of Bobeeg's favorite wrestler, Gorgeous George, when he made a guest appearance at the opening of the A&P. Goldie had long, curly bleached-blond hair, just like Gorgeous George, but with about three inches of black roots showing so people would know she was Armenian by birth not Swedish or Norwegian. Even though she changed her name, she loved being Armenian. "Armenians have passion, kid, and that's something Americans don't know about," she'd tell me. "It's what makes me a winner in the ring and a winner in life." She then flexed her arm to impress me with her winning strength.

Showing passion wasn't for me. I felt passionate about a lot of things, but I tried not to show it. I had already discovered that being cool like Americans rather than showing what you felt didn't leave me half so vulnerable. But I liked Goldie's passion a lot.

Roxie and Goldie reported to me for instructions, even though they were grownups and I was a thirteen-year old. Both were big, strong women, so they would climb the ladders and string lights and ornaments and stretch red and green crepe paper banners from one end of the store to the other. They moved display tables around like they were matchboxes.

"Hey, boss kid, where do you want these sparkly things to go?" Rox shouted down from a ladder top.

"Azad, don't lift that big box, you little squirt," Goldie would say. "Here, let me do it." She followed me around like Mama Jahn would have if she had been there, protecting me from any possible danger, such as boxes from the storeroom falling on me.

We filled the whole place with gigantic glittering Christmas tree ornaments in all sorts of shapes and colors, the kind only seen in banks and big department stores. Auntie Glad got them in a trade for a gambling debt from the bank manager across the street from last year. She didn't believe in using money for things if it was possible. She swapped things for services whenever she could — like pots and pans for credit at the taco stand—and when she had to spend cash for clothes she always bought them on sale —

even buying clothes too big for her because the extra-large size was the same price as the small but you got more fabric for the same price. Her seamstress then re-arranged the extra yardage to make squares for patchwork quilts she sold at the store. Auntie was inventive.

Auntie Gladys decided that this year Marvin's needed a live appearance from the best toy salesman in America: good old Santa Claus. Just the mention of his name seemed to conjure up dollar signs to her. She advertised Santa's arrival weeks ahead of time with a big sign in both English and Spanish, painted on the main window display. A week before Santa's scheduled appearance she added a countdown to the number of days until Santa's arrival until, the day before, the sign announced:

SANTA CLAUS IS COMING TO MARVIN'S
TOMORROW MORNING AT TEN!

The next day by nine o'clock a long line of people—mamas, tias, abuelas, primos and primas, and all their excited niños and niñas—coiled around the block in front of Marvin's waiting for Santa. The "nut man" and the "tamale man" wheeled their carts up and down the street. People were eating and having a fine time visiting in line. The women exchanged ideas of what to buy for their children for Christmas, and talked in eager anticipation of this big event happening right in our neighborhood. There had never been a store with Santa Claus so close to home, as long as anyone could remember. Someone had heard of the dentist across the street wearing a Santa hat and a big white beard when a crying child needed a filling last week. But other than that, all of Santa's appearances were in the big department stores downtown, a long way on the R-car or an hour's ride on the bus.

But at eleven o'clock, still no Santa—and no one knew where he was: Uncle Leo, who was to play Santa, was late. Auntie Gladys called everywhere looking for him, but couldn't find him. She sent people out to his usual haunts, but they came back empty-handed.

How long could her customers be kept waiting before they got tired of standing in line? I could see Auntie Glad picturing beautiful dollar bills flying out the window. She had to think of something quick. It could turn ugly outside if Santa didn't get here right away.

"Never mind, I'll think of something," she barked into the phone. Then, with both eyebrows pointing in towards her nose, she slammed the receiver onto its cradle so hard it made the register ring and the cash drawer open just like I imagined a payoff at a Vegas slot machine.

"Jackpot!" I blurted. Then, as Auntie turned to me with a frown, I covered my mouth. "I'm sorry, Auntie, I didn't mean . . ."

She ignored what I was saying as her eyes took on a calculating look. She sized me up, top to bottom. Now her voice was smooth, winning again. "Azad, you're almost as tall as me now . . . "

Which wasn't much to say, since she was only five feet tall, I thought. But what was she driving at?

"Yes, you've really grown up this year." With a twinkle in her eye she turned to her posse of employees and said, "Ladies, the kid here's our gift from heaven. Azad will be Santa! Come on. Let's get the suit on her."

Goldie was on crowd control outside keeping everyone in good spirits by passing out signed publicity photos of herself in costume, while flexing her muscles for the women, and swinging the children hanging on her enormous arms.

"I think we can get it to fit..." and with a safety pin here, a big fold there, lots of tucks and Scotch tape to pull up the legs, Auntie Gladys announced, "You look darn good to me. Men! Who needs them?"

"But Auntie Gladys," I protested, "how can I be Santa? I'm totally the wrong person... remember, I'm best at decorating the windows not sitting in them . . . I'm just not cut out for this . . ."

"This isn't my fault . . . blame your Uncle Leo. That man; I'm gonna sock him right in the middle of his big fat red nose when I see him."

"But, Auntie, I don't want to do it. I like working behind the scenes."

"You gotta do this for me, Azad, I've got no one else to be Santa. We need everybody available today to work the crowd and ring up sales. It's you or nobody. Hasn't your Auntie Gladys always been good to you? And, you know that if Mama Jahn were here right now, reading your cup, she'd see a big white beard in it because she knows what has to be done."

"Get a grip, kid, you're not alone, we'll watch your back," Roxie said to me between her clenched teeth while sucking on a cigarette, "You're it! Now get out there and Ho, Ho, Ho the crowd."

"Yeah, kid. It's Christmas. Get into the spirit of the thing!" piped in Goldie. "Just think of how you felt when you were with Georgous George. Now it's your turn to make all the little kiddies happy."

I felt my body weaken and resign itself to the challenge. After all, they weren't asking me to be a Turk. Being Santa Claus was actually a huge American honor.

My Las Vegas loving Auntie Gladys put her hands on my shoulders from behind and pushed me forward to the empty chair in the window display and said, "Go get 'em kid. Auntie needs a new pair of shoes."

"Open the doors, Rox," she ordered throwing her arms wide open, and then with a welcoming smile on her face, Auntie Glad greeted the crowd in Spanish saying, "Welcome to your friendly neighborhood gift headquarters!" And in Armenian she said, *Come on in and spend, spend, spend. Let's make Auntie Gladys happy to be alive.*

From my high place of distinction I looked out through the window into the faces of the people pressed against the glass and I saw myself reflected in their eagerness. Can I make believers out of them? I'll shatter their belief in

166

Santa if I come across as a fake. This was an enormous responsibility. I was ready for new experiences of life outside my home, but at the same time I never considered being Santa as a vehicle for self-discovery.

The first child on my lap was about five years old and it was obvious by the way he trembled when he looked up at me that I was believable. When I looked into his dark bright eyes I saw the excitement of my first magnificent window display, the one with the Chinese lanterns and silk scarves fluttering in the breeze. His belief made me a believer—a believer in myself. And, so, in the best, low, grown-up man's voice I could deliver, I asked the most important question of all to a child to which the answer is always correct: "And what do you want Santa to bring you for Christmas?"

He whispered, "A silver Schwinn bike, Santa—that's what I want."

Who wouldn't want a silver Schwinn bike? I wanted a silver Schwinn bike too!

I told him, "Santa" told him, he'd be getting one just like the ones sold at Marvin's, if he was a good boy.

I gave him a candy cane and sent him down off my lap and out of the window display as fast as I could to his mama who was waving the receipt for the bike in her hand for "Santa" to see.

So this is what it's like being God, I thought. God hears the secret desires of the heart, too, just like Santa. The kid was set for Christmas and I made his wish come true just like I had bought it for him myself.

The overwhelmed, awestruck little boy ran back to give me a big hug before leaving. It was clear that I was Santa and all together the entire staff of Marvin's clapped and hooted and Goldie Locks put two of her big chubby neck-cracking fingers in her mouth and let out a loud whistle. I had made a believer out of the little boy, and his belief gave me the courage I needed to believe in myself as Santa for the rest of the day—kind and happy and warm and giving and every kid's best friend—promising them anything they wanted, as long as Marvin's sold it.

But when Auntie Gladys began hitting the bell on the counter in rapid succession and moving her arm up and down, like she was winning big time at the one arm bandit slot machines, it reminded me that Auntie Gladys wasn't just thinking about making children happy. She was a shopkeeper, and her job was to make as much money as she could.

Near the end of the day I began belting out, "Ho, Ho, Hoooooo" as loud as I could with the fervor of the Armenian protestant preachers proclaiming, "Jesus, Jesus, Jeeeesus!" And the gleeful cheers of "*Olé!*" from the crowd every time I *Ho, Ho, Ho'ed* was like a curtain call at the theater. I was center stage at the Pantages and I was the actor everyone was waiting to see.

167

And I was boiling hot in the costume, perspiring like crazy, and couldn't even scratch my nose, because everyone was watching every move I made. I was tired of sitting and I wanted to get up and stretch my legs but I couldn't move. The show had to go on! It was worth it because I was the one who made the kids quiver. When I spoke they cheered. When I promised, everyone believed.

I loved being someone other than myself.

It sounded like this was going to be the best Christmas ever for Auntie Gladys. The bells were ringing and I don't mean they were ringing from the Catholic Church down the street calling people to mass. I could hear the cash register ringing up one sale after another with hardly a pause between the rings, and I saw Auntie bending over behind the counter many times throughout the day as she counted money from the register and stuffed it in the secret pockets Mama Jahn had sewn inside her work smock.

Auntie Gladys sent me my favorite candy, Babe Ruth, burritos, string cheese, potato chips and bottles of Cokes throughout the day to keep up my strength and blew me lots of kisses through the air every time our eyes met.

It was a great day for everyone . . . except Uncle Leo. He poked his head into Marvin's the last hour of the day and Auntie Gladys threw a baseball at him yelling, "Leo, you bum, it's three strikes and you're out! Don't you come around me today, you big horse's ass." Everyone yelled, "*Olé!*"

No matter what happened with Uncle Leo, I knew that I was going to get a fabulous Christmas present from Auntie Gladys for all the hard work I did. She was the best gift giver and she knew I wanted a portable radio. Weeks ago I had stocked the radio I wanted in a place she'd be able to see from the cash register, and I dropped hints about how much it would mean to me to have it for Christmas. And when I saw it was gone off the shelf right after Thanksgiving, I just knew she had put it aside for me.

The next week on Christmas Day, when all the presents were spread out under the tree, I confidently waited for my special gift. It could have been the A-line camel coat we saw at Ohrbach's in downtown Los Angeles or the pearl ring the jewelry salesman showed us two weeks ago. Even though I really wanted that radio, no matter what it was I knew it would be the best gift.

Our family gave out gifts the same way every year. All of us sat in front of the Christmas tree at our house and Auntie Gladys pulled on a Santa hat and announced, "Here comes Santa," as she passed out presents to everyone in the family. This year I patiently waited my turn as, one-by-one, she went around the room giving each person one gift at a time and we all watched it being opened and oohed and ahhed at whatever it was.

I got the ordinary things from everyone else, like a yellow sweater set for school from Hayrig and Mother and a multicolored crocheted afghan from Mama Jahn, a book on Audrey Hepburn from Auntie Zov, and a pink nightgown from my cousin Sossi and slippers from Uncle Mono. And still there was no big gift from Auntie Gladys.

The last gift under the tree was for Raffi. It was an olive green and white clock radio, the newest thing. He went crazy with excitement. I was stunned. As he opened it, I thought, surely this was a mistake…this has got to be my present. But, no, it wasn't mine. I sat there in front of the empty space under the tree, trying to hold back tears from spilling out of me, feeling lost and confused and all of a sudden very betrayed by Christmas and Auntie Gladys. What about my great command performance as Auntie Glady's store Santa?

As we started to move toward Mama Jahn's desserts, Auntie Gladys suddenly fumbled around the back of the tree pretending she was surprised to see one more present.

Too much time had gone by—too much to redeem her, and I wasn't taken in by the fumbling. She pulled out a box with a tag and read aloud, "To Azad, a very good girl, from Santa." While everyone in the room—they were all in on the gag—sat quietly staring at me, I began to open the box, and as I began to open it, I started to cry. I wanted to run out of the room.

Everyone's eyes on me felt intrusive and painful. It didn't matter that it was a red portable radio—just like the kind the American blond, blue-eyed girls all had. It didn't matter that it was gorgeous and beyond my wildest dreams. What mattered was that she had intentionally humiliated me.

This was my Auntie Gladys's idea of a joke. Like a lot of her jokes at the expense of others, it wasn't funny. I tried to laugh, pretending to "get it" for everyone to see that I was "cool," a good American sport, but I wasn't laughing. I was angry at being left out on the most important day for presents, even as a joke, and I was embarrassed about showing those feelings to everyone in the family. A happy response was a lot to ask of anyone, particularly a hardworking thirteen-year-old.

"Look at Azadouhi," Uncle Mono said with pity in his voice. "She's really upset. Why does radio upset her so much?"

"Maybe it's the wrong kind of radio. I don't know. Just stay out of it," said Auntie Zov. Together, they looked at me as if I were beyond understanding.

Everyone's reaction infuriated me. It really did. What girl, or even an adult, wouldn't be crushed to be left out? And after all I had done for Auntie Glad! Why would she want to humiliate me? And now that she had humiliated me, what could I do about it? My jarbig self kicked in.

Later on that night, after dinner, when everyone was busy eating from Mama Jahn's lavish dessert table, where the main attraction was her special Christmas cheorag made with crushed walnuts, I found myself looking at Uncle Leo with new eyes. He had been desolate ever since he angered Auntie

Gladys by not showing up to be Santa, but I considered his position for the first time. It couldn't be easy to be married to such a woman, I thought. If she could do this to me—and I was a little angel by comparison to Uncle Leo—what mental tortures had she inflicted on him over the years? I was a little young to have major insights into adult behavior, but on some level I was putting together a vague impression that my self-centered aunt's mocking might have turned Uncle Leo into the loser he was.

The path to revenge cobbled itself and I sashayed right over it, approaching Uncle Leo sympathetically. Next thing I knew, I had offered him a special Christmas present—the gift of reading his coffee cup. He knew I too had "the gift" of being able to decipher fortunes from all the squiggles and blobs of the dark demitasse coffee sediment. I had learned well from Mama Jahn over the years. He took me up on it. So together we peered into his coffee grounds. And to Uncle Leo's great surprise—miracles of miracles, joy to the world and "tanks be to God"—his fortune was revealed!

Quietly, while everyone was busy with Mama Jahn's cheorag, I gestured to those lines and curves and swirls and said with feigned amazement that, oh, gosh, look at that, they disclosed exactly where he could find the money Santa had made for Auntie Gladys—stashed in the secret pockets of her work smock. Uncle Leo's eyes lit up like our Christmas tree and he started to drool.

I had believed Auntie Gladys and she had used that belief against me. Now, I told myself, it was time to put all my trust in myself. If those children had believed that I, a twelve year old Armenian girl, was Santa—and they had—there was no stopping me. I could forever pretend to be anything I wanted to be, like completely American—amusing and outgoing, the life of the party and always very cool . . . as long as I didn't do so at the expense of others. No one would ever guess I was half and half.

20 THE EXPERIMENT CUP

her hair is long, but her mind is short

Somewhere between junior high and senior high school I began to look like the person I was to become, and luckily that person resembled a TV character named Betty, whose father called her "Princess" in *Father Knows Best*. Everyone at school said so. I didn't have Betty's cute bouncy pony tail, but with my hair pulled back into a long braid you couldn't guess I had curly hair. Since practically all Americans watched *Father Knows Best*, my looks gave me some kind of unearned panache.

During this time of transition, as I fought my way out of the nightmare of puberty, my mother completely shattered my illusion that no one could really see the hair growing on my upper lip except me. I had been bleaching those grotesque facial hairs all summer and thought they had faded away from sight. Clearly, I was wrong because Mother noticed, and if she noticed, the kids at school would too. Princess Betty didn't have facial hairs.

Hirsute women and Armenian women are almost one in the same, so much so that our Armenian deli kept boxes of facial bleach and depilatories on the counter above the feta cheese and Greek olives. The picture of the lady on the boxes was definitely not the lady behind the counter, the original bearded lady. I wanted to try all the hair removal products to see if they really worked, but my mother had other plans for getting rid of my facial hair, using me as a guinea pig for an approach that she herself had never tried.

On a Saturday morning while Mother and Mama Jahn were busy with preparations for a tea party for Der Hayr and the Armenian Church Ladies Auxillary meeting at our home, Mother asked Bobeeg to drive me to an Armenian lady, Digeen Hanoyian, who was a practitioner of the ancient Middle Eastern art of hair removal.

Digeen Hanoyian looked at me through narrowed eyes as she greeted me at the door and ushered me in, a single arm gesture pointing the way to a miniscule room at the rear of an old office building. I was immediately captivated by a black birthmark on her chin, a birthmark adorned with one thin white hair. I wondered why she didn't get rid of it. If not the ugly mole, why not remove that one hair since removing hair was her business?

I sat in an old barber chair as Digeen Hanoyian stood in front of me and produced a strand of red thread from her pocket. It smelled as if she had pulled it from a pickle barrel. Swiftly, with the finesse of an experienced seamstress putting the finishing touches on the hem of a skirt, she used the red thread to twist off the hairs on my upper lip at their roots. I experienced no real pain, just shock as she came as close to my face as a dentist drilling a cavity. Now I knew why she left the hair in the middle of her birthmark—so her clients could stare at it while she did her handiwork on our hairy faces. It was hypnotizing.

When I got home Mama Jahn took me by my elbow and paraded me around the parlor for all the ladies to view my upper lip, as if I were a pet who had just been to the groomer. It was utterly mortifying. "Ah-sheh (look), looking at Azad, everyones. No more sev maz (black hair), on her lip. I very proud to see this day," said Mama Jahn. All the ladies and Der Hayr smiled and nodded their heads in agreement. I wanted to die.

Fortunately, before I was pushed in front of Der Hayr, he returned to his dish of Mama Jahn's preserved figs. She made them every year using the black mission figs that grew on our very own fig tree in the front yard. Der Hayr said the figs reminded him of the Old Country and the joyous memories he had growing up playing in the family orchard.

Mother went to sit next to him and patted his hands saying, "Der Hayr, our tree is laden with fruit during the growing season. Please, help yourself to them when you're driving by our home. We'd be honored if you did." He was touched, as were all the ladies in the room. It was a very nice gesture to offer to our hard working priest. This fig-related largesse took the focus off of my lip, for which I was truly grateful.

After four hair removal treatments I showed my lip to my mother in frustration. "See this hair. It's all come back and it's even blacker and thicker than before! Pretty soon I'll be able to braid it!" Her role in this failed maternal experiment could not be denied.

"That fraud, Digeen Hanoyian . . . I'm not going to throw away money on treatments that don't last. Go back to bleaching," was her advice. "You've always wanted to be a blonde anyway." I really resented my mother, more and more, and her blasé attitude was infuriating.

Not only was there hair on my upper lip, but there was thick black hair under my arm pits. How absolutely animalish, I thought. It was impossible for me to wear sleeveless blouses unless I never raised my arms. And the hair didn't stop there. It was suddenly as if I was made of hair. It grew all up and down my legs and on my arms. Like all my imperfections, I thought, the black hair wasn't a force of nature but was instead an additional unfolding manifestation of the birth curse, a horror that I'd have to live with for the rest of my life until something happened to break the spell. Any time not spent obsessing over my *freakish appearance* was spent in delusion, or that's how it seemed anyway.

Since the day that the Virgin Mary intervened with God when Mama Jahn was dying and broke the spell of her death cup, I'd been waiting for her to save me too. That's what I secretly prayed for and wished for every time I looked in the mirror and many times in between. And being a good Armenian, I kept looking for manifestations.

For several months I singed the hideous hairs growing on my arms over the open flame of the kitchen gas stove, a time-honored approach I had witnessed many times before I ever had any arm hair. Sometimes, when Hayrig came home from work he'd say, "We are either having chicken for dinner or the ladies in the house have smooth arms again."

That *Coral Islands* lipstick had Herculean challenges to overcome. Even the hair on my head was an Augean stable of its own. Here again, Mother had been complicit in various failed schemes to get it under control. She took me to hairdressers who decided the best thing was for my hair to be thinned so it wouldn't stick out. So they chopped away at the layers of thick curly hair and created a bush that stuck out in all directions, a topiary that got bigger and bushier as it grew. By high school, I had rolled it, bobby pinned it, clipped it, flipped it, tugged it, ironed it, under-a-plastic-dryer-bonnet dried it, oiled it, conditioned it, a million times brushed it, into a smelly-rubber-bathing-cap shoved it, clipped it, thinned it, braided it, in-a-knit-cap stuffed it, teased it, and always hated it. While I probed the mirror in a search for better solutions, life went on.

A few weeks after the Digeen Hanoyian debacle, my mother dashed to the living room window, pulled back the sheers behind the curtain and exclaimed, "Look, there's Der Hayr picking our figs again. He's been here every other day for the past two weeks stripping our tree of all its fruit. What a greedy man."

"But you told him he could," I said, taking Der Hayr's side because hadn't Mother already demonstrated that she couldn't be trusted? Not her maternal skills, particularly as they related to my hair, and not her invitation to share figs.

"Yes, but that was just the polite thing to say at the time. What kind of a person would pick someone's fruit? Just like an Armenian."

Like me, Mother had a love-hate relationship with her ethnicity. She stood there, glued to the window, tsking and cursing him in Armenian. No one is as vengeful as an Armenian. It bothered her so much that he was stripping our tree of figs that she had a gardener cut the entire tree down to a stump. Then she waited and watched at the window to catch the reaction of Der Hayr the next time he came for figs. When he drove up the next day he stood at the curb, molleratdz (confused), while he scratched his head and looked around like he was expecting to see the tree in different location.

His apoplexy so delighted my mother that she celebrated by taking me to a beauty shop where she sometimes got her hair done in a French Twist for parties. "Hi, hon, my name is Vivian," the white skinned middle-aged lady with short black, straight hair and a comb and scissors in her hand said to me. "Whatarewegonnadowiththishair? It's a mess!"

Tell us something we don't know, my mother and I thought in unison.

"I don't want it cut short, that's for sure."

"Well, well, this is the biggest hair I've ever seen. Let me see what I can do. Sit back and relax, hon."

Relax, I thought, *how can I relax?* This was the biggest burden of my life and she's asking me to relax?

I acted like I was relaxed as she touched it and tugged at it, walked all around it and while she shook her head and wrinkled her nose at it. Then she took me to a washbowl and I sat as she washed it, massaged it and poured bottles of sweet smelling conditioners over it while she combed them into my hair.

Back to the chair she put in big rollers and put my head under a hot dryer for an hour. When she took the big pink rollers off my head my hair was smooth and bounced as if it were saying, "Boooi-ng, boooooi-ng, booooooi-ng, now this is the real me! This is the hair I'm intended to be. I may not be blond but I am smooth and bouncy."

I didn't break my cool by screaming for joy but I did smile.

"Now, hon, you've gotta come back every week if you want your hair to look nice like this all the time. Will you do that, hon?"

I nodded in the affirmative, even knowing my family wouldn't pay ten dollars a week for me to have a hairdo and I couldn't make that much money babysitting at fifty cents an hour on Friday and Saturday nights.

Anyway, why would I have to go back? The results were perfect. Vivian had fixed whatever was wrong with it all these years, and now it was wonderful. I couldn't stop looking at myself in any mirror I passed by. St. Vivian was a miracle worker.

I went to school the next day proud and happy with my hair for the first time in my life. I went to my first class, physical education, and—wouldn't you know it? It was the first day of swimming.

When I got out of the pool at the end of class, my hair was dripping wet under the bathing cap. As it dried during my second period history class, I could feel its volume increasing overhead. It had returned to its true self— curly and frizzy—sticking out all over the place. For all of tenth grade I looked as if I were wearing a whole Persian lamb on my head.

Still, I was not without potential. My homeroom teacher nominated me for class vice president. He admired me for my intelligence, just like my family. I was the good student and the good girl in school as well as at home, following all the rules and studying hard. That was my job, wasn't it? To repopulate diminished numbers of Armenian intellectuals? Because I'd always been a good student, it was hard to feel puffed up and proud of myself for the nomination. What I yearned for instead was a cute boyfriend first, popularity second.

Nevertheless, the campaign trail loomed. All those nominated had to give a campaign speech at the school assembly. Despite all the chattering I'd done to my friends and at home, I had never spoken in front of a large group before. Our family was a big group but not big enough to fill an auditorium. Still, I was not without resources. Hayrig was used to giving speeches, so I went to him for help.

"Just write what I dictate to you, Azad, and you'll have a winning speech."

So I wrote down everything he said and memorized it for the next day. Then I went to work on my campaign wardrobe.

I put on a powder blue, full felt skirt, a cinch belt in a deeper shade of blue, and a white three-quarter sleeve Ship'n'Shore blouse. I looked sharp. I put my hair in a long braid and that kept it neat, too. And of course, I put on lipstick. I had a new color which I loved, *Cherry Blossom*. The new shoes, the white bucks that I just had to have, looked really neat and sharp too, but didn't fit right. Despite the enlarging blisters on the heels of my feet, I didn't let on. I hoped my careful gait made me look more serious as I walked across the stage. A vice president needed to be serious.

I approached the microphone with confidence that the "best person" would win. Since I was the smartest, I was the best person for the job and I would win the election. Positive thinking in action.

Looking at the sea of faces, I began my short but succinct speech, "If you vote for me I pledge to have your best interests always at heart when I attend student government meetings, and I will work to the best of my abilities to ensure your academic success."

There was polite applause from the student body and big smiles from the faculty.

Then Carla Carter leapt from her chair and bounced over to the podium, her lovely blond hair waving in sync with her hands. She was wearing her short little cheerleading skirt in school colors with white tennis shoes. For a serious position like vice president, I thought, I had it in the bag by contrast to her cheerleader style. The kids would see through her silly gestures and vote for me, the serious, smart one.

Carla started with an exuberant, "Hi, everyone!" She got loud applause and hoots just from speaking in her rah-rah voice. "Vote for me and I'll work with your president, Donnie, to make this a really fun year."

And then she sat down. Everyone knew that Donnie was her boyfriend, running unopposed for president in this same election. There was thunderous clapping, stomping of feet and whistling when she finished. *Fun year?* I sank into my chair considering voting for her, too. She was so darn cute.

The next day Carla won the election by a landslide. She won because she was cute personified—pug nose, white skin, great smile, easy uncomplicated rhetoric and of course bouncy blond hair. She didn't have lipstick but she had cute. And stuck being a smart kid with a good personality but not cute, I couldn't criticize "the cuties" enough. Most of my criticism was inaudible, a running internal commentary on the shortfalls of being an attractive American teenage girl.

My relationship with members of the opposite sex was one of fraternity. The "hiya, Ahzie's" and the "atta-girls," and the light punches on the arm were an expression of their acceptance. As an acknowledged girl jock, I was practically one of them. The boys who weren't athletic, the brainy boys, could relate to me intellectually.

Nevertheless, I was as much a victim of my hormones as any other red-blooded American girl. I was attracted to a boy named Skip who had wavy reddish hair, very light skin, and a great wide smile—obviously not an Armenian. (Already I was making progress on bad ol' Masha's directive, being drawn to odars.) He was the captain of the junior baseball team and a great first baseman. I longed for Skip to notice me, not just as a pal to kid around with, but as a potential girl friend.

I got a great idea from a program I listened to on my transistor radio on the school bus every morning. I listened intently as a psychologist instructed, "Gals, go ahead and ask that certain someone out. He's just too shy to ask you first. Remember, boys like girls with a good personality even more than good looks."

"Great personality" was my middle name. Everyone was always telling me that. I learned to be fun from my Aunt Gladys and television shows. I was especially good at interjecting snappy asides when the kids were talking about something. For instance, when Skip was showing a bunch of us his new rabbit's foot he got for playing baseball, I said, "Lucky for you, but not for the original owner." Everyone cracked up. It happened all the time.

I worked to get up my nerve by memorizing a long list of one-liners — "Can vegetarians eat animal crackers?" "I've been on so many blind dates, I should get a free dog." "I wondered why the Frisbee was getting bigger and then it hit me." So after many days of deliberating over what the psychologist said on the radio, I did it.

The gags worked. Since Skip was laughing and grabbing my arms and tickling me after each punch line, I decided *this was the time*. And with no more preamble, I blurted out, "Hey, how about taking me to the sock hop next Saturday?" Skip blanched and backed away. It was like I had said I had TB. I could see my words just fall in a heap of jagged pieces to the ground. I wanted to reach back into time and take back what I had just said the moment I saw his reaction. I wanted to die. Skip just stood there, stone faced, and said, "I've got other plans." And that was it.

Never, never, never again did I ever think that anyone in high school would be interested in going out with me. I was done with listening to pop psychologists. I would remain the class clown and never try to attract anyone cute. That was it. I swept my obviously hopeless hopes and dreams into a pathetic pile labeled "loser," and muffled them in massive quantities of teenage self-pity and loneliness. No one was like me. No one understood me. My family members, God Bless Them, were each in their own worlds and couldn't help me. No one could.

Not until the eleventh grade did I meet Connie, a science whiz, who was fearless, right up to the point of passing me sharp objects. She gave me a razor and told me to shave the hair on my legs and under my arms using the lather from the bar of soap in the shower. Just like that. I couldn't believe the change in how I looked with all the hair gone. Problem solved. One day soon after, I went to her house to work on a project and she got another bright idea.

"Ahzie, let's straighten your hair. It'll look great straight. I know we can do it using a home permanent kit. We'll just reverse the process. It makes sense, doesn't it? It'll be a snap. We'll just pour it on your hair, comb it through for the same amount of time that a permanent would be on your hair and then wash it out. After that we'll put the solution on it to stabilize it. Just like a perm except we'll comb it straight instead of rolling it up in rollers to get curly. Logical, yes?"

Connie made such good sense. And she got all A's in science, so she must have known what she was talking about.

Of course I said, "Yes, let's do it." The lure of wanting straight hair was strong enough to obfuscate any common-sense questions.

We did exactly as Connie suggested. And after the final rinse, and application of the conditioner that came in the box, when we combed out my hair, it was absolutely and positively as straight and smooth as satin, a lot of satin. It was the exact opposite of a permanent, just as she had predicted. She was smart about what to do with my hair, which looked great for the first time in my life, and I was smart to trust her

The next morning she called me to come over.

"Ahzie, see what I've donated in the interest of science and your good looks? Look at my nails, they've all dropped off."

"Oh, no, Connie...what can we do? Let's soak your fingers in yogurt."

"No Armenian remedies, thank you very much. Just help me gather my nails. We can put them under my pillow for the nail fairy!"

Her nails grew back and were longer and stronger than before. Like the hair on my upper lip, which I continued to bleach.

Connie was a genius. I couldn't believe that my earnest desire for straight hair had finally been realized. Had the Virgin Mary sent Connie? She certainly was a miracle. Even though I admired blondes above all other hair colors, I was content with my dark brunette hair . . . now that it was under control. This contentment harkened back to Veronica and Betty from the *Archie* comic book characters. (I had read *Archie* religiously in the fifth grade. How else was I to find out how to act like an American teenager?) Betty was the unhappy, wimpy one and she was blond. Veronica was the attractive brunette. She was also calculating, sexy and shrewd—all personality traits I admired in my female odar friends, and, in my advancing years, aspired to acquiring myself.

Being convinced that I was still in the grip of the evil eye seemed to give me the go-ahead for becoming calculating, sexy, shrewd and well coiffed. I couldn't help myself. I wanted to be a bad American, not a good Armenian.

21 THE CUP OF ALLEGIANCE

in attempting to fix the brow, do not damage the eye

Straight hair gave me a chance to be a real American.

I celebrated by gazing at my new hair at every opportunity, whether in a mirror, a storefront glass window, a shiny stock pot or the wide edge of a butter knife. I couldn't get over the fact that my cursed hair was now divinely straight instead of a curly, frizzy mess. With straight hair I could do anything. A new world was opening up to me. I felt it not just on my head, but all throughout my body.

When I walked, just a normal kind of walking here and there, my hair swung back and forth. Instead of feeling itchy and scratchy where it rubbed against my neck, my hair now felt like cascading strands of silk caressing my skin. I tossed it out of my eyes with a shake of my head. I touched it often, twirled lengths of it with my fingers and continually combed it. All the lovely sensations I had thought about all my life were now mine.

Back combing hair was a big fad. I'd take a rattail comb, part sections on top of my head and tease them high and then smooth strands over the teasing. My goal was to tease it high so I could look taller than 5' 3". I let the rest of my hair flow over my shoulders.

For this true miracle, I thanked the Virgin Mary and crossed myself many times over. Throughout my life, I had developed the habit of crossing myself in my mind, so that no one could see what I was doing, except at church. That way no one knew how much I counted on God. I was embarrassed that someone would think that I was what Hayrig called a *religious fanatic.*

Nevertheless, I now had proof that Connie was my best friend in the whole world and furthermore that the Virgin Mary was highly reliable, my own personal secret weapon and superhero. When I needed intercession—which was more and more often—I consulted the Virgin Mary to talk to God for me and explain the pains in my heart in a way He would understand. The Virgin Mary and Connie were reliable. My family ever less so.

When Hayrig saw my smooth hair for the first time, he patted my head and said, "I told you that brushing your hair fifty-two times every night would some day produce lovely smooth locks of hair. Proof I was right."

Oh Hayrig, not everything you say is right for me. Can't you see that? I thought, without saying anything aloud. It wasn't worth a long discussion.

Mother was skeptical. She knew Connie had straightened my hair chemically and examined my hair like a doctor examining strands for signs of weakened root shafts and damaged hair follicles and lice. She warned, "It could still all fall out one day as a result of all those chemicals." I wasn't worried.

Nothing she could say would upset me. Hadn't her approaches, what few of them she'd actually deigned to administer, been a total failure?

And Mama Jahn remained sure the latchag she had tied on my head all my young life had done the trick. She liked the looks of my hair, but she didn't like it teased. "You looking like criminal girl with hair that big."

Lovely Mama Jahn. Your latchag is just a rag that has done nothing for me all these years except make my head hot at night.

Aunt Zov, on the other hand, began teasing her hair, too, once she saw mine. Was I finally getting some credibility in the household?

I discovered that straight hair and boys went together, because as soon as my hair was straight and bouncing all around my face, the boys straightened out, too. They paid attention to me in a different way, not like the pals they had been up to then. Were these really the same guys I used to kid around with, who used to punch me on the arm while we told each other jokes? Suddenly, they were nervous around me. They held their heads down when we were together and couldn't put two words together without stammering now.

Overnight I became cute enough to feel like one of the popular girls. I was even voted into the Delta Sigma sorority. It was a huge status thing to have the gold Greek letters hanging from a crowded chain—the blue bead, the gold cross and Greek letters all around my neck. Of course I made sure that the Greek letters were on top of the pile.

In addition to my aptitude in English and P.E., it was easy being funny. I was getting a reputation as a wise ass, the person in the class who said things everyone else was thinking but didn't say. Many of us had hit the phase wherein we thought we were a million times more fabulous than our teachers. Feelings of superiority gave us solidarity. My thoughts made me laugh, so I began to say them out loud when the teacher was talking. I interrupted with flair. Like in homeroom one day our teacher said, "Okay, you kids, get to work. What kind of bad luck do I have that I have all of you jerks in my class?" This led me to say under my breath, "Yeah, you're such a loser, if you didn't have bad luck you wouldn't have any luck at all." It wasn't nice, but it had the desired effect. Those around me cracked up, which made me feel I had the crowd in my hand. Too bad for the teacher, who hadn't heard what I said but knew I'd said something.

Our California History teacher, Mr. Magna, passed gas a lot and seemed oblivious to it. Of course, this played into our hands . . . and into my repertory. Connie would turn to me and say, "Let's count how many times he farts today." Just the thought of it would start us laughing and we'd get in trouble. At my house we called gas attacks "escaping Turks." Not until Connie did I learn that passing gas was called a fart.

So one day, after he let out a big long smelly one, I said what I had heard on the radio that morning: "Better a vacant house than a bad tenant." Everyone in the room went nuts laughing, including Mr. Magna Farter himself.

I never got in trouble for accessing my inner Auntie Gladys either. Sometimes I got dirty looks from the teachers. Sometimes they laughed along with everyone else or they pretended they didn't hear what I'd said.

At home, the reaction to my wisecracking was not enthusiastic in the least.

Hayrig and Mother were discussing choices for a birthday gift to take to Uncle Eddie's party.

"How about the new recording of popular Armenian folk songs they advertise on the Armenian radio hour that just came out?"

"I think he already has it."

"Then what about a book on Armenian poetry?"

I jumped in with: "Hey, what about an electric razor?"

"That's a marvelous idea, acheeg...what do you think, Siroon?"

And before Mother could give her thoughts I came back with, "Yah, his wife can use it too, on her face!" And I proceeded to laugh really loudly at my own joke.

"Azad, that's such an unkind thing to say. I thought you were a sweet girl."

"What is this new side to your personality, making fun of the unfortunate circumstances of others? Amot kez, shame on you."

"Can't you take a joke?"

Mama Jahn added, "Joke-moke, why you saying bad tings about Eddie's wife? You no like her anymore?"

They just don't get it! I thought. *They are so out of it.*

"I'm going over to Connie's. At least she gets me."

"What do you see in Connie?"

"Everything. She's really neat."

"Neat, she no neat," Mama Jahn says. "I see when she come here her clothes. Never she iron. She not neat."

"Mama Jahn, 'neat' means she's 'cool,' she's 'terrific,' 'sharp.' None of you know anything!" And I slammed the door behind me, sure that all their mouths were wide open.

Such were my failed attempts to bring my family into my world. Raffi was a historic irritant, so everything was pretty much the same between him and me. We still hated each other. The adults though—Hayrig, Mother, Mama Jahn, and even Auntie Zov and Uncle Mono—probably felt they had an unfeeling young Turk on their hands. An atmosphere of mutual dread and light treading crept into the household. It was easiest to go undercover.

Towards the end of the semester the drama teacher, Mrs. Peterson, put up a list for the talent show. My name was on it as the person to write the script and be the actor for the time between acts. I was shocked. I asked Mrs. Peterson why she chose me. I was waiting for her to say it was because of my sensational straight hair and instead she said, "I figured you might as well put your joking around to good use."

And now I'm being rewarded for being a smart ass by the drama teacher? Good, I'll show them what I can do. *I'll show myself what I can do* was more like it, because I had no idea what I could do. This was a great challenge. I was thrilled!

Going to the movies was part of my research. One Saturday, on my way to the candy counter for my usual Neccos while the previews were playing, I stumbled over someone's big feet. Looking down in the darkness, I recognized the shoes. Hadn't I polished those shoes last night? I looked up and I saw a man sitting on the edge of his aisle seat, devouring the coming attractions of Gene Autry's next movie. This big guy squeezed into the seat was Hayrig! —the very same man who was always talking about things like going to the movies as frivolous.

Tossing back candy, Hayrig was so captivated he didn't notice me, so I scooted across the aisle to a seat where I'd have a perfect view of him without revealing myself. I thought I knew everything about my father. This was a new one on me. What the heck was he doing here watching cowboy movies? He even had his big Stetson hat in his lap. He kept this memento—from his teenage days working in the Sheaffer Hat Company after his father died—in its big, round hatbox on the top book shelf in his den. What was Hayrig doing, with his cowboy hat, at a Saturday movie with all the kids in town? I didn't know what to think. Was this ahmot or ahmahn? I didn't know!

It was obvious Hayrig wanted to slap his thigh every time Gene Autry prodded his horse Champion to move faster. But he restrained himself. *I should hope so. He's an important attorney*, I reflected. A serious expression came over his face when the shooting began—the good guys against the bad ones.

He didn't take his eyes off the screen. As the good guys wiped out the bad guys who had beaten up the preacher's wife, shot dead the preacher and horse whipped the sheriff, before running over him with the stagecoach loaded with gold that they were now getting away with as they rode out of town, Hayrig remained riveted. As the righteous marshal, Gene Autry, was vindicated, Hayrig let himself relax into his chair. He took out the white linen handkerchief I had ironed a few days before and wiped his forehead. Justice would be served with Gene on the scene.

I wanted to blow Hayrig's cover and ask for serious candy money, but something held me back. Hayrig crept out before the full length movie started. I guessed he was there just for Gene Autry. Hmmm. I had caught him doing something he's always talking against. *Yahdash!*

Later that day, I went up to Hayrig while he was sitting at his desk in his big red swivel chair. When I leaned over and he kissed me on my forehead, I smelled the candy and popcorn on his breath and clothes. I wanted to see if he'd tell me the truth, the truth that he's always talking about that's so important to tell.

"I've been at the movies today, Hayrig. What did you do?"

"Huh, me, what did I do today? Well, acheeges, I spent my time thinking and researching the difference between the Turks, the Armenians of the Genocide and the American western heroes. I'm writing a paper on the subject to read at a conference of attorneys concerned with the rights of oppressed people. That's what I did."

"So did you find out anything interesting?"

"Yes, I think so. The American western heroes stood up for the rights of people who had everything taken from them, even their lives, by people who had no regard for order, justice, peace and in the emerging Old West. Just like what the Turks did to the Armenians. It's the same story, over and over again—the strong and mighty take from the weak. Then a hero comes to the rescue of the weak, and the order of good over evil is restored."

"But it doesn't last, does it, Hayrig?"

"That's right, Azad Jahn. It doesn't last, so we always need new heroes to help the oppressed."

"And that's what you do for our people, right, Hayrig?"

"I try, I try, with God's grace, I try." And with that he kissed me on the head again and I left his office and ambled away into the sunset, to continue my comic research.

I already watched a lot of *Jackie Gleason, Amos and Andy, I Love Lucy, Red Skelton* and *Uncle Miltie* on TV, so I knew about comedy. I mined these resources for inspiration and came up with a lot of funny things to do. I knew I had written great material because at rehearsal all the coolest kids in school were laughing out loud at what I was doing and saying. All those years of being an outsider began to fall away from me. Suddenly, my status as a one-girl Diaspora seemed insignificant. I was still one-of-a-kind, but I was the one my peers loved.

And when the time came to perform the actual talent show to an auditorium filled to capacity with parents, teachers, students and people from the community, including my family, it was an amazing experience to be applauded by thunderous clapping and whistles and cheers when I was on stage. This is what it was like being a true American, and I never wanted it to stop.

Then just before intermission I positioned myself up on the balcony where the spotlights were, way above the audience below. My plan was to have my character falling off the precipice I was clinging to. So I maneuvered to send a stuffed dummy dressed like my character over the side. The gag was great, the entire audience gasped in unison, and even though I burned a hole in my knee on the spotlight when I crouched down and sent the dummy over the edge, my idea worked.

Just as I was congratulating myself, Hayrig's booming voice filled the theater, "Azadouhi, you get down from there right this minute before you kill yourself." I had a split second of mortification, but luckily the audience thought he was part of the act, which produced a second round of laughter and applause. Everything I did was terrific. I could do no wrong. I was a star.

After the performance our school principal, Mr. Dabney, came back stage to find me. I was getting ready to change my clothes. "Azad, I'd like to introduce you to Mr. Mort Weinstein. He's a Hollywood talent agent who was here to see tonight's show."

I thought, A talent agent? I wonder what he wants with me?

"What are your plans when you graduate?" he asked.

"I'm going to college to become a teacher" was my boring reply.

"If your plans change, call me," he said, slipping me his business card. "You are very funny . . . very, very funny . . . another Carol Burnett. Television can use you and I can help you make it big in show business."

Excited beyond belief, I skipped the after show party and went straight home to show Hayrig the talent agent's card and tell him what he said. Hayrig always said that I should be the best at whatever I did, and it was obvious that I'm the best at making people laugh.

I still couldn't believe this was happening to me. Me a television star!

Hayrig, instead of being ecstatic with joy as I expected, showed me a side of himself usually directed towards Turks. He was furious!

"What do you mean—a talent scout has offered you a chance to go to Hollywood? We've lived a few miles from Hollywood all our lives, and if we had wanted you to become an actor, we would have driven you there ourselves."

"So, why haven't you taken me there all these years?" I answered snidely.

"Why? Why?" he yelled, tipping over his ashtray. "See what you made me do with your utter nonsense? The people in Hollywood are not for us. Why don't you know this, Azadouhi? It's an industry built around people who don't believe in doing anything for anyone except themselves. Is this what my daughter has become! It's a completely egomaniacal business based on greed. They are in it for the money and the ego massaging they get from their adoring fans. Is this what you are? Have you ever seen anyone in this family fall all over themselves over a movie star or a television personality?

"Well, actually, yes I have. Auntie Zov. She loves movie stars."

"Never you mind what your Aunt Zov loves. We're talking about you."

Out of the corner of my eye, I saw Aunt Zov quietly slip out of the room. She was a traitor like me.

Mother was listening from her perch on her red velvet reading chair. She quietly made her presence known, "I wouldn't want hundreds of people staring at me on a stage while I did outrageous things to make them laugh. Are you that desperate to be noticed? Anyway, who do you think you are? Lucille Ball?"

It wasn't easy being her daughter.

Uncle Mono and Mama Jahn kept on playing tavloo together, acting uninterested in the ensuing argument. They always deferred to my parents when I was trying to stand up for myself. My hayrig was a formidable presence and no one defied him. Not even me.

And Raffi, who aspired to becoming a fighter, was fully invested in watching the Baron Michele Leoni win his wrestling match with Gorgeous George. Bobeeg Jahn, who watched it with Raffi, didn't say much, because he loved me for me, not what I did. Also, he was a peacekeeper and left problems to Mama Jahn and Hayrig. At least that's what I thought. And Raffi. I certainly didn't expect anything from him.

Nevertheless, I was desperate, so out it came: "I don't see anyone telling Raffi he can't grow up to be a mean, sweaty fighter."

That did it. I was stooping to pick on a little boy.

Hayrig stood up and walked toward me sternly and with clear anger in his voice. "Azad, forget about Raffi. You are the one who carries the Avedisian name, and you have the talent to be a professional like your hayrig." And then he quoted the Bible, which he admired as literature more than spiritual revelation. "From those to whom much has been given, much will be required."

"But I didn't ask to be you, Hayrig!" I yelled as I ran for my room. "I'm *not* you! Have you ever thought that I might have my own plans for my life. It's *my* life. Not yours!"

And thus, this night of excitement, joy and public adulation, beyond anything I could ever have wished for, was erased. It turned out to be a night that no one in the family ever spoke about again. I was going to be a teacher and that was that. My destiny was sealed.

I went to my room, defeated and demoralized. I collapsed in a heap on my bed, sobbing and wailing and grinding my teeth in my sleep. No matter how loud I made my anguish, the volume did nothing to stir sympathy toward my newfound ambition in Hayrig and the rest of them.

It was days before I finally accepted the fact that they would not be moved.

Even Mama Jahn turned a cold shoulder to the idea of my calling the talent agent, after reading my coffee cup that showed textbooks and school bells as well as wedding bells in my future instead of television stars.

I couldn't believe it. "But Mama Jahn, you know I was wonderful in the show. Just like Carol Burnett. You heard them laugh. I was 'bringing the house down,' as they say in English. Let me see the cup, please." So I examined my cup every which way, hoping to find discrepancies in her interpretation. She was right. All the bells were there, staring me in the face.

Was the predictable path my family had planned for me so long ago my jagad or my curse? The only time I concerned myself with my destiny was when I wasn't getting my own way, so inevitably those long, hard looks in the mirror searching for my jagad only took place when I was worried and my brow was wrinkled. My jagad was always the same. It was the outline of a horseshoe, the unlucky side down. I could officially call myself, *Miss Fortune*.

So, as Miss Fortune I'd settle disconsolately into watching *The Carol Burnett Show*. I used to bite my finger nails while I watched TV, but now I twisted and twirled the smooth strands of my straight hair and thought about what was happening backstage. And at Carol's every move, I thought dejectedly, *I can do that. I can do that. And that too!*

It was hard to hold onto the memory of "my 15 minutes of fame" (as Andy Warhol would observe years later) without anyone talking about it. Cups or no cups, I was sick of toeing the line! So I went underground and became sneaky and took up lying to my family. It was the only way I knew how to be myself.

This wasn't like ratting out Aunt Gladys to Uncle Leo. *She* deserved it. My family didn't. So the first time I sneaked, I had to practice the betrayal and force myself to do it. The second time I sneaked, I felt guilty. By the third time, though, I was beginning to think I was a natural. Before long, I was addicted to duplicity.

My treacheries were multi-faceted.

I snuck around and met boys on Saturdays instead of being at the movies with my girl friends and didn't tell my family.

I entertained thoughts about not going to college to become a teacher and didn't tell my family.

I learned to dance watching American Bandstand with Connie at her house after school. There, Connie taught me how to smoke a cigarette. With the first puff I got horribly dizzy. She said it took getting used to as she inhaled a long stream of smoke into her lungs. I was in awe of her. She had the confidence of a movie star, the moves of a movie star, the looks of a movie star and her pulse on the teenage psyche. She was my idol and she was my pal. She hated the cuties as much as I did, but both of us wanted to be like them.

I learned how to curse—*shit, piss, damn, fart-head*—all my best new turns of phrase from Connie. And I didn't tell my family. None of this seems very grave today, or seemed so even a few years later when civil riots started breaking out at American high schools and birth control pills were invented along with psychedelic drugs and the anti-war movement. But acting as I did in defiance of my first generation Armenian family was a dramatic departure for me. And while in the mood for dramatic departures, I enrolled in drama classes at school and didn't tell my family.

At home I was back to being the good Armenian girl dusting, vacuuming, still helping make haladz yegh with Mama Jahn and pretending to enjoy my life with the family. All sweetness and obedience, all the time. This was perhaps the biggest lie of all . . . well, the next to the biggest.

The other change was that I had left off crossing myself, left off praying and—as far as the Virgin Mary was concerned—I was incommunicado, like most lying, cursing sneaks. Hard to carry on a relationship with God when my heart and mind were cutting the ties and making a go of it alone. Or so I thought.

But in high school, every day I was acting like an American teenager. And "acting" was the operative word, because whenever I washed my hair, my inner Azad re-emerged. The hair could only be brought to heel with laborious pressing and fussing several times a week. When it rained on the night of the prom, my hair frizzed up and I called Connie in a huge panic over keeping up appearances. Being a dear friend, she came over with an iron to press my hair straight for the evening and used tons of hair spray to keep it tamed. I was the masked Armenian!

No matter how much I sneaked my way to the real me, deep inside, lurking underneath the perfectly straight strands of hair, was my true identity—I was still the goofy Armenian girl with the horribly frizzy hair who feared going against the wishes of her family. But, hey, I was an actress, wasn't I? I could act like an American girl instead of an Armenian.

Escape became my escape.

22 THE WISHING CUP

don't cut the branch upon which you are standing

Pulling on my white Orlon cardigan over the spaghetti straps of the stunning ocean-blue organdy dress with a great full skirt, which I had begged to borrow from Sossi so as to make a good impression, I snatched up keys to the family Buick and bolted from the house.

"Azad, you come back here this instant," Hayrig barked.

"Not on your life," I shouted back, having the last word.

I was spitting mad at my family for trying to trick me and I had had enough of their reasons why I shouldn't go to Hollywood. There was nowhere to go with my anger except out the door, supposedly to meet my odar friends. *They try to trick me. I'll trick them!*

I had had it with them. Hayrig never relented with the well-phrased plus annotated expectations for my academic ascendance. And my mother was so wrapped up in her books and collecting bits and pieces of the origins of words that she was now writing a book on the subject. All she and Hayrig ever talked about was words, words, words. I wanted to scream some of my newly acquired vocabulary at them, but hadn't been able to get the four-lettered barrage out of my mouth loudly enough for them to hear.

They never wavered. Nice Armenian girls never leave home until they've gotten a gold band wrapped securely around their finger. *Check.* How many times had I heard this? I was destined to live with my family in Los Angeles in my little turquoise bedroom until I was married or dead. *Check.* "You have to be good wife, nice howze lady and never make him nervous." *Check.* It was all in the cups, the horrid little cups!

All my life, I had never been offered choices, except limited and insignificant ones like which color socks to wear—black or white? Or which way to shape the cheorag, in a twist or a round? Which color yarn to use to make my shawl? How much starch for Hayrig's collar? Big life choices were already made for me, most probably because of the evil eye. And there was nothing I could do about that. Every time I turned around that curse bit me on the vodeeg.

No one ever asked what I wanted to do with my life. I might have enjoyed being a baker, tossing flour, yegh and sugar together to make unique pastries and earthy breads hoards of people would line up to buy. But Hayrig would have considered shopkeeping too menial a job for his daughter. I had no alternative but to go to college, and to go to college in Los Angeles. I had been accepted at UCLA, so after summer, off I'd go, driving back and forth to home every day like a good little Armenian girl.

There again, even my coursework at college was already written in stone. There was no way I could follow the advice of the head of the high school art department, who told me to major in art. "You could be the next Arshile Gorky!" he gushed. Arshile who? I stared back at him in confusion, thinking that the only Arshile I knew was the big hairy guy who worked behind the counter at the Armenian Deli. No, I was going to major in education, acquire a lifetime teaching credential and be a teacher. Everyone knew that, and the only person who wasn't a hundred percent convinced and happy about it was, myself, Azad Avedisian.

With this prescription for my future already filled, how could I possibly have called the talent agent who gave me his business card backstage in high school? Hayrig would never have allowed it, but too bad. I was infuriated that my father thought he always knew best.

And that night was no exception. When he had seen me all dressed up and ready to leave, he insisted I stay home and visit with an Armenian family invited for dessert. He presumed without asking that I was going to be home. On the surface of it, this didn't sound so terrible. But when I saw all of Mama Jahn's specialty pastries stacked on silver serving trays and the best gold trimmed demitasse cups out on the counter next to the stove, I realized that this was no ordinary Armenian visit. It had all the trappings . . . and the markings: These people were bringing an eligible son in tow! This was one of my single-minded family's tactics to get me married and, just as important, away from the odars, the odars to which Masha had remanded me. My *friends*, in other words.

So I bolted out the front door and escaped down to the Hollywood freeway and away from Silver Lake and the family, but not to see my odar friends. I was going to The Comedy Club to see some comedy acts with Mort, the talent agent.

I put on the radio and sang *Blue Moon* with Elvis, substituting my own words—"Blue moooon, you see me standing alone, with a dream in my heart, without a life of my own . . ." The Hollywood freeway was, as it always was at night, a long, long necklace of racing headlights and taillights stretching into the distance—a beautiful, electric frenzy to carry me forward into my choices for me. My choices! I was young, talented, and alive. I couldn't sing loud enough. I couldn't drive fast enough.

And without warning, while I was mid-sentence singing, a car lurched into me from the left, and my father's car spun to the right. As my head hit the window, the taillights slid sideways and the headlights came straight at me. I closed my eyes, as the car was struck, seemingly on every side. I didn't open my eyes until the banging and lurching stopped, and only then long enough to realize that I couldn't keep them open. Sensational pain and more pain flooded my head and legs.

I tried to open my eyes, but something was very wrong with my vision. At first I thought I was dead or blind. Then I realized that blood was running down my face; that's why everything was blurry red. I couldn't move. Voices were everywhere, at the window, telling me to hold still. Soon sirens followed. My eyes closed and I waited for the pain to stop. Paramedics' hands and equipment were all over me. They had to cut off my dress to release my smashed legs from the motor of the car. Weirdly, my biggest terrors were that I had decimated Hayrig's Buick and ruined Sossi's lovely organdy dress.

I awakened in the hospital screaming with excruciating pain. Then more morphine arrived in the hands of a creature who floated into the room with large white wings on her head and a long black robe. My own personal nun calmly administered the injection as I screamed bloody murder. The effects of the blessed narcotic instantly lulled me back into a state of calm, and now my head, which was sewn together with 85 stitches, and my smashed legs, in matching casts after emergency surgery to remove all the broken parts of my knees, only hurt when anyone exhaled.

The next time I opened my eyes I saw my family standing in a line at the foot of my hospital bed. I had never seen them so orderly. They looked like they were lined up for a family photo, except no one was smiling. I felt so sorry for Mama Jahn. She looked stricken, pale and red around her eyes, with Bobeeg Jahn's arm around her. I could only imagine how she'd been suffering. I know she'd have enjoyed yelling at me in Armenian if I hadn't been so injured. And Hayrig was beside himself. He couldn't stand still with the others. Instead he was pacing and muttering, "That girl, that girl, what has she done? What has she done to herself?" Auntie Zov was crying. Uncle Mono was somber. Even my usually unsympathetic mother had tears in her eyes.

Every time my eyes opened, their mere presence in my room felt like an indictment for crimes of going against the will of my family. They were like an accusing jury. I closed my eyes. Then, instead of seeing my anxious family, I saw an imposing figure wagging a long, thin index finger at me saying, "See what happens when you run away from your family? See what happens when you lie to your family? Now you've been punished and you'll never be the same. Nothing will ever be the same."

Everything was topsy turvy. The figure's voice didn't know he was making me happy. He didn't scare me. I was woozy and my brain was smashed, but I knew this was a prophetic punishment. Even in this awful, painful mess I was experiencing, the idea of nothing ever being the same seemed strangely appealing. I hadn't liked it the way it was, had I?

While my family was talking with the doctor in a little conference room across the hall, Der Hayr arrived with his cache of divine potions. As he set up his last rites bag on the night stand, I could smell the muron he'd used to anoint Mama Jahn when she was on her "deathbed." I wanted to tell him about the long-fingered phantom who had haunted me about nothing will ever be the same, but I kept losing consciousness every time I tried to talk. I foggily came back into consciousness to hear Der Hayr begin reciting the prayers for the dying and to see him raise his hands, making the sign of the cross over me like I was the body-of-the-week, but I was too weak to resist.

Abruptly, Hayrig rushed in, saying "Der Hayr, stop what you're doing."

"But, Professor, Anoush Azad needing the last rites of her Mother Church."

"I vehemently disagree, Der Hayr. Azad will not die. We will not let her go."

My reaction was just the opposite of earlier that evening. I was actually happy to hear that my family would not let me go. Hold onto me, I said with my eyes to Hayrig and Mother, the only ones not afraid to come close through the array of casts and tubes and imposing medical equipment. On the table next to the bed, I could see a statue of the Virgin Mary holding the Christ Child. My eyes were too droopy to keep open, even for the Blessed Virgin, Hayrig and Mother.

Then Mother spoke to me, "Azad, can you hear me, my child?"

I blinked, trying to communicate "yes." Mother called me "my child"? I closed my eyes as the voice continued.

"Well, then hear me well. I want to remind you that the name I gave you when you were baptized, Azad, means "freedom." Freedom means you are not controlled by fate. You are free to live, Azad. Make up your mind to live."

I blinked again and was startled by the smell of Armenian coffee. Was this real or an hallucination? Was it Mama Jahn's coffee? I struggled to sit up but couldn't. I had tubes stuck in every orifice in my body and I couldn't move. In my confused, drugged up state, I sniffed out the source of the unexpected aroma. I cracked open one eye to get a sense of reality and I saw a figure of a woman, standing at the foot of my bed and sipping coffee from Mama Jahn's demitasse cup.

"Is that you, Mama Jahn?"

Silence.

Opening both of my eyes in stunned disbelief, I realized that this woman looked *exactly* like the Virgin Mary on the bedside table, only she was life size. And she was moving, sipping away as calm as you please. And I didn't see Hayrig or Mother anywhere.

"Mary? Are you the Virgin Mary?"

"Why, yes. Are you the virgin Azad?"

"I am . . . Azad, well, yes, I guess I am the virgin Azad. Am I dead? What are you doing *here*? I'm not a Catholic."

"And I'm not Armenian."

"Why are you here?"

"Everything has a reason and a purpose under heaven."

"That's right. I remember reading that in *Ecclesiastes*."

"Actually, I was quoting Pete Seeger. You know, from *Turn, Turn, Turn*."

"But, you're God—well, er, I mean, you're a goddess or a saint . . . anyway you're a major religious figure. Why are you here?"

"I'm here to see you and give you a message."

"A message for me?"

"Azad child, at a young age I was chosen by God for the most important, life altering job in the world because of one thing, because he knew I would obey."

"I'm not good at obeying . . ."

"No, Anoush Azad not good at obeying now."

Wait! That was Mama Jahn's voice. My eyes flew open in spite of my splitting headache. Now Mama Jahn was close to me and the rest of my family was far away. Mama Jahn's eyes were a ragged red, and she was furiously working Bobeeg Jahn's tesbih with her fingertips. "Tzakus, you going to get well. Don't worry. Everyone going to take care of you. Everyones loveit you. When you better you going to say what you want and we help you to be happy again." Everyone nodded in agreement—even Raffi who was picking his nose in the corner of the room as he watched his shoes.

"You mean I get to do what I want? I don't have to do what everyone else wants me to do?" I was talking to anyone who could hear, but it was the Virgin Mary, in her blue robes and holding a demitasse, who answered:

"You are trying to please everyone instead of the only person who matters."

"Only one?"

"I'm here to tell you that the one person you need to obey in this life is God."

"What does He want from me?"

"What He wants for you is to discover the purpose of your own life. He has given you many talents. Now you must decide what to do with them. All He wants from you is your happiness."

"My happiness. Is that what life is about, finding my happiness?"

192

My family has their ideas for what they want me to be and the blessed Virgin has confirmed that God wants me to figure it out for myself? I blinked again, and instead of the blessed Mother of God, I saw my dinner tray.

It turned out that this was the same hospital I was born in twenty years before, where I received the unexpected and uncalled for curse of the evil eye by Masha.

On the third week in the hospital I was free from the morphine and tubes, and out of the intensive care unit. Instead, I was in a room with three other patients, all of whom snored all day long. After two more weeks, I was more than ready to go home to my own bed, Mama Jahn's cooking and my birthday.

The hospital chaplain came to pray for me. He was Roman Catholic. Before leaving he asked me which was my favorite psalm.

My favorite psalm? What did I know about psalms? Our Der Hayr read them in Armenian. I said the "22nd psalm" because it was the only number I could remember. As the chaplain read the psalm, he looked over his glasses at me sternly. The entire psalm was a list of sins against God! I was mortified to hear him read ". . . and do not surrender me to a shameless soul." I could only hope that the chaplain thought I was still delirious.

It was time to go home. Again.

Just like eighteen years before, Mother was there to help me into the car—this time, not a helpless infant but helpless, nonetheless. I needed a steady arm to lean on as I wobbled and waddled under the weight of casts on both legs from my ankles all the way up to the top of my thighs. Like a porpoise, or maybe in the best of interpretations, a mermaid, I fell across the length of the back seat of our new car, onto an afghan Mama Jahn put there so my casts wouldn't scratch the leather upholstery. It was a white and turquoise blue Chevy Impala with wings and white wall tires. Very luxurious compared to our old Buick.

"What do you think of our new car, Azad?"

"It's beautiful, Mother, but isn't Hayrig upset that I destroyed his Buick?"

"He's so grateful that *you* were not destroyed. That's all any of us care about, and he adores this new car, so there's nothing to worry about. Fortunately the person who hit you had good insurance, anoush."

Mother drove slowly down side streets towards our neighborhood so as not to jar me in the back seat. I craned my neck to get a look at my hair in the mirror. It hadn't been washed since the accident and piles of it were matted with dried blood, especially where the bandages and stitches had been removed the day before. No more lovely straight hair with a Mary Tyler Moore flip, to say the least.

Mother caught me straining to look in the mirror and then heard me gasp.

"Don't worry, Azad, we're going straight to the beauty shop and we'll get your head all cleaned up. Don't you worry." She could not have uttered more reassuring words.

Once back at the chair, Mr. Michel tried to carefully comb through my hair, but it was so painful and unpleasant I gave him permission to do the deed. "Mr. Michel, go ahead, put your precision scissors to work. But please don't take offense. I have to close my eyes. He was quick and sure as he began slicing through all the confused strands of hair.

I hobbled out an hour later with what he excitedly called a pixie cut, with bangs to hide the stitches. The style definitely wasn't me and it was certainly not my dream hairdo, but this was not a dream. I had almost died and I was grateful for God's tender mercies, from wherever they came, Mr. Michel included.

After a long nap in my own bed, which felt like a plunge into marshmallows compared to the hard, plastic wrapped hospital bed, I was ready to get up and hobble around my own home. Everything that usually set my teeth on edge—the plastic bags Mama Jahn washed and spread out to dry on towels on the kitchen counter, Mother's stacks of books all over the place, Hayrig's newspapers and Aunt Zov's angora sweaters drying on the porch—it all looked just great. Best of all, I smelled real food. Mama Jahn's food. And I was hungry for the first time since the accident.

Uncle Mono was proud to lead me to a newly upholstered chair and matching ottoman he made from furniture he had retrieved from the attic. The pattern of the fabric was reminiscent of an oriental rug. The chair and ottoman were just the right height for my legs to rest on while I sat. I would spend the rest of the summer between my bed and this cozy crazy chair, which Uncle Mono put outside during the day and Mama Jahn covered with a clean sheet.

When I woke up the next morning it was officially my birthday. It was also 80 degrees outside. Lugging around casts in the heat was horrible. Nothing else seemed to matter in my life except making my legs stop itching inside the casts. I twisted a wire coat hanger into a scratching rod and shoved it down into the cast. Oh, did that feel good. Such a simple pleasure, to successfully scratch an itch.

I didn't want anything for my birthday except new baby doll pj's to wear, which Mother had bought to give me from Hayrig and herself. They were made of blue and white gingham and edged with a crisp white eyelet trim. The top was loose and comfortable—sleeveless, scoop-necked and A-line. Long enough to skim the top of the casts. The matching bottoms were easy to pull up and down and much cuter than cut-off capris. And cooler. This was all I wanted: to sit on the cool patio in the backyard, scratch my itch, and look at the leaves, stirring under gentle breezes, on the fruit-laden apricot tree, which shaded most of our yard.

The last time I really enjoyed the garden was when I was a little girl and I helped Mama Jahn plant sweet basil seeds from the Old Country. I was surprised to see that she still had that patch of herbs in the same place.

Weeds had tangled themselves around the base of the rose bush. I used to love picking the deep red buds and arranging them with a few stems of deep purple buddleias, white lilies and ferns in canning jars and odd-shaped drinking glasses. I'd put them all around the house to surprise everyone. To me they looked every bit as lovely as the arrangements I saw in the window at the Cinderella Florist in downtown Los Angeles. My bouquets had always made everyone in the family smile. I hadn't thought about these things in years. I guessed that's what five weeks in the hospital did. Made a person nostalgic.

And then, out of nowhere I heard, "Hey, kid, are you out there?"

"Connie, is that you?" I couldn't believe my ears. My best friend Connie was here, coming out the sliding glass door to the back yard. Oh, no, she'll hate my hair, I thought as I tugged at it in a symbolic attempt to make it long and straight.

"Here you are! Ahzie...your hair! It's short!! And it's curly! No one told me that the accident was so bad it made your hair short and curly!"

"I know. It's awful. Look beyond it. I'm still alive."

"Yeah, you had a close call from what I heard. That's why I sent the statue of the Virgin Mary to you, for heavenly support. No visitors were allowed."

"I saw it when I woke up, sitting on my bedside table. I didn't know it was from you. Thanks, Connie. I'll keep it always, kid. Anyway, what are you doing here? No one told me you were coming."

"I wouldn't miss your birthday for anything! Although one of my presents you'll hate and the other one you'll like."

She was right. I loved her first present, *Love Me Do*, the first record from a new singing group from England, the Beatles. I was going to ask Mother to buy it for me first chance she got. I loved the drummer who played the tambourine in this song.

Her other gift was a big rhinestone hair clip I'd use one day when my hair grew out. It was so pretty. Pretty enough to inspire my hair to grow faster I hoped.

The sliding door opened again. It was Auntie Gladys. "Happy Birthday, to my best window decorator." And she was carrying a huge box from Bullocks. "You're looking good, Azad. We were all so worried about you. But I knew you were a lucky gal. I knew you'd make it. Here's something to help you catch up with the newest fashion." Then she noticed Connie, and I introduced them. They were similar versions of each other, each a radical in her own culture.

"Fab, Auntie Gladys, white leather go-go boots! I can't wait to wear them."

"Oh, yeah, Azad, I forgot you have casts on your legs. I can exchange them for go-lo boots instead. They're only ankle length."

"No, I love these. They are so cool."

"Hi, everyone." Out walked Auntie Zov. "I have a little something for your birthday, Azad."

It was a doll. I told Auntie that I hadn't played with dolls in years.

"Tzakus, this isn't just an ordinary doll, it's the newest Barbie. Look, she's so darling. She's wearing a pink satin sheath with a white fur wrap, and best of all she has her 'brownette' hair in a bubble hairdo!!"

Connie was ecstatic. "What great aunts you have, Ahzie. They really know how to shop!! I love this Barbie. She's so stylish, and that hairdo—we have to try it on you when you hair grows out some more. She's a knockout! And the boots are so sharp."

"Where's the family, Azad?" asked Aunt Gladys.

"I have no idea. I haven't seen anyone all afternoon."

And just then, my whole family, my odar school friends and our neighbors appeared yelling, "Surprise!!!" Sossi was carrying a big round birthday cake covered with multicolored roses and a mass of lit candles. It looked to be at least six layers high!

Behind my family were Uncle Eddie and his wife, Sossi's mother, Araxie, Cousin Garo and his young wife and children, some neat kids from my drama class at school and even Der Hayr. They were all singing Happy Birthday to me and carrying platters of all kinds of foods. I was so flustered that I blew out the candles without making a wish.

Mother and Auntie Zov made sure all the platters were placed in order of how the foods were to be eaten—cold mazas first, then warm mazas, then the entrees—on tables Uncle Mono pulled out from the side yard, which had been hidden from sight all afternoon. Mother had decorated them with trails of roses and maidenhair ferns, her favorites because they were so delicate and sturdy at the same time.

All my favorite foods were there. I knew it had taken Mama Jahn many long days to prepare everything. How did she do it without me as her sous chef? Auntie Zov must have stepped in to help.

Bobeeg Jahn placed one of our new TV tables next to me and surprised me with a platter piled high with blini berashki—my absolute favorite food in the entire world and Mama Jahn knew it. She covered them with a kitchen towel so no one would see them because they were just for me.

It was like a wedding feast complete with mazas of every kind—sarma, string cheese marinated with blue cheese, at least twenty varieties of olives, of course bastrauma, lahmajoon, cheese beorags, eggplant prepared in many different styles and piles of homemade breads. Uncle Mono made his famous chee kufta, steak tartare, which many Armenians have said they want for their last supper when it is time for them to die. After tasting it for the first time tonight, my odar friends, who loved it, couldn't believe they were eating raw meat.

Bobeeg prepared his khorovadz which included lamb sausages he made with ground shoulder of lamb, mint and his secret blend of spices, shish kabob and an assortment of grilled whole vegetables.

High over his head, Uncle Eddie carried Mama Jahn's wedding pilaf, which was smothered with raisins and toasted slivered almonds. The dessert table was in the dining room. You could smell the precious yegh that enveloped each morsel of pastry throughout the entire neighborhood that night.

The dancing was a complete surprise. Hayrig put on our Armenian dance records, and everyone started dancing. All the odars dancing with the Armenians was a fantasy come to life. My odar friends and our odar neighbors fit right into the Armenian dancing like they had been doing it all their lives.

All I could do was watch. I watched with the old Armenian women who always sat, taking turns crying and laughing. They were always happiest when there was dancing, which made them sob even harder. They carried too much grief in their hearts to completely rejoice in the moment. I felt like crying, too. I loved watching the energy of youthful bodies stomping the ground in the energetic dance of the *Tamzara*, the twirling and the swaying of graceful arms in the *Chemar Yareh*, and the traditional Armenian style of line dancing to *Gneega*. It was a beautiful sight, which had nothing to do with the dancers knowing the steps or being particularly light on their feet. It was dancing from their souls, pure emotion lit by the fires of passion. It was also beautifully *un*cool.

It wasn't just the Armenians who were passionate; the *odars* were just as seized with the Armenian spirit. No one was ahnlee. And as I sat and watched, the beat of the music penetrated my entire body. The music propelled me up, off my chair and into the dancing circle. I couldn't sit still while the music played. I just couldn't.

I stood, swaying as much of my upper body as I could and moving my hands in the style of our Armenian dancing, twisting my wrists and fingers in circular, delicate motions to the beat of the music. Uncle Mono put a white hankie in my hand for me to twirl and soon everyone made a circle around me, as they danced the *Miserloo*. I kept standing and swaying to the beat of the dumbaghs and secretly gave thanks to God for all these many blessings.

When the Armenian music, Armenian dancing, tavloo playing and eating had come to an end, and everyone had said their goodbyes and given their good wishes ten times over, I was alone with Mama Jahn. She came to sit next to me, a small tray with a demitasse of Armenian coffee for each of us in her hand. We sat together, not talking. She massaged my hands and arms and I allowed myself to feel at peace.

I could see in her face her happiness that I was home. Now I was hers to nurse back to health with her good food and best intentions. Mother would go back to work, knowing I'd be well cared for as I had been all my life with Mama Jahn at home. Hayrig would be able to concentrate on his many clients and commitments to the Armenians in the community now that I was on the mend. Uncle Mono and Bobeeg were planning on hanging around the house to be of whatever help Mama Jahn needed to care for me and the household. Auntie Zov was my amusement with her stories of the movies and movie stars.

After Mama Jahn and I drank our coffees, I turned my cup over away from me and turned it three times before making my wish. I thought long and hard. Unlike the day I was born, there was no rush. The cup had to cool before my fortune could be read and there was no one around to press us.

When the cup was cool, I passed it to Mama Jahn. She held the cup by its sides and gently tugged. It didn't budge. She looked at me and I looked at her and we both smiled. As the last few minutes of my birthday ticked away, Mama Jahn pronounced, "Azad, your wish going to come true."

THE END

GLOSSARY

Aboosh—empty headed
Abrees—long may you live
Acheeg—girl
Acheeges—girl of mine
Achkecht louis—congratulations
Ah-sheh—look
Ahmahn—oh, my
Ahmot—shame, shameful
Ahmot kez—shame on you
Amousteen—husband
Ahnlee—saltless
Anoush—sweet one
Anoushabour—rice pudding
Asdouzo garagit janit tahpee—may the fire of God come down upon
    your soul
Asdvadz—God
Asdvadz kesi byieh—may God keep you
Asdvadz mer—our God
Azad—nickname for Azadouhi (pronounced *Ah-zahd*)
Azadouhi—lit., free woman
Azie—nickname for Azad

Bacheegs—kisses
Badarak—Divine Liturgy
Bagh—cold, frigid
Bastrauma—cured beef with garlic spice rub
Balah Jahn—baby dear
Baligus—baby darling
Batleejahn—eggplant
Beorag—filo dough filled with cheese
Berashki—blini filled with meat
Bobeeg—grandfather
Bocon—crusty, oval shaped rustic bread
Boze—whore

Catah—sweet bread
Catholicos—religious head of Armenian Church
Chee Kufta—steak tartare
Cheesh—urine, urinate
Cheman—a fenugreek and spice mixture for coating bastrauma
Cheorag—brioche type coffee cake
Chi—tea

Dasheeg—high pitched, gleeful shouts made by women during dancing
Dolmas—stuffed grape or cabbage leaves
Der Hayr—priest
Digeen—Mrs.
Duduk—ancient double reed woodwind musical instrument
Dumbaghs—Armenian drums

Eench bes es?—how are you?
Eench ga ses?—what are you saying?
Eench gun es?—what are you doing?
Eench gun es mez?—what are you doing to us?
Eench khidarag—this is horrible
Eench neghoutooin—what a desgrace
El eench?—what else?
Esh, eshag—jackass, assinine
Ei-o—yes

Gahtlets—Russian Armenian hamburgers

Haah—yes
Hadgee—pilgrim to Jerusalem
Haladz yegh—clarified butter
Hahm cha gha—flavorless
Halvah—sesame paste confection
Hanganag Havado—the prayer of St. John of Chrysostom
Hanum—Turkish queen
Harse—bride, wife
Hatz—bread
Havgeets—eggs
Hayr Mer—Lord's Prayer
Hayrig—father
Herishdagas—sweet angel
Hodja—satirical Sufi jokester quoted from middle ages
Hokis—soul's delight
Holy Badarak—the service of the Divine Liturgy, communion service

Jagad—destiny
Janus Jahn—my dear one
Jarbig—clever, quick-witted
Jezvah—long handled pot for making Armenian coffee
Jooge—penis

Kash-heh—drive on
Kesh—ugly, bad
Kezi shad ga serem—I love you very much
Khadayeef—shredded pastry with walnut filling
Khash—healing porridge made with cow parts
Khanamee khapur—fried pastry known as "fool the in-laws pastry"
Khatch—cross
Khelket sirem—I love your brain
Khent—crazy
Khent es?—Are you crazy?
Khent es, eench es?—Are you crazy or what?
Khent guneeg—crazy woman
Khorovadz—grilled meats
Khourabia—cookie covered with powdered sugar
Khunamies—in-laws
Kuftah—stuffed Armenian meatball made with bulghur

Latchag—triangular cotton head cloth
Lahmajoon—lamb flatbread
Lavash—cracker bread
Locum—a sweet candy

Madzoon—yogurt
Mahleb—powdered spice
Manchaghchig—homosexual
Manti—tiny meat pastry
Matneek—ring
Maza—appetizers
Medeem—I'm dying
Meetkeseh—I remember
Menz—big
Menz eshag—big jackass
Molleratdz—confused
Muron—holy oil
Myrig—mother

Nushkhar—holy communion wafer

Odar—outsider, non-Armenian
Oghlavee—a length of wooden doweling used to roll out pastry dough
Oud—Armenian string instrument similar to a lute
Ouz goush—be careful

Paklava—sweet pastry made with layers of filo dough with a walnut filling
Parev—hello
Park Asdouzo—thanks be to God
Pessa—son-in-law
Peece hodadz—low life, rotten
Pilaf—rice

Rahan—sweet basil
Rahki—whiskey
Rojig—walnut grape-pulp roll
Russahye—Russian-Armenian

Sarma—stuffed grape leaves
Sarsakh—stupid
Sev—black
Sev maz—black hair
Shabig—choir robe
Shad lav—very good
Shakar locum—shortbread cookie
Sharagans—religious chants
Shesh-ou-besh—another name for tavloo, backgammon; lit. six [in Persian]
    and five [in Turkish]
Shish kabob—skewered, cubed and marinated leg of lamb
Shoon shan vorti—son of a bitch
Shoud—fast
Simit—sesame seed cookie
Siroon—beautiful, also a girl's name of the same meaning
Soubeorag—cheese filling baked in between layers of pasta
Soud—a lie, false
Sourj—coffee
Sourp, Sourp—Holy, Holy
Surpazan—bishop, your grace

Taboulee—cracked wheat salad
Takouhee—queen
Tavloo—board game, backgammon

Tekelled—spit
Tesbih—worry beads
Tootoum galogh—picklehead
Tornig—grandchild
Tourse ungadz boze—fallen street whore
Tzakus—my darling
Tzaks—slang term of endearment for "hun" as in honey
Tzeezeegs—breasts
Tzeerekt dahlar—may your hands always be blessed

Vardeeg—underpants
Vie!—exclamation of shock, surprise, or joy
Vie ahmahn, ahmotos med-neem—I die of embarrassment
Vodeeg—buttocks
Vostigan—police
Votch—no

Yahdash—I got you
Yegh—butter
Yeghpayr—brother
Yerevan—capital of Armenia
Yertank—let's go
Yes ga khuntrem—I beg of you
Yes kezi shad ga serem—I love you very much
Yorgahn—quilt, comforter

Zatoon—olive

ABOUT THE AUTHOR

Lenore Tolegian Hughes writes and paints at home
in the Santa Ynez Valley, California.

Made in the USA
Charleston, SC
01 April 2013